PRAISE FOR

The Darling Strumpet

"[A] richly engaging portrait of the life and times of one of history's most appealing characters!" —Diana Gabaldon, author of the bestselling Outlander series

"Bawdy and poignant . . . an ebullient page-turner!"

—Leslie Carroll, author of *Royal Affairs*

"Hard to resist this sort of seduction—a Nell Gwynn who pleasures the crowds upon the stages of London and the noblest men of England in their bedrooms. A vivid portrait of an age that makes our own seem prudish, told with verve, humor, pathos . . . and not a little eroticism."

—C. C. Humphreys, actor and author of *Jack Absolute*

"An absolute triumph as a debut novel . . . [It] is an absolutely brilliant addition to the historical fiction genre and might be the best novel on Nell Gwynn ever . . . Nell would have applauded in approval and probably done a little jig to celebrate her tribute." — *Pittsburgh Historical Fiction Examiner*

"Gillian Bagwell's meticulously researched novel takes us from the cobbled, rubbish-strewn alleys of Covent Garden to the Theatre Royal in Drury Lane and into the royal court. She handles the seventeenth-century London street vernacular with aplomb . . . I can thoroughly recommend this book, and look forward to Miss Bagwell's next foray into seventeenth-century England." —*Historical Novel Reviews* (five stars)

"The reader is kept in absolute rapture from start to finish! . . . I enthusiastically recommend *The Darling Strumpet* and if her debut novel is any indication of the fabulousness we can look forward to in future books by Gillian Bagwell then consider me hooked!!" —*Passages to the Past* (five stars)

"For . . . Restoration England lovers this book is a must. . . . The sky is the limit for Gillian's future in historical fiction."

—*Historically Obsessed* (five stars)

"This book was just all around solid. The characters were rich and complex, the plot was paced well and the period language felt natural. . . . I LOVED it. . . If you are a Nell fan, or a fan of historical fiction in general, this is a must read, and if you haven't read much historical fiction, this book would be a great introduction!" —*The Book Buff* (five stars)

continued . . .

"The atmosphere of Restoration London is beautifully rendered in this richly textured novel. Sedan chairs, frost fairs, hot wassail, changeable silks—the details on every page evoke time and place . . . I would definitely recommend *The Darling Strumpet* to anyone looking for a rich and spicy January read."

—*The Misadventures of Moppet*

"Written in the vein of Philippa Gregory's *Other Boleyn Girl* and Tracy Chevalier's *Lady and the Unicorn* . . . Gillian Bagwell is a masterful writer . . . A thrilling and enchanting story that will stay with you long after you turn the last page."

—*The Season for Romance*

"As bawdy and engaging as Nell herself was reputed to be. Bagwell's well-researched novel accurately captures the rowdy, sexy Restoration period . . . Romantics will devour this engaging, sexy page-turner."

—*Dolce Dolce*

"Fans of historical fiction or the Restoration era, or simply desirous of an immersive, fast-paced look into another time, will likely find much to enjoy here."

—*Pop Matters*

"After this fabulous debut piece of work I cannot wait to see what else Gillian Bagwell has for us historical fiction fans."

—BurtonReview.blogspot.com

"I loved it. I sat down and read it in one sitting. Yup. That good. I found myself caught up in the story and just didn't want to put it down . . . This is a very enjoyable book on an extraordinary woman."

—*Broken Teepee*

"Nell claims her place in history and Charles Stuart's heart, a memorable footnote to an era of flourishing theater and outrageous personalities, ever the people's darling. . . . The lusty, good-hearted Nell has secured her place in England's turbulent past, a destitute girl who wins the undying love of the Restoration king. Bagwell does her story justice."

—*Curled Up with a Good Book*

"Bagwell delights readers with tales of Nell Gwynn's escapades in historically accurate detail . . . Nell would have given Madonna and Lady Gaga a run for their money had they been around back then! *The Darling Strumpet* is a well-told historical romance that will be enjoyed by Anglophiles and fans of the days of old alike."

—*Fresh Fiction*

"This is probably not a book I will ever re-read. I don't need to . . . I will never forget it . . . Gillian Bagwell spent twenty years researching this, her debut book. The wealth of historical detail makes it obvious that the time was well spent."

—*Seductive Musings*

Also by Gillian Bagwell

THE DARLING STRUMPET

THE SEPTEMBER QUEEN

GILLIAN BAGWELL

BERKLEY BOOKS, NEW YORK

THE BERKLEY PUBLISHING GROUP
Published by the Penguin Group
Penguin Group (USA) Inc.
375 Hudson Street, New York, New York 10014, USA
Penguin Group (Canada), 90 Eglinton Avenue East, Suite 700, Toronto, Ontario M4P 2Y3, Canada
(a division of Pearson Penguin Canada Inc.)
Penguin Books Ltd., 80 Strand, London WC2R 0RL, England
Penguin Group Ireland, 25 St. Stephen's Green, Dublin 2, Ireland (a division of Penguin Books Ltd.)
Penguin Group (Australia), 250 Camberwell Road, Camberwell, Victoria 3124, Australia
(a division of Pearson Australia Group Pty. Ltd.)
Penguin Books India Pvt. Ltd., 11 Community Centre, Panchsheel Park, New Delhi—110 017, India
Penguin Group (NZ), 67 Apollo Drive, Rosedale, Auckland, 0632, New Zealand
(a division of Pearson New Zealand Ltd.)
Penguin Books (South Africa) (Pty.) Ltd., 24 Sturdee Avenue, Rosebank, Johannesburg 2196,
South Africa

Penguin Books Ltd., Registered Offices: 80 Strand, London WC2R 0RL, England

Cover design by Lesley Worrell
Book design by Tiffany Estreicher

PRINTING HISTORY
Berkey trade paperback edition / November 2011

Library of Congress Cataloging-in-Publication Data

Bagwell, Gillian.
The September queen / Gillian Bagwell.
p. cm.
ISBN 978-0-425-24323-7
1. Fisher, Jane Lane, Lady, ca. 1626–1689—Fiction. 2. Charles II, King of England, 1630–1685—Fiction. 3. Worcester, Battle of, Worcester, England, 1651—Fiction. 4. Great Britain—History—Charles II, 1660–1685—Fiction. I. Title.
PS3602.A3975S47 2011
813'.6—dc22

2010054198

PRINTED IN THE UNITED STATES OF AMERICA

10 9 8 7 6 5 4 3 2 1

This book is dedicated to the
memory of my dear friend Khin-Kyaw Maung.
I miss you every day.

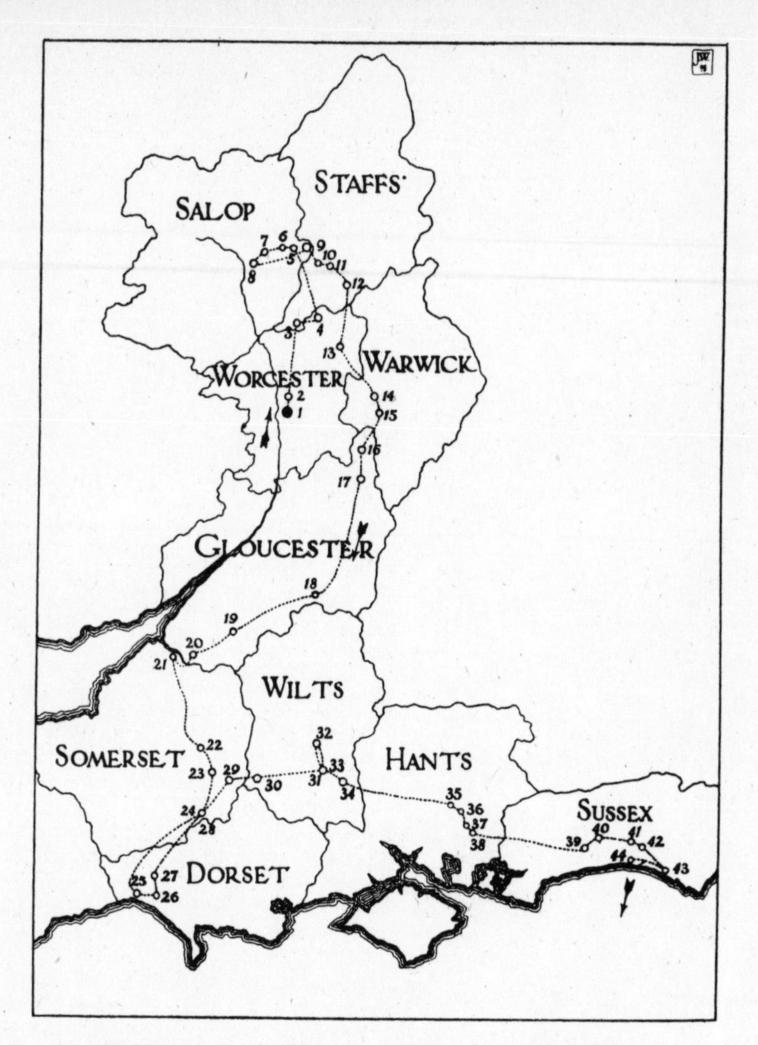

MAP OF THE KING'S FLIGHT FROM WORCESTER TO SHOREHAM

1. Worcester
2. Barbon Bridge
3. Kinver Heath
4. Stourbridge
5. Whiteladies
6. Hobbal
7. Evelith
8. Madeley
9. Boscobel
10. Pendeford
11. Moseley
12. Bentley
13. Bromsgrove
14. Wootton
15. Stratford
16. Long Marston
17. Campden
18. Cirencester
19. Sodbury
20. Bristol
21. Abbots Leigh
22. Bruton
23. Castle Cary
24. Trent
25. Charmouth
26. Bridport
27. Broad Windsor
28. Trent
29. Wincanton
30. Mere
31. Heale
32. Stonehenge
33. Heale
34. Clarendon Park
35. Warnford
36. Old Winchester
37. Broadhalfpenny
38. Hambledon
39. Arundel
40. Houghton
41. Bramber
42. Beeding
43. Brighton
44. Shoreham

CHAPTER ONE

THE AFTERNOON SUN DAPPLED THROUGH THE LEAVES OF THE oak tree. Jane Lane sat in its shade, her back against its stalwart trunk, the Second Folio of Shakespeare's works open on her lap. She had sneaked her favorite book from her father's library and taken it out near the summerhouse, where she could read and dream in peace.

Though what need have I to sneak? she asked herself. *I am five and twenty today, and if I am ever to be thought no longer a child, it must be so today. Lammas Eve.*

"On Lammas Eve at night shall she be fourteen," her Nurse had said of Juliet Capulet. Jane shared Juliet's birthday, the thirty-first of July, but Juliet, at not quite fourteen, had found her Romeo, to woo her and win her beneath a moon hanging low in a warm Italian night sky. *But not I,* Jane thought. *I have come to the great age of five and twenty, and but one man has stirred my heart, and that came to naught.* An old maid, her eldest sister, Withy, would say.

What is wrong with me? Jane wondered. *Why can I not like any man well enough to want to wed him? It is not as though I am such a great prize. Pretty enough, I suppose, in face and form, but no great beauty. Witty and learned, but those features are of little use in a woman, of little use to a man who wants a wife to be mistress of his estate and mother to his heirs.*

What if there will never be someone for me?

She pushed the thought away. Surely there was more to think about, more to do than be merely a wife, exchanging the protection and stability of her father's home for that of a husband's.

She looked down again at the book in her lap, opened to *The Life of Henry the Fifth,* and read over the opening lines spoken by the Chorus, which never failed to thrill her.

O, for a muse of fire, that would ascend
The brightest heaven of invention!
A kingdom for a stage, princes to act,
And monarchs to behold the swelling scene.

Yes, that was what she wanted. A swelling scene, full of romance and adventure, not this dull life in the Staffordshire countryside. She read on.

Then should the warlike Harry, like himself,
Assume the port of Mars, and at his heels,
(Leash'd in like hounds) should famine, sword, and fire
Crouch for employment.

That sort of man would rouse her blood. Sword in hand, armor on his back, astride a great war horse, exhorting his men onward.

Once more, unto the breach, dear friends! . . .
Cry "God for Harry, England, and Saint George!"

Jane sighed. There was no king in England now. King Charles was, unthinkably, dead, at the hands of Parliament, two years since. The war had raged for years, those who wanted there to be no king had won, and now Oliver Cromwell ruled. The king's twenty-one-year-old son, Charles, the exiled Prince of Wales, had been crowned as king in Scotland at the beginning of the year, but Jane's father and brothers and cousins, the neighbors and the newsbooks, whether Royalist or Parliamentary in sentiment, did none of them expect to see a king upon the throne of England again.

Jane's family had mingled with kings since time out of mind. An ancestor of hers had come into England with William the Conqueror more than six hundred years earlier, and Lanes had gone crusading with Richard the Lionheart a century after that, and fought at the side of the Lancastrians in the War of the Roses. Jane's own great-granduncle William Cecil, Lord Burleigh, had been councillor to the great Elizabeth, the Tudor rose that had blossomed from those wars, and in living memory the family tree had born a Countess of Oxford. And many generations back, Jane herself was descended from King Edward I, called "Longshanks" and "the Hammer of the Scots."

But the time for kings had gone, and in their place sat a parliament. What a gray and bleak sound that word had, Jane thought. Would she ever in her life feel excitement again?

The thought again raised the agitation that had rumbled at the back of her mind all day. Her brother John's friend Sir Clement Fisher was coming to dinner, and she rather thought he was likely to ask her to marry him. She didn't want to, really. It was not that there was anything wrong with him. He had served honorably in the wars. It was just that she felt no stirring of passion when she was with him. But if she said no? What were her chances then?

Jane's eyes strayed to the southeastern horizon. Somewhere that way lay London. Throughout her childhood, London had seemed a place of magic, and she had longed to go there. When she was ten, the King's Company of players had given a performance in Wolverhampton, and her father had taken her, all that five miles away, to see them, as a special treat for her birthday. *Henry the Fifth,* the same play that lay open on her lap. She had never been so excited in her life as when that first actor strode onto the stage and began the speech that ran through her mind today.

Afterward, she had begged her father to take her to London, that she might see more plays. "Someday," he had replied, laughing.

But someday had not come soon enough, and when she was sixteen, Cromwell had ordered the playhouses closed, torn down, the plays to be no more. All of Jane's family hated Cromwell, but she felt an especial malice toward him for that. He had not only killed the king, he had killed all the past kings as well—glorious Harry V; his father, Bolingbroke, who had dethroned poor lost Richard II to become Henry IV; and all the rest of them.

"Jane!" Withy's voice cut through Jane's thoughts. There was no time to think of tucking the book away before Withy heaved into view, pink and exasperated in the heat.

"There you are! Reading again."

The verb held a freight of disapproval. Jane was the youngest of the Lane siblings, and Withy, thirteen years her senior, still seemed to regard her as a naughty child.

"Sir Clement Fisher will be arriving before long. You haven't much time to make yourself presentable."

Withy stood looking down at Jane, her broad face damp with perspiration, and Jane could see her own reflection in her sister's face as clearly as in a mirror. She had pulled off her cap, and her auburn hair was curling untidily around her shoulders. Her skirt was dusty, and her face warm in the sun. She was comfortable, which meant almost by definition that she was not properly dressed for company. Especially Sir Clement Fisher.

"You know right well he's like to ask for your hand tonight," Withy said, swatting at a fly that buzzed around her head. "I'd have thought you would want to take some care for your appearance, this night of all nights. You're not like to have many more offers, you know."

"Oh, Withy," Jane protested, but Withy carried relentlessly on.

"You know it's true. How many suitors—perfectly good men—have you turned away? And for what reasons? Too old, not handsome enough, not learned enough. And now you're five and twenty, and Sir Clement is about the only Royalist gentleman left within fifty miles. But I suppose there's something wrong with him, too?"

"There's nothing wrong with him," Jane said. "And yet, I cannot bring myself, though I have truly tried, to have any great desire to be his wife. Or anyone's wife."

"And, pray, what else is there for you to be?" Withy's voice rose in impatience. She stood, hands on sturdy hips, waiting for an answer.

"I don't know," Jane said.

Withy was right. She could be someone's wife, and have a home of her own. Otherwise, she would live on in the homes of her brothers and sisters, never going hungry, never wanting for safety or comfort, but never mistress of her own house or her own life, never with money of her own or the means to be anything other than a spinster relation.

"Well," Withy said. "I beg you to at least not shame the family or discommode Sir Clement. He's riding all this way for your birthday supper, the least you can do is wash your face and try to look more like a lady than a milkmaid."

"And so I shall," Jane agreed, getting to her feet and dusting off the cover of the folio with her sleeve. "But I want to walk first a bit."

Withy rolled her eyes.

"Well, don't be long. In faith, I don't understand you. Any other woman would be counting the hours until supper time." She twitched her skirts in annoyance at the buzzing fly and trudged away toward the house.

Jane regretted not having asked her sister to take the heavy folio inside, but likely the request only would have brought a scathing remark about the foolishness of having brought the book outside in the first place.

The orchard lay up the slope some quarter of a mile north of the house. Jane had always loved to escape from the rest of the world there, especially in summer, when the scent of ripening fruit permeated the air. Apples, quinces, pears, apricots, plums, cherries. The trees were laid out in rows, each kind of fruit with its distinctive leaves. Many of the trees were ancient, had stood for far longer than the seventy-five years that the present Bentley Hall had sat on the site of a previous house by that name. Some of the trees had newer tops grafted onto old trunks and still did not look all of one piece. As a child, Jane had liked to imagine that fairies lived in the orchard and watched her, and that perhaps if she were quiet and wished hard enough, they might come out, and perhaps even take her back with them to visit their magic realm.

Jane stopped beneath a plum tree with particularly wide and spreading branches that she had loved to climb as a little girl, and which for some reason had always given fruit sooner than the rest of the trees. One perfect plum, deep purple and fat in its ripeness, hung within reach. She plucked it, and setting the book down carefully on the roots of the tree where it would not be soiled, she bit into the fruit. It was warm from the sun and a spurt of juice trickled down her chin as she ate. The flesh was satisfyingly firm but seemed almost to dissolve with sweetness. Jane threw away the stone and licked her fingers clean, then wiped them on her apron before picking up the book. She would go to the end of the orchard before turning back, she decided.

She had only been walking for another minute or so when her eye was drawn to movement down the lane between the trees. An unfamiliar horse was tethered to an apple tree, and beyond Jane saw three caravans, with smoke rising from beyond them. Gypsies.

Jane's mother grew tight-lipped with outrage at the thought that the wanderers should presume to camp on the family's property, but from the time she was a little girl Jane had always been fascinated by the Gypsies, moving from place to place, always seeing something new, with nothing to hold them down. This far from the house they disturbed no one, and as far as she was concerned, they were welcome to the fruit they might pick and the stars above Bentley Hall wheeling over their heads for a few nights.

A black-and-white-spotted dog darted out from under one of the wagons, followed by a smaller rust-colored mongrel that nipped at its heels. From beyond the wagons a donkey brayed. The scent of food wafted on the air. Jane couldn't see any of the human inhabitants of the camp, but they were probably cooking the meal or tending to the animals beyond the caravans.

The thought of food reminded her that she should be making herself ready for supper and the visit from Sir Clement Fisher. She turned and made her way toward the house, the heavy scent of fruit in her nostrils. The trees in the orchard were so thickly leaved that they blocked the view ahead of her. A stranger would not have known which way to go. Jane was just remembering a time when as a small child she had gone into the orchard to play and got lost, enchanted by the clouds of blossoms overhead that led her deeper and deeper among the gnarled trunks, when she saw a dark-haired young man sitting with his back against one of the trees ahead of her, his legs splayed out in front of him, his eyes closed. One of the Gypsies, without doubt.

He was not more than ten feet away, and what stopped her in her tracks was the jolt of seeing that one of his hands was in motion in his lap, grasping a stalk of vivid ruddy flesh. Jane had never seen a human phallus and her first thought was that it looked nothing like the somewhat repellent appendages of dogs and bulls, and the second was that it was far bigger than she had ever thought a man's member would be.

The sound of Jane's footsteps on the ground brought the man's eyes open with a start. His eyes met hers with surprise, but no shame. In fact, he tilted his head to one side and smiled at her appraisingly. His hand had stopped its rapid up-and-down movement and now he stroked himself languorously, luxuriating in the sight of her, it seemed. He had the look of a fawn, that sensuous forest creature, half man, half beast. His dark hair fell in unruly curls around his head; his brown eyes, the color of hazelnuts, shone on her warmly. His teeth were vivid white against the florid pink of the tongue that ran along them.

All of this had passed in a flash, less than a second, and Jane stood rooted to where she stood as the young man spoke.

"Come, sit on my lap, sweetheart."

It was an invitation. Not an insult or a taunt or a challenge or a threat. He smiled at her again, his swarthy face flushed and damp, and he opened his hand to show Jane the living wand he cradled.

"Come," he repeated. "And I'll make thee gasp and cry out for more."

Jane felt herself flushing violently, her heart beating in her throat, but she was not afraid. In fact she realized with dismay that she felt a pleasurable thrill at the site of this Gypsy lad, so open in his appreciation at the sight of her, so lazily undisturbed at her intrusion into his solitary pleasure. The realization that she ought to be shocked struck her, and at last brought movement to her feet.

"I can't—"

It was absurd, she thought, to be explaining why she couldn't stay or accept his outrageous offer, and she gathered her skirts and ran from him, away through the trees, his amused laughter ringing in the air.

Out of sight of the young man, Jane slowed to a fast walk. She was shaking. She must calm herself before she reached the house, she thought. She leaned against a tree, willing her heart to slow its pace and her hands to stop their sweating. She felt as though she must bear some visible mark of the encounter, as if Withy or her mother or worse yet Sir Clement Fisher would see as soon as they set eyes on her that she had been touched by some taste of lasciviousness, had given in to the urge as surely as if she had lowered herself onto that purple-headed shaft in the Gypsy's hand and given herself to him like some Maid of Misrule going to a Jack-o'-the-Green on a midsummer night.

AS JANE CLIMBED THE STAIRS TO HER ROOM, NURSE BUSTLED ALONG the upstairs hall with an armful of clean linen, thwarting Jane's hope that she would reach her room unseen. Jane flushed at the sight of the stout figure. Nurse had cared for Jane and her siblings and was now tending her second generation of Lanes, the children of Jane's brother

John, and decades of sniffing out mischief prompted her to peer more closely at Jane.

"And where have you been gadding, lambkin? You look as though you'd seen a ghost."

"Just in the orchard," Jane said. "It's warm out there in the sun is all, and I must hurry if I'm to bathe before supper time."

The reminder about the evening's birthday celebration and the presence of Jane's suitor brought a grin to Nurse's round face.

"Ah, that's it, then. Thinking about that young man. Well, get you to your room and I'll have Abigail bring the tub."

THE TUB FILLED AND ABIGAIL GONE, JANE REMOVED HER CLOTHES, luxuriating in the freedom she always felt when she was released from her tight stays. Her mind went back to the Gypsy lad, and his lazy glance that had raked her from head to toe. She flushed again. He had liked what he had seen, that was clear enough. No man had ever looked at her with such open cupidity and it made her consider herself in a new light.

She went to stand before the long mirror that her father had bought for her at such great cost at Stafford. She had never dared to examine her naked body so closely, and felt a little ashamed, but now she gazed at her reflection, trying to see herself as a lover might. She had always thought her breasts were too small, but they were round and high, her nipples a blushing pink against her creamy skin. She cupped them in her hands, imagining what it might feel like to have a man's hands on her, firm fingers caressing and kneading.

Her waist was slim, her legs long and firm. The soft thatch of reddish brown hair at the cleft of her legs almost but not quite concealed the secret place beneath. She let her hands drift to her buttocks. Her muscles were smooth and sleek from walking and riding. Unwomanly, she could hear Withy saying, but it was good to feel strong and supple and alive.

She dipped a toe into the tub to test the temperature. It had cooled enough to be pleasantly warm, and she climbed in, leaning her back against the high end. The tub was not long enough to let her straighten her legs, and her thighs fell open. She thought of the laughing young man, the look of intense pleasure that had suffused his face in the instant before he had seen her. Was it possible for a woman to give herself the same pleasure?

She usually forbade herself from feeling anything when she wiped herself after urinating, but she knew the sensations that fleeted at the edge of her touch, and now she gave in to the curiosity building within her. She slipped a hand beneath the water, tentatively touching the forbidden place. The bud at the center was engorged under her fingers, throbbing and alive. It felt as though it would jump as she moved her fingers over it, letting the water tickle and tease.

She was breathing hard, and let her hand move in circles, delicately, softly. A tremor was building within her. Was this what it was like to be with a man? But that act involved the man's part, the part of him that melded with a woman. She thought of the engorged flesh bobbing like something alive in the Gypsy's hand, and imagined what it might feel like to have such a thing inside of her. She slipped two fingers inside herself, and found that she was slippery and warm. She moved her fingers deeply in and out as she let her thumb caress the rosebud at her center. What had taken her so long to make this astonishing discovery? She wanted the sensation to last forever, but a wave was building inside her that she could not hold back. She pressed her hand hard, deep into her and against herself, and gasped, holding back the cry that she wanted to voice. She was shocked to realize that within this private little earthquake she wanted to be calling his name, whoever he was. Not the Gypsy, not Sir Clement, or any man she had ever met. Some warrior prince perhaps.

The wave crested and passed. She was alone in a tub of warm water and guiltily removed her hand.

Maybe Withy was right. Maybe such men existed only in plays and fairy tales.

. . .

Dinner that evening was a festive and crowded affair. In honor of Jane's birthday and to accommodate the large gathering, the meal took place in the banqueting house that stood to the east of Bentley Hall. Jane had always loved the banqueting house, built in the eccentric Flemish style with high chimneys and dormer windows—a fanciful edifice designed to surprise and delight. Besides those that lived in the family home—Jane and her parents; her oldest brother John; his wife, Athalia; and their nine children; and her brother Richard, only a year old than she—her brothers Walter and William and their wives were there, as well as Withy and her husband, John Petre; her cousin Henry Lascelles; and of course Sir Clement Fisher, seated beside Jane. Her health was drunk and all were in good spirits.

"I have a special gift for you today, my Jane," her father, Thomas, smiled. The bald top of his head shone pinkly with perspiration, a fluffy cloud of hair standing out above each ear. He handed a little book across the table, and Jane stroked a finger across the soft red calf's leather binding with gilt lettering.

"Oh, Father! How beautiful!" Jane cried, opening the volume. The title page read *Poems: Written by Wil. Shakesspeare, Gent,* and on the facing page was an engraved portrait, the eyes looking out at Jane in a peculiar, almost cross-eyed way.

"I thought it would please." Thomas smiled. "It's got the sonnets, 'A Lover's Complaint,' 'The Passionate Pilgrim,' and a few poems by Milton and Jonson and others. And it's a little easier to carry outside to read than the folio!"

John and Athalia had a book for her, too—*A Continuation of Sir Phillip Sidney's Arcadia.*

"By Mrs. A.W.," Jane murmured.

"Just published," John said. "By a lady author, as you can see. Perhaps you'll become one yourself."

"I can scarce wait to start reading!" Jane exclaimed, beaming.

"Then I guess we'll know to look in the summerhouse should anyone need to find you!" Withy said, to general laughter, passing Jane a length of snowy handmade lace.

There were other gifts—a silk paisley shawl from her mother; yards of fine cloth from her brothers William and Richard; two little purses worked with fine embroidery from John's daughters Grace and Lettice, aged fifteen and thirteen; and ribbons and garters from the younger girls still at home, Elizabeth, Jane, Dorothy, and Frances.

"I haven't got anything for you yet, Jane," her cousin Henry Lascelles called from down the table. He grinned at her and shook a lock of light brown hair out of his eyes. "But come with me to the fair in Wolverhampton next week, and I'll buy you whatever you like!"

"Hmm," Jane mused, her eyes twinkling. "A new horse, perhaps, with a saddle and bridle worked in silver?"

"Ha!" Henry shot back. "Perhaps next year."

"I've made something for you, sweeting." Nurse stumped forward and presented a stout pair of stockings, knitted from heavy gray wool.

"They're plain, but they'll keep you warm," she pronounced. "Not like those silly silk trifles you like."

"Thank you, Nurse," Jane said, kissing Nurse's ruddy cheek and letting herself be enfolded in the capacious bosom. "I will feel even warmer, knowing that you made them just for me."

"I hope you'll accept a little something from me, too, Jane," Sir Clement said.

He reached into the pocket of his dark green coat and pulled out a pair of gloves in fine blue kidskin, which he set beside her plate with a bow of the head. His blue eyes shone at her, a little shy, and Jane was conscious of the family watching her suitor and her reaction to him.

"How lovely," she said, touching the softness of the leather. "Like the color of bluebells. Now I shall welcome the first day of frost."

She met his eyes and smiled. He really was very handsome, she thought. Piercing blue eyes above high cheekbones, a strong jaw, no

trace of gray yet in his wavy brown hair, though she knew he was more than ten years older than she. Why did she feel no thrill of happiness and excitement, nothing but a vague wish that the evening was over and done with?

As the meal went on, the news from the north dominated the conversation. The exiled young King Charles had arrived in Scotland the previous summer from the Netherlands, and in recent months had been massing an army.

"I say His Majesty will not push into England now, or indeed soon at all," Henry declared. "Lambert beat the king's troops under General Leslie scarcely a month ago, and without more men—many more men—he has no hope."

"Exactly," Jane's brother Richard cried. The faint spray of freckles stood out on his cheeks when he was in the grip of a strong emotion, as now, making him look younger than his twenty-six years. "Which is why I say he will cross the border, and that England will rally to his banner. The Papists in the north and his supporters throughout the country know that the time is now."

"What say you, Sir Clement?" Thomas Lane asked, and all eyes turned to the guest. He had served as a captain under John, and Jane wondered if he would fight again if it came to it. He took a thoughtful swallow of wine before answering.

"I agree with Richard. Cromwell has divided the king's forces, and marched on Perth. All is in confusion, but His Majesty may seize some advantage from that by moving decisively now."

"But he has not enough troops to win," Henry argued, his voice rising. He, too, had fought in the wars, serving as cornet in John's regiment. "He must have help from England, but the Royalists who would help him are afraid, have suffered so much already during the wars. John's house and lands were confiscated! My uncle here had all his horses and cattle seized and sold, the profits going to the Stafford Committee. And did not the villains just assess you once more, Uncle?"

"Yes, indeed," Thomas said. "A hundred pounds in January."

His voice was calm, but Jane knew the depth of feeling that lay beneath. Her father had been a justice of the peace, but the title had been stripped from him when the war began and the Lanes had fought on the side of the king, and since then he had regularly been burdened with onerous levies and fines.

"Exactly!" Jane's brother William cried. He pounded a fist on the table, making the silverware rattle. "Those who are known to be for the king must beg for a pass to travel more than five miles from home, have lost their property, and look fearfully on their neighbors, not knowing who is friend and who is foe, and wondering what might be taken from them next."

"The more reason we have to stand now," John said quietly.

At forty-two, he was the oldest of the siblings, and his service as a colonel under the old king gave his opinion further weight. Even his two littlest daughters ceased their whispering, and all eyes turned to him. His blue eyes were grave, and even as he sat still, surveying the gathering, it seemed to Jane that she could see the weight of authority and command on his broad shoulders. A raven's hoarse cry tore through the tense silence.

"I have stayed at home and been silent long enough," John said. "If the king crosses the border and calls for his subjects to join him, I mean to go."

Jane felt a surge of pride as she looked at him. *If I were a man,* she thought, *I would hope to be just such a one as he is.*

A babble of voices greeted John's news.

"Oh, John, no!" Jane's mother, Anne, cried out. "You served honorably and well for years during the wars. Your duty is to your family now."

"If you go, I'm with you, John," Henry said. "When do you think of leaving?"

John glanced at his wife. She had said nothing, but the set of her mouth showed she battled strong emotions.

"It will be no use to go off half-cocked," he said. "I'll raise as many men and horses as I can and ensure that we're well provided, so that when His Majesty summons us we can be of real use."

"Then put me down as one of yours as well, brother," Richard said.

"Not you, too, Dick!" their mother cried. "Two from the family is more than enough."

"I am no child, Mother!"

"But think of the cost!" Anne turned to her husband. "Dissuade him, I pray you, Thomas!"

"Mother, how can you argue that they should not go to the aid of the king?" Jane cried with sudden impatience. "He has need of all the help he can get. It's the crown—the crown and the future of the monarchy. The chance for wrongs to be righted, and the topsy-turvy world to be set back in place. I'd go myself, was I a man."

Her mother gave a little cry of fear and horror, and Withy laughed shrilly.

"I think you would, too."

"The Penderels from Whiteladies might come," Walter mused, hitching his chair close to John. "And perhaps Charles Giffard from Mosely."

"Yes," John said. "And no doubt men from among our tenant farmers, and many others. We'll go to Walsall next market day and make our plans known."

"So openly?" Sir Clement asked. "Do you trust your neighbors?"

"Some of them," John said.

"But others wish us ill," Richard spat, "And will surely report to the Stafford Committee anything they take amiss."

"Then we'll act quickly," Henry said, leaping to his feet, "And be gone as soon as we may."

After dinner, as the ladies prepared to withdraw to the house, Sir Clement stood and walked with Jane to the door of the banqueting house. Her female relatives exchanged significant glances and made themselves scarce.

Wonderful, Jane thought. *No private conversation can take place but I will be expected to report the results.* Sir Clement smiled as if understanding her thoughts, and spoke in a low voice.

"Will you not visit with me a little, Jane, now that we have a moment to be alone?"

Jane had known he'd be likely to speak his mind tonight, and had hoped to put off the conversation, for she had no clear answer for him, and no wish to cause him pain. He stood looking down at her, his blue eyes solemn, and she nodded. They strolled toward the house in silence. The western horizon was pale pink, shot with gold, and the first stars were just beginning to twinkle in the deepening blue overhead. A hush hung over the land, and Jane inhaled the scent of blossoms heavy on the breeze. Soon it would be autumn, but tonight was a perfect summer evening and she didn't want to go inside.

"Let's sit in the summerhouse," she said. "No one will disturb us there."

They sat side by side on an upholstered bench. The men's voices drifted from the banqueting house, still rising and falling in excited conversation.

Clement took Jane's hand and looked at it, as though he had never noticed it before.

"So small," he said. "And yet so strong. You'd make a fearsome soldier, Jane, and I honor your courage and your spirit, no matter what your sister may think."

"Withy has no good opinion of me, whatever I do."

"I think you know already what I mean to ask. I've long had such admiration and affection for you, and it would make my life complete if you were more to me than a friend, but a cherished partner. Jane, would you grant me the supreme happiness of consenting to be my wife?"

Jane forced herself not to sigh or to withdraw her hand. She looked into his eyes, shining at her in the shadows, kind and calm. Why could she not just say yes?

"You do me great honor, Sir Clement. You possess all the qualities women prize in a husband, and I probably have no need to tell you that my mother and sisters are all aflutter to hear what they hope

will be happy news very shortly. And yet I must ask you to indulge me by allowing me some time to consider."

"Of course. I have no wish to hurry you."

His lips were set as if in pain, and Jane's heart contracted. He was a good man, honorable, brave. What was wrong with her?

"I beg you to tell me," he said, "if there is some fear that you have, or some flaw in myself that I may mend?"

"No. The flaw is in me. I long for—I know not what. For adventure, I would say, did I want to leave myself open to your mockery."

"I would never mock you, my dear. I don't know what adventure you hope for, but no doubt you're right that I cannot offer you vivid excitement. I'm thirteen years your senior, no dashing young suitor to carry you off. I watched, enraptured, as you turned from a charming girl into a lovely young woman. I offer you my esteem, respect, and love. I can provide for you a comfortable home, even a grand one, if I may say so with modesty. I would protect you, honor you, and endeavor to make our life together as happy as it may be, but more than that I am powerless to give."

He looked off into the deepening shadows, silent. *For God's sake, give him something,* Jane thought miserably.

"That in itself is a world, which any woman should be overjoyed to accept. I shall think on your offer most seriously. May I answer you at Michaelmas?"

"At Michaelmas, then," he smiled. "And I will possess myself in patience during those two months as best I may."

"YOU WHAT?" WITHY CRIED.

"Asked him to wait?" Jane's mother breathed. "Sir Clement Fisher, and you asked him to wait?"

"Jane!" Athalia looked as shocked as though Jane had said she'd stuck a fork into Sir Clement's hand. "Has John not told you of the house? And the miles of parkland in which it sits?"

"Here are two of your nieces, younger than you, and betrothed!"

Jane's mother scolded. "He does you such honor, and you fling it away!"

"I know!" Jane cried, throwing up her hands. Their words echoed the fears ringing in her head. "I know. He is all that I should want, and yet I cannot make myself love him."

"Love the deer park," Withy snorted. "Love for the man may come hereafter."

Later that night, when most of the household had gone to bed, Jane found her father reading in his little study, peering over the rims of his glasses in the flickering candlelight. He looked up as she came in and reached out a hand to her. She took it and sank onto the fat little hassock next to his chair, on which she had spent so many happy hours as a child keeping him company as he worked. During his years as a justice of the peace she had observed in silent admiration as he counseled friends and neighbors and resolved complaints and disputes, most frequently with all parties happy at the outcome.

"You look troubled, sweetheart," he said, kissing her hand. "What's amiss? Or do you care to discuss it?"

"Mother and the others are vexed that I asked Sir Clement to wait."

"Ah, that," he said, his eyes twinkling.

"And have you not lost patience with me, too, Father? Are you not afraid I'll end a sad old maid?"

"Never in life." The love and comfort in his voice soothed her agitation. "And come to that, I'd rather you were happy and unwed than a miserable wife."

"I wish I'd been born a man." Jane sighed. "Or at least that I had the choices a man does. Look at Richard—only a year older than me, yet he can set the course of his own life, go where he wills. While I must keep at home and wait, though for what, I know not."

"I'd not have you other than as you are. Sir Clement is a good man, and if you can be happy with him, he'll make you a good husband,

I have no doubt. But whether you wed or no, you'll never want for a comfortable home here with us, or with John and Athalia once your mother and I are gone."

"I know." Jane squeezed her father's hand. "What are you reading?" she asked, standing to look over his shoulder.

"Virgil. Something about these times puts me in need of the classics."

"Nothing but bad in the newspapers," Jane agreed. "And though the ancient folk had their share of woes, they somehow seem less dire in rhyming couplets."

Thomas laughed, his eyes disappearing into the wrinkles around his eyes. "Well put, honey lamb. Now, never fret. We'll find something to distract your mother with, and let you think in peace."

CHAPTER TWO

THE DAY AFTER JANE'S BIRTHDAY, SHE FELT AT A LOSS. THE CELEBRATION was over and Clement was put off a few weeks. It was what she had asked for, and yet she felt discontent, with herself and the world. What on earth did she want? she wondered, looking at her reflection as she brushed her hair.

"You have a letter, Mistress Jane." Abigail appeared at the bedroom door, letter in outstretched hand, and Jane took it from her eagerly.

"It's from Ellen!" Jane cried. "Mrs. Norton. Ellen Owen as was."

"Oh, I hope she's well," Abigail smiled, her dark curls bobbing. "I always did like that lady."

Jane sat on the window seat and broke the seal on the letter. It was not often she received mail, and it made the day seem special. Her dearest friend Ellen had married the previous year and gone to live at her husband's grand home, Abbots Leigh, near Bristol, a hundred miles away. When Ellen lived nearby, she and Jane had visited each other frequently, sharing their hopes and dreams, and it seemed that

Ellen's dreams had come true. George Norton was everything she had wanted in a husband—handsome, rich, earnest, and above all, passionately in love with her. In November her happiness was to be crowned with the birth of a baby and her letter was full of her joy at impending motherhood.

> *I feel so peculiar and yet so wonderful that I don't think I can describe the sensation with any justice. My belly has begun to swell, and with marvel I run my hands over it and know that within lies a copy of my dear George (for I am sure it is a son, and my mother writes that carrying a baby low as I do is a sure sign that the child is a boy). My bosom, too, has grown, though surely it is too early for milk to be there, and though perhaps it is indecent of me to put it to paper, George seems to take even more delight in my body thus than he did when we were first wed.*

An image of the grinning Gypsy flashed into Jane's mind. She wondered what it would be like to lie with a man, and then wondered whether she would ever find out.

> *Oh, Jane, I wish that you were sitting next to me so that I could whisper to you these thoughts and feelings that I blush to write. Nothing would give me more joy than were you to come to visit when I am brought to bed and remain for some time after the baby is born. Though in name I am mistress here, in truth I feel as if I am still the guest of George's mother. I have no real friends and long for your company.*

I will go, Jane thought. *Perhaps Ellen can tell me what I'm waiting for, and whether I'm a fool to wait. There must be some sign she can point to, something that will tell whether I should marry Clement or no.*

She ran to find John and discovered him in shirtsleeves in the stables among a crowd of grooms and stable hands. The big stallion

Thunder was out of his box, and the gate was open into the stall where the pretty new dappled mare stood, whinnying and jerking nervously at her halter. The men looked embarrassed to see Jane, and she realized they must be about to put the stallion in to cover the mare, but she was so excited at the prospect of the trip that she couldn't wait.

"Ellen wants me to visit her when she has her baby! I so much want to go."

The scent of the mare in his nostrils, Thunder blew out a great whuffling breath and reared, and the boy holding his bridle narrowly avoided the slashing hooves.

"Have a care there, Tom." John turned briefly to Jane, but his attention was on the horses. "You'll need a pass to travel, you know."

"Oh." She had not thought of that. "But surely you can arrange it?"

"I daresay." He laid a calming hand on the shying mare. "But let's speak of this later, when I'm at leisure."

He sounded impatient, and as Jane made her way back to the house, she realized that perhaps it was because the arrangements for her travel would have to be made with the governor of Stafford. John had been governor of that town, as well as nearby Lichfield and Rushall. But Stafford had fallen to the enemy and the Parliamentary colonel Geoffrey Stone, once John's friend, was now governor, though even the rebel officers regarded John with respect.

She had her own reasons for feeling uneasy about a meeting with Colonel Stone. Just before the war had begun, when she was fifteen, young Geoff Stone, then twenty-three, had begun paying court to her. The matter had not gone so far as an engagement, but Jane had liked him very much, as had her family, and it had been painful and embarrassing for everyone when it became apparent they were on opposite sides of a disagreement that would be settled on the battlefield.

THE NEXT MORNING JOHN POPPED HIS HEAD IN JANE'S BEDROOM door, booted and his coat over his arm.

"I'll ride to Stafford today and see Geoff Stone. I don't think he'll give us any trouble about letting you visit Ellen. Someone must travel with you, though. I'll ask him to make the pass for you and a serving man, and we'll settle later who is to go."

"Thank you," Jane said, standing on tiptoe to kiss his cheek. "It means so much to me to see Ellen. And I'm just as glad not to have to see Geoff myself."

John was so much older than she that it was almost like having a second father, Jane thought. And while she revered Thomas Lane for his gentle wisdom, John was a big bluff soldier in his prime, and with him she always felt that nothing could hurt her.

"It's little enough I can do," John said. "The wars brought trouble in so many ways, we must find our way back to as many ordinary pleasures as we can."

That evening he returned with the precious pass, authorizing Mistress Jane Lane to travel the hundred miles from Bentley to Abbots Leigh, accompanied by a serving man.

"Colonel Stone asked me to send you his compliments and best wishes for a safe journey," he said. "He's a good man, for all that I disagree with him about the governance of the country."

On an afternoon a week later, Jane heard the wagon rumble up the drive and then excited voices in the stable yard. John and her father had set out for Wolverhampton for the weekly market, but they had hardly been gone long enough to accomplish their business. She peered out the window and saw Richard and her cousin Henry listening intently to John, though she couldn't catch the words.

She ran downstairs and out the door on the heels of her mother and Athalia.

"What is it, Thomas, what's happened?" her mother cried. Her father turned to them, his eyes burning with emotion.

"King Charles has crossed the border at Carlisle with his army and was proclaimed king at Penrith and Rokeby."

Jane's heart thrilled. Something real was happening, after all the rumor and uncertainty.

"How many men does he have?" she asked. "Is it the Scots, or has France or someone sent troops?"

"It's mostly Scots so far," John said. "But yesterday the king issued a general pardon and oblivion for those who fought against his father, and is calling on his subjects to join him and fight."

He took a printed broadsheet from his coat pocket, and Richard pulled it out of his hands.

"Dear God," Jane's mother moaned. "More war."

"But this will be the end." Richard's eyes were gleaming. "This is our chance to defeat the rebels for good and all."

"Let's not stand here to discuss it," John said as a groom took the team of horses by the bridles and led the wagon away. "Come inside and we'll talk."

As the family gathered around the table, servants edged in from the kitchen to hear the news.

Jane had seized the Parliamentary *Mercurius Britannicus* newspaper her father had brought home, and snorted in disgust.

"They've set forth in the most alarming terms every invasion of the Scots since 1071. 'Un-English,' they call those who would join the king, and say they deserved to be stoned."

"Hardly surprising from that source," Henry said. "But hear what the king says. Read it, Dick."

"'We are now entering into our kingdom with an army who shall join with us in doing justice upon the murderers of our royal father . . .'"

"It's really happening!" Jane cried. "He's coming to take back his throne!"

"'To evidence how far we are from revenge, we do engage ourself to a full Act of Oblivion and Indemnity for all things done these seven years past, excepting only Oliver Cromwell, Henry Ireton,

John Bradshaw, John Cooke, and all others who did actually sit and vote in the murder of our royal father.' "

"That's only right," Henry said, to murmurs of agreement.

" 'We do require some of quality or authority in each county where we shall march to come to us . . .' "

They were all silent for a moment, and then John spoke.

"I'll go to Walsall tomorrow to begin to form a regiment. We'll send word around tonight. And we shall hasten to the king's side as soon as we may."

Oh God, that I were a man! Jane wished. *Then I, too, could rally to his side and fight, instead of sitting here to await the outcome.*

As summer ripened, the emotional temperature of England seemed to rise. Every day there was more ominous news. The Catholics of Lancashire had failed to rise for King Charles. Parliament ordered the raising of militias in each county. A month's pay was provided to the militiamen who were flocking to support the Parliamentary army, and the generals Cromwell, Lambert, and Harrison were harrying the king's forces as he moved southward. The government clamped down, ordering that all copies of the king's proclamation were to be turned over to the authorities to be burned by the local hangmen. Public meetings were forbidden. The already stringent restrictions on travel were tightened.

"You cannot think of going to Abbots Leigh now!" Jane's mother cried over supper on a warm evening toward the end of August. "Soldiers everywhere, and thousands of Scots among them!"

"The Scots are with the king, still far to the north," Jane responded. "It's the Roundheads and the militias I would run into, and in any case, my pass provides for a manservant. I'll take one of the grooms with me."

"That's scarcely better. John, you must accompany your sister."

"You know I can't, Mother."

"Or you, Dick." Anne rounded on her youngest son.

"No more can I," he said, doggedly tearing into a piece of bread. "I mean to join the king as soon as we are provisioned."

"I'll get a son of one of our tenant farmers to travel with Jane," Thomas Lane intervened. "Some great strapping lad who'll make sure no harm befalls her."

Jane's mother shook her head in exasperation. "That's a step in the right direction. But, Jane, surely Ellen would understand if you cannot come?"

"I would not ask her to understand." Jane tried to keep the irritation from her voice. "She wants my company, and I would not miss the chance to be with her for anything."

JOHN, RICHARD, AND HENRY WERE DAILY AT WALSALL, AND THE TROOP of men and horse they would take to the king's aid was growing as the people of the surrounding countryside took heart at the prospect of his return to the throne. Jane joined her brothers and cousin in the parlor after supper each evening to hear about the events of the day, and shook her head in disgust as she read the latest proclamation, "An Act Prohibiting Correspondence with Charles Stuart or His Party."

" 'Whereas certain English fugitives did perfidiously and traitorously assist the enemies and invaders of this Commonwealth and did set up for their head Charles Stuart, calling him their king'!"

"The more frightened they are, the harder they strike out," Henry said, his booted feet propped on a stool before him. John lit his pipe and blew a smoke ring, watching it dissolve into the shadows before he spoke.

"They've made it a capital offense to give aid to the king in any form. There will be no middle ground. If we're defeated, the repercussions will be bloody and terrible."

"The king has reached Worcester!" Henry crowed a few nights later. "He summons all men between the ages of sixteen and sixty to rally in the riverside meadows near the cathedral."

Richard tilted the newly printed broadsheet toward the firelight.

"He promises the Scots will return home once the war is done. Perhaps that will mollify Mother."

A few days before the end of August, Jane heard the men return home earlier than usual, and ran down to the kitchen to hear the news. John was bathing his face with water from a bucket near the door. Henry and Richard stood nearby, their faces ashen.

"What's happened?" she asked, her heart in her throat.

"The worst news we could have hoped for." John shook his head, drying his face and hands. "The Earl of Derby had stayed in Lancashire to defend against Cromwell's advance. Cromwell's men caught up with him at Wigan. It seems he may have escaped, but more than two thousand have been taken prisoner, including the Duke of Richmond and Lord Beauchamp."

"The enemy had word of where he was," Henry said, sinking in despair onto a stool. "There must be spies in the ranks. Some of the Scots are abandoning the king now, and making for the border."

"The king was already outnumbered," Richard fretted, slamming his fist onto the big worktable. "The battle could come any day. John, we can't wait any longer."

"Another two days," John said. "Mistress Hawkins has promised a dozen horses, and we'll need every beast we can get."

"Let me leave tomorrow," Richard insisted. "With the men and horses we have now."

Oh, that I could be riding with you, Jane thought.

"Very well," John said. "Henry and I will follow the day after."

THE NEXT EVENING AFTER SUPPER JANE SLIPPED INTO THE PARLOR to find her brothers and cousin huddled together near the hearth, their worried looks and low urgent conversation presaging some further bad news.

"What is it?" she asked.

"Come in and shut the door," John said. He handed her a printed broadsheet.

"'We do hereby publish and declare Charles Stuart, son to the late tyrant, to be a rebel, traitor, and public enemy to the Commonwealth of England,'" Jane read. "'And all his abettors, agents, and complices to be rebels, traitors, and public enemies, and do hereby command all officers civil and military in all market towns and convenient places, to cause this declaration to be proclaimed and published . . .'"

She let the proclamation drop to the floor, suddenly wishing that she could bar the doors of the house, locking out danger and keeping these men she loved so much safe at home.

"It's not that I mind risking my life," Richard said, his cheeks flushed with anger. "But if we fail and are captured, the dogs will take the house, the land, and we'll not be here to protect Mother and Father."

I can't strap on a sword and a pistol and ride to Worcester with them, Jane thought. *But there is something I can do.*

"I'll take care of Mother and Father," she said. Her brothers and cousin looked at her. "And your family, too, John, if it comes to that. You must go."

"How can you?" Richard shook his head. "Your love won't feed them nor yet put a roof over their heads if Cromwell's men burn the house."

The reference to burning hung heavy in the air. An earlier Bentley Hall had been burned down seventy years ago by the mayor and members of the corporation of Walsall during a dispute over common rights, and during the wars many houses had been destroyed by troops on both sides.

"I can marry Clement Fisher," she said.

She felt numb and then consumed by panic, as if her air were being cut off. *Don't be stupid,* she told herself, swallowing back tears. *If they can risk death on the battlefield or scaffold, how can I hesitate?* The men were all staring at her, and she squared her shoulders and swallowed the sobs that were rising to her throat.

"If you go, we will stand firm here at home, whatever comes."

John came to her and wiped a tear from her cheek with his thumb.

"Thank you, Jane. It's a weight off my mind to think so. But let's pray the battle ends with the king on the throne, and it doesn't come to such a pass."

RICHARD AND PART OF THE NEWLY FORMED WALSALL ROYALIST REGiment set off to join the king on the first of September. Cromwell had arrived at Red Hill outside the city walls of Worcester, his New Model Army augmented by local militias from across England, and the battle must begin any day. On the third of September, John and Henry rode northward with another hundred men and horses. The house seemed eerily empty and quiet as the family gathered for dinner.

"It was a year ago today that young King Charles met Cromwell's forces at Dunbar," Thomas Lane commented, and Jane shivered, recalling her despair at the news of the terrible rout, and Cromwell's subsequent subjugation of Scotland.

Jane felt restless all afternoon. She tried to read but found no pleasure in it and could not make herself sit still, so she gave up and went outside. Clouds hung overhead and the air seemed to crackle with tension. She felt lonely, but there was no one to talk to, no one who would satisfy her longing for easy companionship. Maybe she would stay with Ellen for a month or more, she thought. Maybe she would feel happier with a change of scene. *And perhaps*, a voice at the back of her head whispered, *perhaps you will meet a man there.*

JANE LAY AWAKE THAT NIGHT, HER MIND AND SPIRIT DISTURBED. SHE had only begun to drop off to sleep when she was startled into wakefulness by the furious pounding of horses' hooves and dogs barking. She ran to the window. There was no moon, and by the silver starlight she could barely make out fleeting shapes in the blackness as several men on horseback pelted into the yard as though the forces of hell were after them.

"All of them into the stable!" It was John's voice calling out hoarsely.

"Quick, man, quickly, away!" And that voice was Henry's, low and urgent. Something must be terribly wrong, that they should be back so soon.

Her heart pounding, Jane threw a heavy shawl around her shoulders and ran downstairs, meeting her parents, Athalia, Withy, and Withy's husband, John Petre, as they converged in the kitchen just as John slammed the door shut and dropped the bar into place. Henry had collapsed onto a stool at the great table, and was slumped forward, his breath coming in ragged gasps.

"What is it, John?" Thomas Lane asked, striking a flint and lighting the lantern. Its blue glass panes bathed the kitchen in a spectral glow.

"There's been a great defeat at Worcester," John said, his face haggard. "We got no further than Kidderminster before we began to meet soldiers fleeing. We left it too late to join the king. The battle started this morning."

"Richard!" Jane's mother shrieked. "What of Richard? Is he with you?"

"Alas, no," John said. "We turned back as soon as it was clear there was no longer a battle to go to."

"Cromwell's men are scouring the country for the king's soldiers even now," Henry said. "It was all we could do to get back before we met any of them."

"And the king?" Jane cried. "What of the king?"

John and Henry exchanged glances.

"We heard that he was killed," John said heavily. "But also that he had been taken prisoner."

Jane's heart sank. If young King Charles had been captured, he would surely be executed as his father had been, and the Royalist cause would be lost indeed.

"Everything is chaos." Jane thought Henry seemed near tears. "All that is certain is that the king's forces were greatly outnumbered, and the day was lost after fierce and terrible fighting."

Outside a gust of wind shook the trees, and Jane heard the patter of rain against the window, invisible against the icy blackness.

"I'll go into Wolverhampton for news tomorrow," Thomas said at last. "Though I fear me none of it will be good."

All through the night and into the next day it rained. In the gray light of dawn, Jane stood huddled in her shawl, staring out an upstairs window. A quarter of a mile away, the Wolverhampton Road was thick with the traffic of the disaster. Wounded men limped or were carried by their fellows. The rain beat down relentlessly, turning the road into a sucking stew of mud. Jane hoped against hope that she would see Richard walking up the lane to the house, and prayed that he was alive and unwounded. She turned as John came to stand beside her, unshaven and with dark circles under his eyes. She was startled to see how gray was the stubble on his cheeks.

"Can we not help those poor men?" she asked. "Give them water and food, at least? Perhaps somewhere someone is doing the same for Richard."

In a short time the bake house behind Bentley Hall was bustling as servants dispensed water, hot soup, bread, and ale to the stream of refugees, along with bread, cheese, sausages, and apples to carry away with them. In the kitchen, the women of the house did what they could for the wounded. Washing away the blood and mud and binding the men's wounds with strips of linen and herbal decoctions to slow the bleeding and soothe the pain made Jane feel that she was making some difference, and it gave her the opportunity to ask about Richard.

"Richard Lane? No, Mistress, I don't know him." The young soldier, one arm in a bloody sling and his face gray with pain and dirt, shook his head. Jane closed her eyes and tried not to imagine Richard's body stiffening in the cold rain.

"Though to be sure," the lad continued, gulping water from a tin cup, "by the end it was like hell itself, and I would have been hard-pressed to know what happened to any man."

"Tell me," Jane begged. She sat beside him on the bench next to the big kitchen table. Across from her, Nurse was sponging blood from the ragged scrap of flesh that was all that remained of the right ear of a redheaded boy who was doing his best not to cry.

"I was just to the north of Fort Royal, up on the hill," the young soldier said, "and when the rebels captured the fort, we were cut off from the rest of the king's forces. Outflanked, and trapped outside the city walls. We tried to get to St. Martin's Gate, but Cromwell's men—the Essex militia it was—came after us."

He shook his head, as if trying to puzzle something out, and his voice was hollow as he continued.

"There was no question of capture. They just wanted to slaughter all of us they could. Of course, once they overran the fort, they had our cannons. Men were falling all about me and the dead were huddled in piles against the city walls. By some miracle I reached the gate and got through."

A heavy rumble of thunder sounded, rattling the windows, and the rain seemed to renew its fury.

"And then?" Jane prompted gently.

"All was confusion. The enemy must have broached the other gates of the city, for they seemed to be coming from all directions. They were riding men down, cutting them down as they fled. I saw the king almost trampled by our own horse, running in so great disorder that he could not stop them, though he used all the means he could."

"Alas," Jane said. "Would they not stand and fight?"

"I'm sure most did as well as they were able, Mistress. But by that time even those who still had muskets had no shot, and were trying to hold off the enemy horse with fire pikes—burning tar in leather jacks fixed to the ends of their pikes. Dusk was falling and with it the end of any hope. I fled out the gate, my only thought to head northward."

He drained the last of the water and stood, slinging his canvas sack on his shoulders.

"I thank you for your kindness, Mistress. And I hope your brother is safe and on his way home."

Jane heard similar stories throughout the day. The king's army had known to begin with that they were outnumbered, but fought with the desperation born of the knowledge that today was their only hope. At the fort, at the city walls and gates, in the streets, it had been brutal, exhausting, confusing mayhem, ending in defeat and despair.

"We were beat," a grizzled sergeant said. "It was not for want of spirit, nor for want of effort by the king. Certainly a braver prince never lived."

"What does he look like, the king?" Jane asked.

The sergeant blew out his cheeks. "Like a king ought to, you might say. I was proud to look on him, and to be sure, I could tell that all around me felt the same."

Jane thought of Kent in *King Lear. You have that in your countenance which I would call master . . . Authority.*

"What else?" she asked.

"He's a big man, over six feet, and well formed." He noted the look in her eyes and smiled. "Yes, and handsome, too, lass." Jane blushed. "Of a dark complexion, darker than the king his father. He was wearing a buff coat, with an armor breastplate and back over it, like any officer, but finer, you know. And some jewel on a great red ribbon that sparkled like nothing I've ever seen."

Although the fight must have been terrible, Jane wished desperately that she could have seen the king.

"He was right there among the men in the battle?" she asked.

"Oh, to be sure, Mistress. He hazarded his person much more than any officer, riding from regiment to regiment and calling the officers by name, and when all seemed lost urging the men to stand and fight once more."

Exactly like King Henry V, Jane thought.

Once more unto the breach, dear friends, once more;
Or close the wall up with our English dead . . .

"He had two horses shot from under him, he did."

Jane could imagine the young king so clearly, and she choked back a sob as she remembered that he might well be dead.

"I was there to near the end, I think," the old sergeant went on. "When there remained just a few of us by the town hall."

We few, we happy few, we band of brothers . . .

"All that kept us going was the word that the king had not been killed or captured, so far as any could tell. It was full dark by then, and I was able to slip away by St. Martin's Gate, which our horse still held."

MANY OF THE FLEEING SOLDIERS WERE SCOTTISH HIGHLANDERS, the upper part of their great kilts drawn up over their heads against the rain, and Jane fancied she saw in their faces bleak despair that went beyond their hunger, discomfort, and defeat in battle. By midday Parliamentary cavalry patrols thundered by on the now-deserted road, and in the afternoon Jane watched a detachment pass with a string of captured Royalist soldiers, their wrists bound, soaked to the knees in mud.

"What will happen to them?" she asked John.

"The Scots will likely be transported to Barbados, or maybe the American colonies. As slaves, more or less, to work on plantations."

"Inhuman," Jane whispered in horror. "And the English?"

"Prison. Likely execution for the officers. The men may be spared their lives."

"Richard," Jane said. "It breaks my heart to think where he may be. Wounded, perhaps, lying in some field, wet and hungry and in pain."

Or worse, she thought, but did not speak the words, as if giving them voice had the power to make them real. John put a hand on her shoulder and pulled her closer to him.

"Let's not think that yet. It may well be that he escaped in safety and is on his way to us even now."

He kissed the top of her head, and the familiar scent of him, the pungent smell of tobacco smoke, mingled with his own sweat and a slight layering of horse, made Jane feel calm and safe.

THROUGHOUT THE DAY AND EVENING, NEIGHBORS CAME TO CALL AT Bentley to exchange news.

"A Scottish soldier that passed this morning said he had heard the king had been taken prisoner near sunset," said John's friend Matt Haggard from Lichfield. "But another swore he had seen the king with his own eyes well after dark."

"A Parliamentary patrol stopped at the house just at dawn," said old Mr. Smithton. "The captain said he'd seen the king dead, wounded through the breast by a sword. But he looked like a lying whoreson to me."

Jane chose to believe what the gray-haired sergeant had heard late in the evening, that the king was still free and unharmed. For to let herself think anything else overwhelmed her with grief and terror.

After supper Jane and her father sat side by side reading before the fire in his little study. His companionship, and the persisting in everyday activities, comforted her, helped her believe that all was well or yet might be. The rain beat down outside, and she tried not to think of where Richard might be. John came to the door, and smiled to see his father and sister look up with identical expectant expressions.

"Mother's gone to bed," he said. "And Athalia and the girls."

"Good," Thomas said. "Better to take comfort in sleep than worry needlessly."

Jane was surprised to hear the whinny of a horse outside. She ran to the window and peered out, and in a flash of lightning could make out a rider on the drive, leading a second horse behind him.

"It's not Richard," she said.

"Who can that be, now?" her father wondered.

"I'll see to it," John said, and to Jane's alarm he took a pistol from a drawer of the desk before he made his way downstairs. He reappeared a few minutes later with William Walker, an old Papist priest that Jane knew as a friend of Father John Huddleston, the young priest who acted as tutor to the boys at neighboring Mosely Hall.

"You're wet to the bone, sir," Thomas cried. "Come down to the kitchen to dry yourself."

"I thank you, Mr. Lane." The old man shivered. "But better I ask the favor I've come for and be on my way." He glanced at Jane.

"You can speak before my sister," John assured him. "And to tell you true, if I send her away she'll only pester any news out of me once you've gone."

Old Father William smiled at Jane, as a drop of water gathered on his nose and fell to the carpet.

"Well, then. I've two horses below, and Mr. Whitgreaves asks if you would take them into your stable for the night, and mayhap for a few days." He lowered his voice. "There's a gentleman at Mosely who's come from Worcester fight. He can be hid well enough, but the house lies so close to the road that any strange horses are like to be noted."

"Of course," said John, with a glance at his father.

"Maybe this gentleman will know news of Richard," Jane cried.

"Just what I was thinking." John nodded. "Of course we'll take the horses, sir. But as Jane says, the household is in great fear for my brother, who was at Worcester. Pray tell Mr. Whitgreaves that I'll ride over tomorrow night, to learn what I can of the battle, and how we may help his fugitive. But come, let's get those horses out of sight."

"Oh, Father," Jane said as John and the priest disappeared down the stairs. "The poor old man, walking all that long way back to Mosely in the rain."

"Old he may be, but he's a man still, and he'll not melt. He's doing what he can for our cause. I would I could do more, could have gone with your brothers to the fight." Jane, standing behind her father's chair, leaned her head onto his and put her arms around him. The thought of him fleeing from Worcester in the night was more than she could bear.

"I know you'd go to fight, but I'm glad you didn't. What would we do without you here at home?"

He patted her hand and nodded. "Yes, yes. But it's your brother I'm worried about."

"No doubt we'll hear more tomorrow," she said.

JANE AND ALL THE HOUSEHOLD PASSED THE NEXT DAY IN A FEVER OF anxiety about Richard. John went into Walsall and returned with newly printed broadsheets.

"'A Letter from the Lord General Cromwell Touching the Great Victory Obtained Near Worcester,'" Jane read as Henry and her parents listened.

"I'll warn you, it makes grim reading," John said, sinking into a chair before the fire in the parlor.

"'We beat the enemy from hedge to hedge, till we beat him into Worcester,'" Jane read. "'He made a very considerable fight, and it was as stiff a contest for four or five hours as ever I have seen.'"

"And I make no doubt he's seen some bad fighting," John said, his face grim.

"'In the end we beat him totally. He hath had great loss, and is scattered and run. We are in pursuit of him and have laid forces in several places, that we hope will gather him up.'" Jane read it over again. "Then they haven't captured the king yet. At least that's something."

"Not yet. It's hard to see how he can escape being taken, though."

Athalia came in with a mug of something steaming. She brushed a lock of golden-brown hair from John's forehead as she gave him the drink, and he kissed her hand and smiled up at her, his face tired.

"Here's another," Henry said, "'A Full and Perfect Relation of the Fight at Worcester on Wednesday Night Last.'"

"I don't want to hear it," Jane said. "It makes me too angry and sad."

. . .

Jane was eager for night to come so that John could make his visit to Mosely Hall, and she waited up long after the rest of the family had gone to bed for his return, reading in the kitchen by lantern light. She found it difficult to keep her mind on *The Aeneid,* and realized that she had been staring unseeing at the same page for several minutes, filled with anxiety about what tidings John would bring. It was near midnight when she finally heard his horse, and ran to the kitchen door to meet him.

"Richard's alive and unhurt, or was two nights since," John said as soon as he came in, unwrapping his heavy scarf and hanging his coat on a peg near the hearth.

"Thank God," Jane cried. "Where is he? Did you learn more news of the battle?"

She added hot water and lemon to brandy and brought mugs to the table for both of them.

"Ah, that warms me," John said, drinking. "Thank you, Jane. Yes, there is much news. It's my old commander Lord Wilmot who has taken refuge at Mosely. He was in the thick of the battle, at the king's side."

He glanced around, as if spies lurked in the shadows, and lowered his voice.

"Jane, the king is alive and nearby."

Jane smothered a gasp and leaned closer to John as he continued.

"When it became clear that the fight was lost, the king took flight from Worcester with the remains of his cavalry. A few hundred men, Wilmot said. Most of them headed for Tong Castle, having got word that General Leslie and what was left of the Scots infantry had gone there. Richard went with them, but Wilmot heard that all were taken prisoner before ever they reached Tong."

Jane felt a cold knot form in the pit of her stomach. Richard a prisoner. He could be dead even now, perhaps shot or hanged with no deliberation or trial. She felt furious at her helplessness.

"And the king?" She spoke so low that she could hardly hear her own voice.

"The Earl of Derby urged the king to make for Boscobel, where Derby had been concealed after his defeat at Wigan. Charles Giffard of Boscobel was with them, though, and said that it had been searched but lately, and that Whiteladies might be safer. So the king, with only a few companions, rode through the night and reached Whiteladies about three in the morning."

The hairs on the back of Jane's neck stood up to think of the king being so near. The old Whiteladies priory, now owned by the Giffard family, was only some dozen miles away.

"There are cavalry patrols looking for him," John continued, his voice rough with exhaustion and emotion. "So the Penderel brothers hid him in the wood nearby, and there he spent the day."

"Dear God, in the rain."

"Better wet than captured. Wilmot would not say more than that the king is now being helped by other good neighbors of ours, and with God's grace will soon be on his way to safety."

"What will Lord Wilmot do?" Jane asked. "He, too, must be fleeing for his life."

John's eyes met hers and he paused before he answered.

"Now must I tell you that we can help him. That you can help him."

"How can I help him?" she asked in surprise.

"He must get to Bristol, where he can arrange for a boat to take the king to France." Bristol. Only a few short miles from Ellen Norton's home.

"My pass to travel."

"Yes. Wilmot must play the part of your serving man, and ride with you to Abbots Leigh."

The news took Jane's breath away. She felt a thrill of fear, but it instantly gave way to excitement. An adventure. Lord Wilmot, friend of the king. She had never met the man, but his name conjured in her mind an image of a handsome and dashing officer. He would sweep her into his arms and together they would ride through peril. Once at Abbots Leigh, he could doff his disguise. By then perhaps he would be smitten with her . . . Jane checked herself. How ridiculous to be carried off in foolish fantasies, with all that lay at stake.

"Will I wait for Lord Wilmot at Ellen's house until he has found passage for the king?" she asked. "Or return without him?"

"You'll not ride alone. It's far too dangerous, and moreover it would raise questions if you were stopped, especially as your pass is for you and a manservant. I'd go with you but my name and my face are too well known to the rebel commanders, and I'd put you in greater danger still. But we'll find a way. If you're willing." He looked at her searchingly. "You need not do it."

"Of course I'm willing! How could I do otherwise, when the life of the king is at stake?"

CHAPTER THREE

"You cannot go!" Jane's mother cried, her hands fluttering in dismay.

Jane stood at the foot of her bed, folding three pairs of stockings into a nightgown and packing them into a satchel.

"With all those soldiers on the road?" Anne Lane paced, heels tapping on the floorboards, and then swooped to Jane's side. "And Scots, most of them! You'll be ravished and murdered."

"I shall have protection, Mother," Jane sighed, frowning as she noticed a small tear in the sleeve of her favorite shift. "John will arrange for one of our tenants' sons to ride with me."

"Small comfort! He may be worse than the soldiers, for all we know."

Jane's heart softened at the sight of her mother's face, pink with agitation beneath her white cap, and she pulled Anne to sit beside her on the bed.

"Ellen is expecting me. Her first baby! I promised her as soon as she knew that she was with child that I would be there for her lying-in and to keep her company after. I cannot disappoint her."

Jane's mother sniffed and dabbed at her eyes with her lace-edged handkerchief.

"I don't know what John is thinking of. And your father. I should never have considered such a thing when I was a girl, and you may be sure my father and brothers would have had none of it."

Jane's favorite uncle, Hervey Bagot, was a colonel in the Royalist army, and his son Richard Bagot had been mortally wounded at the Battle of Naseby. She thought that they would certainly have been in favor of her doing whatever she could if it would save the king, but she merely took her mother's hand and kissed her cheek.

"All shall be well, Mother. Cromwell's men are too busy searching for the king to bother with me. And the poor Scots are fleeing for their lives, exhausted and hungry. I would be in more danger if I were a turnip."

On Saturday night, John returned to Mosely Hall to make plans with Wilmot for his escape to Bristol with Jane and to bring Wilmot's horses back to Bentley. Once more Jane waited for him in the kitchen, sitting at the big table in the middle of the room. She had brought knitting to keep her hands busy, but the activity didn't still the turmoil of her mind, and she threw down the needles and yarn and went to the window again. The sliver of moon cast a faint silver glow over the stable yard and outbuildings, and all was quiet.

The big case clock in the great hall struck two when Jane finally heard John's footsteps. She pulled the door open, and he moved heavily as he came in and threw off his coat. His whole aspect was one of despair and worry, and prickles of fear ran down her spine.

"What's amiss? Is it Richard?"

"No," he said, pulling a chair close to the fire and warming his hands above the flames. "I have no news of him."

Jane put a mug of brandy and hot water into his hands and he inhaled the steam and drank before he spoke again.

"The situation is grown more perilous than it was. The king set out for Wales on Thursday night with one of the Penderels, but the crossing of the Severn is guarded by two companies of militia and all the boats have been seized. There was nothing for it but to return last night, and he's back at Mosely."

The king, only six miles away, and still in danger. It was like something out of a play, Jane thought.

"Oh, no," she whispered. "What will he do?"

The firelight flickered orange on John's face, and it seemed to Jane there were lines around his eyes that had not been there only days earlier. His voice was hoarse when he spoke again.

"Jane, I am loath to say what I am about to because I would not put you in danger, but I can see no other way."

Jane stared at him. What could he mean?

"The king must ride with you to Abbots Leigh. Not Wilmot, but the king himself."

The shock was so great that Jane found she could say nothing.

"He's already disguised himself, Wilmot says, cut his hair and changed clothes with a poor woodsman so that none would know him."

Jane tried to picture the dashing young king who had rallied his troops at Worcester, grimy and unrecognizable.

"We can clothe him in better apparel, and hope that he'll pass as your serving man. But, Jane, this is far more dangerous than riding with Lord Wilmot."

"I must help him if I can."

John stared into the fire, and shivered despite its warmth. "When the king's friends parted from him at Whiteladies," he said, "they begged him not to tell them his plans so they could not be forced to reveal them if they were put to torture. Jane, if you were to be taken . . . The danger is great."

Jane swallowed. She was very much afraid at the thought of what might happen to her. But if she did not help the king to escape, surely he would be found and captured soon.

"I'll do it."

"Someone else must go with you."

"Henry." Jane had always felt that in the company of her cousin

Henry she could come to no harm, and she felt the more so now that he was a soldier. She recalled the steely determination in his eyes when he had set off with John the few days earlier that now seemed so long ago, and his bitter disappointment when they had returned in confusion, having left too late to join the battle.

"Yes. Henry would go, and I'll have less fear knowing that he's with you."

"But when shall we go? Surely soldiers will be searching the houses hereabout and are like to find the king?"

"Mosely has a priest hole, so the king is well hidden. But still he must fly soon."

Jane had been shown a priest hole once, in the house of a Catholic friend. It was a little space, not more than four feet square and three feet high, just big enough to hide a man or forbidden articles such as crucifixes, the entry hatch concealed beneath a close stool in the floor of a closet. It had made her skin creep to think of climbing down into it, with no air and no light save for a candle, and her heart went out to the young king.

"Wilmot will send tomorrow to know if you'll undertake the journey. Think it over."

"I don't have to think," Jane said, pushing her fears aside. "Nothing could stop me."

The next day after noontime dinner, John stopped Jane as she was heading upstairs to her room.

"Henry's in the orchard. Come join us for a little chat."

She grabbed a shawl and hurried out with him, relieved that Withy and her nose for secrets were nowhere to be seen. Henry was swinging by his arms from the branch of a great apple tree, and drew himself up higher before he dropped to the ground, dusting off his hands on the knees of his breeches. He was almost thirty, but there was something very boyish about the way his whole face was lit at the prospect of adventure, Jane thought.

"I'll ride to Mosely again tonight," John said, "and bring Wilmot back so we can make our final preparations, but let's consult between us now." He turned to Henry. "Jane's pass is for her and a manservant, no more. I'm concerned that if I go back to Colonel Stone and ask to add someone else, it will draw attention we'd better avoid."

"Agreed," Henry said. "I'll chance it. If we're stopped and the king is recognized, the lack of a pass will be the least of our worries." He grinned at Jane, eyes shining. "Didn't think when you woke up a few days ago that we'd be saving the king's neck, did you?"

"No," Jane smiled.

"Are you sure, Jane?" John asked. "If you're having second thoughts, better to voice them now."

"I'm having no second thoughts. And if I were, I'd go through with it anyway. For what other way is as sure to get the king out of danger?"

"Spoken like a true soldier." Henry tweaked a curl that strayed from Jane's cap, the same as he had done since she was a little girl and he a dashing older boy. "But it's as well I'll be with you, to protect you from the king as much as for anything else."

"Why, what a thing to say!" Jane cried in astonishment. "What may you mean by that?"

"Only that he's a man like any other, and used to having his way."

"Careful, Henry," John warned.

"John, if she's to travel with him, she should know to be on her guard." John shrugged in acquiescence, and Henry continued. "He's already got a bastard son by a wench on Jersey, and there are whispers that he got at least one child on the daughter of the governor there, too."

Jane felt a little shock at such licentiousness, but she was more annoyed at the sight of Henry, clearly expecting her to be outraged.

"Brisk work for a lad of twenty-one," she said coolly. "But I'm sure His Majesty will have more on his mind than attempting to debauch me."

She smiled inwardly to see that Henry looked disappointed at her lack of reaction.

"It's too cold to tarry here," she said. "We'll talk more tonight. I'm going in."

. . .

HENRY WAITED WITH JANE IN THE DARKENED KITCHEN THAT NIGHT. John had a book of maps that had been prepared for Royalist officers, and Henry studied it by the lantern light.

"An exceeding useful thing to have," he said. "The maps will save us asking our way. The less attention we bring to ourselves the better."

Jane paced, going to the window to peer out into the blackness. The pale curved crescent of the moon had risen into view before they heard the clatter of horses' hooves. A rush of cold air gusted through the kitchen as John came through the heavy wooden door, followed by a stocky figure wrapped in a bulky cloak, and Jane shivered as the reality of what she was planning to undertake hit her.

"My lord, may I present my sister Jane? You know my cousin Henry Lascelles, I believe."

"Your servant, Mistress. A pleasure to see you, Lascelles."

As Wilmot pulled off his hat and bowed to her, Jane saw that he was a big man with a spreading paunch, near on forty years old, and nothing like the dashing hero of her imagination. But still he looked the part of a soldier, and Jane knew from John's service under him that he was a capable and shrewd commander. She brought warm drink to the table and sat down with the men. Wilmot's buff coat was splattered with mud, the collar of his shirt was grimy, and his unshaven face was stubbled with gray, and Jane remembered that like the king, he had been on the run from Cromwell's men for five long days.

"Henry will ride with my sister and—your master," John said, his voice low.

Wilmot nodded his understanding.

"An extra man will not go amiss in case of danger," John added. "And you and I may be of help, too, my lord. We can give out that we go to visit Clement Fisher at Packington. The way lies in the same direction the others will travel, and we can keep in sight at least through the morning."

"Well bethought," Wilmot nodded. "The greatest danger probably lies closest to here, so the more men to hand the better. And I shall be glad to see Fisher again."

"The situation has fallen out well for our purpose," John said. "I had planned to send the son of one of our tenant farmers to accompany Jane, and it is such a man your master must feign to be. We'll provide suitable clothes and instruct him in what he needs to know."

"I've already made arrangements to stop with family at Long Marston on the way," Jane said, looking at the men's shadowed faces. "And they'll not question my having a serving man with me."

"Long Marston's a long day's ride," Henry said, "but if all goes well we should be able to make it, and to reach Abbots Leigh in another two days' travel."

"Good," Wilmot said. "I'll ride from Packington, and meet you all at Abbots Leigh."

"Then we're agreed," John said. "We'll be ready to leave when you think fit, my lord."

A thrill went through Jane's stomach. It was really happening. A greater adventure than she could have imagined.

"Let us make it as soon as it may be," Wilmot said. "The danger grows with every hour. I'll bring him here tomorrow at midnight, and we'll leave at daybreak." He stood and threw his cloak over his shoulders. "Until tomorrow." He bowed to Jane. "I honor your courage, Mistress. And I know I can speak for our master in giving all of you his profound thanks."

LATE THOUGH IT WAS, JANE LAY STARING INTO THE DARK, UNABLE TO stop her mind from whirling. She could scarcely believe that before the next day was out, the king would be at Bentley, and that the following morning they would be on their way toward Bristol, riding to save his life and any hope for the future of England's monarchy. She had never traveled farther than Stafford, less than thirty miles away, and now she was setting out on a journey of a hundred miles, every step fraught with peril to her own life as well as that of the king. Her cat, Jack, lay purring at her side, and she reached down to stroke his head.

"How has it come," she asked him, "that an undertaking of such moment should rest on my shoulders? Will I be able to surmount the difficulties and terrors that are sure to lie along the way?"

Jack shifted against her, his purring rumbling deep within his chest.

I shall have to, Jane murmured to herself. *God give me strength.*

The next morning Jane looked out her bedroom window to see a man hastening to the kitchen door. She recognized him as one of the five surviving Penderel brothers, who lived in and around Whiteladies and served the Giffard family at Boscobel, a few miles away in the woods of Shropshire. The family had fought for the king, and a sixth brother had been killed at the Battle of Edgehill. Jane saw John slip out to the stables with the man, and a few minutes later she heard his footsteps on the stairs. He put a finger to his lips imploring her silence as she opened her door to him.

"John Penderel's just come from Whiteladies. Colonel Ashenhurst was there last night with a party of soldiers. They'd been told that the king was at the house, and they tore the place apart and used Charles Giffard very roughly."

"Dear God," Jane whispered, closing the door and leaning against it in alarm. "The king wasn't there, was he?"

"No," John said, sinking onto a chair. "But it maddened them not to find him. A soldier captured after Worcester had led them there, and they beat him badly. They have the scent of the king now, and will hunt until they find him. And look at this." He dug a folded paper out of his pocket. "It's being distributed to every parish in England."

Jane stared at the broadsheet, headed "A Reward of a Thousand Pounds for the Capture of the Traitor Charles Stuart." A cloud covered the sun outside, and she felt a cold shadow of fear pass over her heart.

"Then we had best get him out while we can," she said.

"Jane, are you sure?" John came to her side and they stood looking out the window. In the yard below, a servant trundling a barrow of barley toward the brew house stopped to exchange words with one of the grooms, and their laughter drifted upward.

"Yes," Jane said. "Yes. We cannot turn back now."

"Very well. Then Lord Wilmot and Whitgreaves will bring him here tonight, and you'll set off in the morning."

Jane suddenly wondered when she would return. Maybe with things so unsettled at home she would not linger at Abbots Leigh as she had thought, but return as soon as Ellen's baby was born.

"Another thing," John said. "We must keep this between ourselves and Henry now."

"Doesn't Father know?"

"He knows about Wilmot's horses. He may suspect more, but he hasn't asked and I've told him nothing. Nor Mother or Athalia either." John's face was grim. "And better we leave it at that. They cannot be forced into betraying information they do not have."

"Forced?" The image of her aged father and mother brutalized by Cromwell's men rose to Jane's mind, and that gave her pause as nothing else had done.

"They're desperate now to find the king. I know some of these men and I'd like to think they'd use our people civilly, but we cannot count on that."

"Then Mother and Father shall know nothing," Jane agreed.

THAT AFTERNOON FATHER JOHN HUDDLESTON ARRIVED ON FOOT looking harried and shaken. John ushered him into Thomas's little study, nodding to Jane to follow them. As it was a capital offense to be a practicing Catholic priest, Huddleston was dressed in the coat and breeches of a country gentleman. He was young and sturdily built, and Jane recalled that he had fought in the wars under the Duke of Newcastle, following in the footsteps of his grandfather, who with eight brothers had raised two regiments for the first King Charles.

Huddleston waited until John had shut the door behind them before he spoke.

"Southall the priest catcher was just at Mosely with a troop of soldiers."

"The king?" Jane and John spoke at once.

"Is hidden yet." Huddleston's voice was barely above a whisper. "The officers accused old Mr. Whitgreaves of having been at Worcester, but neighbors gathered and attested that he had never left home. The soldiers were out of humor at having been misinformed, and beat some men who stood up to them." The priest's brown eyes were hot with anger.

"Did they not search the house?" Jane asked.

"Mr. Whitgreaves did a wise thing. Upon hearing that the soldiers were coming, he opened all the doors of the house to show he had nothing to hide. They searched anyway, but found nothing. One of them promised an ostler working in the stable yard he should have a thousand pounds if he could tell where the king was."

"Oh, no." Jane could barely breathe.

"He didn't know the king was there," Huddleston said. "And he might not have told if he did."

"But the offer of a so great a reward may prove too terrible a temptation for some poor soul," John said. "Every moment increases the danger."

"And the soldiers?" Jane asked, looking from Huddleston to her brother. "Will they come here now?"

"We must be prepared," John said.

WORD OF THE EVENTS AT WHITELADIES AND MOSELY SPREAD, AND at supper the entire household seemed on edge, though no soldiers had appeared to search for the king. Jane was lost in thoughts of the next day's journey and did not at first hear Withy speaking to her.

"Do you hear me, Jane?" Withy repeated, rapping Jane's wrist sharply with her spoon. "We've decided to leave with you in the morning."

"What?" Jane put her wine glass down hard, sloshing a few drops onto the tablecloth. "I thought you weren't going home until next week?"

"We hadn't planned to," Withy said, shaking her head and dabbing at the spilled wine with her napkin. "But after these past days I'd rather be at home, and I'd prefer the safety of traveling in company than taking to the road on our own." She speared a piece of meat from her plate and popped it into her mouth.

Jane's heart sank. Setting off with the fugitive king disguised as a tenant farmer's son would be difficult enough without Withy traveling along, sure to stick her nose where it had no business. What could she say to dissuade them? She cast a glance at Henry, listening from across the table. He seemed to read her mind.

"If I were you, John Petre," he said to Withy's husband, "I'd hold off a few days before taking your wife abroad. By then Cromwell's men are sure to be fewer on the ground, and the roads will be safer."

"That's true," Jane said.

Withy's husband opened his mouth to speak, but Withy cut in. "Then why don't you wait?"

Jane could think of no answer and flushed in consternation, and to her annoyance, a knowing smile crept over Withy's red face.

"Maybe Jane is in such a hurry because she plans to elope," she simpered to the table. "It's not Ellen Norton but some lover she's riding off to!"

Her scornful laugh made it only too clear that she considered the idea ridiculous, and Jane bit her lip to keep from flying out at her sister with angry words.

"Nonsense. Of course it's Ellen I'm going to see. How could it be otherwise with Henry along? I would delay my travel myself did not Ellen expect me every day. Of course you're welcome to ride with us, Withy."

Withy looked put out at Jane's capitulation, but only turned to her husband and said, "That's settled, then. We'll leave in the morning."

. . .

JANE WENT TO HER ROOM AFTER SUPPER TO FINISH HER PACKING. SHE could not carry much, only what would fit in the saddlebags, and she was debating whether to bring along the book of Shakespeare's sonnets when there was a quiet knock at the door. John slipped in, shutting the door behind him.

"I'll be off to Mosely about ten," he said. "And return with Lord Wilmot and—and the other gentleman. You have the clothes?"

Jane took from a large chest the gray broadcloth suit that had been made as Sunday best for one of the servants but had never yet been worn, and a pair of shoes belonging to Richard, who had the biggest feet in the family.

"Good," said John. "Those will do well. He can have a bath and shave in the kitchen and sleep in the servants' quarters, and keep out of sight until we're on the point of leaving."

"I'll make all ready," Jane said, "and have food waiting when you come back." She turned back to her packing, but John put a hand on her arm.

"Jane, it would be better if you didn't see him until morning."

"But I want to make him welcome and see that he's comfortable," Jane said. "It's little enough to do."

"I know," John said. "But if you don't meet with him tonight, then if it comes to it, you can truthfully claim you never laid eyes on him until he brought out your horse, and you knew not who he was. If we're discovered, that could be the difference between life and death for you."

They stood in silence for a moment, listening as the case clock in the hall below struck eight. Fear lurked in the pit of Jane's stomach, but she looked up into John's worried eyes and spoke calmly.

"I had rather be hanged for a sheep than a lamb. I'll heat water for his bath and give him his supper." She gave a wry smile. "And beg his pardon in advance for the nuisance Withy is sure to make of herself."

"Well, that can't be helped. But they'll part from you before the end of the day. Between you and Henry I'm sure you can keep her off the scent for a few hours."

It was near midnight when Jane heard the soft whinny of a horse in the darkness of the stable yard. John was back from Mosely. She could hardly believe that the king would really be in the house in a moment. She lifted the candle to view herself in the mirror above her dressing table. She looked anxious and white-faced, her eyes wide in the darkness of the room. She attempted a smile. Better. She wondered if she should change clothes. She had pondered what to wear. It was the king, after all, whom she would be greeting, and yet she would be meeting him in the kitchen in the middle of the night. She had settled on her favorite gown, a brocade of dusky rose, set off by the lace-trimmed sleeves of her shift. Her bosom swelled at the neckline of the bodice, and she draped a white kerchief around her neck and then tossed it away. It was the king, and she would look as pretty as she could, whatever the circumstances. She tucked a stray curl into place, and crept silently out of her room.

As Jane approached the kitchen door, she could hear men's voices. She paused to listen, her heart beating fast. John's voice, quiet and steady, but intense with emotion. Wilmot's tenor whisper. And a lower voice, speaking only a few words, which could only be the voice of the king.

She took a deep breath and entered the kitchen. The men were huddled near the warmth of the fireplace, their faces eerie in the flickering firelight. She stared with shock at what appeared to be a tall scarecrow standing between John and Lord Wilmot. Beneath a greasy and shapeless gray steeple-crowned hat, bloodshot eyes shone from a face that was freakishly mottled sooty black and greenish brown and creased with sweat and dirt, dark hair hanging lank and damp on either side. A threadbare green coat, too small for the broad shoulders, stretched over a battered leather doublet and ragged breeches, and the stockings of coarse yarn were heavily darned at the knees.

The king it must be, but if Jane had not known otherwise, she would have thought him some desperate beggar or Tom O'Bedlam. The men were looking at her and she collected her wits enough to curtsy deeply.

"You are most welcome, Your—" she began, but the scarecrow hastened to her and raised her, whispering fiercely, "No formalities, I pray you, Mistress. I thank you for your hospitality, but the less said the better for all."

Jane looked up into the shining dark eyes of the king. She was astonished to see him summon a weary smile, and she found herself smiling back, her nervousness melting away.

"Then I will say only I pray you sit, sir, while I get you some supper."

Wilmot's serving man settled himself on a stool by the fireplace and the others sat at the kitchen table, seeming near to collapse now that they were safe inside. Jane drew a pitcher of ale and put it before them with slipware mugs, and then dished stew from the kettle that hung on a hook to the side of the fire. She was pleased at the smile on the king's face when she set a steaming dish before him, and when she came back a minute later with bread, cheese, and butter, he had already eaten most of the stew.

"Forgive my animal nature, Mistress," he said, meeting her eyes. "It's little I've had to eat in the last days, and this meal is the best that I can recall in my life, it seems."

Jane blushed, and took up his empty dish. "Then I beg you let me give you more, sir."

The king consumed the second plate of stew hungrily while John and Wilmot and Wilmot's man ate at a slower pace. Jane lit some more candles, and as the light fell on the king's feet, she was shocked to see that his shoes had been slit around the sides, and that his protruding toes were bandaged and dark with dried blood. What a terrible ordeal he had already passed through in the last few days, she thought, and what unknown dangers lay ahead of him.

"My brother has fresh clothes for you, sir," she said, setting another loaf of bread upon the table. "And water for a bath is hot and ready."

"The happiest words I've had in a week." He smiled, and she was pleased that so simple a thing probably was the most welcome gift she could give him at that moment.

"Then I will bid you good night," she murmured, with a half curtsy.

"And I will see you on the morrow, a changed man."

Jane turned to go, but the king took her hand and spoke again. "I thank you, Mistress Lane, most humbly, for your kindness and your bravery."

Jane felt herself lost in his eyes, and was conscious of the other men watching her.

"Not at all, sir," she murmured. "I'm happy to do whatever I can in your service."

The king raised her hand to his lips and kissed it, and she felt as though a bolt of lightning had shot through her. She tried to speak but no sound would come, and she could only nod and smile as she fled into the darkness of the hall.

IN BED, JANE LAY LOOKING AT THE STAR-FLECKED NIGHT SKY OUTSIDE her window. She touched the back of her hand, where the king had kissed her. She seemed to feel the imprint of his lips on her skin and shivered. She was excited, but a thrill of terror was roiling her belly. Only a few days ago she had been longing for adventure, but what lay ahead of her was no story out of a book, but a real journey fraught with danger. The plan that had seemed thrilling now felt like madness. The king was a big man, not easily disguised. What hope was there that they could make their way undetected along a hundred miles of roads teeming with enemy troopers, and pass among countless common people for whom a thousand-pound reward would mean a life of security?

Guide us and protect us, Lord, Jane prayed. *Make clear our path and cloud the vision of our foes. Preserve the king, that he may live to protect our beloved England. And help me to have the courage to see the journey through, whatever may come.*

CHAPTER FOUR

It was still dark when John knocked on Jane's door the next morning. Her stomach felt shaky with nerves as she washed and dressed, and she tried to shut out Withy's chatter as she breakfasted. Henry seemed in good spirits, which helped to calm her. He would know what to do if trouble came, and of course the king was a capable soldier. All she really had to do was sit behind the king on a horse, she thought. And keep her head about her.

As the first streaks of pink dawn shot through the gray clouds, John came into the dining room, pulling his coat on.

"It's time you were off," he said. "Jane, your horse stands ready."

When Jane emerged from the house a few minutes later, Withy and her husband and Henry were already mounted, and John and her parents stood waiting to bid them farewell. Jane stared. The young man who held the bridle of her gray mare was unrecognizable from the ragged fugitive of the night before. A bath, a change of clothes, and further cutting of his hair had transformed the king. He was strikingly handsome, his face shaved clean and the mottled brown scrubbed away. His dark hair was now evenly trimmed so that it just brushed his jaw and was combed neatly back. If she had not known the truth, she would have regarded him warily as a Roundhead.

The new suit of clothes in gray wool Jane had provided fit his tall frame admirably. His snapping dark eyes met hers as he pulled off his hat and bowed to her, the very picture of a deferential retainer.

"Good morrow, Mistress. William Jackson, your humble servant."

"Thank you," Jane replied, probably too curtly, in an effort to conceal her discomfiture.

The king swung himself into the saddle and offered her his arm—his right arm, the wrong one to enable her to mount easily, and there was a moment of awkwardness as she tried to hoist herself into position. John saw the difficulty and managed a laugh as he came forward to help her.

"The other arm, fellow. You must not be awake yet."

The king ducked his head in apology and offered his left arm.

"I'm sorry, Mistress," he said easily. "You're right, sir, I must still be half dreaming."

Jane heard her mother give a snort behind her and mutter, "Blockhead."

John helped Jane settle herself on the pillion behind the king, her feet perched on the little planchette that dangled against the horse's belly. The king sat astride, facing forward and away from her, but she could not help that her side brushed against his back, and she was intensely aware of his presence. He smelled like soap and wool, and she wondered how long it had been before the previous night that he had bathed or put on clean clothes.

At Jane's side, John spoke quietly.

"Lord Wilmot and I will follow shortly. We'll catch up to you and keep within sight of you as long as we may before we branch off toward Packington."

He gave an almost imperceptible nod to the king, and went to stand beside his wife.

"Travel safely, sister. And Henry."

Henry touched his hand to his hat in salute, and spurred his strawberry roan gelding into a walk, the dappled mare bearing Withy and her husband following.

"Have a care!" Jane's mother called as Jane's gray mare fell in behind the other horses. "Go with God!"

And the journey had begun.

THE SKY WAS PEARLY GRAY, AND A LIGHT BLANKET OF MIST LAY OVER the fields that stretched away on either side of the road. The calls of sparrows and wrens echoed in the crisp morning air and a breeze stirred the drifts of brown and golden leaves. The horses' hooves sounded dully on the muddy road, but Jane was grateful that no rain clouds threatened overhead, and it appeared they would have a fine day for their travels.

Henry spurred his horse to a faster walk, and Withy's husband, John Petre, followed his lead. As the horses quickened their pace, Jane realized that she had never ridden pillion behind anyone but her father or one of her brothers. She was grasping the little padded handhold of the pillion, but to be really securely seated, she needed to hold on to the king in front of her. What to do? Surely she could not simply slip her arms around the royal person, uninvited? The king seemed to sense her quandary, and turned his head over his shoulder to speak low into Jane's ear.

"Hold tight to me, Mistress Lane."

The sudden pressure of his back against her shoulder, the warmth of his breath, and the low rumble of his voice sent a tremor through Jane.

"Yes, Your—yes, I will, thank you."

She reached around him with both arms and held fast. Her lower body was facing sideways, but of necessity her right breast was pressed against the king. Dear God, she had never been so close to a man before, she thought, and this sudden physical intimacy jolted her into a new awareness of her own body. Her heart was fluttering in her throat and she swallowed hard, wondering if the king was similarly taking note of the sensation of having her close against him.

The road was mercifully free of many travelers at this early hour, and they passed through Darlaston, Pleck, and Quinton without running into neighbors.

As the sun cleared the horizon, the misty light of dawn gave way to a glorious day. The sky arching overhead was a cloudless blue, and it seemed to Jane that the leaves of the trees, radiant in their autumn golds and reds, stood out more clearly than she had ever noticed before. On either side of the road, the stubble fields and red earth rolled away in gentle waves, broken by the lines of dark stone walls.

"The day could not have been finer had we ordered it," Jane said to herself.

"Mistress?" The king tilted his head toward her inquiringly.

"Oh! I only remarked how splendid the day."

"It is indeed. My heart soars with hope, I find."

He glanced ahead to see if they were overheard, but the thud of the horses' hooves on the clay of the road covered the sound of their voices. A conversation with the king. Jane's heart soared, too, and she began to sing softly.

"The east is bright with morning light
And darkness it is fled,
And the merry horn wakes up the morn
To leave his idle bed."

The king laughed with pleasure. "I've not heard that since I was a boy." He joined in for the chorus, his deep baritone a counterpoint to Jane's treble.

"The hunt is up, the hunt is up
And it is well nigh day,
And Harry the King is gone hunting
To bring his deer to bay."

The cheerful mood was catching, and the others sang along as Jane and the king continued with the next verses.

"Behold the skies with golden dyes
Are glowing all around;
The grass is green and so are the treen
All laughing at the sound."

The cool autumn breeze whispered by them, redolent of hay, livestock, and the deep earthy smell of the fields.

When they had been traveling for only an hour, Henry pointed to two figures off in the distance. John and Lord Wilmot, with hawks on their wrists and John's hounds tumbling and barking around them as they rode through the open fields.

"Excellent," the king murmured. "Two good men within sight, should we need them."

THE PARTY HAD BEEN SOME FOUR HOURS TRAVELING, AND JOHN AND Lord Wilmot had only just disappeared from view, when Jane's horse cast a shoe.

"What a nuisance," Withy huffed. "Did not this mooncalf Jackson examine the shoes before we left?"

She glared at the king and he dropped his head to avoid her eyes.

"Bromsgrove lies not far ahead," Henry said swiftly. "A smith can soon put us to rights, and we'll not lose much time."

He glanced at the king, and Jane knew they shared her apprehension about stopping and being seen, but there was no hope of riding as far as Long Marston without the horse being reshod.

As they rode into the little village, they came to an inn posted with the sign of a black cross, and the sound of a blacksmith's hammer rang out from a small smithy behind it.

"We'll take the ladies inside for some refreshment, Jackson," Henry said, helping Jane dismount. He handed the king some coins.

"Wet your whistle while you wait for the smith, and fetch me when he's done."

"Aye, sir," the king said.

Withy and John Petre were already entering the inn, but Jane hesitated. Would the king know what to do? Had he even been in a smithy before? He gave her a smile and nodded infinitesimally as he led the gray mare toward the stable yard.

Jane turned to follow the others inside, but her eye was caught by a broadsheet nailed to a post before the inn, its heavy black letters proclaiming "A Reward of a Thousand Pounds Is Offered for the Capture of Charles Stuart." Glancing around to see if she was observed, Jane edged closer and read with a sinking heart.

"For better discovery of him take notice of him to be a tall man above two yards high, his hair a deep brown, near to black, and has been, as we hear, cut off since the destruction of his army at Worcester, so that it is not very long. Expect him in disguise, and do not let any pass without a due and particular search, and look particularly to the by-creeks and places of embarkation in or belonging to your port."

Jane moved quickly away from the signpost, desperately wondering what to do. Surely the smith, the grooms and ostlers, all the people of the inn and the town had seen the proclamation, and it must be the same in every village through which they would pass. How could they hope to arrive at Abbots Leigh without the king being discovered?

She had to warn the king, she decided. She walked around to the back of the inn, where the sounds of the blacksmith's hammer had rung out. The privy was likely to be back there as well, she reasoned, and she could use that as her excuse for skulking in the stable yard should anyone wonder.

As she rounded the corner of the inn, she saw that she was already too late. The smith was examining the gray mare's shoeless hoof, and the king leaned nonchalantly against a post, watching with apparent interest. He glanced up and smiled when he saw her, seeming completely at ease.

Jane could not think what to do, and needed to relieve herself anyway, so she ducked into the little house of office. No ideas had occurred to her when she emerged a couple of minutes later. A bucket of water and a pannikin of soap stood near the outhouse, and she used the excuse of washing her hands to assure herself that nothing disastrous had happened yet.

So far, all appeared to be well. The king was holding the horse's hoof while the smith fitted a shoe to it. Shoeing the horse should only take another minute or two. If the smith would only keep his eyes on his work, perhaps they would escape without discovery.

Her heart stopped as the king spoke.

"What news, friend?" Jane was astonished at how naturally he had taken on the accent of a Staffordshire country fellow.

"None that I know of," the blacksmith answered, reaching for a handful of nails. "Save the good news of the beating of those rogues, the Scots."

Jane gulped in fear, but the king just nodded.

"Are there none of the English taken that joined with the Scots in the battle?"

"Oh, aye, to be sure," the smith answered, tapping a nail into place. "But not the one they sought most, that rogue Charles Stuart!"

Jane dropped the soap into the bucket, and the king and the smith glanced her way. She dared not meet the king's eyes, and busied herself with retrieving the soap.

"You have the right of it, brother," the king said. "And if that rogue is taken, he deserves to be hanged more than all the rest for bringing in the Scots."

"You speak like an honest man," the smith grinned. He squinted at his handiwork, and nodded to the king to let go the horse's foot. "Well, friend, yon shoe should hold you to wherever you're bound."

WHEN THEY WERE SAFELY ON THEIR WAY, JANE WHISPERED URGENTLY to the king about the posted proclamation.

"I would have liked to take to that villainous smith with his own hammer," she fumed.

"I take his words as no indictment of me," he shrugged. "The people are weary of war, and want only to go about their lives."

He began whistling "Jog on the Footpath Way." Jane wanted to say more, to tell him she was quite sure that most of his subjects passionately shared her desire to have him back on the throne, but mindful of Withy and John Petre, she said nothing. They would be branching off toward their home in Buckinghamshire at Stratford-upon-Avon, which they should reach by midday, and then the journey would be less strained.

The ride continued uneventful for another hour or more, when an old woman working in the field by the side of the road called out, "Don't you see that troop of cavalry ahead, Master?" She seemed to be addressing the king, rather than Henry or John Petre, and Jane looked at her in alarm. Could she have recognized him? The old woman only nodded slowly, an inscrutable smile on her toothless mouth, and, eyes still on the king, tilted her head at the road before them.

Jane's eyes followed where the old woman indicated, and to her dismay she saw that about half a mile ahead, a troop of fifty or more men and horses were gathered on both sides of the road. Henry and Withy's husband slowed their horses and came side by side.

"We must go another way," John Petre said to Henry.

"They've seen us already," Henry objected. "To turn off now will bring suspicion upon us. I think it safer to continue as though we've nothing to fear. And we must cross the river here."

He started forward, but John Petre grabbed his arm and shook his head obstinately.

"You weren't beaten by Oliver's men like I was a while back, for no reason but that they suspected me to be a Royalist. I don't relish more of the same, and I'll not take Withy into danger."

Jane could sense the king's tension. He leaned back and spoke into her ear.

"Lascelles is right. If we turn back now, it will bring them down upon us. We must go forward." He clucked to the horse and they pulled abreast of Henry.

"Surely we must ride on," Jane said to Henry urgently.

Withy turned over her shoulder, shaking her head. "You ride where you've a mind to, Jane, but we'll take a different way."

"But they see us," Jane pleaded. "Look."

They were within a quarter of a mile of the troops now. Men sat or sprawled in the shade of trees, their horses munching at feed bags, and faces were turned toward the approaching riders.

John Petre reined to a halt. "The road we crossed not half a mile back will bring us into Stratford by another way. We'll take that."

He doubled back the way they had come.

Henry shook his head in frustration but turned his horse, and there was nothing for it but for the king and Jane to follow. Jane fretted inwardly, but she and Henry had no convincing argument for their urgency, and the king could say nothing.

The road was narrow and led into a wood, but John Petre seemed to know where he was going, and when no sound of pursuing hooves followed them, Jane began to relax again. In half an hour the track curved to the right, passed through a tiny hamlet, and the village of Stratford-upon-Avon lay before them. Soon they would be across the river and free of Withy and John Petre.

"Hell and death," the king muttered as they rounded a bend.

Jane glanced ahead and felt her stomach drop. The narrow road through the village was thick with horses—the same troop of cavalry they had turned off the road to avoid. Jane's instinct was to flee, but the soldiers had spotted them, and now there was truly no way but forward without giving the appearance of flight. Henry and the king exchanged the minutest glance and nod, and Henry held back the roan gelding and fell into place behind the gray mare.

The troops were just ahead now, and Jane noted with horror that the broadsheet with the woodcut of the king and announcing the reward for his capture fluttered from a post at the side of the road. Her arms tightened around the king's waist.

The troopers were turning to look at the approaching party. One officer leaned toward another and they exchanged words, their eyes on the king. Henry took his reins in one hand and the other dropped toward his pistol.

Don't be a fool, Jane thought. *If you draw now, we will all die.*

There was some shuffling movement among the mounted men. *This is it,* Jane thought. *We've not come even a day's journey, and already we are lost.* An officer raised an arm, glancing around him, and she felt the king stiffen, bracing for an attack.

"Give way there!" the officer cried.

John Petre checked his horse, but the officer's eyes were on his troops.

"Make way there! Way for the ladies!" he called.

The troopers parted, clearing a narrow lane between them, just wide enough for a single horse to pass through. John Petre and Withy were between them now, and Jane could see that Withy was clutching her husband tightly.

"Good day to you, sir," John Petre greeted the officer as they passed, his voice strained.

"And you, sir," the officer replied. Suddenly he frowned, and put up a hand. "Hold, sir, if you please."

His eyes took in Withy and her husband, Jane and the king, and Henry behind them.

"Where do you travel, sir?"

"Home, sir," John Petre said. "From a visit to my wife's family."

He dug in the pocket of his coat and pulled out the pass for his and Withy's travel. Jane could see that the back of his coat was dark with sweat. *Don't panic,* she willed him, *and all will be well.*

The officer glanced at the paper and handed it back.

"Very good, sir, travel on."

His eyes moved to Jane and the king and she held her breath. Perhaps the officer would not trouble himself to check to see that all of them held passes. Her stomach tightened as she recalled that Henry had no pass. She and the king were nearly past the officer now, and he was making no move to stop them. But it could be a trap, she thought.

The cavalry could easily close in around her and the king, and it would be futile to fight. She felt the eyes of the men on either side of the road following her.

She forced herself to look into the officer's face, and gave him a bright smile, trying to still the beating of her heart. He swept his hat from his head and bowed.

"Your servant, Mistress."

She nodded in reply. The smile froze on her face as the officer's hand went to the pommel of the saddle.

"Hold, fellow."

The king reined in the horse. John Petre halted ahead, and Henry of necessity stopped as well. They were surrounded now, their way blocked by the mounted cavalrymen ahead and behind them.

The officer glanced at the king and then at Jane.

"I'm sorry to trouble you, Mistress, but I'm obliged to ask if you have a pass for your travels. These are dangerous times for a lady to be abroad without good reason."

"I—yes," Jane stammered. "My—my cousin bears my pass."

She looked to where Henry sat on the roan. Why, oh, why, had she not carried her pass herself?

Henry rode forward, his face pleasantly bland.

"This is the lady's pass," he said, reaching into his pocket. "And here is my own."

Jane held back a gasp of surprise.

The officer glanced at Jane's pass and then at her.

"You travel to Abbots Leigh, Mistress?"

"Yes, sir."

"That's quite a ways from Staffordshire. What might take you so far?"

Jane strove to keep her voice calm. "I go to see a friend, who is shortly to be brought to bed of her first child."

She knew her face was flushed, and hoped that the officer might interpret it as embarrassment at having to speak of something so indelicate.

"I see." His eyes flickered down the paper. "Well. I know the hand to be Colonel Stone's."

He glanced at Henry's pass, and then at Henry.

Please, God, Jane prayed. *Please let us go on.*

The officer shook his head and spoke to Henry. "Well, I suppose Colonel Stone thought he had good reason, though was she my cousin, I'd not risk her safety on the road just now, even with a manservant along."

"Your concern is much appreciated," Henry said smoothly. "But I assure you, I'll let no harm come to the lady."

The officer brushed away a fly that threatened to land on his face, and shrugged, apparently satisfied.

"Then I'll detain you no further. And I bid you good day. Mistress."

He bowed again as the king clicked to the mare, and now other officers were nodding and bowing to her. She forced a smile as they rode forward. And then they were past the soldiers, and ahead of them lay the sparkling water of the River Avon, and the bridge over it.

NOT FAR ON THE OTHER SIDE OF THE RIVER, WITHY AND JOHN PETRE'S way southeast parted from the road toward Long Marston, and they took their leave. Jane, Henry, and the king rode on some way in silence, as though fearing they were not truly alone. It was not until they had continued half a mile or more, the open country stretching away on either side of them, that the king finally laughed out loud in relief, and Henry and Jane joined in.

"I've never been so frightened in my life," Jane cried. "I'm glad we were a-horseback, for sure I would never have been able to stay steady on my feet."

"Amen to that," said the king.

"Henry, what on earth did you show him?" Jane asked.

"Why, a pass, cousin," Henry smiled. "Yours was easy enough to copy, I found."

The king whistled. "Then were you cool, indeed, sir, while the rogue examined a forged pass. But all's well that ends well. Now that the danger has passed, I have a great hunger, I find. Would it be agreeable to halt for a rest?"

Their saddlebags were packed with a roasted chicken, bread, cheese, and fruit, and they spread a blanket beneath a tree and ate while the horses grazed. Jane felt the tension leave her. She squinted up at the sun slanting through the golden leaves above and breathed in the sharp autumn air, and the king smiled to see her pleasure.

"Well, despite everything, this feels almost like a holiday. An adventure toward, and a fair companion."

Jane felt herself blushing, but smiled back, and noted the look of surprise, not altogether happy, on Henry's face.

It was nearly dark when they reached Long Marston, a village of small thatched cottages, and Jane was relieved that they had no trouble finding the home of her mother's cousin John Tomes and his family, a substantial half-timbered house near the river. As the king took the horses to the stable, the Tomes family appeared to greet the visitors.

"Cousin Jane! Cousin Henry!" Amy Tomes's round face shone as she welcomed them into the warm parlor. "It's a weight off my mind to have you safely here. I wondered if you might choose not to travel, what with the grim news from Worcester."

"Any trouble on the road?" John Tomes's expression was grave.

"No," Henry replied. "Plenty of soldiers, but they let us be. And of course we had Jane's man Jackson with us."

"A likely-looking lad!" Amy's blue eyes twinkled at Jane. "He's just come into the kitchen, and the cook and the maid are already elbowing each other out of the way to stand next to him. I think we'll bed him down in the stable, away from the field of battle!"

She laughed merrily and Jane felt a twinge of unease. She had reckoned on staving off Roundhead soldiers, not round-heeled kitchen wenches. But at least her cousins accepted the king as her servant without a second thought.

Upon hearing that Richard Lane had been arrested after the battle, John Tomes produced a printed list of prisoners of war.

"It only names officers," he said. "But perhaps you'd like to see it."

Jane read over the names—seven pages, closely printed—from Robert, Earl of Carnworth, down through colonels, majors, captains, lieutenants, cornets, and ensigns, and finally "a list of the king's domestic servants," including his apothecary, surgeons, and secretaries. Next to many of the names was the notation "wounded," or "wounded very much." She shivered, thinking of Richard.

"Richard's probably well," John Tomes comforted her. "If they've got organized to print a list of the officers, no doubt more news will come soon."

"Look at this, if you want something of a lighter cast," Amy urged.

Jane struggled to maintain a neutral expression as she read the heading on the broadsheet, "A Mad Design or Description of the King of Scots Marching in His Disguise."

"Silly, isn't it?" Amy asked. "I pray it may be otherwise, but I fear His Majesty must surely have been slain at Worcester, or we'd have heard of his being taken."

AFTER SUPPER, JANE WENT UPSTAIRS TO THE SMALL ROOM THAT AMY had made ready for her. It was cozy, a fire dancing in the fireplace, and the soft feather bed and plump pillows called to her. But weary and aching though she was, she longed to see the king before she slept. From the window she could see the stable, and the soft light of a lantern shone from it.

It is my duty to see that he is well bestowed, she thought, *that he has all he needs, for he can scarce ask for anything himself.* But she knew it was more than that. She wanted to feel the warmth of that smile, the bright light of pleasure and appreciation in his eyes when he looked on her, to hear his laugh.

The house was quiet. Henry was in a room at the other end of the hall, and would not hear her if she crept out. And why should she care if he did know? There was nothing wrong in making sure that her sovereign would spend a comfortable night. But she felt secretive, and was glad that all was dark and still as she opened her bedroom door and slipped down the stairs and out into the yard.

The door of the stable was shut and Jane stood for a moment uncertainly before she gathered her courage to knock. The door swung open in a moment, and the king stood there in breeches and shirt, a blanket wrapped around his shoulders.

"Mistress Lane!" He was surprised to see her, she could see, and she felt foolish.

"The night is cold." She spoke quietly and then dropped her voice to a whisper. "Your Majesty. Is there anything you lack? Were you well fed?"

"It is cold. Pray come in where it is warmer."

He held the door open for her and she stepped past him. In the golden glow of the lantern she saw that another blanket lay in a nest of straw, and the warmth from the horses made the place comfortable. The gray mare snorted softly to see her, and the king chuckled.

"I'm not the only one pleased to have a visit, I find."

He grinned down at Jane. She was suddenly intensely aware of the animal warmth of him, his bare skin glowing in the lantern light where his shirtfront fell open on his chest.

"I have clean clothes, shoes that do not torture my feet, a warm place to sleep, and a belly full of good food. I lack nothing but the pleasure of your company for a few minutes. Come, sit with me."

He gestured to a bale of straw in as courtly a manner as if he were inviting her to sit upon a silken cushion. Jane sat and he dropped into his nest in the straw and smiled.

"Thanks to you, my spirits tonight are higher than at any time during this last hellish week. Perhaps since I left Jersey more than a year and a half ago."

"But all that time you were in Scotland. Proclaimed king, and with an army at your back."

The king snorted in disgust. "Proclaimed king, yes, but kept like a prisoner. The only way the Scots would help me was if I agreed to swear to their Covenant, not only for myself but for all Englishmen, which was much against my conscience to do. And they kept me at my prayers from morning till night, and I swear to you that I exaggerate not one jot. Into my very bedchamber they followed me, hounding me with my wickedness. Truly, I thought I must repent me of ever being born."

"A foul way to treat one's king," Jane said.

He shrugged. "I minded it not so much on my own behalf, but they would have me admit the wickedness of my poor martyred father, and that was beyond enduring. But the worst of it was that I was so alone."

He looked at her as intently as an artist might his subject, and Jane blushed.

"Alone? Surely not."

"I assure you, yes. For the Scots deemed my dearest friends more wicked than I, even, and would not countenance their presence. I have been a great while without congenial company. To say nothing of the fact that I have scarce looked on a female face or form in more than a year."

The air between them seemed to quiver. Jane knew she should go, that somehow she had got into dangerous waters, but she could not make herself move. The king stood and came to her and pulled her gently to her feet, and she went to him as if in a dream. She shivered to feel him so near, his desire palpable, and she felt she could hardly breathe as he put his arm, her hand still in his, behind her, and drew her to him. She looked up at him, his dark eyes shining in the flickering light of the lantern, and it seemed the most natural thing in the world when his lips met hers, feeding delicately upon her. Her free hand reached around his neck and she pulled him closer, feeling the roughness of his close-cropped head in her palm. She smelled his scent and the faint musk of horses, mingled with the wood smoke from the fire and the heavy aroma of the tallow candle.

The kiss seemed to last forever but at last the king straightened and looked down at Jane, his hand stroking her cheek.

"I'm sorry, sweet Jane," he murmured, kissing her hand. "I shouldn't have, but I was quite overcome. You'd best go now."

Jane didn't want to part from him, but knew that he was right. Reluctantly, she stepped back toward the door.

"Good night. May good rest attend Your Majesty."

"Charles," he whispered. "When we are alone so, call me Charles."

In her bed, Jane tossed fitfully, feeling Charles's hands and mouth on her, recalling his taste and scent and the feel of his body against hers. She longed for him with every particle of her being, wished that he would creep to her bed in the quiet dark, and was quite appalled at the fierceness of her desire and her complete lack of care for any consequences that might follow should things go further between them. Between her and the king.

Jane's first sight of Charles in the morning was at the breakfast table. He came in from the kitchen with a large pitcher, and he caught her eye and smiled as he went to Henry's side.

"Cider, sir?" he asked.

"Thank you, Jackson, yes," Henry said.

"Good morning, Mistress."

Charles's sleeve brushed Jane's arm as he reached for her mug, and she felt herself flushing at the sound of his voice and feel of him so close. She kept her eyes on her plate as he poured for her, but felt that Henry had given her a quick and curious glance.

They set off soon after breakfast, with their noon meal packed in the saddlebags so that they could keep from inns and public eating houses until they reached Cirencester that night.

It was a spectacular day, the air crisp and fresh. With Henry riding ahead of them, whistling happily, Charles reached down and pulled Jane's hand to his lips and kissed it. She tightened her arms around his waist and felt her heart soar. The sky rose in a vast blue arc above them, before them lay a landscape tinged with rosy sunlight, and all things seemed possible.

They soon left the village behind, and rode on between stubbled fields. The beautiful half-timbered houses of Mickleton gave way to meadowland, and then to substantial houses of pale stone as they reached Chipping Camden, its vaulted stone market stall packed with sheep, and a crowd of traders around the market cross. Leaving the town, the road sloped downward to an open valley.

"Beautiful country," Charles said. "I haven't been just here before."

Jane longed to ask him a thousand questions, about his life, his family, his hopes and plans for what he would do once safely out of England, but didn't want to seem too inquisitive.

"You have seen much of the country, have you not?"

"Yes, some. During the war, of course. And before the war, for most of the year my family moved between Whitehall, Hampton Court, Windsor, and the other palaces not far from London. But during the summers the king my father and my mother would go on progress throughout the country, staying in turn at other palaces and the homes of nobles on their way, and when I was old enough to travel, I joined them."

Jane imagined the royal retinue making its way around the countryside. "A traveling holiday! Where did you like best?"

The king laughed. "Anywhere that I could get out and ride or swim or play!"

Of course, Jane thought, his memories of those travels were all from when he had been a child. He couldn't have been more than about twelve when his father's royal standard had been raised at Nottingham for a battle that both sides had hoped in vain might settle the king's quarrel with Parliament.

"And during the wars?" Jane asked.

"I was with my father to begin with, headquartered in Oxford, and moved where he moved. Then when I was not quite fifteen, I was made general of the Western Association, and went to take up my duties in Bristol."

"A general at fourteen?" Jane asked in amazement.

"In name only, to speak truly. My cousin Rupert was really in command, but I learned much from him, and it was the start of making me into a man. And a king." His voice was sad, and no wonder, Jane thought.

"And then?" she asked.

"Then we lost Bristol, and I moved westward into Cornwall, and then to the Scilly Isles and thence to Jersey, and then to France and the Low Countries. The next time I set foot on English soil was when I crossed the border from Scotland a month ago."

"But you'll be back," Jane whispered fiercely to him. "I know you will."

"I will," he nodded, straightening in the saddle. "But God knows when or how."

They rode on in silence for a little way. Jane watched a flock of sparrows swoop overhead, then plunge and divide, settling on the branches of a large sycamore.

"Will you sing to me, Jane?" Charles asked. "Your good spirits cheer me."

Jane began to sing "Come o'er the Bourne, Bessy." Henry slowed his horse to come along side them, and sang the man's part as they came to the second verse.

"I am the lover fair
Hath chose thee to mine heir,
And my name is Merry England."

Charles laughed in delight as Jane sang in response.

"Here is my hand,
My dear lover England,
I am thine with both mind and heart."

. . .

THE MORNING WAS BLESSEDLY UNEVENTFUL COMPARED TO THE PREvious day's ride, and at midday they stopped beneath a huge oak tree to eat. Jane was very conscious of Charles's hands on her waist as he helped her to dismount, and she could feel her cheeks going pink at the vivid memory of his lips on hers the previous night.

"I had a close call of it last night," Charles said when they were settled comfortably with their meal spread on a blanket, and Jane's heart skipped before he broke into a smile.

"The cook told me to wind up the jack," he said, taking a swallow of ale from the leather bottle. "And I had not an idea what she meant."

"Oh, no," Jane laughed. "It's a spit for roasting meat, that winds up like a clock."

"So I know now, but she must have thought me a thorough idiot when I looked around the room to see what she could mean. She pointed to it, and I took hold of the handle, but wound it the wrong way. Or so she told me, with a glower and a curse. 'What simpleton are you,' she asked, 'that cannot work a jack?' I thought quick and told her that I was but a poor tenant farmer's son, and that we rarely had meat, and when we did, we didn't use a jack to roast it."

Henry laughed, but it was to Jane that Charles was looking with a smile on his face.

AS AFTERNOON DREW TOWARD EVENING, A TALL CHURCH SPIRE ROSE in the distance ahead.

"That will be Cirencester," Henry said. "The Crown Inn is said to be friendly and comfortable, though right at the marketplace and heavily traveled."

"Then the Crown it is," Charles said. "I'll keep to the room and keep my head down when I must pass among strangers."

The Crown lay just off the main road and only feet from the medieval stone church. As they rode into the inn yard, Jane was alarmed to see that it was full of soldiers and that another party of troopers were right behind them.

"Never fear," Charles murmured, dismounting. "Leave it to me."

He helped her to the ground, and after an exchange of glances, Henry tossed him the reins of his horse as well. To Jane's astonishment, Charles swaggered forward into the crowd of red-coated soldiers, bumping into shoulders, stepping on feet, and provoking a hail of oaths as the men scrambled to avoid being trampled by the horses.

"Have a care, you clotpole!"

"Poxed idiot!"

Jane made to step forward, but Henry's hand on her arm stayed her. Charles glanced around as if in astonishment, his mouth gaping open.

"Beg pardon, your worships."

His accent was thickest Staffordshire, as if he had grown up in the country around Bentley Hall. A burly sergeant, tall but not so tall as Charles, shoved him hard and glowered at him.

"You whoreson fool! Do you need teaching manners?"

He pulled back his fist, and Charles flinched as though in fear.

"Kick him like the dog he is, Johnno," another soldier called, and there was a chorus of laughs.

Charles plucked his hat from his head and hung his shoulders in sheepish apology.

"I'm sorry, your worship. Most sorry, sir."

Johnno stood sneering at him, as if deciding whether to strike him or not, but then shrugged.

"Well, get on with you, then. And let it be a lesson to you for next time."

"Oh, yes, sir," Charles said, tugging at his forelock and grinning like a child reprieved from a whipping. "Thank you, sir."

Nodding at the muttering soldiers to either side of him, he ambled toward the stable with the horses.

"I still say you should have thrashed him," a second sergeant called out to Johnno.

"Not worth dirtying my coat."

The men laughed, and turned their attention back to whatever they had been doing when they were interrupted.

"WITH ALL THESE SOLDIERS I'VE ONLY BUT TWO ROOMS LEFT," THE landlord said. "And not even room for your servant in the stable. He'll have to sleep on a pallet in your room, sir." He had witnessed the scene in the stable yard, and grinned at Henry. "Perhaps it's just as well you keep the fool out of harm's way."

They ordered food to be brought upstairs rather than going down to the taproom to eat, and by the time Jane had washed her face and hands, the men were already waiting in Henry's room. Charles, in breeches and shirtsleeves, was lounging on a chair near the fire, his long legs stretched before him and his feet propped on a stool. He looked like a great cat, Jane thought, watching the play of his muscles beneath the linen of his shirt. There was something catlike about the glint in his eyes, too, as he gave her a lazy smile.

"Well," he grinned. "I reckoned that blundering among the troops would anger them so that they'd not think to look beyond their rage, and so it did. But the ostler had keener eyes. As soon as I came into the stable, I took the bridles off the horses, and called him to me to help me give the horses some oats. And as he was helping me to feed the horses, 'Sure, sir,' says he, 'I know your face.'"

Jane gasped and Henry looked at him in alarm, and Charles nodded wryly.

"Which was no very pleasant question to me, but I thought the best way was to ask him where he had lived. He told me that he was but newly come here, that he was born in Exeter and had been ostler in an inn there, hard by one Mr. Potter's, a merchant, in whose house I had lain at the time of war."

"What ill luck!" Henry exclaimed.

"I thought it best to give the fellow no further occasion of thinking where he had seen me, for fear he should guess right at last. Therefore I told him, 'Friend, certainly you have seen me there at

Mr. Potter's, for I served him a good while, above a year.' 'Oh,' says he, 'Then I remember you a boy there.'"

Jane laughed at Charles's impersonation of the ostler, nodding in sage satisfaction.

"And with that," Charles continued, "he was put off from thinking any more on it but desired that we might drink a pot of beer together. Which I excused by saying that I must go wait upon my master and get his dinner ready for him, but told him that we were going for London and would return about three weeks hence, and then I would not fail to drink a pot with him."

"Quick thinking, Your Majesty," Henry grinned.

A knock at the door heralded the arrival of dinner. Once the kitchen boy was gone, Jane made to serve Charles, but he waved off her attentions and begged her and Henry to sit and eat with him.

Riding pillion for so many miles was wearying, and Jane's body ached in unaccustomed places. The men appeared exhausted as well, and hot food and warmed wine brightened their spirits and revived their energy.

"Do you know"—Charles smiled over a leg of chicken—"I begin to think that I may be safe after all. Only one more day of riding, and we shall be at Bristol."

"And nothing will hinder us from getting you there, Sire," Henry said, "though it costs my life."

Charles looked from Jane to Henry. "I can only hope that I will see the day when I can honor you as I wish for the help you have given me. I have been much humbled by the love and care shown to me by so many of my people these last days. Most of them have been poor folk with little enough for themselves, but they've risked their lives to keep me safe, and offered all they have. Indeed, one of them gave me the shirt off his back, quite truly."

He plucked at his shirt, now grimy from the ride but clearly new.

"The people love you, Your Majesty," Jane said. "And pray for your return."

But none of them love you so well as I do, she thought, watching the flickering firelight play on his face.

Charles looked around the room, cozy with the fire crackling, its light chasing the shadows away, and smiled.

"A bed to sleep in tonight! I will ne'er take such comfort for granted again."

"Of course you shall have the great bed, Your Majesty," Henry said, "and I will take the pallet."

"Even a pallet would be welcome," Charles laughed, "and a great improvement from doubling myself up in priest holes, and a day spent sleeping in a tree."

"In a tree?" Jane asked in astonishment.

"Yes," Charles said. "When I was at Boscobel, the Giffards feared I would be discovered if I stayed within, even in the priest hole, so I spent a long day in an oak some little way behind the house, my head resting upon the lap of one Colonel Carlis, who I think you know?"

"Yes, an old friend," Jane said.

"Cromwell's men were searching in the woods nearby, and it scarcely seemed possible that we should escape detection. And yet despite all that, I was so tired, having gone three nights without sleep, that I slumbered, my head resting on the good colonel's lap."

"Will you tell us of the fight at Worcester, Your Majesty?" Henry asked, pouring more wine for all of them. "We've only heard pieces of the story, and none from any who know what happened so well as you."

Charles's eyes darkened, and Jane thought of the stories of confusion, despair, and horror she had heard from the soldiers fleeing from the battle.

"It was a desperate venture, in which people were laughing at the ridiculousness of our condition well before the battle. We had been three weeks marching from Scotland, with the rebels pursuing us, when we limped into Worcester. We knew Oliver was on his way with thirty thousand men, and I had but half that number, hungry, sick at heart, already worn out, many lacking even shoes to their feet."

Jane thought of the ragged survivors on the road past Bentley the day after the battle. It was a wonder any had survived at all, she thought, if they had begun in such desperate condition.

"We needed every advantage we could get. We blew up the bridges leading to the town, dug earthworks, built up the fort, and waited. When at length Cromwell came, he fired upon the city, but made no further move for three days."

Charles was on his feet now, pacing. Jane could imagine only too well the tension of the young king and his soldiers, knowing the battle would come but not when, having to stay vigilant and ready despite their exhaustion and apprehension.

"He was waiting, you see, for the third of September." Charles turned to them, a bitter smile creasing his face. "A year to the day since he beat us at Dunbar. And when that day dawned, he moved."

"John Lane and I were on our way to Worcester on that day, even as the fight was under way," Henry said. "I would we had reached you in time to be of use."

"I would you had, too. Had we had but a few thousand more so stouthearted, perhaps the fight would have ended differently."

He leaned a hand on the mantelpiece and stood staring down into the fire. Jane tried to imagine how a battle started.

"How did it begin? How did you know what to do, how to place your men?" she asked.

"I began the day atop the cathedral with my officers," Charles said. "Where we could see for miles in every direction. My heart was in my throat, I can tell you, to see the enemy off to the south, so numerous."

Jane's throat tightened to think what he must have felt, seeing the possibility of death and destruction marching inexorably toward him.

"I cannot say whether our hopes or fears were greatest that morning, but we had one stout argument—despair. For we knew that everything rested on the outcome of that day, and for me it would be a crown or a coffin. I took a last look at that great sweeping view, the wind on the river, my men massed and waiting, and went down to fight."

Jane pictured him, mounted and armed, raising his sword aloft, rallying his men to battle.

Follow your spirit; and upon this charge
Cry "God for Harry, England, and Saint George!"

"If bravery and determination alone were enough, you would have won," she said.

"You held the fort and the city walls for most of the day, did you not, Your Majesty?" Henry asked.

"So we did. The tide turned, alas, when they overran the fort, and turned our guns against us. The Duke of Hamilton, who led the Scots so valiantly, was grievous wounded by a cannonball."

Jane winced. A cannonball could easily take off a man's head or cut him in two.

"His men held off the charge at Sidbury Gate as long as they could, but once the enemy was within the city walls, the day was lost."

"My lord Wilmot says he never saw a fiercer fight," Henry said.

"My men made a last stand near the town hall, and I hope I may never see such a sight again as the red of the setting sun on the blood in the streets. But it just gave me time to get to my headquarters, cast off my armor, and bid Wilmot to meet me outside the gate with fresh horses if it could be done. As it was, I heard them breaking down the front door even as I slipped out the back, and though it was only steps to St. Michael's Gate, it was a near thing that I got out."

His look of bleak despair chilled Jane's heart, and she wished she could take him into her arms and comfort him.

"There was no other way, surely," she said, "but for you to fly?"

"No," Charles agreed. "My life and any hope for the future of the kingdom would have been lost had I tarried but five minutes longer. Outside the walls, Wilmot and I encountered some of our troops. I tried to rally them to go back and try once more, but it was no use, and it would probably have done little but let me die fighting instead of fleeing."

The fire was burning low, and Jane was exhausted with the day's riding. She longed for a minute alone with Charles, but there seemed no graceful way to manage it, so she rose to leave. Charles's eyes met hers, and she felt their heat.

"Let me light you to your room, Mistress Jane," he said, picking up the candle from the table.

"I'll do it, Your Majesty," Henry said, rising.

"Sit, Lascelles," Charles said, and it was not a request. "I said I'll light the lady's way."

Henry bowed his head in assent, though Jane could practically hear the questions and protests in his mind.

"Good night, Henry," she said demurely, not meeting his eyes. "I'll see you on the morrow."

Candle in hand, Charles led the way down the passage. He loomed before her in the darkness, the candlelight silhouetting him in its golden glow. In a moment they would be alone. Her heart beat faster at the thought of his arms around her, his mouth on hers. But to Jane's disappointment, when they got to her room he opened the door for her but did not follow her inside. She looked up at him, not quite daring to reach out a hand to touch him, to tilt her head back and draw him into a kiss. He took her hand, turned it over, and the feel of his lips on her palm made her belly contract with desire.

"I'll go back to your cousin now, sweet Jane."

No, Jane thought, *don't go.*

Charles smiled and stroked her cheek, as if reading her thoughts. "Henry has hazarded his life for my safety, and I would not cause him unease or make him think I regard you with less than honorable respect, which indeed I do not."

"Then good night, sir," Jane said, turning.

"But, Jane," Charles said, stopping the door with his foot, "I'll see you in my dreams, make no mistake."

CHAPTER FIVE

THE WAY TO ABBOTS LEIGH LAY THROUGH BRISTOL. THIS WAS THE most dangerous part of the journey yet, as Charles had spent some months there during the war and might be recognized, though he had aged from the sixteen-year-old boy who had left to the man he was today. Still, it was risky. Henry rode ahead, and Jane could see his shoulders tighten with tension as the increased traffic on the road told them they must be close to the city. His hand strayed to feel for the pistol at his belt, and he eyed passing strangers warily, as though a bent old woman with a flock of geese might be hiding a Parliamentary trooper beneath her skirts.

At length the towering city walls with their arched gates rose ahead.

"Lawford's Gate," Charles said over his shoulder to Jane. "The last time I was here the mayor met me with a crowd of dignitaries to welcome me."

"Better we find our own way today," Jane said.

Charles pulled his hat lower over his brow as they followed Henry through the massive portal and into the open marketplace, with a castle beyond. The streets were bustling with people on foot and on horseback, with wagons and carts, and with sheep and cattle. Wolverhampton was the biggest town Jane had ever been in, and this was far bigger, she realized with excitement.

"Is London like this?" she asked in Charles's ear.

"London?" he laughed. "No, this is nothing to London. It's a good city, though; I liked it here and was sorry to leave. Do you know, I have a month's mind to see what progress was made on the fortifications since then." He spurred the horse forward to ride up next to Henry.

"We've plenty of daylight left to reach Abbots Leigh," he said in a low voice. "Let's ride to St. Michael's Hill to see what became of our works after Oliver took the city."

Henry glanced around them. People everywhere, including many soldiers. Jane could see him forming his words carefully.

"Is it wise? The sooner you are safely out of the city the better."

"But half an hour," Charles said cheerfully. "Humor me. Come, I cannot tell when I may chance to be in Bristol again."

Before Henry could answer, Charles rode ahead and set off on a street branching away from the marketplace. He seemed infused with a new vigor and excitement, his head held higher, his back straighter. Despite his plain clothes, he looked like a king, Jane thought with both pride and alarm as she wrapped her arms tighter around him.

"The Royal Fort." Charles pointed as the walls to the northwest of the city came into view. "We rebuilt that when we took the city in '44, and did much else to strengthen the line of the defenses."

Henry rode beside them, his professional interest as a soldier overcoming his caution, and Charles carried on his commentary in a low voice. It was a beautiful day, a fresh breeze blowing off the water, feathery clouds scudding above, the river full of shipping, the quays swarming with sailors and with dockworkers loading and unloading the ships that rode at anchor.

"My lodgings were just there," Charles said, pointing out a tall house that rose on a hillside. "And look, there's the fish peddler my cook used to buy from."

"Then perhaps we had better ride further from him," Jane murmured.

"You're right. And probably time that we made for Abbots Leigh anyway."

"High time," Jane heard Henry mutter.

Charles wheeled his horse away from the fort. The hilly streets wound up and down, and just as it seemed to Jane as if they must be heading back the way they had come, Charles reined in and came to a halt. Henry rode up next to him with an inquiring glance.

"Hmm," Charles said. "I was sure this was the right road." He glanced behind them and then ahead. "But it doesn't look at all familiar now. Of course the city has changed . . ."

Passersby were noting them and Jane felt very conspicuous. She glanced anxiously at Henry and saw that his jaw was tight and his face reddening.

"Let me see now," Charles muttered. "There's the sun, so that's west. We want to go west and north, more or less, once we cross the river, but surely we must go further south first. No, I must have missed a turning."

He rode confidently back the way they had come and turned into another street about halfway down the hill, and then into another. But they seemed no nearer the river, and Jane could feel Henry's increasing agitation. A few minutes longer and she was truly worried. The map had shown the general route to Abbots Leigh, but she had no idea how long it would take them to reach it, and the sun was dropping low over the horizon.

"Perhaps we should ask someone," she ventured, but she wasn't sure it was the wisest course. As urgent as it was to find their way, any interaction with strangers could bring calamity upon them. Suppose they had the ill luck to speak to someone who recognized the king's face? The thousand-pound reward was a mighty inducement to betray him, and if they were lost they would have no hope of escaping if they were pursued. She glanced around to see what passersby looked least threatening, and was alarmed to see a small party of soldiers emerging from a tavern a little way ahead, their voices ringing out with boisterous laughter.

"No, I'm sure this must be right now," Charles said, spurring the horse into a trot down the hill. The road did bring them to an area more heavily peopled, and Jane thought they must be near the quays now, but once more Charles stopped. An inn stood at one side of the road, and a sturdily built ostler was just unhitching a horse from a cart.

"Good even, brother," Charles called out, and the man glanced up. No light of recognition showed in his eyes, Jane was relieved to see, as they rode closer.

"Like a fool, I've lost my way," Charles said, his words thick with the accent of Staffordshire. "Would you be good enough to tell me how to find the Redcliffe Gate afore my mistress boxes my ears?"

It didn't take much acting for Jane to look thoroughly annoyed, and the ostler's red face creased in a grin.

"Not much used to cities, art thou, then, hayseed?"

"No, truly," Charles laughed with an embarrassed shrug. "I've ne'er seen so many houses and people in my life."

"Well, look you," the fellow said, and Jane, Henry, and Charles paid close heed to the directions he gave.

"Thankee, friend," Charles called with a farewell wave. "And I hope to do you a good turn someday."

"Not likely, boobee!" the stranger laughed. "But I thank you for the thought."

Jane was relieved when once again the city walls came within view and a high stone gate loomed before them.

"That's it," Charles said. "We'll cross the river at Rownham Passage. It's not far now, and we can't miss it."

This time he was right. The road sloped down to the muddy banks of the Avon, and a ferry was crossing back from the opposite side. The ferryman nodded at them as they rode aboard and Henry counted out their fares, but he didn't give Charles a second glance. Jane looked in awe at the magnificent deep gorge between two rocky cliffs, through which the river passed on its long journey from Stratford toward the sea.

"It's only two or three miles now." Henry sounded relieved as they reached the far bank of the river. "We could take the main road, but according to the map there's an old Roman road that goes up through the orchard."

"Then let us use that," Charles said. "For in this instance, the only way to go is up, and the more private we can be, the better."

The main road lay before them, climbing a steep hill, the late-afternoon sun slanting down through the canopy of tall trees that lined the road, but Henry led them off to the right, and they easily found the track that wound up through the apple trees, heavy with their red and gold fruit. Jane inhaled the scent, thinking of the orchard at Bentley.

"Boobee?" Charles mused, turning his head over his shoulder to speak to her. "What did the fellow mean by calling me that?"

"It's a song," Jane laughed. "All about a country clodhopper that goes to London."

"Ah." Charles grinned. "Then I can congratulate myself that I've pulled the wool over the eyes of at least one proud man of Bristol. Still, I don't relish another evening in the kitchens as I spent at Long Marston. It might be more prudent to contrive some way to keep me apart from the household at Abbots Leigh."

"True," Jane said. "We could say that you're ill and not fit to mix with the other servants."

"That would serve," Charles agreed. "And I've no doubt I look pale and haggard, what with the miles of riding and walking, and the lack of meat and sleep over the past week."

They were near the summit of the hill now, and Jane was pleased to think that they were so close to having accomplished what they set out to do—get the king in safety to where he could wait while Lord Wilmot found him safe passage from England—but she felt a pang at the realization that their arrival meant her time with Charles was growing short. How long would it take Lord Wilmot to arrive and then to find a boat? Would she have another evening with Charles? Two? What heartache it would be to turn for home and ride back to Bentley behind Henry. She tightened her arms around Charles's waist, and he patted her hand.

"Tired?" he asked. "We must be nearly there now."

"I am weary of riding, but not of your company."

His hand brushed hers, and his lips tickled her ear as he spoke, his voice a husky whisper. "I shall not let you part from me just yet, sweetheart."

The horses seemed to sense that they were near the end of their journey, and they pressed on despite the steepness of the hill. Soon a high stone gateway with a two-storied gatehouse rose ahead.

"That must be it," Henry said, turning. He slowed so that Charles and Jane pulled even with him. "It's a big household and there will be grooms enough to deal with horses," he said, his voice low. "It would be safer for you to wait near the stables while Jane makes arrangements with her cousin to lodge you somewhere quiet."

As they passed through the arched gateway, the road curved, and the great house stood before them, perched on the summit of the hill. Jane let out a little cry.

"What a grand house!"

It was fine house, its imposing front three stories high, with a row of a dozen gables along the roof, its vast lawns rolling away downhill in all directions. On the green before the house, eight or ten people were playing at bowls, and two or three more lounged on the wide front steps to watch the game's progress. Jane was just as glad that she did not see Ellen among those gathered; she could ride to the back of the house with Charles and Henry and make a more quiet entrance than if she had had to stop to greet Ellen before all those people.

Henry had been right, and as soon as the horses approached the stables, two boys came running out to take the horses by their bridles while the riders dismounted.

"Wait here, Jackson," Jane said, "while I find Mrs. Norton."

She didn't have far to look, however, for a voice from above called out happily.

"Jane! You're here!" Ellen leaned out a window, beaming. Jane laughed with pleasure to see the familiar tousled blond curls and rosy cheeks.

"Ellen! How radiant you look!"

"Stay just where you are," Ellen called. "I'll be down directly!"

She appeared a moment later at the back door, and Jane rushed to embrace her, careful of her bulging belly.

"Come in, come in," Ellen urged. "You must be worn out with the ride, and I'm so big I can scarce get about."

"Ellen, you remember my cousin Henry Lascelles?" Jane asked. Henry and Ellen bowed to each other as Charles hovered in the background. "And I wonder if I might beg a favor. My man Jackson here has been ill of an ague. I would take it most kind if you would let him have a good chamber with a fire so that he might go early to bed, or I fear the boy will never recover."

"Of course, of course, the poor lad," Ellen agreed, giving a vague smile in Charles's direction. "I'll have Pope see to him directly. But come with me, dear Jane, I want all the news from home."

Jane had just time to settle herself in her room, visit briefly with Ellen, and wash her hands and face and change her clothes before it was time for supper. She insisted on carrying a dish of broth to her ailing man herself, and the butler Pope showed her the way to the garret room where Charles was lodged.

"Mrs. Norton has asked Dr. Gorge to look at your man after supper, madam," Pope said as they climbed the stairs.

"Oh," Jane faltered, "that's most kind."

She tried without success to think how she could plausibly refuse the offer and decided she would just have to warn Charles. Fortunately, Pope left her at the door of Charles's room, and she slipped in to find him stretched on a bed before a blazing fire. He sat up as she came in, grinning at the sight of the steaming bowl.

"Your friend is very kind to accommodate me so well," Charles said. "Please give her the humble thanks of William Jackson, and let us hope that I can make more suitable thanks later."

He tilted the bowl and drank hungrily, reminding Jane of a ravenous dog.

"Ah, that's good." He sighed in satisfaction.

"Don't worry," Jane smiled. "I'll tell the butler you're up to proper food, and I'm sure he'll see to it that you're well fed. But there's a doctor visiting the house, and Ellen has asked him to look at you."

Charles shrugged. "It's not much of a part I have to play, being wan and weary."

"Good," Jane said. She knew she must hasten to the dinner table, but she was loath to leave him. "Shall I look in on you later, to make sure all is well?"

She said it carelessly, but wondered if Charles could hear her heart thumping in her chest.

"I would take it most kind," he said, taking her hand, and she cursed herself because she knew she was blushing as she took the empty dish from him and went out the door.

The household at Abbots Leigh was large, consisting not only of Ellen and George and George's mother, but of sundry siblings and cousins and friends, including the clergyman and physician Dr. Gorge, who had been watching the bowls when they arrived, and seemingly dozens of servants.

Over supper the discussion turned inevitably to the battle at Worcester and speculation about the fate of the king. Jane was glad Charles had suggested being kept secluded, and as soon as she could excuse herself after supper, she slipped up to his room. She was alarmed to find him with a bloody handkerchief pressed to his nose.

"What's amiss, sir?" she cried.

"It's nothing." Charles waved off her concern, pulling the handkerchief from his nose to see whether the flow had stopped. "I get nosebleeds from time to time, with no rhyme or reason to them, but I suffer no ill effects beyond the inconvenience." He patted the bed. "Come, sit with me."

She sat beside him, very conscious of their being alone. He turned to her and took her hand, and she felt suddenly shy.

"Did the doctor come?" she asked, a trifle too brightly.

"Indeed he did. And as soon as I caught sight of his face, I knew him."

Jane caught her breath in alarm.

"He was chaplain to my father when I was a boy. I kept to my bed, and as much as I could, turned my face from the candle so that I should be in shadow, and I don't think he knew me." He gave a wry smile. "Perhaps it was foolish to say I was ill. It's made me an object of many kind attentions. The butler himself brought my dinner, and a maid came, too, with a warm posset to speed my recovery. Maybe it's only my fancy, but I felt that they looked on me strangely."

Jane's stomach tensed in panic. "Oh, dear, what shall we do?"

"Nothing for now. Wilmot should be here tomorrow, and with any luck he'll have news of a ship for me."

Jane remembered with a catch in her heart that this might be the last time she would have Charles's company alone. He seemed to read her mind.

"Oh, Jane," he said, brushing a curl from her cheek and letting his hand trail down her jaw. "Would that I might keep you with me a little longer. I have been so much alone."

She looked up into his face, seeing both the warrior king and lost little boy, and felt overwhelmed by desire and tenderness.

"When the war started," he said, "my family scattered. I was twelve. I went with my father, and I tried to be a man. I tried most pitifully when I was parted from him three years later. It was in Oxford. It was raining, and I hoped that the raindrops would conceal the tears on my face. No ocean could have hidden my tears if I had known that I would never see him again."

Jane saw that tears glistened in his eyes. He took her hand, and kept it resting on his thigh.

"His death was a cruel shock to England," she said. "I cannot think what an unbearable grief it must have been to you."

"I was told that on the scaffold he said just one word," Charles said. "'Remember.'"

A shiver ran though Jane.

"Like Hamlet's father."

"Yes. And here I am, like Hamlet, charged to avenge my father's murder and the loss of his crown."

"But you are not like Hamlet. You do not hesitate."

"No, I need no *Mousetrap* to know where the guilt lies. And when the way seems hard, as now, I think to myself, 'Remember thee? Ay, thou poor ghost, while memory holds a seat in this distracted globe.'"

He bent his head to Jane and kissed her, taking her head in his hands and pulling her close to him, and she responded hungrily, sinking back onto the bed as he moved toward her. He showered her with kisses, her eyes, her ears, her throat, then back to her mouth, and she burned for him with an intensity of feeling she had not known was possible. This was what she had been longing for—passion and love, lifting her above the dreariness of daily life.

Charles pulled away from her, hand stroking her throat, his breathing rapid.

"Go from me, Jane. I should never have touched you so."

His eyes were searing into her, his touch hot on her skin, and she had never felt so alive. This was what she had feared she would never know, this rush of rapture and fever of excitement throughout her body. She had torn herself away from him the night before, but to do so again, knowing that they would likely part on the morrow, called for more strength than she possessed.

"I will not go from you, Your Majesty," she murmured, her hand trembling as she laid it on his chest. She felt his heart thudding and saw his throat move as he swallowed.

"Jane," he whispered, nuzzling her ear. "If you stay, I cannot answer for the consequences. I've not been with a woman in a year and a half. My blood quite overcrows my scruples, and if I am much longer in your presence, I will lose mastery of myself entirely."

Jane took his hand and kissed it.

"It is well lost in such a cause. I give myself to you."

"Jane."

His voice was husky. He pulled her to him, kissing her deeply as they sank together onto the bed. His hands were lifting her petticoats, and he was on top of her, parting her legs with his knees.

It was wrong, Jane knew, but she didn't care. She would have let him take her though the mouth of hell gaped before her. His fingers were caressing, exploring, making his way easy. She gasped to feel the hard flesh pressing against her, entering her, driving deep within her. She pulled him into her, rising to meet his thrusts until a wave built and crashed within her, and he put a hand over her mouth to stifle her moans. A moment later he arched his head back and his whole body gave a convulsive shudder. Then he was still, and rolled to the side to hold her close, and they lay panting in each other's arms.

"Oh, Jane, forgive me," he whispered at last. "I should have stopped myself, no matter what you said."

"I didn't want you to stop," she said into his ear, her hand stroking his sweat-soaked back. "I don't want to lose you. After tomorrow I will see you no more, but I can always remember tonight."

"Stay with me," Charles said. "Don't leave until morning, if this night is all we have."

As the light of daybreak crept through the window, Charles and Jane made love again, this time more slowly, unencumbered by clothes or hesitation. Jane looked up at Charles, memorizing each detail of his face, the dark stubble of his beard on his flushed cheeks, the heavy lashes of his eyes, the fall of dark hair. She found her hands grasping him to her and marveled at the hardness of his muscles, their tightening as he moved within her.

When they had both spent, she lay nestled in his arms, not wanting to move. But Henry or Pope the butler or someone else could come to the door at any moment.

"I must go," she said, kissing his chest and inhaling his scent. "Before I am discovered."

"And I will brave the kitchen," he said, reaching for his breeches. "Perhaps I may hide better by going among the household than by staying mewed up here. But I beg you, come back in an hour or two, and tell me what news you hear."

She pulled on her clothes hastily, and he bent to give her a last kiss before she tore herself from him and crept out the door.

Jane and Ellen walked out after breakfast, Ellen happily showing Jane the gardens and the sweeping views downhill in all directions.

"Breathtaking," Jane said, gazing at the shadowed fields and forests far in the distance.

"Yes," Ellen agreed. "I do love it here, as much as I miss you and my family." She put her arm through Jane's. "Oh, Jane, I hope you will stay for a long visit."

"I'd like to." Jane smiled. "I've missed you more than I can tell you, and have longed for your advice."

It was true, she reflected, though now everything seemed to have changed. A few weeks ago she had wondered if she would know love if it came to her. Now she knew without a doubt that she was in love, but she could certainly not confess it to Ellen or anyone else.

"Good." Ellen squeezed her hand. "There will be plenty of time for confidences."

A little later, Charles answered Jane's soft knock at the door of his little room and drew her in swiftly, holding her to him and kissing her.

"Oh, Jane, I feel so alive in your arms."

Her head swam at the intensity of his presence, the taste and smell and feel of him.

"And I in yours." She thought she had never felt so vibrantly aware of her body or been swept by such emotion as she felt now looking up at him.

"Come," he said, drawing her down to sit beside him on the bed.

"I must consult with you. I feel like a hare being chased by hounds, and I don't know whether to hide in the thickets or run for it."

"What's happened?"

"I went down to the kitchen after you left, having a very good stomach after such a night." He cocked an eyebrow at her and she blushed and smiled.

"The doctor saw me, and asked what news I had of Worcester. It took me by surprise and I scarce knew how to answer, and seeing my hesitation, he said, 'I am afraid you are a Roundhead, but I will try what mettle you are made of.' Then what should he do but takes me into the buttery and drinks me the king's health in a glass of wine! So what could I do but drink as well, wishing myself good health, did he but know it."

"Then he didn't know you last night!" Jane felt a surge of relief.

"It would seem not, but things only got hotter from there. I went to the buttery hatch to get my breakfast and the butler Pope was there with two or three other fellows. We fell to eating bread and butter, along with some very good ale and sack he gave us. One, that looked like a country fellow, sat just by me, and began to talk of the fight at Worcester, giving so particular an account to the company that I concluded he must be one of Cromwell's soldiers."

Perhaps her relief had been premature, Jane thought.

"I asked how he came to know so much, and he told me he was in the king's regiment, by which I thought he meant one Colonel King. But questioning him further, I perceived he had been in my regiment of guards, in Major Broughton's company, that was my major in the battle."

"My cousin!" Jane exclaimed.

"Is he? No wonder you are so valiant, coming from such a family of warriors."

He shook his head in admiration, and Jane felt herself glow at the compliment.

"So I asked the fellow what kind of a man I was," Charles continued. "To which he answered by describing exactly both my clothes and my horse, and then looking upon me, he told me that the king was at least three fingers taller than I."

Jane burst out laughing at the absurdity of the situation.

"Upon which," Charles said, "I made what haste I could out of the buttery, for fear he should indeed know me, being more afraid when I knew he was one of our own soldiers than when I took him for one of the enemy's."

"I shouldn't wonder," Jane said, her mind whirling. What on earth should they do? Was the danger too great to wait for Wilmot? Must they make their escape now?

"So Pope and I went into the hall," Charles said, "And just as we came into it, Mrs. Norton was coming by. I plucked off my hat and stood with it in my hand as she passed, and Pope looked very earnestly on my face. I took no notice of it, but put on my hat again, and went away, walking out of the house into the field."

"Probably the best thing, but if he thinks he knows you, others might, too! Surely we must get you out of here? Shall I find Henry?"

"I don't know. Wilmot should be here tonight, and I will need his help, whatever comes next."

Jane nodded, thinking. "Then perhaps it's best if we can wait until he's here, but be prepared to fly should anything change."

The uncertainty did not last long. That afternoon, Henry pulled Jane aside and whispered to her urgently.

"We must talk with the king. I'm afraid the butler knows him."

Her spine went cold with terror, and they hurried to Charles's room. He looked grave when Henry repeated his story, running his hands through his hair distractedly so that it stood on end.

"He says very positively to me that it is you, but I have denied it," Henry said.

"Do you think him to be an honest man?" Charles asked, pacing.

"Yes, most certainly," Henry said. "He was a trooper in your late father's regiment of guard, in our cousin Major Broughton's company, and then served at Lichfield under Jane's uncle Colonel Bagot."

Charles shook his head in amazement and turned to look at Jane.

"Bagot your uncle? It seems your family has been more help to me than any host of angels."

"Pope has been always upon our side," Henry continued, "and I would trust him with my life."

"Then I shall have to do the same," Charles said. "I pray you bring him to me."

A few minutes later, the door of the little room safely shut, the butler John Pope knelt and kissed the king's hand. Jane was touched to see him wipe tears from his eyes before he raised his grizzled head to look into Charles's face.

"Your Majesty," he said, rising a little stiffly from his knee, "I knew you at the first. For I was falconer to Sir Thomas Jermyn when I was a boy at Richmond, and saw you often."

"Of course," Charles said, "for Jermyn was groom of the bedchamber to my father. I am very glad to meet you, and upon the word of Mistress Lane and Lascelles, I will trust you as I would an old acquaintance."

"Then I beg Your Majesty to tell me what you intend to do." Pope spoke urgently. "I am extremely happy to know you, for otherwise you might run into great danger in this house. For though my master and mistress are good people, yet there are at this time one or two here who are great rogues, and I think I can be useful to you in anything you will command me."

Thank God, Jane thought. Pope might save them from unforeseen dangers.

"Then here is how it lies," Charles said. "I have come hither with the intent of taking a ship from Bristol to any French or Spanish port. Lord Wilmot is to arrive today, and you can help him look for a ship." Pope looked alarmed.

"Then I am even more glad you have taken me into your confidence, Your Majesty. For there are many in the house who would certainly know Lord Wilmot, and know he was at Worcester with you, and might put two and two together. With your permission I will endeavor to meet him on his way and bid him wait until tonight when I can bring him into the house secretly. And once that is done, I shall go to Bristol myself to seek out a ship."

CHAPTER SIX

THE SUN STREAMED INTO ELLEN'S LITTLE SITTING ROOM, JUST off her bedroom. Jane, reclining on a chaise with her feet up, only a few feet away from Ellen on her daybed, luxuriated in the coziness of the small chamber.

"If I had such a wonderful room as this, I don't think I'd ever leave it!" she exclaimed.

The afternoon was too warm for a fire and it still felt almost like summer. The sky outside the window was a cloudless and brilliant blue, and before settling herself on the chaise, Jane had marveled at the views, sweeping away down hill to distant farms and pastures. A small table beside the chaise was scattered with books, and a maid had placed a tray with cups of chocolate and small cakes on another table within arm's reach of the two women.

"I do spend much of my time here," Ellen smiled, biting into a cake. "Oh, this is good. Two more advantages to being with child. I can eat anything and everyone is only too happy to indulge me in whatever I fancy, and whenever I want to be alone in my own little domain here, all I need say is that I am feeling in need of rest and quiet and no one disturbs me."

"Are you not happy here?"

"Oh, happy enough, I suppose. Everyone is kind, but so polite. I have no true friends, really, and no chance to make any, as I cannot go out in society like this."

"Perhaps once the baby is born."

"Yes, perhaps then. But, Jane, it brings me such joy to see you. Tell me all your news."

"News have I none, really," Jane laughed, looking down. She longed to tell Ellen about Charles, and was afraid her friend would read her heart in her face. "Sir Clement Fisher has asked me to marry him."

"You call that no news?" Ellen's cheeks dimpled in a smile.

Jane shrugged.

"I've asked him to wait. I don't know, Ellen, I hoped you could advise me. Did you know right away when you met George that you loved him?"

"I liked him," Ellen said, considering. "I thought him kind and gentle, and from the first he treated me as though he valued me above his life."

"That sounds like true friendship and contentment," Jane said. "And perhaps that is all that one needs. But did you—did your heart thrill?" She lowered her voice to a whisper. "Did your belly ache to have him within you?"

Ellen gave a little gasp of half-shocked delight.

"What a thing for a maiden to say!" Her face became thoughtful. "No, not at first. Not until I knew that I would be his wife. But you have always been braver than I. Perhaps you need a fiercer kind of passion than I do. And if so, I hope you find it. But don't wait too long, Jane. You don't want to be a perpetual guest in Athalia's house once your parents are gone, but mistress of your own home."

. . .

"TELL HENRY THAT POPE WILL BRING WILMOT HERE TO MY CHAMBER at midnight," Charles said, tucking into the bowl of stew Jane had brought to his room. "We'll learn what he's been able to do about finding a ship, and lay our plans."

Jane smiled. The pretense of Charles's illness had been resumed after his adventures in the buttery that morning, and she had brought him his supper. If everyone was to meet in his room that night, it gave her a perfect excuse to spend the evening with him. Charles obviously thought the same.

"Come back, though, after you tell Henry, won't you?" he grinned. He mopped the last of the stew from his bowl with a chunk of bread. "Your friend has a very good cook. I count myself lucky to be fed, much less fed so well."

He reached out his hand to Jane, and she took it and went to sit next to him on the bed. Outside the window the moon, in its first quarter, shone golden in the deep aquamarine of the evening sky.

"It near broke my heart," Charles said, pulling her into his arms and leaning his back against the wall, "those days at Mosely, watching the soldiers on the road below, knowing they were hungry, and being able to do nothing for them."

Jane thought of the ragged men she had watched limping by on the Wolverhampton Road. They were the lucky ones, who had not been killed or injured so badly they could not walk, or taken prisoner, but the desolation she had seen in their faces haunted her.

"Mrs. Whitgreaves did what she could for them," Charles said. "Patched their wounds and fed them. They were most grateful, she said. They told her they met with great hostility from most of the country people, and that they were living on cabbage stalks and pea straw, whatever they could find that was nearly edible."

"We did the same," Jane said. "Fed them and gave them water, poor men."

"They were so close I could see their faces as they passed. I recognized a man from my own regiment of Highlanders, McLelland by name, a fierce and hardy soldier. So loyal, as all of them were, and not a thing could I do to ease their misery."

Jane's head was pillowed on his chest, and she could feel the vibration of his voice as he spoke. She reached up to touch his face, feeling the roughness of the stubble on his cheek.

"And you had marched so far before the battle."

"Yes. Down the hard way, by Carlisle, through rough and barren country. The way that so many armies before us had marched to their defeats."

"How did you feed the army?"

"With difficulty." Charles grimaced. "We had wagons of supplies with us, but only enough to keep the men on short rations. And yet I could not afford to outrage the people as we went. They have little enough as it is. I ordered that there was to be no pillage, no looting. And I was forced to hang a man for stealing apples."

"For so little?" Jane cried, appalled.

"An example had to be made, else discipline would have fallen by the wayside, did the men not believe I meant what I said. He was a good man, too. I liked him. I had rather it had been almost any but him."

"Like Bardolph."

"Bardolph?" Charles's eyebrows rose in surprise.

"Yes, in *Henry the Fifth*. Prince Hal must hang him for stealing. His friend, from so many adventures. And the prince had done worse himself."

"Exactly. But how do you know Prince Hal and Bardolph so well?"

"I have always been a great reader," Jane said, putting her hand palm to palm with his and marveling at the size of his hands. "We have the plays at home."

"And so did we," Charles mused, closing his fingers around her hand. "My father had a great bound copy of the Second Folio."

"So does mine!" Jane laughed. "The very same. I always loved to read and dream about the adventures of kings."

"And now you know firsthand," Charles said, pulling her to face him, "what do you think about the adventures of kings, Mistress Jane? Not so full of pageantry as mud, at least for this king."

"'And what have kings, that privates have not too, save ceremony?'" Jane quoted.

"True, too true," Charles said. "But it's precious little ceremony I'm like to have in the days to come, I fear."

Deep thoughts were within his dark eyes, and Jane was amazed once more to think that it was indeed the king with whom she spoke so easily. His majesty had been stripped from him on the field at Worcester, but she would give him what ceremony she could. She knelt before him, took his hand in hers, and kissed the finger where his ring should be. He looked down at her in surprise.

"My liege," she said. "Take my homage and know that I give it you on behalf of thousands more who would bend their knees to you if they could."

"Jane."

His voice was husky with emotion. And with desire, too, for he placed his hands on her shoulders and ran them down over her bosom, then leaned down to kiss her deeply. Her breath came quickly and she stood and let him pull her onto the bed. She felt none of the pain or doubt of the first time they had lain together, and she gave herself to him without hesitation. They lay together after, and Charles laughed softly as he stroked Jane's hair.

"What a marvel of a woman you are."

"Me?"

"Yes. Beautiful and brave and spirited, a tender lover, and learned, too. Quoting Shakespeare, forsooth."

They watched as the points of shining stars pricked through the deepening blue velvet of the night sky.

"I wish my sister, Withy, could hear you say that," Jane said. "She says too much learning is wasted on a girl."

"But your parents did not feel the same?"

Jane shrugged. "I was lucky. My brother Richard is only a year older than I, so when my father schooled him he schooled me, too. It warmed his heart that I had a passion for poetry and plays, and enjoyed learning Greek and Latin, as Richard never did."

"Greek and Latin, too?"

"In for a penny, in for a pound," Jane laughed. "My father set me to translating Virgil's *Aeneid* when I was but twelve. I loved the fire of it, the sinew and muscle of the poetry. 'Hecate, howled to in cities at midnight crossroads.' Isn't that marvelous stuff?"

Charles grinned and took up the quote.

> " '*You avenging furies and you gods of dying Elissa,*
> *Acknowledge this. Direct your righteous will to my troubles,*
> *And hear my prayer.*'

"And the plays?" he asked. "Did you ever see one?"

"Once. When I was ten the King's Company came to Wolverhampton. My father took me to see *The Life of Henry the Fifth*."

"The year of the plague," Charles said. "We went on an unusually long progress that summer, and the players were with us because the London theaters were closed. Just think, we could have met." He kissed her, and then laughed. "But I was only six, so I doubt I would have been able to make much of an impression on you. Though perhaps I could have, too. I had my own company of players."

"Did you?" Jane cried in delight.

"Yes, from the time I was a year old. They played in the Cockpit at Whitehall and toured, too. Though they were only actors from the old Red Bull, not so good as my father's men, of course."

"Oh, how I wish I could have seen more plays. But the players never came so close again, and then the war began . . ."

"Yes," Charles said. "And the players put down their lutes and slapsticks and went to war, like all the rest."

"If you do one thing for England," Jane begged, "bring back the playhouses."

. . .

JANE WENT TO HER ROOM AND SET HER CLOTHES AND HER HAIR TO rights before returning to Charles's room, and by the time Henry knocked on Charles's door, no one would have known that she had spent the evening making love with the king. Pope arrived with Wilmot a few minutes later.

"Your Majesty." Wilmot bowed before Charles pulled him into an embrace.

"Wilmot, you're a welcome sight." He turned to the two men who had slipped into the room with Pope behind Wilmot. "And you, good lads."

"My man Swan you've met," Wilmot said. "And Rogers, servant to Mr. Winters, at whose house I lay last night. You may trust them as you do me."

"You are both most heartily welcome, gentlemen," Charles said gravely as they made their bows. "And now, sir," he said, turning to Pope. "What cheer?"

"Alas, Your Majesty," Pope said. "My news is not so good as I had hoped. There will be no ship sailing for France or Spain from Bristol for a month to come. But there are other ways, if you will hear me."

"Come, sit," Charles said. "All of you, and let us take our soundings."

They drew into a little circle by the fire, Charles on the only chair, Jane sitting between Wilmot and Henry on the bed, and Pope, Swan, and Rogers squatting on their haunches. The light of the fire flickered on their worried faces, reminding Jane of the secret meetings in the kitchen at Bentley in the days before she had set out with Charles.

"Here is my thought, Your Majesty," Pope said. "We are but two days' ride from the Channel coast. There are many boats setting forth from there, though they be smaller than the merchant vessels at Bristol. But that may be just as well, for the enemy will find it very troublesome to search every fishing boat that puts out from the little southern ports."

"And between here and the coast you move through country

friendly to our cause," Wilmot said. "Somerset and Dorset, whence sprang the Western Association."

"A day's ride from here lies the village of Trent," Pope continued. "The home of Sir Frances Wyndham."

"Of course!" Charles cried, clapping his hands. "The Wyndhams! I know honest Frank, though not so well as his brother Edward, who was governor of Bristol, and of course dear Christabella."

"Yes, dear Christabella," Wilmot said with a meaningful smile. With a twinge of jealousy, Jane wondered who Christabella might be, and whether it was to Wilmot or to Charles that she was dear.

"I know the way to Trent well, Your Majesty." Rogers leaned toward the king, his eyes shining in the shadows. "For my mistress is sister to Mrs. Wyndham."

"Your Majesty could lie hidden at Trent while Lord Wilmot seeks out a boat for you at Weymouth," Pope said. "It would surely be safer than remaining here, for there are those in the house that I fear might be dangerous should they know who you were."

"The road south is good, Your Majesty," said Rogers, his ruddy face lit with earnest enthusiasm. "It's the old Roman Fosse Way, and I know it like the back of my hand."

"It's well traveled, but as safe a way as we are like to find," Wilmot agreed. "And truly I think it your best choice."

"And of course we'll go with you, Your Majesty," Henry said. "You'll want as many men along as possible."

To Jane's relief, Charles nodded. She had feared that one of the men would suggest that her presence was no longer needed and she had been prepared to argue that she and Henry should not turn back until Charles was settled at Trent.

Charles looked around at the little group, a pleased smile on his face. "Just when I think I am dished, another escape presents itself."

"I know Edward Kyrton, steward to Lord Hertford, at Castle Cary," said Pope. "That's but a few miles from Trent. He would go to his death for Your Majesty. I can send word to him that he should expect two gentlemen and a lady who need quiet lodging for the night, while Lord Wilmot goes on ahead to Trent to give warning to Sir Frances that you are coming."

"Swan and Rogers and I will lie in the village tonight and set off in the morning," Wilmot said. "And meet Your Majesty at Trent on Monday."

"Then it's settled," Charles agreed. "I cannot thank you all enough for the pains you have taken on my behalf. You've saved my bacon once again."

Wilmot, Rogers, and Swan departed with Pope, and Jane remained with Henry and Charles.

"I am sorry to impose still further on your goodwill, Lascelles," Charles said. "And Jane. You had thought your service was at an end, having got me safely here, but I hope you will not find it too troublesome to travel with me to Trent."

"No trouble is too great, Your Majesty," Henry said. "I am thankful that my cousin and I may be of service to you."

"Then I bid you good night and good rest," Charles said.

His eyes flickered toward Jane as Henry bowed, an invitation in his glance, and she smiled her acquiescence. But Henry stood holding the door for her, and she followed him out, intending to return to Charles when Henry was safe in his room.

"More of an adventure every day, isn't it?" Henry said in a low voice as they reached the door of Jane's room.

"Indeed. But all in a good cause. Good night, Henry."

She shut her door and listened to his footsteps continuing down the hall to his room. She was sure Charles was expecting her to return, but how long should she wait to be sure the coast was clear? She counted a hundred slowly, and then again, more impatient with every second to be in Charles's arms. Softly then, she opened the door of her room. All was quiet and dark, and shoeless, she crept to the narrow staircase that led to the garret where Charles's room lay. A shadow loomed before her and she stopped short with a gasp of surprise.

"And where might you be going, cousin?" Henry's voice was quiet, but there was no mistaking the steel within it.

"Nowhere," she faltered. "I mean, I—I remembered something I need to ask the king."

"Indeed. And what could be so important that you creep to his room in the wee hours, on stocking feet? He may be the king, but I'll not have you playing the whore to him, Jane."

The word struck Jane as hard as if Henry had given her a blow to the face.

"How dare you?" she whispered fiercely. "It is none of your concern what I do."

"You don't even bother to deny it, then?" he demanded, grasping her forearms with hard hands.

Jane shook herself free. She could protest her innocence, but what was the point?

"I don't answer to you, Henry Lascelles," she spat. "I am no child. And if I choose to go to the king's room or to the king's bed, it's my own business. Now let me pass."

They stood facing each other in the dark a moment, their labored breathing the only sound. Henry's rangy form blocked her way, but she would not turn back. At last he stood aside, but he seized her by the shoulders as she moved to pass him, and spoke low and angry into her ear.

"You're right, I cannot stop you, without I lock you in your room. Were he any other man than the king, I would challenge him. And even though he is the king, I'd do the same, though it meant my death, were it not that on his head rests the future of the kingdom. But your father and your brother shall know of this, and the shame you have brought on our family."

He thrust her away from him and she nearly lost her balance as he stalked down the stairs past her. She felt herself flush with anger and humiliation, and a new sense of shame as she saw how he must think of her, and how anyone else would, too, did they know how things stood with her and Charles. She leaned against the wall, trying to still her galloping heart. It was not fair for Henry to chastise her so, she thought. In ordinary circumstances, she would never behave as she had done for the last several days. She had lived virtuous and quiet her whole life. But these were not ordinary circumstances. It was the king to whom she had lost her heart. And he didn't treat her like a whore, but like an admired friend or even sweetheart.

Didn't he? Cold panic surged through her stomach. She felt suddenly as if she had been swept into a raging river, the cold water swirling her deeper into trouble. What if Charles did not care for her beyond taking pleasure in her body, and would forget her as soon as she was out of his sight? Fear and humiliation swept over her at the thought. And, oh, God, if Henry did tell John and her father . . . The king's cast-off whore. That is what she would be forevermore.

She found she was weeping, and knuckled away her tears. She couldn't let Charles see her like this, but neither would she miss the chance of going to him, for who knew whether they would find another chance to be alone before they parted. *Well,* she thought, squaring her shoulders, *if I'm his whore, another night won't make a difference.* She straightened her dress and climbed the stairs.

Charles was waiting in the dark when Jane slipped into his room and shut the door softly behind her.

"I thought you'd changed your mind," he said in her ear as he lifted her skirts. His hands were eager on her flesh and his fingers sought the place between her thighs. Her heart felt like ice. She loved him, loved him with her soul. But maybe Henry was right, and this was all she meant to him.

"Treat me like a whore," she said, her voice hollow.

He jerked away from her.

"What?"

"I am your whore, am I not? So use me as you would do a whore."

Charles looked down at her, peering at her face in the moonlight. Did he see the traces of tears on her cheeks?

"What's got into you, Jane? Why do you say such a thing?"

"Do you care for me?" she asked, regretting the words as soon as they were out.

"Of course I do. You've risked your life—"

"I don't mean that. Do you care for me? Would you care for me, were things not as they are?"

Tears welled in her eyes as she waited for him to speak. It seemed a long time, and she shivered, her skin going to gooseflesh in the cold night air.

"Sweetheart." Charles took her into his arms and kissed her eyelids. "I care for you. You are sweet and courageous, and I pray I may get the chance to tell all England how good you have been to me."

She longed to melt against him, but stayed rigid, as if by controlling her body she could control her heart and soul.

"But after tomorrow, or soon, you will be gone, and I'll never see you again."

Charles sighed and shook his head. "What would you have me say? I must be gone, if I value my life and my country. You know that."

"Yes, I know that. And I have been a fool to let myself love you as I do. So do not use me as a lover. Use me as you would a whore. As rough and uncaring as you please."

"Jane . . ."

"Do it." She marveled that she could speak so to the king.

"Very well." He let go of her and stood motionless a moment. "Then onto your knees and serve me."

"I don't know how."

Now it had come, she was afraid, far more afraid than she had been. What had she sought to prove?

His voice sounded like that of a stranger when he spoke. "It's easy enough. Come, wench, onto your knees."

He grasped her hair and forced her down as he unbuttoned his breeches. His cock stood hard and he pulled her mouth onto it.

"Suck. Yes, like that. That's what a whore does."

Jane let him guide her movements. She felt a twist of shame, and then wondered why it should be so. He had done the same for her, and it was a gift of exquisite pleasure. But this was different somehow, and she knew it. She heard his breath come quick, heard him stifle a low moan, and then he pushed her onto the bed, rucking her skirts up behind as he entered her. He thrust hard and she knew he sought his pleasure only. It gave her pleasure, to know she pleased him so, and there was a power in it, too, though it did not have the sweetness of love.

He spent soon and rolled off her. They lay in the dark silently for some time, not touching, and she listened to his breath slow to its normal rhythm. Finally he spoke.

"I cannot think of you as a whore, for you are none."

He pulled her to him, cradling her against his chest, and his eyes shone in the dark as he caressed her, brushing a strand of hair from her face.

"Oh. I am glad." Her heart was thawing, and she stroked his forehead, feeling the dampness of the sweat and the dark curls around his ears.

One flyspeck more blotted Jane's happiness. Better speak of it now than leave it to torment her with uncertainty later, she thought.

"Who did Lord Wilmot mean, when he spoke of 'dear Christabella' so smilingly?"

Charles stirred restlessly beside her.

"She was my nurse."

"Your nurse?" She looked at him in astonishment, trying to see his face in the dark.

"Her husband was governor of Bristol during the war, and when my council came to Bridgewater, she was there. I hadn't seen her in many years, since I was a child. She petted and cosseted me, as she used to do, and people talked, as they will."

Jane remembered Wilmot's raised eyebrow and the insinuation in his voice.

"But you were not a child."

"No. I was, though, little more than a boy—not quite sixteen—and trying to do the job of a man. I was lonely and sad and terrified, and she gave me comfort."

"In her bed?"

Charles sighed. "Yes. She was a very handsome girl, not yet thirty, and she taught me that in her arms I could forget my cares for a little and find sweet oblivion."

Jane's heart contracted. Of course he had had other women, but to hear him speak of one made it particular, not general. It was her own fault, she knew. She had asked.

"And where is she now?"

"With her husband. I haven't seen her in five years and more."

They lay silent for a little while, until Charles pulled Jane to face him.

"Jane, our time is short and my life and future are not my own. But in my heart you are my queen, and I swear it ever shall be so."

She laughed softly and laid her head on his chest.

"If I am a queen, then am I like Dido. You will treat me as cruel Aeneas treated her, going off in pursuit of your crown and leaving me to my grief, and I shall go mad of a broken heart at your faithlessness, as Ophelia did."

"You won't go mad," Charles snorted. "You have far too much sense. And you're much stronger than poor Ophelia. You might curse me, but you'd never do away with yourself.

> "'*May he not enjoy his kingdom or the days he longed for,*
> *But let him die before his time, and lie unburied on the sand.*'"

Jane smiled and took up Dido's curse.

> "'*Then, O Tyrians, pursue my hatred against his whole line,*
> *And the race to come, and offer it as a tribute to my ashes.*'"

"That's my girl," said Charles. "Come, kiss me, and let me kiss you as my love."

CHAPTER SEVEN

JANE WAS RELIEVED NOT TO RUN INTO HENRY AT BREAKFAST after their encounter the previous night. She and Charles had agreed that there were too many people about for it to be safe for her to spend time in his room during the day, and in any case she was glad of the chance to visit with Ellen while she could. She had said nothing yet of their plans to depart on the morrow, and dreaded it, but thought she would pass it off as some whim of Henry's to visit farther south, assuring Ellen that they would return in a day or two.

"Shall we walk out this morning?" she asked Ellen as they finished the morning meal alone in Ellen's little sitting room.

"Perhaps in the afternoon," Ellen said. "I'm feeling tired and my belly is a bit unsettled." Jane noted with concern that Ellen's face was unusually pale.

"Are you well? Should I find Dr. Gorge?"

"Oh, no." Ellen brushed off her worry. "I'm sure it's nothing. No doubt if I lie down for a bit, I'll feel better by and by."

So Jane walked by herself, out through the great walled garden where gardeners toiled among the espaliered fruit trees and into the open meadows that sloped down toward the sea. Great spreading chestnuts and maples dotted the land, little winged flying seedpods twirling down to the earth in the breeze. They made Jane think of fairies, and the stories her grandmother Bagot used to tell her when she was a child about the little people who lived in the woods.

It was a spectacular estate, and it brought to mind Sir Clement Fisher and his lands. She had not yet visited Packington Hall, but John assured her that it was a beautiful and stately house of red brick, surrounded by miles of parkland. There would be something quite wonderful, Jane thought, about being mistress of all that she could see. But she knew that she would cast off the possibility of lands and property in a moment if she could keep Charles with her, could have always the excitement and pleasure she felt in his company.

Ellen did not appear at dinner, and Jane went upstairs to find her. Ellen was lying with her eyes closed on her daybed, an open book beside her.

"Shall I read to you?" Jane asked. Ellen opened her eyes and smiled.

"Yes, I'd like that. Do you know, I don't think anyone has read aloud to me since my mother when I was little."

"I always loved it when my father read to me," Jane said, taking up the book. She had barely begun to read when Ellen gave a little groan. Jane looked up and saw that Ellen's face was covered by a sheen of sweat and contorted with pain.

"What is it?" Jane cried. "Are you in labor?"

"No, no, no," Ellen cried, "It's too soon. It cannot be. Oh!" She gasped as with a sharp pain. "Oh, Jane, something is quite wrong!" Jane saw with horror that a crimson stain was spreading across Ellen's skirts.

"I'll run for the doctor," Jane said, dropping the book as she started to her feet.

"No, don't leave me!" Ellen cried. She rose and tried to go to Jane but collapsed to the floor.

"Help!" Jane shouted, yanking the door open. "Fetch the doctor quick!"

She sank to the floor beside Ellen, who was now unconscious, the front of her gown soaked in bright red blood.

Two hours later Dr. Gorge emerged from Ellen's bedroom, his face gray. Jane waited there with George Norton's sister and a few others of the household. At the sight of Dr. Gorge's face her heart sank.

"Is she dead?" she cried.

"No. But the baby is lost, poor thing. And Mrs. Norton is very weak and in grave danger, I fear. She may recover, but only time will tell."

"Can I see her?"

"For a few minutes. Don't talk of the child, if you can avoid it."

Jane was shocked at Ellen's appearance. She had been washed and dressed in a clean nightgown, but her color was so pale as to be almost blue, and though the covers were pulled to her chin, she was racked with shivers. A maid, tears running down her face, carried away a basket with bedclothes soaked in blood. No one else was in the room.

"Oh, Ellen."

Jane sat on the chair at Ellen's bedside and took her friend's hand in hers.

"Jane." Ellen's voice was a croak. "I've lost the baby. What will George say?"

"He will say how lucky he is to have you, sweetheart, that's what he'll say."

"I hope," Ellen sobbed. "Oh, Jane, I wish I was at home. I wish my mother was here."

"Perhaps when you're well you can come for a visit," Jane whispered. "When you're strong enough to travel."

"It's so far," Ellen said, her voice choking. "Oh, why did I ever come so far from home? Don't leave me, Jane. You're all that I have right now."

"What about George?" Jane asked, stroking Ellen's damp brow.

"He loves me but I cannot let him see me like this. Promise you'll stay with me."

Jane's mind raced to Charles and Trent and the Wyndhams, but the king's needs paled in comparison to Ellen's beseeching eyes. He would have to go without her.

"I promise," Jane said, holding Ellen's hand in hers. "I'll stay."

When Dr. Gorge's sleeping draft had taken effect and Ellen was soundly asleep, Jane slipped from her room. She felt a hundred years old and wanted only to lie herself down and weep for her friend's pain and grief. But Henry stood in the hall outside her room.

"We must talk," he said quietly as she approached. "No, not about last night. This is far more serious. He's waiting in the orchard and we must consult about what to do now."

Jane felt scarcely in her right mind with her sorrow over Ellen, but she knew Charles must be desperate to speak if he summoned them this way in broad daylight.

The household was distracted with the tragedy of the lost baby, and no one gave Jane and Henry a second glance as they made their way past the garden and down into the orchard. Charles was pacing beneath a great pear tree. He looked up as they approached and glanced around to make certain that no one was near.

"Truly, Jane, this is a sad turn of events," Charles said. "But we must be gone in the morning."

"I cannot!" she cried.

She could still feel the imprint of Ellen's feverish hand clutching hers, and the sound of Ellen's sobs echoed in her ears.

"I cannot leave her," she said more quietly. "She needs me. And even if she did not, how am I to excuse it? We have planned for months that I should be here. I cannot now pack up and be gone when I am scarce come."

"But no more can His Majesty remain here," Henry said. "No ship is to be had from Bristol, and we must try another way."

"And we shall," Jane agreed, striving to remain calm. "But can we not wait a few days?"

Charles and Henry exchanged glances.

"Jane, you heard what Pope said. Every day I tarry makes it more likely I shall be taken," Charles said.

"And Lord Wilmot is already gone," Henry added. "He'll be at Castle Cary tonight, and at Trent tomorrow."

"If I do not arrive," Charles said, "he'll fear the worst. He might be brave and foolish enough to get Frank Wyndham to raise some men to come to find me. Such a party would raise attention. They would surely be taken before they got here, which would cost their lives, perhaps under torture to disclose where I am. And if they managed to reach here unchallenged, their presence would sound the alarm. In either case, I would certainly be captured, and many more along with me."

Jane knew he was right, but she struggled to think of some other way.

"Jane, I know it is hard, but it must be done," Charles said.

"Can you two not go and leave me here?" she pleaded.

Henry shook his head impatiently.

"What explanation is there for your manservant riding off in haste without you at break of day? There have been questions already, wondering looks. Such an action would be the tinder to the fire, and would jeopardize His Majesty immensely."

"And the pass," Charles said. "The pass is for you and your manservant. You are the greater part of my disguise, Jane. If I were taken alone, I should be undone."

The two men pressed close to her in their agitation and desire for secrecy, and Jane felt as if she were being smothered.

"Then go you with him!" she cried at Henry. "Make up some story to excuse it! Dress yourself in my skirt and cap if you must, but leave me here!"

Charles had lowered his head at the pain in Jane's voice, but now he looked up at her, with a new light in his eyes.

"A story it shall have to be, and I have hit on it. You shall receive a letter purporting to be from home, telling you that your father is gravely ill, his life is feared for, and begging you to haste you home."

"That will serve," Henry nodded. "And Pope can deliver it."

Jane looked from one of them to the other in disbelief.

"It sounds like something out of a play."

Charles smiled grimly. "It does in truth, but unless you can think of a better way, we shall have to try it."

Jane fought the tears and rage that were building within her. She thought again of poor Ellen, lying limp and frail in that dark room, all joy and will to live drained from her with the lifeless child. To leave her would be callous and a betrayal of their long friendship. To tell a lie to excuse leaving her would be treachery beyond bearing, and these men, they didn't understand. She looked from one to the other, wondering whom she hated most at the moment, and began to sob. Some moments passed. Henry glanced warily around, and Jane knew that whatever happened, they could not stand much longer arguing in the orchard, or someone would surely hear them and wonder at the strange scene. At length Charles sighed and spoke.

"Jane, there is no other way. The circumstances are hard, I grant you, brutally hard, but without you I am lost. And more than that, the kingdom is lost."

It was true, Jane thought. There was no other way, but her mind grappled with it still.

"Jane." Henry's voice was as hard as the hand that grasped her arm. She looked from his steely blue eyes to Charles's dark eyes, and saw there only the reflection of her powerlessness. For Charles she had cast her safety and reputation to the wind, and now she must abandon her dearest friend, who might be dying. Cold anger at both of them overtook her grief. She pulled her handkerchief from her sleeve, dried her eyes, and blew her nose.

"Then so be it," she said. "I will do what I must."

Charles moved as if to take her hands, but she stepped back and looked into those dark eyes, those eyes that had pulled her in so deep and held her still.

"I will do what I must for the future of the kingdom," she repeated. "But as for you, Charles, you may go hang."

. . .

"JANE." ELLEN'S EYES, SUNKEN IN DEEP SHADOWS, LIT AS SHE SAW HER friend's face, and then darkened. "What's wrong?"

"Oh, Ellen," Jane whispered, tears welling from her eyes. "I must go. My father is ill, most gravely ill. I had a letter."

She dropped her head, unable to meet Ellen's eyes, and wept. Surely there was a place in hell being readied for her now for such a lie.

"Oh," Ellen said. "I'm sorry, dear. Then of course you must go to him."

She turned her face to the wall and Jane saw that she was trying not to cry.

"I'm sorry," Jane whispered desperately. "Oh, Ellen, I'm so sorry, so sorry, so sorry."

AS JANE PREPARED TO LEAVE IN THE MORNING, SHE WAS GRATEFUL that her tearstained and swollen face would be attributed to her grief and anxiety over her father and Ellen. The servants were solicitous, and the rest of the household was too taken up with poor Ellen to pay her much mind.

At supper the previous night Charles's plan had been carried out without a hitch. Pope had brought a letter to Jane at the table, and as Jane had read Charles's handwriting, informing her that her father lay at death's door, her distress at leaving Ellen had welled up and it had not required any acting for her tears to flow. Pope had taken Charles his supper, and she had not seen or spoken to him since she had walked away from him the previous afternoon.

She stepped out the front door to see the Nortons' groom leading Henry's horse with the baggage, and Charles leading the mare with its saddle and pillion. He smiled at her, as if he had not a care in the world. She was stunned. How could he smile? Had he already forgotten Ellen and how deeply it pained Jane to be leaving her? Her anguished rage boiled to the surface once again, and the thought of mounting the horse behind him and putting her arms around him—she wouldn't do it, that was all.

"Change the saddles, Jackson," she snapped at Charles.

Henry, standing on the porch beside her, stopped with his arm midway into his coat sleeve and glanced at her in astonishment.

"I beg your pardon, Mistress?" Charles asked, keeping his eyes and his voice low after a fleeting instant of unguarded surprise.

"I'll ride with Mr. Lascelles today," Jane said curtly. "Take the pillion from the mare and put it on the roan. Now, if you please."

Jane felt a perverse pleasure as she watched Charles's helplessness. Surely no one had ever spoken to him that way before. His face flushed and she saw him struggle not to answer her back, but she had him squarely. He could do nothing but obey her.

"As you wish, Mistress."

He silently unbuckled the pillion and secured it behind Henry's saddle, moving the baggage to the gray mare.

"Jane," Henry began, but she cut him off.

"And may I not ride with you, cousin? Fie, why should it be a matter of such concern on which horse's arse I am jounced today?"

Henry glanced at Charles, but said no more. He swung up into the saddle, reached down to help Jane mount, and clicked to his horse, and they were off, Charles trailing behind on the gray mare, thunderclouds brewing behind his dark eyes.

Jane had no wish to be close to Henry either, and as they set off toward Bristol she obstinately held only to the handhold at the front of the pillion rather than putting her arms around him. She kept her face turned toward the road ahead so that Charles, riding behind them, was out of the field of her view. But as they headed south, the country grew hilly. A steep hill rose before them, and as they began the ascent, Jane came near to losing her seat.

"For God's sake, Jane," Henry said over his shoulder, "hold on to me. I know you're in a temper, but it's only yourself you'll hurt if you take a spill."

So she held to him, hating him, hating Charles, hating herself for betraying and abandoning Ellen. She wept as silently as she could, made more miserable still by the dust of the road collecting in the wet rivulets on her face. Henry and Charles spoke not a word to her or to each other. By the time they stopped for their noontime meal and to rest the horses, her head ached desperately, her face was a grimy mess, and she thought she had never felt more unhappy in her life.

Henry laid out the food and with perfunctory politeness invited Charles to eat. Jane stalked off some distance to find a hedge behind which to relieve herself, and when she returned she moistened a handkerchief and washed her face as best she could. The men were eating in sullen silence. Jane's body ached from the ride, and she wondered how much longer she could bear it.

"How far to Castle Cary?" she asked no one in particular.

Henry glanced at Charles and answered her.

"About fifteen or twenty miles yet. We need to change horses, Jane. I don't care who you ride with, but the pillion must go on the roan. The mare cannot carry the load of two people so long."

They were perched on boulders by the side of the road, atop a high hill, with a breathtaking view of the countryside below. The air was fresh and clean, a breeze sweeping away the clouds above. The road ran steeply downward, meandered through the valley below, and was lost as it climbed the next hill in the distance.

"I am truly sorry, you know, Jane," Charles said softly. "If there was any other way—any other way—I would have taken it."

She sniffled and wiped her nose on her sleeve. Her heart still ached for Ellen, but almost as much at the effort of holding on to her hatred for Charles.

"I know," she said, not looking at him.

"And I am sorry, too," Charles added, "for any offense I have given you, Lascelles."

Henry stiffened. Jane had said nothing to Charles about Henry's words the night before, but he must have guessed at something like the truth.

"I hold Jane in great esteem," he continued. "This time, this journey of ours, is like nothing I could have imagined. It seems not wholly real."

"And so the rules do not apply?" Henry spat. "Or do any rules apply to you, Your Majesty?"

Charles gazed off into the distance. "Look at this great country before us," he said. "My country, in name. But the fact just now is that every man in England has the power of life or death over me. Breathe but a word in the right ear, and farewell Charles."

> "'*For God's sake, let us sit upon the ground*
> *And tell sad stories of the death of kings,*'"

Jane quoted, her voice barely above a whisper.

"Yes," Charles said. "'How some have been deposed, some slain in war.' If Shakespeare were yet alive, he could write the tale of this our journey. Of the three of us. 'We few, we happy few, we band of brothers.'"

"Do you mock me, Sire?" Henry demanded, springing to his feet, his voice sharp in the thin air.

Charles hastened to his side. "No. By no means, Lascelles. I only mean that for the moment, my life is not my own and I am not myself. I have no path to guide me for such a sojourn as this has been. I am a man like any other, and like any other man who is weary and fearful and in despair, I have sought solace in the arms of a lady who is tender and kind, and the nearest thing to a guardian angel I am like to see this side of heaven."

He reached out to Jane and she put her hand in his. He raised it to his lips and kissed it. The wind whipped higher, rattling the trees and sending loose golden leaves cascading down the hill. Henry stood with his back to them, gazing out over the landscape below, and Charles spoke again.

"Before God I swear that if by His grace the day comes that I sit upon my throne and rule this land, I shall do all within my power to honor you both for what you have done for me. In my present straits I can offer no more. And if that is not enough, but give me the loan of a horse, and I will go on to Trent alone. I will make certain that you are recompensed for the beast."

In the silence Jane watched a hawk soar high overhead, coasting in a lazy circle, its harsh cry echoing against the rocks.

Finally Henry turned to face Jane and Charles, who still sat hand in hand.

"I have sworn to see you safe and I will do it, come what may. I bear the name of eight kings, and would not shame it by abandoning my sovereign."

Charles stood and went to him. "Then give me your hand, brother Henry. We will go forward together, and I am honored to have such company."

POPE HAD DRAWN A MAP SHOWING THE PLACEMENT OF THE MANOR house at Ansford, just north of Castle Cary, and Rogers had taken word to Edward Kyrton of the impending arrival of the travelers. Rogers was waiting at the gate into the stable yard, and Kyrton burst from the house and came forward to greet Jane as Charles helped her to dismount and took the horses' bridles. Kyrton's eyes lingered on Charles's face a moment too long, and Jane knew that he must surely have recognized the king, but he only bowed to her and Henry, murmuring, "Come, come, you are welcome all," as he ushered them into the house.

"Pope asked me to give you quiet lodging for the night," he said smoothly. "The chambers at the back of the house are most private, and I myself shall bring up food and aught else you may need."

Jane was grateful for a few minutes alone. She was exhausted with riding and the day's intense emotions. She washed in the basin Kyrton provided, the grit of the road muddying the water and leaving the linen cloth streaked with dirt. Kyrton laid out supper in a small parlor, a bright fire dancing beneath the great stone mantel. When he had gone, Charles stood at the window, watching the setting sun tingeing the horizon with pink and orange.

"That's Glastonbury Tor, if I'm not mistaken," he said, pointing, and Jane went to his side. "Where Arthur and Guinevere are supposed to lie. During the war one of Cromwell's men chopped down the Holy Thorn, the hawthorn tree on the Tor that they say grew from the staff of Joseph of Arimathea. A soldier at Worcester told me that he had it from a man who was there that the ruffian was blinded by a flying splinter. I wonder."

They were all exhausted, and as soon as they had done with supper Henry withdrew to his room. Alone with Charles for the first time since the previous afternoon, Jane felt apprehensive. Her rage had dissipated, leaving only sorrow and weariness. But was he angry at her after she had treated him so harshly? Her fears were relieved when he came to her side and bent to kiss her.

"Jane," he said, lifting her chin to meet his eyes. "Would you lie alone tonight? I know you are weary, and perhaps you cannot forgive me yet."

"No," she said, standing and folding herself in his arms. "I will lose you soon, and would not waste a night I might spend by your side. I shall have all the time I want to be angry at you when you are gone."

CHAPTER EIGHT

THEY ROSE AND WERE ON THEIR WAY EARLY. IT WAS ONLY TEN miles to Trent, but it seemed that all of them felt an urgency to be there as soon as they could, as if the king's hoped-for refuge might disappear into the mists as they approached. The road wound through fields and pastures, with hedgerows rising over the hills and sheep dotting the meadows. In places the branches of the trees at the sides of the road met in an arch overhead, and they rode through a green tunnel. Gray stone cottages with thatched roofs stood here and there. Swallows flew in raucous flocks, swooping and darting beneath the lowering clouds.

"We must be near now," Henry said as they met a boy with a herd of goats.

The road was very narrow, hemmed in on either side by tall hedges, and Jane felt as if she was in a garden maze like the one at her grandparents' house, Blithfield. The goats passed between and around them, bleating, the bells suspended around their necks jangling. A cart drawn by a donkey approached, the lanky lad with the reins in his hands whistling. Charles pulled his hat lower over his brow, and nodded in response to the boy's cheerful "Good morrow to you."

The hedges by the roadside dwindled and came to an end, and orchards stretched away on either side. Jane saw a church steeple rising ahead, and knew they must be nearing the manor house. Suddenly a couple stepped from behind a stone wall beside the road. The man raising his arm in greeting had the erect bearing of a soldier.

"Frank, Frank, how dost thou do?" Charles called out, reining to a halt as the man came to his side. "And Mrs. Wyndham, I make no doubt." He nodded to the pretty dark-haired young woman smiling beside Wyndham.

"Aye, sir," Sir Francis Wyndham said, his voice low. "I cannot tell you how gratified we are to see you, but let us waste no time in getting you inside." He glanced down the road toward his house. "The servants are all abroad this morning, but we must be wary of our neighbors. It will be safest for you to take the horses to the back and slip in the kitchen door while we welcome Mistress Lane and Mr. Lascelles at the front of the house."

He nodded toward the manor house. "The drive curves around the back, and Swan and Rogers are there to take the horses."

"As you say, then," Charles agreed.

A tavern with the sign of the Rose and Crown stood across the road from the great gray-stone manor house with its thatched and gabled roof, and half a dozen red-coated soldiers were gathered in the stable yard. Jane was conscious of their eyes turning to watch as Charles helped her dismount and led the horses away.

"Good morrow, gentlemen!" Henry called out, bowing.

"And to you, sir," one of the soldiers answered. They watched for a moment more, and then turned back to their circle and continued their talk.

Colonel and Mrs. Wyndham must have walked uncommon fast, Jane thought, for they threw the front door open as though they had been inside all the while.

"Why, cousin!" Mrs. Wyndham cried. "I pray your journey has not been too uncomfortable?"

"Not too bad, all considered," Jane responded.

She kissed Mrs. Wyndham's cheek and took her arm fondly, reflecting that Mrs. Wyndham appeared to be a few years younger than she was, and that they did indeed look as though they could be cousins.

"But I am perishing for a drink of something cool."

She felt like an actress walking offstage must do, she thought as they entered the house. A gray-haired older lady, her eyes goggling, shut the door behind them, and another girl about Mrs. Wyndham's age hovered nearby. Colonel Wyndham hurried away, and a moment later reappeared with Charles and Wilmot.

"If it please you, come upstairs," Colonel Wyndham murmured to Charles. "We will endeavor to make you as comfortable as may be."

He led the way, Charles and Wilmot with him, and Jane and Henry following with the three Wyndham ladies. It was a handsome house, Jane thought, glancing around the great hall as they climbed the stairs. The chamber into which Colonel Wyndham ushered them was beautiful and cozy. Sun flooded through the tall windows, casting warm rays across the gleaming oak planking of the floors and the honey-colored wall paneling.

The door of the room safely shut, Wyndham bowed deeply. "Welcome, Your Majesty. May I present my wife, Anne, my mother Lady Wyndham, and my cousin Juliana Coningsby."

"I thank you for your hospitality and kindness, ladies," said Charles, smiling.

The black-haired Juliana Coningsby was as young and pretty as Anne Wyndham, their faces were flushed with excitement as they curtsied, and Jane felt an unreasoning surge of jealousy as Charles smiled at them.

"Allow me to name Mistress Jane Lane and Mr. Henry Lascelles," he said, "who have been my saviors, as you are now." Jane and Henry exchanged bows with the Wyndhams, and it seemed to Jane that the ladies eyed her with barely suppressed curiosity.

"We think it best to lodge you here in my mother's rooms," Colonel Wyndham said. "They are the most removed from the rest of the house and the most private, and there is a priest hole, should it be called for."

"What could be better?" Charles said, beaming. "I would say that you cannot guess how grateful I am for your kind shelter, but that I am sure you can."

Anne Wyndham dimpled a smile at him. "Please excuse me, Your Majesty," she said. "I beg you to make yourself comfortable while I bring some refreshment."

She and Lady Wyndham bustled from the room, and Charles sank onto one of the chairs around a table near the fireplace, and gestured to the others.

"I pray you all, be seated." He turned to Jane and Henry. "Frank here has been most active on our behalf. He was governor of Dunster Castle during the war, and with Sir John Paulet he formed the Western Association, its members gathering under cover of a race meeting."

"Though to no avail," Colonel Wyndham said, seating himself on a bench near the fireplace. "Our rising last December was discovered almost before it had begun, and I have only just been released on parole from imprisonment."

Jane noted that he was thin, and his face lined and shadowed, as though he had been ill. She realized that he was probably only in his thirties, though she had at first taken him to be older.

"I cannot tell Your Majesty what inexpressible joy it gives us to see you well," Colonel Wyndham said. "The news we had from Worcester was that your life had been lost, and we knew no different until my lord Wilmot's arrival last night."

"Perhaps that is to the better," Charles said. "If the people hereabouts think me dead, they will have no reason to look for me."

"True," Colonel Wyndham agreed. "But if it please Your Majesty, it will be safest if you remain within these rooms. This morning I sent forth most of the servants on various pretexts against your arrival, but they will return, and the fewer people that see Your Majesty, the better. With your permission, we will make your presence known to our man Henry Peters, and two of our maids who have all been with us for many years and whose loyalty is beyond question. The rest of the household will remain in ignorance."

"I will follow your judgment in all things, Frank," Charles said. "Providence has showed me the way to your door, and I trust will show me when it is safe to step forth."

Anne and Lady Wyndham returned with the two maids, Eleanor and Joan, both middle-aged women who sank to their knees to kiss the king's hand, expressing their determination to do anything in their power to help him and make him comfortable. They left and came back a few minutes later with bread, cold meat, cheese, fruit, and ale. After the meal, Anne Wyndham turned to Jane.

"Shall we withdraw and leave the men to their planning, Mistress Lane? I am sure that you must be weary from your journey and would be glad to leave the business to the gentlemen."

Jane had no wish at all to leave the business to the gentlemen and desperately wanted to be in on their discussion, but as the men rose and the Wyndham ladies waited smiling for her, she felt trapped, so with a pained smile at Henry and Charles, she departed.

"This will be your room, Mistress Lane," Anne Wyndham said. "Near to the king so that you may confer easily if need be."

"How charming," Jane said, with genuine pleasure, for the room was not only lovely but just a few steps from Charles's door. She turned to find Juliana Coningsby gazing at her, her dimpled cheeks rosy and her bright blue eyes glowing with excitement.

"What an adventure you must be having!" Juliana cried, speaking for the first time since greeting the king.

"Yes!" Anne Wyndham giggled, clapping her hands. "We did not know the king was so handsome a man!"

"And to be a-horseback with him on such a journey!" Juliana gushed. "Like something from a fairy tale!"

They stared at her as if she might do something marvelous and unexpected, and Jane laughed uncomfortably, wondering if her feelings for Charles showed clearly on her face.

"Indeed, it has been an adventure," she said. "One that I scarce looked for, and that came upon me so suddenly that even now I hardly know what to think of it."

"Come, girls," old Lady Wyndham said, shooing the younger women toward the door. "I'm sure Mistress Lane is tired. There will be plenty of time for talking later."

Jane was more tired than she had known from the strain of the last few days, and when she was alone, she gladly dropped onto the bed, soft with feather beds and down-filled pillows, and was soon asleep.

JANE, HENRY, AND WILMOT JOINED THE WYNDHAM FAMILY FOR DINner, and seeing the size of the household, Jane thought it was much the best course for Charles to stay out of sight. With assorted family members and servants, she reckoned there must be more than twenty people under the Wyndhams' roof. The old maid Eleanor beamed at her and Jane smiled back, unaccustomed to such adulation.

After the meal she went to Charles's room and was happy to find him alone, reading over the little catechism he had been given at Mosely. He took her into his arms and kissed her, then led her to the window seat.

"What a lovely room!" she said, admiring the garden below and the view beyond, down the hill and southwest, the sun slanting over the fields. "I could stay forever here!"

"Let us hope you shall not have to, and nor shall I." Charles laughed.

"What did Colonel Wyndham say?" she asked. "Can he help you?"

He grinned, seeming more relaxed than she had yet seen him. "He has a friend who he is confident can get a boat for me, and will go to see him tomorrow. Oh, Jane, I am almost home free."

"Yes," said Jane. "Almost there," and her heart contracted. "Oh, Charles, what shall I do without you?" She looked to him, love and longing welling up and filling her as she gazed on his face.

He chucked her under the chin and took her hand. "Why, sweetheart, you shall do very well, just as you did before ever I came to disrupt your life."

Jane tried to smile but tears filled her eyes and she choked back a sob before she replied.

"But now I know what life can be, what happiness is, how can I return to things as they were?"

Charles looked down at his feet, scuffing a leaf from the sole of one shoe with the toe of the other, and he sighed.

"It cannot be helped, sweeting. You know it as well as I. You have hazarded your life for me already as it is, and now you must return to your family and safety."

"I know," Jane wept softly. "But I don't want to."

He kissed her hand and brushed the tears from her cheeks. "No more do I. But let us not think on it until we must." He cupped her chin in his hand and kissed her. "We have tonight at least."

"I don't want to wait until tonight," she said, desire racing through her at the heat of his lips on hers. "Lie with me now. I ache for your touch."

"I need no second invitation to a repose so sweet," Charles murmured. He pulled her to him and kissed her deeply, his hands entangled in her hair. He rose and led her toward the little bedchamber that lay a step up from the main room, but before they reached the stair, they were startled by a sudden loud clanging of bells. It was not a simple tolling of the hour but a wild clamor, and now shouts and singing could be heard. They went to the window. Smoke rose near the church steeple that stood only a few dozen paces away, but the trees obscured their view of whatever might be happening. The noise of the unseen crowd grew louder, and Charles hastened to the door of the chamber.

"Eleanor," he said to the maid who waited outside. "Pray find out the cause of that noise. Belike it tokens some important news."

The bells jangled on, ringing out the same cascading peal over and over. Ten or fifteen minutes passed before Eleanor reappeared, her broad face red with emotion.

"Oh, Your Majesty," she whispered. "It is people from the village here, met to welcome a crowd of soldiers just come. They have lit a bonfire and are dancing. They are rejoicing . . ."

She stopped and began to weep.

"At what?" Charles prompted. She looked at him, her eyes dark with sorrow and anger.

"At the news of your death, Your Majesty. There is one great ruffian, a soldier in a buff coat, roaring that he slew you and took the coat from your body. And the villains, they drink his health and cheer him."

She wiped her eyes with her apron, shaking her head in disbelief.

"Alas, poor people," Charles said softly. He took the maid's hand, and she raised her eyes to his. "Let it trouble thee not, good Eleanor, for your care and kindness outweigh what they do in their ignorance."

Jane took her supper with Charles in his chamber, feeling like a queen as Eleanor and the other maid, Joan, hovered solicitously. Wyndham, Wilmot, and Henry joined them at the table after supper.

"I doubt not that we shall find a boat for Your Majesty within a day or two," Wyndham said, lighting a long-stemmed clay pipe and blowing a puff of gray-blue smoke.

"And the sooner the better," Wilmot said. "Your Majesty, being forth today I have learned ill news."

Jane felt her stomach heave with worry. Had Charles's presence been discovered? If he was not safe here, where could he hide, with so many soldiers nearby, and the people of the village still celebrating his supposed death?

"The Earl of Derby was arrested near Kinver after he left us at Whiteladies," Wilmot said.

"Ah, dear God, no," Henry groaned.

"He was taken first to Whitechurch," Wilmot continued, "and then to an inn at Banbury. He tried to escape when he was being removed to Chester Castle, but was caught."

"Was he killed?" Colonel Wyndham asked, his face white. Wilmot shook his head.

"No. But he is to be tried on charges of treason on the first of October."

Charles rose and went to the window and stood staring out. The moon, almost full, was just rising golden next to the church steeple, its bells silent now. Charles exhaled heavily, and ran a hand through his hair in agitation before he spoke. "A trial that must surely end in his conviction and death."

They sat silent for a few moments. The fire crackled and hissed, and a burning log shifted with a snap. The sweet scent of Wyndham's tobacco mingled with the tang of the cool night air.

"And, I am sorry to say," Wilmot continued softly, "the Duke of Hamilton died on Friday of the wounds he had at Worcester."

Jane sent up a silent prayer for the duke, one more life given in service of the king. Was it all for nothing, this suffering? she wondered. *Please, God, let it not be in vain.*

"On Friday," Charles said, his voice hollow. "The day we came to Bristol." He bowed his head as if in prayer. "Alas for Hamilton and for Derby. God, that so many brave and good men should lose their lives for their help to me."

"I doubt not that they go to their deaths willingly," Colonel Wyndham said. "Knowing that the cause they serve is great."

Charles sat and took Jane's hand in his. She noted the other men take in the gesture. Colonel Wyndham's eyes showed a brief flash of surprise. Henry breathed in sharply and looked away. Wilmot only raised an eyebrow and gave her a faint smile.

The king's whore . . . Was that what they were thinking? she wondered.

Wyndham drew on his pipe and blew out a smoke ring.

"Before these wars began," he said, "my father, knowing he was ill and soon to die, summoned my four brothers and me. He put us in mind of the many years of peace England had enjoyed under her last three monarchs, but bid us prepare for cloudy and troublesome times ahead. 'I command you to honor and obey our gracious sovereign,' he said, 'and at all times to adhere to the crown, and though the crown should hang on a bush, I charge you forsake it not.' "

"Well remembered," Charles nodded. "That the crown so hung upon a bush on the field at Bosworth when Richard fell, and that Henry Tudor plucked it forth and raised it once again to honor."

"Just so," Wyndham said. "And when my honored father's prophecies came true and war rent the land, we heeded him. Three of my brothers and one of their sons fell in fighting for Your Majesty's father." Henry and Wilmot murmured in sympathy.

"God grant that I may be worthy of such sacrifice," Charles said, clasping Wyndham's hand. "And live to do your family the honor it deserves."

"Amen to that," Wilmot said.

"Give me but ten or twelve thousand men as stouthearted as those by the name of Wyndham, Lane, and Lascelles," Charles said, looking from face to face, "and I will return and sweep all before me, and pluck the crown from the bush once more."

"We will stand with you, Sire," Henry said, "when that happy day comes. But what may we do now to help Your Majesty to safety? Will we ride with you to the coast?"

"Henry," Charles replied, "you and Jane have done such signal service that there are none could hope to do more, and I hope that I may live to thank you as I would. But I think that your task is now at an end." His eyes met Jane's, and she knew he was about to speak the words she dreaded to hear.

"Colonel Wyndham and good Wilmot have the matter in hand," Charles said, "and I do not wish to endanger you further than I already have."

"But surely there is something we can do?" Jane cried. She could hear the note of desperation in her voice, and saw Wyndham and Wilmot exchange a glance.

"No," Charles said softly. "Go home and be safe. That is what you can do for me now, Jane."

"Then we'll ride tomorrow." Henry nodded. "And keep you in our prayers until we learn of your safe deliverance to France."

Jane went to her own room when the men departed, but when the house was dark and quiet, she crept down the hall to the chamber where Charles lay. She scratched softly at the door, and he opened it, his eyes luminous in the dark. He stood in nothing but his breeches, the moonlight falling softly across the white of his skin, and she threw herself into his arms, her hands urgent on his chest, his back, pulling her to him, offering her mouth up to his. He took her head in his hands and kissed her deeply, his mouth moving to her throat as she arched against him, her insides turning to liquid fire. He stripped the nightgown off over her head and cast it away, his hands caressing her breasts, sweeping down over her belly, her hips and buttocks.

"You are so very beautiful," he murmured, and she moaned, wanting him inside her, inside her body, her heart, her soul. He knelt and pulled her to him, kissing the thatch of soft hair at the base of her belly, warm fingers sliding into the cleft of her thighs, caressing the slick wetness so that she whimpered with desire. He swept her up into his arms and carried her to the bed, threw off his breeches, knelt between her legs, and entered her so hard that she cried out. He stifled her mouth with a hand, and she gasped as he thrust, filling her, staking her to the bed with his passion.

"I cannot wait, my sweet, my sweet, you are so sweet," he whispered, moving inside her, and she found herself arching up to him, pulling him down to her, wanting him so deeply inside her that it felt as if they were one. She tore at his back with her fingernails and he rode her hard, urgently, slamming into her so that she felt the insides of her thighs bruising from his battering thrusts.

A wave rose and rose within her, colors swam in her head, and she gasped and bucked, almost weeping with the intensity of the pleasure. The same wave was carrying him, and they exploded together, his mouth on hers, devouring her even as he groaned in his crisis.

They lay still joined, his weight crushing her, his hands caressing her face as their breath slowly returned to normal. She felt the damp of their commingled sweat cool in the breeze from the open window. He stirred to move, and she pulled him tight to her, grasping his buttocks, wanting him never to leave the haven of her body. He looked down at her and kissed her again, moving his hips against her, and she felt him rising to hardness again. She reached down and took him in her hand, marveling as the shaft became engorged and stiff, pulsing between her fingers. She guided him into her again and he gasped as he slid into the tight scabbard of her flesh. This second coupling was slower, endless, wordless, their eyes holding each other's even as their bodies merged.

"Oh, Jane, I love you."

He spoke so low that she could scarce hear him, but he had said the words, and she grasped him to her.

When at last they had spent again, they lay entwined in each other's arms, the moonlight spilling across the bed, Charles murmuring endearments through the tangle of Jane's hair. Through the night they made love. Jane climbed astride Charles, riding him, moving herself up and down his length, first slowly so that he groaned with aching for more, then faster and faster, his hands pulling her down onto him so that she felt impaled there. She took him into her mouth as he had shown her until he grew hard again, wondered as he guided her to lie on her front and slipped a pillow beneath belly, shuddered as he thrust deep within her, touching places she had not known existed. She wondered if she would ever feel so alive again.

At last, at long last, drained and exhausted, they wrapped themselves around each other and slept, until the first birds began to call their greetings to the morning and the golden dawn began to lighten the windows. A bird sang, and Jane thought of Juliet, waking on the morning after her wedding night.

It is the lark that sings so out of tune,
Straining harsh discords and unpleasing sharps.
Some say the lark makes sweet division,
This doth not so, for she divideth us.

Charles stirred, and eyes still closed, pulled her close against his chest. She inhaled the scent of his hair, his skin, trying to store it in her memory so that she could keep the sense of him close to her when he was gone. She lay with her belly and breasts pressed against him, her arms tight around him, listening to the growing chorus of the birds and feeling the room brighten with the rising sun. The day was coming, and could not be kept at bay, and she felt her heart breaking in her chest.

O, thinkst thou we shall ever meet again?

"Will you give me something of yours?" she whispered. "Your handkerchief? Something that smells of you for me to keep always by me."

Charles opened his eyes and kissed her lips, her cheeks, her eyelids, before untying the handkerchief he had wrapped around his throat against the cold. He draped it around her neck, and then let his hands drift lower to whisper across her belly and buttocks. His cock was growing again, rising against her, and she stroked its length with delicate fingers. Charles laughed softly.

"You shall have that again if you wish it, too, my sweet, but I have something more lasting to give you." He reached for his waistcoat hanging on a chair next to the bed, and pulled from the pocket a tiny leather case, studded with silver in a looping pattern. He opened it and drew forth something chestnut-sized and silver.

"My watch," he said, putting it into her hand. "When I cast off my own clothes at Whiteladies, I gave my Garter and my George—Saint George and the dragon, you know, in gold and diamonds—to Colonel Blague to keep safe for me, and I gave my rings, my snuffbox, all the money I carried save a few shillings to the poor people who were helping me. But though I knew I ought, yet I could not bear to part with this. My father gave it me the last time I saw him." His eyes shimmered with tears and tenderness filled Jane's heart.

"Oh, Charles."

She touched the little engraved silver case, overcome at the thought of his giving her such a gift of himself.

"It is precious to me as you are," he said. "Wear us both near your heart."

"I will. Always." She knotted the watch into the handkerchief and pinned the little bundle to the inside of her stays, retrieved from where they lay on the floor.

"See? It will lie in my bosom." She stroked his cheek, and he kissed the tips of her fingers. "Think of me and know that however far away you may be, yet you are part of me."

He held her to him, kissing her lips, her face, her hair. His cock stood hard and throbbing against her belly now, and his breath was coming fast.

"May I take my farewell of thee thus?" he breathed, his hands parting her thighs as he rolled himself atop her once again.

"Yes, my love. With all my heart. Take me, for I am yours."

They were both crying, and their tears mingled on their cheeks, the taste salty as they ran into Jane's mouth. Their joining this time was urgent and hungry, and was over soon. Morning light flooded the room.

More light and light, more dark and dark our woes . . .

"You must be gone," Charles whispered.

Let me be ta'en, let me be put to death
I am content, so thou wilt have it so . . .

Jane knew that the moment of parting she had dreaded could be put off no longer. She knew she must rise, but buried her face against his chest once more.

"Don't forget me." Her voice was thick with grief.

"Oh, Jane, I couldn't if I tried," he murmured, his voice husky in her ear. "You have given me my life. You are my life, as much as my breath and heartbeat."

CHAPTER NINE

JANE'S GRAY MARE WAS SADDLED, THE PILLION GIRDED ON, AND the Wyndhams' servant Peters stood holding its bridle. They were leaving the strawberry roan for the king, and Jane thought she heard its nickering from the stable. Henry swung himself into the saddle and held his hand out, and with Peters's help, Jane climbed up and settled herself on the pillion, her feet on the little planchette and her skirts smoothed down over her legs.

"Go with God," Colonel Wyndham said, "And may your way home be safe."

JANE AND HENRY WOULD TAKE A DIFFERENT ROUTE HOME, BOTH because the more direct route was shorter than the way they had come, and because it would be safer not to pass through Bristol, Cirencester, Stratford-upon-Avon, and all the other towns where they had ridden with Charles, on the chance that someone had noted and wondered about the tall dark servant and might recall them.

They traveled more slowly, too, as they could not switch off the heavier weight of the two riders between the horses. They rode north from Trent as if toward Castle Cary, but turned east after only a few miles, and at the end of the first day's travel they had reached a village called Mere.

The George Inn was the sole place of lodging, and Henry had no sooner procured them two rooms and ordered supper than Jane heard the thunder of horses' hooves on the road. There was a shouted order, the jangle of bridles and creak of leather as men dismounted, laughter, voices, and the sound of still more horses. The door of the inn flew open and several booted Parliamentary officers strode in and hailed the landlord.

"A whole troop of cavalry," Henry said under his breath to Jane.

"Shall we ride on?" she whispered.

"No. It would only draw attention to us if we left now, and besides, there's no telling how far we would have to ride to find another inn. It's nearly dark as it is."

The eyes of some of the officers had lighted on Jane and Henry, and he raised his voice to greet them.

"Good even, gentlemen."

They nodded to him and bowed to Jane, and she gave them a distracted smile before dropping her eyes.

"I'll thank you if you would bring our food upstairs," Henry said to the landlord. "My sister is ill at ease in the presence of so many soldiers."

"Right enough," the landlord agreed. "Lucky you came when you did, or there'd have been no room at all."

JANE LAY AWAKE FAR INTO THE NIGHT, LISTENING TO THE SOUND OF the soldiers drinking and talking below and thinking of Charles. It was a miracle he had got as far as Trent, she thought.

Keep him safe, she prayed. *Keep him safe and get him to the coast and France. And let me see him again.* But she knew she would not see him again anytime soon, or maybe ever. She clutched the knotted handkerchief to her, inhaling Charles's scent, holding his precious watch close to her heart.

THE NEXT AFTERNOON'S RIDE BROUGHT THEM DOWN FROM THE HILLS and onto the rolling plains of Salisbury. From far off Jane spotted a strange shape, which as they drew closer she saw was a circle of great standing stones.

"What is that?" she asked.

"Stonehenge," Henry answered. "The Giants' Dance, some call it. Very ancient. No one knows why it is there or what it is for, but it will stand long after we are forgotten."

"Can we ride closer?" she asked as they drew even with the stones.

Henry turned off the road. It was only a short distance to the circle, and he rode around it. Some of the massive pillars had fallen and lay on the ground. Henry reined the horse to a halt and they gazed westward into the blaze of the setting sun, the great upright stones casting long shadows. The wind whipped across the grass of the plain, and Jane shivered.

"Where can they have come from? We've passed no stone outcroppings or anything in the land like this."

Henry shrugged. "Who knows?"

"It seems almost like a church," Jane mused. "Like the columns down the aisle of the nave, but in a circle."

"And so it might be."

Jane stared. The stone circle seemed to draw her in, to emanate some deep sense of power or protection, and she didn't want to leave.

"Let's stop for the night," she suggested.

Henry glanced at the setting sun and at the vast emptiness around them. "It's not much further to Amesbury," he said. "With an inn, and beds."

"There will be beds on other nights. Please?"

Henry shaded his eyes against the setting sun as he gazed silently at the stones, and Jane felt that he, too, sensed their power. He nodded, helped her to dismount, and tethered the horse, and they walked in silence around the perimeter of the great circle. Jane stood and watched in awe as the fiery orb of the sun seemed to balance atop one of the pillars. Deep blue shadows slanted across the gray of the stones. The sun sank toward the horizon, darkness drawing down across the whispering plains.

They gathered brush and wood and built a fire near the center of the circle, but ate cold food they carried with them. The full moon rose gold in the purple of the sky, and Jane felt somehow, swathed in her blanket beside the fire, with the stones looming black around them, as if she was at the very center of the universe, and at one with all people since the world had begun.

"Let's say a prayer for the king," she whispered. "I almost feel that from here our words will reach straight up to the ear of God."

Henry nodded, and reached for her hand. They bowed their heads, each in silence offering up their pleas.

They lay down to sleep, huddling close together on the ground, the fire sending its bright sparks heavenward.

Jane woke with first light, the clean autumn air sharp in her nostrils. She gathered her blanket around her, and crept barefoot away from where Henry lay snoring beside the cold remains of the fire. The grass was damp with the dew, and the feel of the moisture on her feet after the days of riding made her feel vibrantly alive.

The horizon to the east was shot with pink and purple, the sun not quite showing above the rim of the plain. She picked her way along the ditch encircling the stones, marveling at how their appearance changed depending on where she stood. A tall stone stood just outside the northeast perimeter of the circle, leaning in as though pointing the way to the center.

"Good morning!" Henry's voice broke the silence. He stood grinning at her, his blanket draped over his shoulders.

"Good morning yourself," Jane laughed as she went to him. "Isn't it glorious?"

She twirled, admiring the horizon, still dark purple to the west, and the east now rosy gold.

"Look!" she exclaimed. "How the sun appears just there, in that break between the stones. Almost like a doorway for the sunlight to pass through."

They watched in silence as the sun rolled higher above the leaning stone just outside the circle.

"What can be the purpose? I wonder," Jane mused.

"Perhaps we'll never know," Henry said. "But I'm glad we stopped."

"Yes. Here among these stones I feel as though the power of the universe is with me, rising up from the center of the globe and through my feet, rooting me to the very earth."

She reached her arms toward the lightening sky, in salutation to the new day.

"I will have to try to keep this power within me. I feel that I could face anything with the strength of the stones flowing through my body."

The day's ride took them north to Marlborough and they spent that night in Burford. It was all new country to Jane, but Charles's absence was a constant ache. She longed to be sharing the journey with him, to have him solidly in front of her on the horse, admiring the view, passing the ride with singing and talking, and warming the nights with love.

On Friday the twenty-second of September they reached Evesham. It was only forty miles from Worcester, and had quartered thirty thousand of Cromwell's soldiers before the battle. Many of them were back again, and here Jane felt more immediately than she had since Charles arrived at Bentley the threat to his life and the completeness of the defeat of the Royalist cause. The royal arms had been chiseled from the stone market stall and lay in a heap of shards of brightly painted plaster, and on the wall was pasted the broadsheet offering a reward of a thousand pounds for the capture of "Charles Stuart, a black-haired man six feet two inches in height."

The town was full of rumors of the king's whereabouts. As they ate supper in the taproom of the inn, Jane and Henry listened to three soldiers arguing.

"He's somewhere not far off, mark my words," a big fair-headed lad asserted. "In some lurking hole."

One of the others shook his head vehemently. "Don't believe it. He's long since slipped across the border to Scotland."

"He'd have had to be in disguise to do it," claimed the third soldier, a little bandy-legged man with a red face.

"And there's some that say he was," the first man chuckled. "Dressed as a wench, I've heard."

Jane kept her eyes on her food. Cromwell's men had not given up the hunt, it was clear, but it also seemed they did not know the truth. She put a hand to the front of her bodice, feeling the lump of the watch pinned there, and said a silent prayer for Charles's safety.

It would be a long day's ride to reach Bentley without stopping another night, but both Jane and Henry were eager to be home, so they rose in the dark and set off north, using a different road than the one that had taken them through Bromsgrove.

When they turned off the Wolverhampton Road onto the lane that led the quarter mile to Bentley, and the house was at last within sight, Jane felt as though she had been gone for a century. The dogs barked excitedly as they rode into the stable yard, and soon the whole household had come out to greet them.

"Praise be to God, you're safe!" Jane's mother cried, kissing her cheeks. "But where is the other horse? And that farmer's lad?"

"He stayed at Abbots Leigh to work on the harvest." Now that Jane spoke it, the story she and Henry had concocted to explain the king's absence seemed feeble and suspicious.

"Then it's a good thing your cousin was with you!" her mother clucked, hugging Henry. "Else would you have been at the mercy of every ruffian on the road. I didn't like the looks of that boy from the first I set eyes on him."

"We did not expect you so soon," Jane's father said quietly, embracing her. His gray eyes were worried as he looked into hers. "Is all well?"

"No. Ellen—Ellen lost the baby."

Tears coursed suddenly down Jane's cheek.

"Oh, poor girl," Nurse cried, enfolding Jane against her capacious bosom. Jane's strength left her, and she began to sob, for Ellen and her dead child, for Charles, for herself.

"I'm so sorry, Jane." John was beside her, his eyes full of concern. "For Ellen, of course, and that your journey was harder than it should have been. Go rest yourself now, and Henry can tell me all about it."

For days Jane felt utterly drained both in body and spirit. Her whole body was battered and bruised from the many days of riding, and several times she soaked in a tub of hot water, letting it unknot the tension that seemed to grip every part of her. She ached with the loss of Charles, the fear that perhaps he had not got to safety after all, and apprehension that her part in his escape should become known.

And Michaelmas was only a few days away. She had promised Clement Fisher an answer to his proposal on that day, but she felt a sense of helpless despair when she thought of what she could say to him, for her whole life—her very being—had changed irrevocably in the intervening weeks. Her heart and mind were so full of Charles that it was hard to find room for anything else.

And another worry gnawed at the back of her mind, further complicating the question of what to say to Clement. Her monthly courses should have begun, and they had not. She tried to remember exactly when she had last bled. It had been at least a week before they received news of the battle at Worcester, she was sure, but more than that she could not recall. Could she be with child? How would she know? There must be signs, but she didn't know what they might be. Perhaps the signs were there to see for someone who knew what to look for—Nurse, her mother, Athalia, her other sisters-in-law, the servants. There was no one she could ask.

If she accepted Clement's offer and married him right away, at least she would have a husband if it proved she was with child. But it would be unkind and ignoble to do so without telling him the truth, and if she told him, it was very likely he would no longer want her. And even if he agreed to take her with another man's get in her belly, wasn't it likely that the baby itself would proclaim the truth? Anyone with an eye in his head would look twice at a dark-haired, dark-eyed child of Charles's, and fair, blue-eyed Clement.

She agonized about what to do, and did not even feel right praying about it. She hoped that she was not with child, and then felt guilty about that. Might it not be even more sinful than lying with a man to wish that no child resulted? Especially if that child was the king's?

At last Jane wrote to Clement, telling him she was still exhausted from her journey and distraught over Ellen's loss of the baby, and asked if he would give her another fortnight, until the fifteenth of October, before he came for his answer. Maybe her path would become clearer by then.

In Jane's absence the family had learned that her brother Richard had been arrested and imprisoned after Worcester. He was likely at Chester Castle, but they did not know what his fate would be.

Bentley was not the only local household left reeling after the battle. Many men had been injured or killed or captured, or had managed to escape arrest but had since fled across the sea.

Jane strolled with John in the orchard one morning, eager to be able to speak privately. The early fruit had been harvested, and only the apple trees were still heavy with their red and gold bounty. A cool breeze rustled through the trees, and russet leaves drifted in the wind.

"Charles Giffard says that Colonel Carlis was at Boscobel when the king was there," John said, stopping to examine the entrance to a badger sett, the burrowed tunnel leading toward the roots of an apricot tree. "Giffard was under Carlis's command at Worcester, and they were in the thick of the fighting at Sidbury Gate and High Street. Carlis just got out of the city with his life, and now is gone to the Low Countries." He dusted his hands on the knees of his breeches, and they resumed their walk. "Giffard was taken with the Earl of Derby, but managed to escape. He fears he may be taken yet, and thinks of going to France."

"Any word of the king?" Jane whispered.

John shook his head. "In Walsall the other day I heard tales of his being gone to the United Provinces or Scotland. But it's all rumor. Cromwell's men are still searching round here, and in Worcestershire."

"Thank God," Jane breathed. "He should be in France by now. Will you take me to town next time you go? Perhaps there will be news. And as glad as I was to be home, now I am restless to be out and doing."

John smiled. "Your journeys have given you a taste for novelty and bustle."

He had given no indication that he knew what had passed between her and Charles, so Henry must have thought better of his threat to tell him, Jane thought with relief. She could not bear the thought of her adored older brother regarding her with scorn and disapproval as Henry had.

"Maybe so," she agreed. "All I know is that I feel like a bird in a cage, and long to stretch my wings."

A LITTLE MORE THAN A WEEK AFTER JANE AND HENRY HAD RETURNED home, Jane accompanied John to market day at Wolverhampton. There had still been no news of Charles, and each day's passing increased her agitation. If all had gone as he expected, he should be in France, and word should have reached England by now. She was glad of the opportunity to distract herself with such mundane business as matching a color of embroidery thread for her mother and gazing with admiration at the fine horses for sale. She tried to ignore the troops everywhere throughout the town.

A new book would be a good thing to occupy her mind, Jane thought, and she made for the bookseller's stall where she and John had agreed to meet. Before she could begin to examine the books, however, her eye was caught by stacks of a broadsheet headed "Last News of the King of Scotland."

Her eyes raced over the words. The king had fled into Scotland to Lord Belcarris, it said, and Cromwell's men were in pursuit. Surely it was not possible, Jane thought. He would hardly have left Trent, so close to the southern coast, and ridden north, back into danger.

She bought a copy of the Parliamentary newsbook *Mercurius Politicus,* but found no comfort there. The Earl of Derby, who had been captured shortly after leaving Charles at Whiteladies in the hours after the battle, had been tried, despite having been given quarter when he was taken, and had been found guilty of treason for aiding the king. Jane thought of Charles gazing out the bedroom window at Trent, staggered with the thought of Derby's apprehension and what it would mean.

"Jane."

She turned at the sound of John's voice, and held the newsbook and the broadsheet up noiselessly.

"I know," he said. He took her arm and led her away from the bookseller's stall, glancing over his shoulder to see who might be watching them, and spoke in a low voice. "Francis Yates, who guided the king from Worcester to Whiteladies, was arrested. He's been—questioned—but refused to tell where he left the king or where His Majesty is like to have gone."

John's face was grim, and Jane could imagine the likely brutality of the interrogation.

"Yates will be hanged here next market day."

Jane's eyes went to the gibbet at the center of the marketplace and a cold knot of fear gripped her stomach. Yates had done far less to help the king than she had, and he would die there in a week's time. She clamped a hand to her mouth, suddenly faint and nauseated, and John steadied her, his hands on her upper arms, his eyes clouded with worry.

"Here, sit."

He led her to a stump and sat her down, took his little flask of brandy from his pocket, and handed it to her. Jane grimaced at the smell of the spirits but took a drink, feeling the fire of it warming and calming her belly.

"Jane, I must be here when he dies."

"Why?" she cried in horror.

"He must have the comfort of friendly faces in the crowd. He served under Carlis at Worcester, but Carlis is gone abroad, as is Giffard and many others who were his comrades. He's married to a sister of the Penderels, but they would put themselves in grave danger to be there. I would not have him die without knowing that what he did and its consequences are valued and will be remembered."

How awful it would be to die alone in the midst of a hostile crowd, Jane thought. She shivered at the thought of watching Yates hang, but met John's eyes.

"Then I shall come with you."

John looked away from her, his gaze following a knot of red-coated soldiers.

"There's another reason, too. He'll need a friend to pull on his legs and hasten his death. A broken neck is better than strangling at a rope's end for a quarter of an hour."

Jane felt herself sway on the stump and dropped her head into her arms.

"Take me home, John. Please, get me out of here now."

THE NEXT MARKET DAY JANE STOOD WITH JOHN, HENRY, AND HER father at the front of the crowd that had come to Wolverhampton to see Francis Yates die. Despite the danger, the Penderel brothers were all there, their weathered faces lined with grief and anger. Many others in the crowd were also there in support of Yates, to let him know that he would not be forgotten. But there was a hostile element, and they were emboldened by the presence of so many Parliamentary soldiers. As the cart carrying Yates approached, a group of boys followed along, shouting derisively and throwing refuse and stones.

Yates's hands were bound behind his back, and he sat in the cart without looking to either side, as if his enemies were not present. The cart drew up under the gibbet, where a platoon of soldiers stood in ranks. They parted to let the cart pass, and then ranged themselves in a square around the gibbet, their muskets pointed out toward the crowd, bayonets fixed. The boys who had dogged the cart pushed to the front of the crowd.

"You'll be in hell before dinnertime, Yates," one redheaded young ruffian sang out.

"Sooner than that, Neddy," one of his friends shouted. "You'll meet the devil while the shit's still running down your legs, you traitor!"

"No traitor he, but a braver man than thou wilt ever be!" roared one of the Penderel brothers, shoving the second boy so that he fell to the ground.

The boy jumped to his feet, and his friends closed around him as Yates's family and friends rushed forward to stand on either side of the farmer. Shoves were exchanged, the crowd surged forward toward the gibbet. The soldiers swung their bayonets at the advancing mob and their captain shouted for order above the babble of angry voices. Henry pulled Jane behind him to protect her as the melee threatened to envelop them. Yates, in breeches and a shirt stained with sweat and dirt, had been pulled to his feet by a soldier in the cart with him, and stared silently out at the riot breaking out on his behalf.

A shot shattered the air, halting the skirmish.

"This will be your only warning!" roared the red-faced officer, smoking pistol in hand, still pointed toward the sky. "Whosoever causes further disturbance will be arrested."

Royalist and rebels backed away from one another, exchanging final shoves and sneers, and the crowd subsided into muttering.

"Proceed with the punishment!" the officer barked. "Lieutenant!"

A young lieutenant stepped forward, and read from a printed broadsheet, his voice cutting into the silence.

"The Parliament of the Commonwealth of England have thought fit to enact and declare that no person whatsoever do presume to hold any correspondence with Charles Stuart, son of the late traitor, or with his party, or with any of them, nor give any intelligence to them, or to any of them, nor countenance, encourage, abet, adhere to, or assist them or any of them, not to voluntarily afford or deliver, or cause to be afforded or delivered to them or any of them, any victuals, provisions, arms, ammunition, plate, money, men, or any other relief whatsoever, under pain of high treason."

A few hisses and shouts of "boo" rang out, and the lieutenant glanced at the crowd and took a breath before continuing.

"Whosoever shall offend against this Act and Declaration, shall or may be proceeded against by a Council of War, who are hereby authorized to hear and determine all and every the said offenses, and such as shall by the said Council be condemned to suffer death, shall also forfeit all his or their lands, goods, and other estate, as in case of high treason."

Jane had read the words of the proclamation when it was published in August, which now seemed a lifetime ago. But how vastly different to hear read aloud each offense of which she and her family were guilty, with Francis Yates standing not twenty feet away and about to die merely because he had guided the king to Whiteladies in that dark night after the battle.

"Drummer!" the captain shouted, and the drummer started into an ominous roll.

The soldier beside Yates placed the noose that hung from the gibbet around his neck and tightened the rope.

"Let him speak!" someone shouted at the back of the crowd.

"Aye, let him speak!"

The cry was taken up and the crowd was roaring now. They far outnumbered the soldiers guarding the gibbet, and Jane saw sweat rolling down the face of a fair-haired young soldier who stood a few feet before her. She looked beyond him to Yates. He was near tears now, but not of fright. He nodded at familiar faces, pulling at his bound arms as though he would have waved and saluted in response to the cries.

"God save the king!" he shouted, and the crowd called back.

"God save the king!"

"We won't forget thee, Frank!"

"You've a heart of oak, lad! Your name will live in England forever!"

Yates held his head high, his brimming eyes bright with emotion.

The drummer played furiously, in a futile effort to drown out the yells of the crowd.

"Drive on!" the captain bellowed.

The driver of the cart lashed the horse, and the cart started forward.

Francis Yates, nothing beneath his feet now, jerked and bucked at the end of the rope, his face contorted in desperation and agony, his eyes bulging, his tongue rolling forth as he struggled for the breath that would never come.

Henry thrust Jane back against her father as he and John rushed forward, followed by the five Penderel brothers. There was a moment's hesitation as they confronted the soldiers who faced them. Then the soldiers' eyes snapped away from them, not seeing them, deliberately not seeing as Henry and John strode to the foot of the gibbet, and the Penderel brothers ranged themselves in a half circle, facing the howling crowd. John and Henry each seized one of Francis Yates's legs, their eyes met and they nodded, and they pulled with all their strength, a sharp and brutal shock. Yates's body twitched, but he struggled no more. Sobs and cries echoed in the cold air. John looked up at Yates's face, purple but still, then stepped back and saluted the swinging corpse. Henry mirrored him on Yates's other side.

Sobs tore Jane's throat, and she clung to her father. He clutched her to his chest, and she could hear that he was weeping, too, and the enormity of what danger she had brought upon him, her mother, and all her family as well as herself swept over her. If her part in the king's escape were discovered, she would die just as Yates had, with John and Henry likely dangling at her side, and her old parents would lose their house and lands and all they had.

God, keep them safe, she prayed. *Let my deeds never come to the light, that Henry and John and my parents and those I love do not suffer for what I have done.*

CHAPTER TEN

THE SPECTACLE OF FRANCIS YATES'S EXECUTION HAUNTED JANE'S dreams. Adding to her anxiety was the fact that as yet, the newsbooks, broadsheets, and proclamations carried no news of Charles. When she parted from him, he had been within a day's ride of the coast, and Frank Wyndham had been confident that his friend would find him a boat and get him safely on his way. He should have reached France long since. Even if the worst had happened and he had been taken, that news would have been proclaimed far and loud. The only reasons she could think of for the silence were ominous. He could have been killed by robbers or in some accident on the road, or set to sea only to be drowned. Perhaps it was even possible he had been captured by Cromwell's soldiers and was now in some prison, silenced from communication with the outside world, the fact that he lived too dangerous to be made known. And if that was the case, he would spend the rest of his life, however short or long that might be, locked away from all hope and happiness.

. . .

Jane's courses had still not come, and her body felt strange in many little ways that were so subtle she could not quite put them into words. She felt almost certain now that she must be with child, but she did not know of any way to ascertain either that she was or that she wasn't, and if she was, there was nothing to be done about it. How long would it take before her belly began to show? She didn't know.

Nurse was solicitous of her these days, knowing that she was distressed over Ellen Norton's miscarriage and endangered health. That was true, of course, but Jane longed to be able to confide in Nurse about her love for Charles, her fear at the lack of word that he had reached safety, and the possibility that she might be carrying his child. As Nurse brushed her hair one evening, singing a lullaby that brought Jane back to the times of her earliest memories, she leaned back against the pillowy bosom, tears in her eyes. Would Nurse understand if she spilled forth her secrets? She might. But Jane bit back the words. If it came to pass that she knew without question she was with child, then she would seek Nurse's help. But until that day came, she must wrap her love and fear close to her heart, though she felt she would choke.

A fortnight after Francis Yates's hanging, John was going into Wolverhampton to sell a load of coal and pay a levy to the local committee, and Jane went with him, hoping that there might be news of Charles and seeking distraction from her worries. But there seemed to be even more troops in the streets and marketplace than there had been a few weeks earlier, and she felt vulnerable and frightened. She and John had just left the town hall when a man's voice called to him.

"Colonel Lane!"

They turned and Jane was surprised to see that the man approaching them was a Parliamentary officer. It took her a moment to realize that it was her old suitor Geoff Stone. She had not seen him in years.

He was even more handsome than she remembered, with the same smiling green eyes and curling brown hair, but he had acquired an air of maturity and command that he had lacked in the days when he was courting her.

"Jane."

He bowed, and for a moment it seemed as if the war and all that had passed since they had last met had never taken place.

"Geoff." Jane was annoyed with herself that her voice betrayed her vulnerability and the mixed emotions she had upon seeing him.

"Good afternoon, Colonel Stone," John greeted Geoff, and the two men bowed and shook hands.

"I'm pleased to see you safely returned from your journey to Bristol," Stone said, gazing at Jane, and something in his tone made her uneasy. He seemed on the verge of speaking again, but held his silence.

"Yes," Jane said. "I thank you for your pass, that I might see my friend."

"I trust you found her well?"

"I—no."

The tears welled in Jane's eyes as she thought of her last sight of Ellen. She had received a letter from Ellen a few days earlier, assuring Jane that she was feeling much better and asking after the health of Jane's father, and her loving selflessness made Jane feel like a monster for having abandoned her.

"I'm most sorry to hear it," Stone said. "She recovers?"

"Yes," Jane said. "Thank you, she will do well enough in time."

It was odd to be having a normal conversation with a man in the uniform of what would always seem the enemy to her, and yet Geoff's gentle voice and kind eyes brought back very clearly their mutual affection of long ago. She could not quite think of him as the enemy. And yet if he knew how she had passed the second half of September . . .

"What news, Colonel Stone?" John asked, sensing Jane's unease.

"None that will be welcome to you, I fear, Colonel Lane. The Earl of Derby will be executed tomorrow at Bolton, I hear."

There seemed nothing to say to that, and there was an awkward silence.

Stone glanced around. The marketplace was busy with soldiers, country people, and town folk, but no one was nearby. He took a step closer to Jane and John, and when he spoke his voice was so low that Jane could hardly hear him.

"There are stories going about that Charles Stuart escaped with the help of a lady."

The hairs on the back of Jane's neck stood up.

"I've heard no names, nor anything definite," he continued, glancing from John to Jane. "But the rumors are there."

Jane stared at him. Surely he was not merely passing along gossip. Was this a threat? A warning?

Geoff stepped back smartly and bowed.

"A pleasure to see you, Jane. Always happy to be of service to you. Colonel."

He nodded to John and walked away without another word.

"Dear God," Jane whispered. "He knows."

"He cannot know," John said, watching Stone disappear in the crowded street. "But he suspects. You're right about that."

"What shall I do?"

"Nothing yet. But I fear we must give thought to what may come."

The next evening shortly after dark Jane heard a horse thundering up the drive to the house. She did not recognize the cloaked rider who threw his reins to a groom and ran toward the back door. Alarmed, she hurried down the stairs and was astonished to see Geoff Stone striding toward her from the kitchen, his hair on end and his face wet with the rain.

"Jane, thank God you're here," he said, grasping her by the arms and glancing wild-eyed behind him. "You are discovered. The Council of State in London has issued a warrant for your arrest. You must fly, and quickly."

Jane gaped at him, too shocked to reply. He put a wet hand to her cheek, kissed her briefly on the mouth, and was gone.

JANE, JOHN, AND HENRY SAT IN THE BANQUETING HOUSE, THE DARK broken only by the fractured beams of light cast through the perforated tin sides of a lantern.

"Many have gone to the Low Countries," Henry said. "Of course the king's sister's court is there."

"But the king was going to France," Jane said. "If we are to flee, let us go to where he is."

"We don't know that he has reached France," Henry said.

"We would have heard if he had been taken," Jane argued. "And his mother is in Paris, and his brothers."

"My thought," John said, "is that you will both be safest if you do not travel together. If they know that both of you were with the king, they will be looking for both of you. Each of you alone is less recognizable."

Alone. The word thudded into the pit of Jane's stomach. Fleeing for her life was bad enough, but to face it alone—where would she find the courage?

"You're right," Henry agreed, "And the more false scents we can drag across our trail, the better. I can give out that I am going to Scotland, and make it seem as though I go to join the king there."

"But go somewhere else in truth?" Jane asked. "Where?"

"Don't say," John cut in. "You'll be safer, Jane, if you don't know."

"So I'm to fly alone and not even know where to find Henry?" Jane cried, feeling that it was all too much to bear.

"You will not be alone," John said. "I'm going with you."

"But your family . . ." She thought of John's wife, his eight girls and little boy left without his protection.

"It can't be helped," he said. "First, I landed you in the fire and I must keep you from being burned by it. Secondly, if they know you were with the king, they surely know I had a hand in the scheme."

Jane looked from John to Henry. Their grim faces were eerie in the shadows.

"When shall we go?" she asked.

"As soon as we may," John said. "Tomorrow early, before the household is stirring."

"Tomorrow!" Jane gasped. "But everyone is abed already; there will be no time for good-byes."

A cold draft blew through the room, making the flame in the lantern gutter and waver.

"It's better so," John said. "They'll come looking for us. Remember how they treated poor Giffard at Whiteladies when they thought the king was hidden there. They beat him and laid waste to the house. They dishonored the women, searching their persons. It will be safer for those we leave behind if they truly do not know where we are, and cannot be forced to give us up."

Jane shivered and began to weep quietly. When she had first declared she would gladly do whatever she could to help the king, it had not occurred to her that she might have to leave family and home without a farewell. She thought of her father's distress and surprise when he would find her gone, her mother's fear for her safety. She thought of Clement Fisher, and her promise to give him an answer in a day or two. She thought of her cat, Jack. She had missed him during her journey with Charles, and he had slept with her every night since her return, as if doing so could keep her from going again. Who would love him as she did?

"You're right," Henry said. "I will be gone before daybreak."

John stood with him and they embraced.

"Jane," Henry said, dropping to one knee before her. He took her hands in his and looked up into her eyes. "You have more pluck than many a soldier. You have already done a hero's work, and I am sorry that now you are called upon to do more. But John will be with you and you will be well. And even without him, I'd put my money on you against any man of Cromwell's."

Jane had been through so much with Henry in the weeks past that she was filled with desolation at the loss of his company.

"Oh, Henry," she cried, holding him to her. "I will scarce know what to do without you. Thank you. For all you have done for me. Go with God. And if He is willing, we shall see each other across the sea."

And then Henry slipped out into the cold blackness, and was gone.

"We must go afoot," John said. "And it will be safer to go a different way altogether than you have already been. To Yarmouth, I think. We can find a boat there for France."

"Yarmouth." Jane knew it was on the east coast of the country, but no more. "How far is it?"

"Two hundred miles, perhaps a little more. The map will guide us. Leicester to Peterborough to King's Lyn to Norwich, and thence to the sea. But, Jane, it will be rough traveling. You must not look like the lady who was seen riding with the king. We must accoutre ourselves as country folk, and travel on foot."

Jane thought of Rosalind and Celia preparing to set forth for the Forest of Arden, and almost laughed out loud despite herself as a thought struck her.

"What?" John asked.

"'Were it not better,'" she murmured, "'because that I am more than common tall, that I did suit me all points like a man?'"

John looked at her as if she were mad.

"As You Like It," she explained. "But, John, it's a good idea!"

"For you to put on man's attire? Certainly not!"

"They will be looking for me! A woman! With such a face and of such a height, and hair of such a color. But if they see a lad they will not think to question it."

"Absolutely not." John shook his head impatiently.

"It worked with the king. He passed right under the noses of soldiers, blacksmiths, ostlers, kitchen maids, and none took him for other than what he pretended to be. If he can do it, so can I."

John buried his face in his hands and groaned. "It's not a lark we are setting out on, Jane."

"I know it, John. I know it well. My life is at stake and yours, too. I laugh because if I do not I will cry."

"Very well," he sighed.

"I will at least write a letter," Jane said. "I cannot break Father's heart."

"No," John agreed. "Nor would I break Athalia's. Write a letter, then, but we must be gone before sunup."

CHAPTER ELEVEN

In the end it was Jack the cat from whom Jane took leave in person, and she found the parting almost unbearable. She kissed and cuddled him, and he responded as always with his rumbling purr.

"I'll be back as soon as ever I may," she whispered, rubbing his round belly and jowls. "Don't forget me, Jack."

He blinked and purred deep in his chest, and she gave his sleek coat one more stroke before taking up the leather satchel that held all she would take with her and slipping from the room.

John was waiting at the banqueting house, heavily cloaked and holding a stout wooden staff. He took in her appearance with a shake of the head.

"Here," he said. "If you're putting on the person of a lad, you might as well be armed like one."

He held up a dagger.

"If you're threatened face-to-face and can get to the knife, aim for the throat. Straight up, just under the chin."

Jane stared at him and thought of herself plunging cold steel into a man's gullet.

"I'll teach you more later," John said, handing her the staff. "And in the meantime, remember that a stick comes in handy for defense as well as for walking."

Jane hefted the tall oak stick in her hand. It was heavy enough to do real harm if she swung it with all her strength.

"Come," John said. "It will be light within the hour, and we must be past Walsall and as far beyond as possible by then."

They set off down the lane toward the Wolverhampton Road, and a few minutes later Jane turned to look at the house, but it was already invisible in the blackness of the night.

LATE MORNING FOUND JANE AND JOHN APPROACHING THE VILLAGE of Little Aston. They had met a few other travelers, country people driving animals to market, and Jane was thankful it was a cool day, for already she had walked much farther than ever she had in her life, but the thought that every step took them farther from the danger of being arrested helped her press on. They had brought food so they would not have to enter an inn or tavern for their noon meal, and they walked a little distance off the road to eat, sitting beneath a great chestnut tree. There was a crossroads ahead, and John pointed at the track that headed south into the fields.

"That's a Roman road. We'll take it—it will be less traveled than the main road. Odd to think, isn't it, that we still tread the same paths that men walked more than a thousand years ago?"

Jane gazed at the narrow road disappearing into the horizon. Her legs and buttocks already ached with the unaccustomed exercise, and her shoulders with the weight of the bag.

"Somehow," she said, "it gives me strength to think of them. Roman centurions marching across the countryside as we do now."

John smiled. "A good thought."

"Where will we stay the night?" Jane asked, brushing bread crumbs from her lap.

"Round about Tamworth. I don't know whether to chance an inn. We don't look like the sort who should have the money for such lodgings."

It was true, Jane thought, looking at her brother. His clothes were those of a rough country fellow, coarse brown wool breeches and coat over a battered leather jerkin, with his cloak draped over all. He wore heavy yarn stockings and shoes with hobnails in their soles, and his felt hat was battered and shapeless. Jane was dressed much the same. She had found a voluminous shirt that would not show her shape even with nothing over it, but it was covered by a woolen waistcoat and a heavy skirted coat in dark green that muffled any hint of a bosom or waist and fell to below her knees. She wore the rough woolen stockings Nurse had knitted for her and stout shoes. She had not quite been able to bring herself to cut off her hair, so she had stuffed it under a tight-fitting cap and clapped a gray slouch hat over it.

"We might see if we can pay for supper and a place on the floor with cottagers," John said. "Though we're still close enough to home that I would be more comfortable did we not have to speak to anyone if we can avoid it. If we can find a barn or other shelter, it would be the safest thing for tonight. I have oiled canvas to rig a tent if we can find no place indoors. How are your feet? Can you keep walking for some time?"

"Yes," Jane said, thinking of the Roman soldiers.

"Brave girl." He smiled, and standing, reached out a hand to help her to her feet.

THE SKY DARKENED AS THE DAY DREW TOWARD DUSK. EVERY PART OF Jane's body ached, and a chill wind rattled through the trees and bushes along the road. She longed for hot food and a soft bed, and braced herself for the possibility that they might have to sleep on the bare ground if no shelter offered.

"There should be a village not far ahead," John said, looking up from his little book of maps. "We'll stop there."

The village was little more than a cluster of houses and a church, but lamplight and voices spilled from the doorway of a tiny alehouse.

"What do you think?" Jane said, her stomach growling at the smell of food.

"I think we can venture in for a meal," John said. "But the less said the better. Son," he added, grinning.

Six or eight men in the rough clothes of farmers were gathered at a couple of tables in the tavern, and they ceased their talk as John and Jane entered. Jane was keenly conscious of their eyes on her. Could they tell she was a woman? It was dark in the little taproom and her coat stood out from her body, but still she feared they would discover her.

"Good even, friends," John said, and Jane nodded to the strangers. She thanked God for John's presence. He was a big man and moved with the authority and bearing of a soldier, and she was sure most men would think twice before starting trouble with him.

"And you, friends," one of the men answered, and the others murmured their greetings.

"My boy and I have had a long day of walking," John said. "And would welcome a whet and a meal."

Jane was relieved that none of the men seemed to recognize John or question his description of her as a boy.

"Then you've stopped at the right place," said a barrel-chested man with sparse gray hair, moving toward the bar with its mugs and barrels. "There's stew and the finest brown ale you'll find for many a mile."

His grin reassured Jane, and she gave him a smile as she unslung the heavy bag from her shoulders.

The hot stew, as well as the loaf of brown bread and the pint of honey-colored ale, were good, and she gave them her attention and let John do the talking.

"Where have you come from?" asked the landlord. "And what news?"

"From near Wolverhampton," John said. "No news there but the old news—soldiers everywhere, and all in uproar."

"It's the same everywhere, we hear," nodded a little man with a pocked face. "Looking for the king, under every bush and haystack."

With studied innocence, he whistled a few bars of "The World Turned Upside Down." The words most usually heard to the tune in recent years were "When the King Enjoys His Own Again." John carried on with the tune, and the atmosphere in the room relaxed perceptibly.

"Confusion to Oliver," said the publican, raising his mug. "And good health to the king."

"Good health to the king," John agreed, and Jane murmured, "The king," pitching her voice low.

"Where are you and the lad bound?" a little bald-headed man in a tattered brown coat asked.

"Near Desford way," John said. "My sister's man died, and we go to help her settle his business and bring her back home again."

Murmurs of sympathy arose, and the publican refilled their mugs.

"We've need of a place to sleep for the night, if you've a room."

"The room we sit in is all there is," the publican said, "but I've a couple of pallets we can lay before the fire."

"We'll take it and gladly." John nodded.

After another hour of talk, the men drifted home, and the publican closed and barred the door and laid out two straw-stuffed pallets before climbing the stairs to his own bed. Jane rolled herself in her blanket, clothed except for her shoes, and was asleep almost as soon as she was settled.

JANE AND JOHN WERE ON THEIR WAY EARLY. JANE HAD SLEPT SURPRISINGLY well for the roughness of the accommodation, and with each mile they moved eastward and closer to escape, her spirits rose. They walked through Tamworth, a market town huddled around a castle on the riverbank. No one appeared to take undue notice of them, and the road once more passed between open fields. It was colder than it had been the day before, and Jane's shoes were chafing at her heels.

"Let me stop a few minutes so I can tend to my feet," she said.

She sat on a fallen tree and pulled off her shoes and stockings to find that her heels were blistered and angry red. She had brought a little pot of salve, and smeared it onto the blisters.

"A bit of lambs wool should help," John said. "Here, let me fix it for you."

His big hands moved surely and tenderly as he laid soft pads of wool against the chafed spots and tied them in place with strips of linen. Jane watched him, thinking again how grateful she was for his presence. She fitted her silk stockings over the bandaging before putting on her heavy wool stockings and shoes, and John helped her to her feet.

"How's that?"

"Better," she said, standing and trying her weight on alternate feet.

They filled their leather bottle from the river and drank of the cool water before setting forth once again. It was late afternoon when Jane heard the rumble of horses' hooves on the road behind them, and turning, saw a blur of churning red in the distance. A cavalry patrol. She glanced around in a panic. The fields on either side of the road offered no hiding place.

"Nothing for it but to keep on, and bluff it out if they should stop us," John said, his eyes narrowing as he squinted into the sun to watch the soldiers.

They moved to the side of the road, and Jane prayed that the patrol would pass on. Her stomach clutched in fear when the hoofbeats slowed.

"Hold, there!" a voice called, and the lead rider, an officer whose face was almost as red as his coat, rode past them and then wheeled his horse back to face them. Jane glanced around. Another half-dozen mounted soldiers were behind them. They were trapped.

"Where are you bound?" the officer demanded.

"Near Leicester, sir." John's voice was slow and even, as untroubled as a farmer on his way to a holiday fair.

"Your business?"

"Well, sir, I'm taking my boy here to be apprentice to a silversmith."

The officer squinted at Jane and frowned. "He looks old to be starting an apprenticeship. How old are you, boy?"

"Six-sixteen, sir." Jane thought she managed to keep her voice level.

"You're right, sir," John said, shaking his head as though in despair. "He is old, at that. But the silversmith wanted a bond, you know, for the lad's food and lodging and clothes, and all he might need, come to that, and well, I've been sore pressed to scrape together what he asked for. We had a bad harvest last year. The oats weren't so bad, now, but the wheat—"

"Never mind about the wheat, fellow," the officer barked. "Have you seen a lady, her hair brown to reddish, tall and fair, perhaps five and twenty years of age? She might be riding with a man, an inch or two below six feet, with brown hair and blue eyes?"

"Faith, no sir."

I heard myself proclaimed . . .

The line from *King Lear* ran through Jane's mind. It scarcely seemed real. The officer's eyes snapped to Jane's face and she felt her palms start to sweat.

"And you, boy?"

. . . No port is free, no place
Does not attend my taking.

The other riders had circled close in around them now, the horses snorting and pacing restlessly. *They know,* Jane thought. *They know it's me, and I'm going to hang.* She thought of Francis Yates's livid face, the terror in his bulging eyes as he jerked frantically at the end of the rope.

"No, sir." Her voice was scarce above a whisper, and she kept her eyes on the ground.

"Look at me!" The red-faced officer snarled. Jane felt John bracing himself beside her, as though for a fight. But it wouldn't be much of a fight, she thought. He would be lucky to get his pistol from beneath his coat before he was shot.

"Are you simple, boy?" the officer prodded. "I say, are you simple? Look at me, boy!"

He rode around them in a tight circle. Had he seen that she was a girl? Jane willed her heart to be still and raised her eyes to look into his face, streaked with sweat and the dust of the road. He smelled her fear, like a dog, and she must throw him off the scent somehow.

"No, sir. It's only—could I be a soldier, sir?"

She hadn't planned what to say, and her words astonished her. John and the soldiers appeared to be equally amazed. Then the officer burst out laughing.

"You?" He spat on the ground and his men guffawed. "The Protector would be scraping the bottom of the barrel indeed, to take such a milk-faced weed as thee, boy." He turned back to John, sneering. "Quite the fire-eater your boy thinks he is."

John nodded, and Jane knew that the befuddled expression on his face was unfeigned.

The red-faced officer sighed wearily, as though the encounter had taxed his patience to the limit and beyond. He clicked to his horse and began to move off, and just when Jane was about to breathe a sigh of relief, he turned back toward them again.

"I almost forgot. You'll not have seen a tall black-haired fellow, six feet two inches high? He's—he's a gentleman, but he might be disguised as someone of meaner birth?"

"No, sir," John said. "No one like that."

"Nor I, sir," Jane piped up. "What's he done, sir? Is he a highwayman?"

The soldiers exchanged looks and laughed.

"No. Not a highwayman." The officer shook his head and spurred his horse, and the patrol clattered off, clods of mud flying behind them.

Jane forced herself to remain on her feet until the riders were out of sight. Then she sat down heavily on the road, her belly heaving, and vomited onto the damp earth.

THE TERROR OF THE ENCOUNTER WITH THE SOLDIERS HAD LEFT JANE feeling drained. She wondered where Henry was and whether she would ever see him again. The blisters on her feet had broken and every step was painful. She wanted only to stop, to rest, to hide and feel safe, but she knew that the only way to reach safety was to keep moving forward, so she shut her mind to her fear and discomfort and thought of Roman soldiers.

The sun was low on the horizon when they stopped to rest again. John drank deep from the leather bottle and passed it to Jane while he pulled the atlas from his bags and studied it.

"It's still some miles to the next village. How are your feet?"

"I can keep on," Jane said.

"The night should be clear," John said, looking at the cloudless horizon. "My thought is that perhaps it might be better to keep an eye out for some shelter in the open country than go among people. That was a good performance of yours, but now we know they're looking for you and Henry . . ."

"Yes," Jane agreed.

Her stomach contracted again with the panic she had felt at the red-faced officer eyeing her so closely.

They walked on for a mile or two, and John pointed out a small structure a little way off the road. Exploring, they discovered that it was a shepherd's hut, empty but for the heavy smell of wool and wood smoke. A blackened fire pit lay beneath a hole in the roof.

"Good," John said. "At least we can have the warmth and light of a fire."

Jane let her pack fall heavily in a corner of the hut.

"Don't drop just yet," John said as she pulled off her coat.

He was rummaging in his bag, and drew forth one of his pistols along with a small leather case and powder horn.

"I want to teach you to shoot," he said, to Jane's inquiring glance, and she laughed without humor.

"Perhaps I really can go for a soldier boy, then."

Jane had not examined John's pair of pistols closely before. He had bought them at the growing Gun Quarter in the little village of Birmingham, not far from Bentley, and she had heard him speak of their superior manufacture and reliability. They were beautiful, she thought, admiring the silver scrollwork. And big. The barrels were as long as her forearm.

John showed Jane how to load the pistol—put the hammer at half cock, feed the powder and ball and wadding into the barrel, tamp it down with the ramrod—"Always ram it well home, or the barrel could explode," he warned—and prime the pan with a pinch of powder.

"Now it's primed and ready. You can carry it like that, so you're prepared in case of trouble. When you're ready to fire, you bring it to full cock, like this. You'll want to practice that a lot. You don't want to fumble when you need to shoot."

He handed her the weapon and she was surprised at its weight.

"You can hold it with both hands," he said, demonstrating. "Or brace the barrel against your left forearm. Try it both ways."

There was a quince tree nearby, and he set one of the golden-green fruits, heavy with ripeness, on a boulder.

"Aim for that," he said. "Both arms out straight this time. Squeeze the trigger slowly. And keep your feet well apart and braced; that pistol has quite a kick."

Jane did as he said but was still astonished at the power of the weapon's recoil and the deafening roar. But the quince was gone, blown into pulpy pieces.

John whistled and grinned at her. "Do that again and you can take Cromwell's shilling and join the army."

Jane warmed at her brother's praise. He had made quite a name for himself during the wars, leading such successful raids on supply trains that the Parliamentary army had ordered that travel be suspended on the road from London to Coventry.

Jane sent four more quinces to meet their Maker before she and John repaired to the shepherd's hut, where John laid small branches and kindling for a fire and lit it with his flint and steel. They ate cold meat and bread, but heated water in a small tin pan and mixed it with brandy, and Jane felt more comfortable as the drink blurred the edges of her mind. She thought about the soldiers they had encountered that afternoon, and the pistol and the dagger she wore sheathed at her waist.

"Have you killed men?" she asked.

John picked up a branch and poked the fire, and they watched the sparks fly upward to the black hole in the roof before he spoke.

"Aye. It would be hard to see as much fighting as I did and not have it so."

"Was it hard? Were you afraid?"

"The first time I had no time to be afraid or to think whether it was hard. We had taken Rushall Hall, but the rebels wanted it back, and badly. They scaled the wall and charged the house after dark when we were not expecting them. I was in bed, but fortunately I was reading and had the lantern still lit. I heard footsteps outside the door and had my pistol in hand when he came through. He had the light in his eyes and the split second it took for him to spot me was enough time for me to shoot him before he could shoot me."

Jane tried to imagine herself in John's place, firing on a stranger to save her own life. Her stomach tightened with fear and she hoped she would never be in those circumstances.

"I caught him full in the breast," John said, "And he looked at me with such surprise. Almost with outrage, as though I had taken some unfair advantage. Then he fell. I could hear shouting and pistol shots and I knew I should reload, but my hands were shaking so badly that I could not. So I stood there and looked upon him. He was very young, and resembled our Richard a bit. He didn't move and I thought at first that perhaps he was only shamming. But then blood ran from his mouth, down his cheek and onto the floor, and I knew he was dead."

He poured more brandy into their tin cups and topped it up with hot water. Jane wrapped her fingers around the cup, feeling its warmth. Her stomach was fluttering, and she rubbed the cup over her belly.

"Feeling ill?"

"Just a little queasy," Jane said. "It'll pass." *Please let it pass,* she thought. Whatever would she do if she was with child? She pushed the worry to the back of her mind. She would face that trouble when she had to. She drank, feeling the brandy lighting its way down her throat.

"The first time, you said. There were more, then."

"The next was the hardest," John said. "For I knew him."

Jane thought of Geoff Stone, and pictured him and John facing each other over loaded pistols.

"We had word of a convoy of wagons heading for Coventry and were lying in wait just off the road. It was a beautiful summer afternoon, the kind of day that would have been well spent fishing. We heard the rumble of the wagons and waited until they came around a bend in the road. I could hear them laughing. One of our lads got off a shot just as they came into sight. Then all was merry hell. There was an armed man next to the driver of each wagon, and they were shooting at us, and our men were shooting at them from both sides of the road. I saw one of our lads go down, a blossom of blood on his belly, and aimed at the man who had shot him. He turned and took aim at me just as I was squeezing the trigger, and I saw that it was Christopher Hobbs, from Walsall. He had been in my mind not a quarter of an hour past, for I had spent just such an afternoon fishing with him. He knew me, too. The recognition flashed in his eyes. But he fired. He missed. I fired. It took his jaw away. He dropped the gun and fell to the road and a wagon ran over him as he lay there, and that finished him if he wasn't dead already."

John exhaled hard and closed his eyes, and Jane saw his mouth tighten with the effort not to weep.

"I pray the king is safely in France," he said. "And if he comes back to England with an army at his back, I'll go to his side once more. But I thank God now that He sent me eight girls, and only the one boy, so I don't have to fear I'll see them fight and die."

He looked at Jane, her hair, loosened from its tie, falling free over her shoulders, but her shape hidden by her heavy wool waistcoat, and he bowed his head.

"Oh, Jane, I did wrong to bring you into this. You should be comfortable at home."

"No," Jane said. "You did right. For what is my comfort, or my life, come to that, against the safety of the king and kingdom?"

THE NEXT AFTERNOON A DRIZZLING RAIN BEGAN. JANE WAS CHILLED to her bones and her feet were in agony. They had passed no houses since midday and she was beginning to fear they might have to sleep out of doors, when John gestured to a pinpoint of light in the deepening dusk ahead. As they came closer they could see that the light shone from a tiny alehouse with the sign of a red lion swinging above the door, and that there were a few houses scattered nearby.

"We'd best stop here if we can," John said. "It'll be full night soon."

They entered the little tavern to find a dozen men gathered at a few tables. Having passed herself off as a boy for three days, Jane was much more at ease than she had been when they entered the alehouse on their first night traveling. Still, she left most of the talking to John. Over supper he exchanged pleasantries with the locals and then asked for any news. They told of a cavalry patrol that had come through the previous afternoon, surely the same that John and Jane had seen. They had stopped and questioned the village folk, looking for a man and a woman traveling together on horseback, and for the king, a tall dark-haired man in disguise.

"Charles Stuart they called him," a lean-faced farmer scoffed.

He eyed Jane and John, and apparently thought better of speaking further.

"What place might this be?" John asked, when they had finished their supper.

"Bosworth," the landlord said. "Where Richard the Third lost his crown, and Henry Tudor found it."

Jane thought back to Francis Wyndham's tale of his father, exhorting his sons to honor the crown though it hung on a bush. The bush might be right outside the door, and it was Charles's several-times-great-grandfather who had put on that crown and passed it down.

They were in luck that night, as the inn boasted a room to let. It had but one bed, but it was warm and dry, and to Jane it was a welcome refuge. She bundled herself in her cloak and blanket by John's side and was soon asleep.

The gray light of dawn woke Jane, and she groaned, feeling all too plainly now the effects of three days of walking. Her whole body felt odd, too, she thought. Her breasts were tender, and the rough fabric of her shirt chafed against her nipples. She was exhausted, and bathed her face in cold water to rouse herself.

"We'll reach Leicester today," John said as the road took them along between fields dotted with sheep. "But there's like to be many troops there, perhaps even handbills with your description, so it's probably safest for us to pass through and get as far past it as we can tonight."

Jane didn't argue with that logic, and John was right—the town was full of soldiers. The proclamation offering a reward of a thousand pounds for the king's capture was posted in the market, and Jane blanched at the heading of another broadsheet fluttering from a post, "The True Speech Delivered on the Scaffold by James, Earl of Derby." She went closer, and was even more startled by the second heading in smaller letters—"Likewise, the Manner How the King of Scots took Shipping at Gravesend on the Fourth of this Instant October with Captain Hind, Disguised in Seaman's Apparel and Safely Arrived at the Hague." She beckoned wordlessly to John, and he came and read over her shoulder.

"It couldn't be," she said. "Could it?"

He shook his head, frowning as he read over the notice. “Hard to see how. Gravesend is at the mouth of the Thames near London. A very long way from Trent.”

“Perhaps it’s just another rumor.”

“Like enough.” He glanced around and kept his voice low. “Too many soldiers about for my comfort. Let’s buy what provisions we need and be on our way. If it’s true, no doubt we’ll hear more about it soon.”

They stayed in the marketplace just long enough to buy some pies to eat and bread, sausages, cheese, fruit, and nuts to carry with them, and Jane was relieved when they passed through the city’s eastern gates and were once more in open countryside.

The road between Leicester and Peterborough was much more heavily used than their way had been so far, and a small roadside alehouse gave them the opportunity to exchange news with other travelers.

“Aye, I heard of that same broadsheet,” said an old farmer in a dirty smock. “But I don’t believe it myself. I fear the king was killed at Worcester fight.”

Jane looked around the little taproom, and reflected that as John had not shaved since they left and neither he nor Jane had bathed or changed their clothes, they were beginning to look authentically the country folk they pretended to be.

“I heard in Peterborough,” asserted an itinerant mender of pots, “that the king is hiding under a red periwig, and acting as serving man to a soldier in Cromwell’s army.”

“Don’t believe that flimflam,” scoffed a stout woman with a goose under her arm. “I spoke to a man yesterday swore he had seen the king dressed as a woman in London not a week ago.”

“If he’s taller than two yards and as swarthy as they say”—John smiled—“he must make a very ugly wench.”

“It’s the truth you speak,” the woman cackled. “But perhaps in London the girls are so ugly that the people there take no notice!”

John and Jane walked on, through barren fields and bare-branched trees and scattered villages, the north wind biting through the layers of their clothes as they grew nearer the sea. The days were getting colder and wetter. Frequently now the road was muddy or even flooded when it was near a stream, and then they had to make their way as best they could, sometimes leaving the road altogether to find dry ground. On their eighth day walking John fell ill of an ague, miserable with running eyes and nose, aches, and a cough deep in his chest. In the late afternoon they came upon a great house, and going to the kitchen door, asked to sleep in the stables. The round-faced cook clucked in sympathy at John's red nose and wan complexion.

"Sit you down and I'll feed you up well, poor dear," she exclaimed, and in the heat of the great fireplace John's shivering ceased.

The stables were warm with the heat of a dozen horses, and nests of straw provided a more comfortable bed than they had had in days. In the morning John was no better but insisted he could press on.

"It's Sunday," Jane pointed out, looking at him in dismay as he forced himself to a sitting position. "A day of rest, and heaven knows we deserve one. Besides, we'd likely draw attention to ourselves, traveling on the Lord's Day."

"You're right there," John agreed, blowing his nose. "Perhaps we should plan to lie low on Sundays."

They slept for most of the day, and at mealtimes Jane slipped back to the kitchen, where for a few pence the cook was happy to feed her and send hot food back to John. After two nights of rest John was well enough to travel, and they set forth again.

In Peterborough they heard more rumors of the king's whereabouts—he had gone to the Isle of Man, he was in disguise and in the company of a highwayman near Coventry—and saw another broadsheet, "The Declaration of Major General Massey Upon His Deathbed at Leicester and the Manner How Charles Stuart Forced His Passage and so Escaped Toward Scotland."

"At least we have not heard of his capture," Jane said as they made ready for bed on a cold night in the village of Eye, just north of Peterborough. "That argues that perhaps he is safely abroad. And yet I wonder why there is no word of his being in France if he has reached there?"

"No telling," John said, frowning as he studied his map book. He had been silent and glum that evening.

"Are you feeling ill again?" Jane asked, searching his face.

He shook his head wearily. "Just thinking of Athalia and the girls." His voice was thick with emotion, and Jane put a hand on his shoulder and kissed the top of his head.

After they had blown out the candle, she lay awake for a time, thinking of her parents and family, of Nurse and the rest of the household, of Jack's odd creaking call when he greeted her. They were all so far away, and no telling when she would see them again. She wondered where Henry was, and said a prayer for his safety and comfort.

The confusion of rumor about Charles worried her, too. Surely he should have reached France long ago? Why had the news not come to England? Perhaps he had wished to keep his presence secret for some time. But what if he had been apprehended? Or been forced to change his plans? If he really had gone to Scotland or London, then what would become of her and John when they reached France—if they reached it? They had not yet gone half the way to Yarmouth, and the thought of walking another hundred weary miles with winter coming on brought a chill to her heart.

Another fear was becoming hard to put from her mind. She had still not had her monthly courses, and in so many ways, her body felt different. She felt thicker at the middle and heavy somehow, her lower body ached, and she was exhausted. But of course, she tried to reassure herself, the aches and tiredness could be put down to the endless miles, sometimes scant food, uncomfortable sleeping conditions, and constant worry. John would likely know how a woman felt in the first weeks of being with child, but she could certainly not ask him. She dreaded the thought that if she was carrying Charles's baby, they would not reach France before her condition became obvious.

The road led north now, toward King's Lyn, near the Wash of the

North Sea. Every day the sun rose a few minutes later and set a few minutes earlier. Between the condition of the road and who they might meet, it was not only dangerous but virtually impossible to travel in the dark, so each day they covered a little less ground.

On the afternoon of the third day on the road from Peterborough, a tribe of Gypsies passed them by on the road, their carts and caravans accompanied by a scrawny cow and a few sheep. They nodded their greetings to the wanderers, and a little black-eyed girl stared at Jane from the safety of her mother's arms. Jane thought of the Gypsy lad in the orchard at Bentley. She wondered whether the chance encounter had led her to behave in such a reckless manner with Charles, giving herself to him though she had known she might never see him again.

It had drizzled throughout the day, and as dusk drew on, the heavens opened and cold rain drove down, turning the road into a soup of mud. They struggled on, Jane becoming fearful about whether they would find shelter. They stopped when they came to a place where the narrow road disappeared beneath a flowing stream that crossed it.

"Now what?" Jane asked, looking in dismay at the swirling eddies.

John squatted by the stream's edge and thrust his staff into the clouded water. When he pulled it out it was wet fully two feet up from the bottom. He glanced to either side and shook his head.

"Here, across the road, is likely to be where the water is shallowest," he said. "We could follow the stream and look for a better place to ford, but it will be dark soon."

On the other side of the stream the road wound on into the deepening gloom, the landscape barren of trees or anything that promised shelter.

"Then let's chance it," Jane said. "Nothing to be gained by waiting."

"Take your shoes and stockings off," John said. "No use getting wetter than we need to."

They rolled up the bottoms of their breeches, wrapped their shoes and stockings into their blankets, and slung the bundles high across their shoulders. John went first, using his staff to steady himself, and reached a hand back to help Jane. She grasped his hand and stepped into the stream, feeling the shock of the cold as the water swirled around her knees. They made their way slowly, the mud soft and slippery beneath their feet and the rain slanting into their faces.

Suddenly Jane found her feet sliding out from under her. She cried out as she floundered, trying to break her fall with her staff, but she lost her balance and sat, bringing John down with her. He struggled to his feet and helped her up, and they continued step by slow step until they reached the relative solidity of the far side of the stream.

Jane looked down at herself and at John with consternation. They were both soaked up to their necks, their clothes sodden and dripping. Worse, their satchels and blankets were soaked.

"Let's see the damage and what can be salvaged," John said.

He opened his bag and pulled out its contents piece by piece. The ship's biscuit was a soggy mass of crumbs. The raisins and nuts and cheese were wet, but would be edible. The powder for the pistol was useless. John shook his head over the little atlas, its pages stuck together in one wet mass.

"If I try to pull the pages apart now, they'll only tear. What it really wants is careful blotting."

He groaned in despair over the tinderbox. The dry fungus inside that was used as a punk to catch the sparks of the flint and steel was spongy with water, and the little bag of straw and sticks he carried as emergency tinder was also soaked.

Jane looked around, fighting down feelings of hopelessness. Night was falling rapidly, they were wet through, they had little food, and now there was no way to build a fire to warm and dry themselves. She felt tears coming on, and struggled to hold them back.

"Come," John said, helping her to her feet and putting an arm around her shoulders. "Nothing to be done but go on and see what we find. It's like to keep raining all night; we must get to some shelter."

Mechanically, shutting down the part of her mind that wanted to simply give up and lie on the muddy road, Jane put her dripping stockings and shoes back on and picked up her sodden satchel, and they went forward.

After an hour of walking that felt like an eternity, the scent of wet wool in her nostrils, the rain driving down, Jane saw a flickering light ahead, and smoke rising.

"Look!" she pointed.

They moved on rapidly and soon the light resolved itself into a campfire beneath a spread of canvas tethered between two wagons, with people squatted around its warmth. It was the Gypsies they had passed earlier. The smell of cooking wafted toward them and Jane's stomach turned over with hunger.

"What do you think?" John asked. "Shall we ask if we can buy supper and a place at the fire?"

"Yes," Jane said without hesitation.

She could not stand the thought of spending the next day or two in wet clothes and shoes, and with the exhaustion they both already suffered, she knew they were ripe for falling ill.

John flung his cape back over his shoulders so that the butt of his pistol peeked out from the front of his coat, and they made their way to the Gypsies' camp. The group eyed them as they came into the circle of firelight.

"Greetings!" John called out.

There were four or five women, ranging from a young mother with a baby at her breast to a withered crone, a dozen children tumbling and playing, and five or six men seated near the fire. Jane saw with a start that one of these was the lad who she had seen in the orchard at Bentley on her birthday.

"We've had a misfortune, as you can see," John said, gesturing at their clothes and satchels. "Wet clean through, with our food and tinder ruined." He held up a small coin. "We'd be grateful for supper and the chance to warm ourselves and dry our clothes."

The men squatting by the fire glanced at one another, and after a muttered conference, the eldest of them nodded and held out his hand.

"Welcome, then."

John gave him the coin, and the Gypsies rearranged themselves to make room for the strangers, offering up stools so they would not have to sit on the ground. Jane draped her cloak over a wagon wheel, removed her shoes, and peeled off her wet stockings. She hesitated before pulling off her coat and hat, but it couldn't be helped, for they would never dry when they were on her. She went back to the fireside in her breeches and shirt, and laid her wet things close to the fire before seating herself next to John. It must be obvious that she was a woman, and she felt the men's eyes on her, but no one made any comment.

One of the women brought them tin plates of stew with chunks of bread, and Jane ate ravenously.

"Where are you bound?" one of the older men asked, his accent sounding musical to Jane's ears.

"King's Lyn," John said. "Not too far. And you?"

"Where the road takes us." The Gypsy grinned, the orange light of the fire and shadow playing across his face. "Perhaps further north."

Jane noticed that the Gypsy lad was looking at her curiously from across the fire. She smiled in a way that she hoped was friendly without being too inviting.

The rain had fallen off now, the drops a mere patter on the canvas overhead. A bottle of something was produced, and Jane accepted a cup of amber liquid that seemed to be some kind of brandy.

One of the men fetched a little guitar from one of the caravans and began to play, singing as he strummed. It was a mournful tune, and though Jane couldn't understand the words, it seemed to be a song of loss, perhaps of love, perhaps of death. She thought about Charles and wondered where he might be, praying, as she did so often, that he might be safe.

The women took the children off to bed in the wagons, and the fire burned lower. The rain had stopped, and stars were winking in the blue-black spaces between the clouds. The young Gypsy disappeared, returning a few minutes later with blankets, which he laid out beside the fire. He examined the blankets that John had hung up and turned them, holding them up to show that they were already drier than they had been.

John was speaking to the man on his other side, and the young Gypsy came and sat beside Jane.

"I remember you, lady," he said, his voice low and his eyes glowing.

Jane blushed but met his eyes.

"I remember you, too."

"You are a long way from home. And you would have the world think you are a boy. Are you in danger?"

Jane nodded. "Yes. We had to leave home, my brother and I."

"Ah, your brother." The answer seemed to please him and he nodded, staring into the fire. "Then he will care for you, keep you safe."

"Yes," Jane said. For she knew that whatever came, John would protect her, though it might put his own safety at risk.

"Thank you for the food and the fire," she whispered. "It would have been a miserable night without your kindness."

The young man shrugged. "Perhaps you would have done the same for me."

"Yes," Jane said. "I would. And if I am ever able to go home again, you are welcome at Bentley. In fact, even if I am not there, you go to the door and say that Jane and Colonel John bid them give you what you need, and that you may stay on the land as long as you like."

"I thank you, lady." He bowed his head, then took her hand and kissed it. "I wish you sweet rest and safe travels, if our paths do not cross again."

CHAPTER TWELVE

A WEEK AFTER JOHN AND JANE HAD LEFT PETERBOROUGH, THE heavy gray-stone gate leading into the walled town of King's Lyn rose ahead. The town itself lay on the east bank of the River Great Ouse, which flowed northward another mile or so toward the North Sea, but Jane could smell the salt of the water and the brackish odor of the fens.

"I'm thinking we might risk an inn," John said. "There's not much between here and Norwich. It's likely our last chance for a hot meal unless I shoot something to cook. And tomorrow's Sunday. We could make it a real day of rest."

"Yes," Jane said. Her body ached everywhere, her feet were burning in her stockings, now stiff with dirt, and she felt as if she would never be comfortable again. "Do you think we look the sort of people who can afford to pay for a hot bath?"

John smiled. "Perhaps we'll chance it."

They found an inn off the market square, and judged that the extravagance of a hot bath would make them conspicuous enough without the additional luxury of separate rooms, so John sat in the taproom while Jane waited in their little chamber for the tub and buckets of hot water to be brought up.

Alone and with the door barred, she stripped off her clothes. She had not been naked since they left Bentley, and she was dismayed at the grayish cast of her skin and how dirty the water became when she lowered herself into it. She stirred the tub with her hand and the hot water lapping against her skin felt as though it was washing away the hardships of the past weeks. On Monday they would be on their way once more, with the loneliest part of the journey ahead of them. But no need to let that spoil tonight.

She scrubbed herself with the rough cloth and soap, luxuriating as the itch of sweat and dirt left her skin. She let her hands linger on her breasts and belly. She was not sure she could see any difference, but she was almost certain now that she was with child. Charles's child. What would he think? What would he say? Would he be glad of the news as a distraction from his cares, and welcome her? And what if he did not? She pushed the thought away, bringing to mind instead the picture of his face so close to hers during those magic nights when they had journeyed together, his eyes shining at her in the dark, his hands warm and urgent on her skin.

When she had bathed, she put on the cleaner of her two shirts and washed the other in the tub. She had washed them as well as she could in turn every week or so when there was water to be had, hanging the washed shirt to dry overnight, and carrying it tied about her if it was not fully dry by the time they left in the morning. She had two pairs of heavy stockings but had not washed them, as she needed the extra layer of protection between her feet and the unyielding leather of her shoes. They were nearly stiff with dirt, and she took the opportunity to wash them now, grimacing at how rapidly the water turned nearly black.

Jane had just hung up her shirt and stockings to dry when John came upstairs from the taproom, his face grim.

"What is it?" Jane asked. "Soldiers?"

Perhaps they had been mistaken to think that she would be less likely to be hunted on this remote north coast of the country.

"No." John sat heavily on the bed. "I was talking to some sailors just come into port. They spoke another ship yesterday that had heard from a fishing vessel come from the south that the king was drowned on his way to France."

Jane stared at him and then staggered as if the breath had been knocked out of her, and John caught her and steadied her.

"Aye, it's terrible news," he said.

She sank onto the bed.

"But how can they be sure? We've heard so many rumors."

"That's true," John said. "But they say the news came from a Channel boat, who had heard it from other vessels down that way. The officers believed it, though there's been no official word."

The initial shock was wearing off and Jane began to sob. Charles. She could bring him to mind so clearly, feel his weight on top of her, smell the scent of him, hear his voice. It wasn't possible that he could be gone, that after all they had gone through to save him, he could be lost from mere drowning.

Jane felt she couldn't get her breath. She was shaking and her sobs had turned to racking gasps for air as she curled into herself on the bed.

"Jane!" John cried in alarm, brushing her hair off her face. "Breathe deep and slow if you can."

She tried but felt herself slipping into a void of terror and despair. John held her to him and stroked her head.

"I know what grief you must feel, having traveled with him as you did. My God, what grief to the whole country."

"No," Jane sobbed, finally able to speak. "It's more than that. Oh, John, we were lovers. I am with child by the king."

John pushed her from him with such force that she almost fell off the bed. He stared at her, disbelief warring with outrage and anger as he saw the truth of it in her face. He stood and paced, running his hands through his hair in agitation, then turned on her.

"How could you have behaved so?"

"I love him!" she cried, her grief outshone for the moment by building rage.

"Love!" he snorted. "Love? You were a maid and you gave yourself to a man who could never wed you even if he would. He was the king, whether covered in mud or no. Did you not think of the shame you would bring to the family?"

"The family? Is that all that concerns you, brother? Shame to the family? At your behest I put myself in mortal peril to help him. And now England is not safe for me, and what lies ahead of me, I know not. My life is a shambles, and you have no sympathy for me, but worry about your honor."

She spat the word at him.

"No sympathy for you?"

John strode toward her, eyes blazing. She had never seen him so angry.

"I left my wife and family, not knowing when I may see them again, because I could not abandon you to make your way alone to safety. Have you thought of that? And what are we to do now?"

"Go on to France, what else?"

"You say it as though it were no small matter! God knows how long it might have taken us to reach France, did all things smile on us. But your—condition—changes all. What if you are taken badly? What if we do not reach France before you are brought to bed? Or if we do? How shall we look, creeping to the queen and the French court, you big with the king's bastard?"

Jane slapped John across the face.

"Then leave me!" she shrieked. "Leave me to my grief and myself! I had rather make my way alone than with you if you think so little of me!"

She shoved him so that he stumbled back against a chair, and he made as if to strike her, but mastered himself, and leaned on the chair, breathing hard, his hands clutching it as if it were the only solid thing in a heaving ocean. Jane slumped onto the bed, hugging her knees to her chest as she sobbed.

At length John sat, breathed more calmly, and spoke.

"There is nothing for it but to go on and hope that all will be well."

All well? Jane thought. Nothing would ever be well again, for Charles was dead, England was not safe for her, and she must go on to a strange land where she knew no one.

"I'm sorry," John said after some time. "For all of it. For putting you in the king's company and in danger, for what has come to pass, and for my harsh words."

Jane didn't answer, and he went and sat beside her.

"You must eat. I'll go down and have food brought up."

Jane bathed her face in cool water while John went downstairs. They ate together by the fire, and the hot food soothed her, but her tears kept surging to the surface.

"Perhaps he is not dead," John said, and she nodded numbly, holding to that shred of hope.

Jane's dreams that night were terrifying, full of cold ocean water crashing onto her in waves. She woke herself with crying out, and John took her in his arms and held her as she wept.

In the morning Jane felt as though she had been beaten with sticks, so weary was her body and so defeated her spirit. She was desperately glad they had decided not to leave until the next day, and passed the day drifting in and out of sleep, her dreams torn with grief and fear.

"Can you travel tomorrow, do you think?" John asked over their supper.

"I'll have to. The sooner we set off, the sooner we shall be in France."

THE ROAD TOWARD NORWICH AND YARMOUTH TOOK JANE AND JOHN east through swampy fens, the salt smell of the sea heavy in their nostrils. Buzzards and crows called shrill in the biting air. After the first hour of walking they passed no one. The land lay before them, vast and empty.

At late morning they passed a windmill, its great arms creaking as they turned.

"Then someone else must be alive out here," Jane said.

In the afternoon they came to a crossroads. A village lay a little off the main road to the north, and to the south the little road ran straight through the rustling brown grasses and met the horizon.

"Another Roman road," John said, and Jane almost thought she could hear the tramp of feet on the damp earth as ghostly legions moved in the mists.

"It's All Hallows' Eve," she remembered, and wondered if it was true, as Nurse had told her when she was a child, that on this day the barrier between this world and the next was thin, and spirits walked.

The road turned to the southeast and climbed into rolling hills. Walking on the incline made Jane's thighs and buttocks ache. Dark clouds were gathering ahead, and she glanced at the sun dropping lower in the sky behind them.

"We'll not walk too much further tonight," John said. "When we find anyplace likely, we'll stop. But it may be we sleep rough."

Jane nodded. This would be the hardest part of the way, the long march toward the sea through barren silent lands.

The road sloped down out of the hills, and onto a broad flat plain with sheep downs stretching away on either side, dotted with high shrubs and outcroppings of rock. Another hill rose ahead, and Jane's spirits began to flag. She stopped, and John waited while she pulled the leather bottle from her bag and drank, and then handed it to him. They walked on. A brown hare bounded across the road in front of them, and then another. Jane looked out into the scrub and saw movement here and there.

"Well, look at that," John exclaimed. "When we reach those rocks at the bend of the road ahead, you sit and rest for a bit and I'll see if I can shoot one of the little creatures, and perhaps we might have a hot dinner."

When they reached the stones, Jane sank onto a boulder and rested her back against a high wall of rock behind her. Long-eared hares scampered everywhere. John laid down his pack and staff and checked his pistol. He had bought powder and shot in King's Lyn, and the pistol was primed and ready. He walked a few yards off the road and squatted near some shrubbery. He was absolutely motionless, and Jane watched in fascination as a hare loped toward him and then stopped, its nose and whiskers twitching as it sniffed the air. John's pistol was pointed at the furry head, and she watched as he squeezed the trigger slowly. There was a roar and the hare flew backward in a little shower of blood. John lifted it by the feet and held it up for Jane to see.

"Well done!" she cried.

The thought of meat for dinner and the warmth of a fire energized her, and she hopped off the rock as John made his way toward her. Suddenly someone was beside her. The man had stepped from where he had been hidden behind the tall outcropping of rock, and his pistol was pointed at Jane's head. He was a big man, perhaps thirty years old, wearing a red soldier's coat, but it was ragged and filthy, and his face was covered with a golden haze of stubble. A deserter, he must be.

Jane stared at the man, too surprised to react, and felt rather than saw John stop where he stood, some twenty paces away.

"I thank you," the man said to John. "You've saved me the trouble both of taking your pistol from you and shooting dinner. Now throw down the weapon and the cony just there, along with your purse."

John hesitated and the man grasped Jane roughly by the arm.

"Come, friend. Surely your boy here means more to you than whatever coin you're carrying."

John silently tossed the hare and his pistol onto the ground, and reached to open his coat.

"Slowly," the big man barked. "So I can see you don't have a second pistol at your belt."

Jane tried not to start. John didn't have a second pistol at his belt, she knew, because it hung at her own waist, concealed by her coat, which fell unbuttoned around her. Could she get to it?

John slowly pushed his coat aside, showing that he had thrown away his only weapon. He pulled the purse of coins from his coat pocket and held it out for the man to see. There were still some gold coins sewn into the lining of his coat, and Jane prayed that the man would be content with the purse and not think to look elsewhere. John dropped the purse onto the ground, and the man glanced at Jane.

"Now you, boy. Does your daddy let you carry any coin or weapon? Open your coat so I can see."

He straightened his right arm to point the pistol toward John as he turned Jane to face him. She saw a flash of surprise in his eyes, followed by a leering grin.

"Well, I'll be poxed. You're no boy."

He licked his lips and reached his free hand toward Jane's breast. Then everything seemed to happen at once. John shouted, the man turned his head sharply away from Jane, and in that instant she yanked the pistol from her belt, bringing it to full cock, thrust it up into the hollow below his chin, and fired.

The man's body flew backward as Jane staggered back from the recoil of the weapon. John ran toward her, but the deserter lay in a pool of brains and blood. John clutched Jane to him, nearly sobbing.

"Oh, Jane, Christ, oh, Christ."

She held on to him, shaking, and he helped her to the rock, where they sat clasped together, John rocking Jane in his arms, murmuring soothing words into her hair. After a time she lifted her head to look at the man she had killed, the place where his face had been staring up into the darkening sky.

"What will we do with him?" she whispered.

John glanced around.

"I'll drag him into the bracken there and cover him over. The birds and the beasts will take care of the rest."

He bent and searched through the dead man's pockets, coming up with a purse and a bag of shot and powder, which he laid on the rock next to Jane. He threw off his coat, grasped the corpse's booted ankles, and hauled it bumping over the rough ground into the gorse. Jane's stomach was heaving, but she forced herself to stand and to kick loose dirt onto the trail of blood to cover it.

When John came back, dusk was falling.

"Come," he said, putting on his coat. "It will be dark soon."

Jane needed no urging. She wanted to put as much distance as possible between herself and the dead man.

"There's something ahead." John pointed when they had gone about a mile.

As they drew near Jane saw that it was an ancient crofter's hut, low walls built of stacked slabs of peat topped with a thatched roof. The little door hung loose on its leather hinges, but the hut was dry inside and would provide shelter from the elements and whatever night-walking things might be about.

"You rest," John said, and Jane did so gratefully, comforted by the sound of him moving around outside as he built a fire. She drowsed and woke to the smell of roasted meat. John came in with the cooked hare. She was hungry but her gorge rose at the sight of the little legs stretched out in their darkened skin.

"I can't," she said, lying down again and turning her face away. "I'm sorry."

"You must eat something," John insisted gently. "At least some bread." The bread they had bought that morning in King's Lyn was still fresh and good, and Jane found that the bland softness was just what she wanted.

The night was full of noises—the harsh call of a barn owl, the shriek of some small animal taken by a predator, the wind rattling through the bushes—and as the fire before the hut died out, Jane heard little scrabbling feet in the dark. The wind sighed outside and she shivered in her blanket, seeing the stubbled face of the deserter and then his inert form lying so still on the dirt, and she wondered if his spirit had followed them and hovered nearby.

In the morning they set out early. The road ran through open heath, but they passed two or three windmills, and here and there little tracks crossed the main road, leading to tiny clusters of cottages in the distance. In the late afternoon they came to a small hamlet, and learning that there were no houses on the road for several miles ahead, decided to stop for the night, bedding down before the hearth in the village's sole tavern.

The next night the road offered no shelter but a blacksmith's shop. A village lay a mile or so to the north, the smith told them, but dark was coming on fast and it would be easy to lose their way, so they wrapped themselves in their blankets and cloaks and slept warmed by the residual heat of the forge.

The next day a cavalry patrol passed them on the road, riding fast and apparently not finding them worthy of suspicion. Still, worried that the soldiers might be searching for a woman of Jane's description, they slept in an old barn some way off from a great house, with only hard ship's biscuit and cheese and tough strips of dried venison to eat. Jane was exhausted and wanted with her soul to spend a day lying down instead of walking, but she was afraid and insisted they move on. Besides, the day was bitterly cold, and walking kept her warm.

The road now took them through vast and lonely country. The dull brown of the heath stretched endlessly toward the horizon. Here and there a rock outcropping broke the flatness, cutting upward into the gray sky. The land seemed strangely hushed, listening, waiting. Their footsteps on the road sounded harsh, intrusive. Neither Jane nor John had spoken in some time and Jane felt almost that she would not be able to speak if she tried, as if her voice had somehow been taken from her in the oppressive silence that surrounded them. She looked off to the right, to the left. Nothing but empty land, sparsely covered in heather. They might have been the only people left on the earth, as far as she could tell.

And then suddenly she saw that a few feet ahead of them, just off the road, was a human shape, and she gasped and stopped in her tracks. It was an old woman, bent and knotted, swathed in garments so ragged and of such indeterminate color, and standing so still, that she might have been the twisted trunk of a dead tree. The woman had not been there the moment before, Jane was sure of that. John had come to a halt beside her.

"Hail."

The voice was soft, scratchy, almost inaudible, but Jane felt the hair on the nape of her neck rise at the line that floated up from somewhere in the back of her mind.

All hail, Macbeth, hail to thee, Thane of Glamis.

Could she have imagined it, that this crone had actually addressed them so? She glanced at John and was simultaneously relieved and frightened to see that he looked just as discomfited as she. She found her eyes darting around her, as if there might lurk two more hags, sprung as if from the ground. John found his voice.

"Well met, Mistress. It is a barren stretch of country we've been passing through. Is there a village nigh?"

The woman shook her head, her eyes fixed on them keenly. Surprisingly clear and blue eyes, Jane thought, for one so aged, and then realized that she really could not tell how old the woman was. Her hair was shrouded under a cap, and her skin, pale and taut over the bones of her face, looked translucent as fine vellum. She could have been forty or a hundred.

"No, Master. No village hereabout or for many a mile."

Jane's heart sank. John glanced around and Jane could sense him searching for his next words.

"But you, Mistress, surely you do not live in such wild country alone?"

The fierce eyes blinked and Jane thought of a hawk. Perhaps the question had frightened the old woman. After all, what could she do against two strangers who wished her ill and who had ascertained she was on her own? But the woman looked fearlessly back at them, with an odd little smile, almost a look of careful patience.

"I live where I am."

There seemed nothing to say to that.

"We seek shelter for the night," Jane said. "And had rather stop sooner if there is shelter to be had than walk on after dark to we know not where."

"We all of us walk to we know not where. Young Mistress."

Jane involuntarily drew a sharp breath, and the woman nodded slowly.

"Aye, I see you what you are."

The woman's eyes dropped to Jane's belly, and as loudly as if she had spoken it, Jane heard the words.

Thou shalt get kings, though thou be none.

Jane shivered.

"There be a shepherd's hut," the woman said. "A little off the north side of the road. You'll pass a stone cross before it. Some four hours' walk, perhaps."

All three of them glanced at the sky. The clouds threatened overhead, growing blacker by the minute.

"It will be rain tonight."

At the old woman's words another echo pounded through Jane's head.

Let it come down.

"Then must we make for shelter, Mother," John said. "Will you not do so, too?"

"My time is not yet. But yours is coming nigh."

She drew her cloak closer about her, turning from them, like a bat folding its wings about itself, Jane thought, and with surprising rapidity she moved away across the barren landscape.

Jane thought they must have been walking for more than four hours, but they had seen no sign of a hut. Her lower body was clenching in pain. It seemed she had been walking since the world began.

Night was falling. The gray clouds looked pregnant with rain, and the air seemed to crackle. A wind blew up, shaking the leafless branches of the trees. A crow, winging its way rapidly south, cawed loudly and Jane looked up.

Let us withdraw, 'twill be a storm.

The line from *King Lear* came unbidden into her mind and cold fear seized her heart.

"Shelter." It came out as a whisper almost. "I don't think I can go much farther, John." He glanced at her with concern, and scanned the rocky surroundings.

"Here, let me take your pack."

He lifted the heavy sack from her and slung it over his shoulder along with his own. The relief from the weight only made Jane conscious of how weak and weary she was suddenly feeling. Her head began to swim and she stumbled against him. He caught her as she sank, supporting her in his arms, his eyes wide with alarm.

"I'm sorry," she murmured.

"No need to be sorry."

A drop of rain splashed onto his face and his eyes darted frantically from the sky to the barren wilderness that surrounded them.

"There must be something hereabout."

Jane nodded, her mind flooded with the pain that was gripping her from somewhere below, reaching up to pull her down into its jaws. She forced herself to move, willing herself forward. The heavens had opened of a sudden, and now rain was slanting down, icy knives cutting into her face. *Keep moving,* she told herself. *Keep moving.* But for how long could she keep herself on her feet? It was almost dark now, and soon they would not be able to find the shepherd's hut even if they were near to it. They might pass it by. And what then? She shut the thought from her consciousness, focusing her entire being on putting one foot in front of the other. She was almost hanging on John now, could barely keep her other hand curled around the staff. It was so heavy, so heavy. She smothered a sob.

"I think I see something ahead there," John cried. "Can you make it that far?"

Jane glanced where he pointed, a little distance ahead and off the road. It was barely visible in the deepening shadows, and appeared to be a fallen tree, but she was too weak to question him, all will of her own was gone. She nodded and held to his arm, and together they plodded forward. The rain battered down and a heavy gust of wind swept leaves into a swirling dance around them.

"It's a hovel of some kind," John said as they drew nearer. "Perhaps the shepherd's hut she meant. Whatever it is, it will have to do."

Jane could see now that it was a primitive structure, no more than four corner poles with walls of wattle and daub and branches laid over the top with rough thatching tied into place, but it was out of the wild weather. She crouched to push aside the sheepskin hung over the low door and almost fell through, overcome with weariness and pain. There was a pallet of sacking stuffed with straw, and she crawled onto it. John followed her inside, pulling after him the two packs and staves. He unrolled a blanket and laid it over her. It reminded Jane of so many nights when Nurse had tenderly tucked her into bed and she longed for home desperately. Tears welled from her eyes.

"What's amiss?" John asked anxiously. "Are you taken ill or is it just weariness with walking?"

"I don't know," she whispered. "I'm weary, yes, but it's more than that. I hurt. Inside."

She closed her eyes and tried to locate the pain, discern its cause. It was low in her belly, somewhat akin to the twisting cramps she sometimes felt when she had her monthly courses, but worse. She was afraid to voice the dark terror taking hold of her mind, as if speaking her fears would bring them to pass.

"I'm going to gather some firewood before it's all soaked through," John said. "I'll only be a few minutes."

He ducked out the door. Jane tried to breathe deeply to calm herself. Maybe she had been mistaken and she was not with child. Maybe it was only her monthlies starting again, and it was painful because it had been so long. *It must be that. Let it be that,* she prayed. She drifted into sleep for a few minutes, and roused at the sound of John coming back with a bundle of kindling and some branches, which he laid beside the little door.

"I can scarce light a fire in here," he said, "without smoking us to death. If the rain lets up, I'll build a fire before the doorway. Are you cold?"

Jane nodded, her teeth chattering, and John wrapped his blanket around her.

"Have a drop of brandy. It'll warm you for now. And some food."

She drank and felt the liquid move down her throat and into her belly, and ate a few bites of bread, and it did give her some strength.

Outside the rain was pelting down with a sinister hiss, pattering against the roof of the hut, and cold drops leaked through, dripping onto the floor and onto Jane. The wind rose to a shriek. No fire would have burned before the door in such a wind, and the drafts coming through the feeble walls would have blown any fire inside onto the tinderlike wattle and daub and the dry straw of the pallet. It was full dark now, and Jane could no longer see John, but found comfort in the sound of his breathing.

Suddenly a sharp pain twisted within her, searing her, and she let out a wild cry of torment and fear.

"Jesu, Jane, what is it?"

John was next to her, his hand seeking hers. Jane felt a rush of wetness and warmth and gasped. She fumbled at the blankets, struggling to throw them off.

"Pull the covers from me, John."

He yanked them aside and she leaned forward, feeling urgently between her legs. Her breeches were soaked and her hand came away sticky. The sharp smell of blood was in the air, and Jane had a vision of Ellen Norton, her skirts soaked with a flood of bright crimson.

She was losing the baby. In the instant the knowledge came to her mind, sure and terrifying, there was a flash of light from outside the hut. Jane's first fevered thought was that lightning had struck. But no clap of thunder followed. Instead, the flap of sheepskin covering the door was pushed aside and a bobbing light entered, followed by a formless shape.

"Ee, here's no place for thee on such a night as this," the shape said. "Can you carry her, Master?"

The lantern swung toward Jane, and by its flickering light she could see the face of the old woman who had appeared beside the road. The woman clucked and shook her head.

"And here's blood, too. Quiet your heart, lamb, all will be well. Come out of the storm."

Jane felt John scoop her into his arms. She huddled against him as he carried her out into the darkness, the cold sharp stabs of rain mingling with the warm tears on her face, and then blackness flooded up and she knew no more.

WHEN JANE WOKE, SHE WAS LYING IN A SOFT BED OF SHEEPSKINS, AND swathed in a woolly blanket. A fire was burning, and by its light she could see that she was in a low-ceilinged cave. John sat nearby on a stool, a bowl of something steaming and savory smelling in his hands, and the old woman was humming to herself as she stirred a pot on a hob over the flames. She threw in a handful of dried leaves, and the aromatic scent took on a deeper cast. Jane tried to place the smell. Exploring with her hands, she found that her man's clothes were gone, and she was clad in a shift of some kind, clean and dry. Beyond the mouth of the cave, some fifteen paces off, she could hear that rain beat down and wind howled, but the fire lay between her and the outdoors, and she was warm. There was some small but heavy weight at her side, and lifting the cover, she discovered that it was a cat, a gray tabby with white on his chin and throat and the tips of his paws, regarding her with glinting gold eyes. She stroked his fur, and a deep purring greeted her touch.

John looked up at her movement, and setting the bowl down, came and knelt at her side.

"How are you faring, sister?"

Concern was in his eyes, and Jane took the hand he gave her.

"Better." She was surprised her voice sounded as strong as it did. "How long have I been here?"

"A few hours."

The old woman came to her with a mug of whatever had been in the pot.

"Drink this, lambkin. It will give thee back some of the strength thou hast lost."

Jane took the mug and inhaled the steam, and sipped. Some decoction of herbs, sweetened with honey. John stood as the woman knelt to peer at Jane, and he moved away to the other side of the fire, looking out toward the blackness of the night.

"I don't have to tell you that you've lost a babe," the old woman murmured, her eyes intent on Jane's. "I could see it within thee when we met, and also that its spirit wavered, undecided whether to stay or no. And more than that could I see as well."

"What—what did you see?"

"The son of a king it was. How it should be so, I know not, but I saw it clear as day. And that you travel to find this king."

Jane stared at the woman, wanting to ask a hundred questions but afraid, too, of asking.

"Over the water." The woman spoke as if in a trance. "Far over the water."

"Then he lives?" Jane cried.

"He lives."

John had turned back toward them at the sound of her exclamation, and the woman glanced over her shoulder and then back to Jane.

"Your brother knows it, too, the truth of this babe, and the love that got it. He knows it in his heart, though he has not yet let it in his mind."

She nodded, and put a soothing hand on Jane's. "He mislikes it, and tries to keep it from coming clear into his head, but the misliking is not more than the love he has for you."

JANE CONTINUED TO BLEED AND CRAMP OVER THE NEXT FEW DAYS, but she slept much of the time, the oblivion healing the grief of the lost child and the pain of her body. When she woke, the old woman, Marjorie, was never far away, and the cat, Beastie, was usually curled next to her.

"How came you to be here?" Jane asked one evening as Marjorie sat next to her, spinning a fine gray yarn on a spindle. "Have you no family?"

"No, no more," Marjorie said, her eyes far away. "They're all long gone. Burned out, my house was, during the wars. So the Beast and I made for the heath, to find peace and safety."

Jane glanced around the cave. It was cozy, perhaps twenty feet deep and a little narrower. The fire toward the front warmed the place and frightened off animals, its light flickering on the slanting rock walls above. Marjorie kept a few sheep, and their skins and wool provided soft nests for sleeping.

"Do you not get lonely?" Jane asked softly. "For human company, I mean," she added as Beastie nestled closer to her side.

Her eyes and Marjorie's were both on the spindle, spinning, spinning, dropping lower as the thread formed from the handful of soft wool in Marjorie's lap.

"Sometimes. But perhaps I'm not made for keeping company with others, or perhaps I'm past it. A witch, they said I was."

Her pale blue eyes turned to Jane, unblinking.

"Some folk fear what they do not understand," Jane said, and Marjorie nodded.

"Aye, that's the truth of it."

John came in from the outside, his breath visible in the cold air at the cave's mouth, stamping his feet to get warm.

"It'll freeze tonight," he said. "Snow can't be far off."

"I'll be well enough to travel in a day or two," Jane said.

She wished they didn't have to leave, but the miles that still lay ahead before they reached Yarmouth would only get harder to travel as the weather grew colder and the days grew shorter. She thought of Henry. Surely he must be safely out of England long since.

It was past the middle of November when Jane was at last strong enough to face the remainder of the journey. Her breeches had been soaked in blood, and it seemed somehow a travesty to put on the clothing of a boy when she had so recently passed through the ordeal of a woman. Marjorie brought out a skirt in gray brown homespun and heavy knitted stockings, and insisted that Jane put them on.

"My daughter's," she said. "She died in childbed. She would be pleased to know that they were warming thee."

Jane worried about leaving the frail old woman on her own in the desolate landscape with winter coming on.

"Will you not travel with us?" she asked, the night before they were to set out. "Come to France."

A faint smile lit Marjorie's face.

"To the king? Thinkest thou he'd welcome an old witch to his little court? No, the Beast and I will keep at home here, waiting for the day."

"The day?" Jane asked.

Marjorie looked at her sidelong.

"When the king enjoys his own again."

"Then you truly do not think he's dead?"

Marjorie shook her head.

"Nay. His road is long and furrowed with troubles, but he's not dead."

CHAPTER THIRTEEN

Marjorie's cave was less than a day's walk from Norwich. It was the biggest city through which they had passed, and likely to be garrisoned with soldiers, so they would not stay longer than they needed to buy food for the rest of the journey and to hear what news they could. Jane tucked her hair into a white cap that tied beneath her chin and put her hat over that, and shrouded as she was in her coat and cloak, she was confident it would take a sharp eye indeed to discern in her the tall and handsome lady sought for helping the king. She glanced at John. He, too, could probably pass now among people who knew him and never be taken for Colonel John Lane of Bentley Hall. His face was hidden by gray whiskers, his coat was stained and torn, and his hands were browned by exposure and the dirt of the road.

They entered Norwich through St. Martin's Gate. The city, sprawled around the castle and cathedral, seemed a bustling metropolis after the empty heath. At the market they bought bread, cheese, and apples for the journey, and some meat pies to eat on the spot.

"What news?" John asked the pie man. The man glanced at him and took in his traveler's garb.

"None so great since the news that the king has reached Paris, but perhaps you've heard that?"

"The king has reached Paris?" Jane gasped.

"Some two or three weeks since," the man nodded, gratified at being the bearer of such astonishing information. "Joined there with the queen his mother and his brother the Duke of York."

He looked around and lowered his voice.

"Oliver's men are fit to lie down and die with rage and frustration, for they'll never reach the king now. I've the newsbooks with the tidings, if you can read."

He brought out copies of *Mercurius Politicus* and *The Weekly Intelligencer of the Commonwealth* from a fortnight earlier, both bearing the news that Charles Stuart had reached Paris more than a week before then.

"Thank God!" Jane cried as they stepped away from the pie man's stall. "Alive and well. Oh, John, it has not all been for naught! But when Henry and I left him on the eighteenth of September, he was within a day's ride of the sea and there was every hope of a boat. What can have taken so long?"

"We'll learn when we get there," John said. "But at least now we know he's safe, and moreover, we know we will find him when we reach France."

Happiness suffused Jane's heart and the very sun seemed to shine more brightly. Charles was safe, and she would be with him again when this difficult journey was at an end.

"How far is Yarmouth now?" she asked.

"Close on thirty miles," John said, studying the map. "Another three or four days, depending on how much you're able to walk."

"And then how long to get to France?" Jane asked.

"I don't know. It depends on what sort of boat we're able to find and how difficult that may be. The herring boats go out from there, and there's other shipping as well. But all sailors are at the mercy of the weather, and so are we, too."

. . .

They crossed the river at one of the great stone bridges, and a mile or so out of the city the road sloped down to the river, rushing green in its muddy banks. The land was more populous here, and the way took them past enclosed fields on both sides of the road, and an occasional windmill, but it was bitterly cold.

In the afternoon, about four miles out of Norwich, they came upon that sure indicator of a well-traveled route, a blacksmith's shop. The friendly blacksmith told them they could undoubtedly get supper and a place before the fire at the house of his daughter and son-in-law, which lay a little way ahead.

"I say we stop there," John said. "No need to wear yourself out."

Jane readily agreed. She was feeling much stronger after two weeks of rest, warmth, and food in Marjorie's cave, but now her legs were not so hardened to the walking, and the skin of her hands was cracked with exposure to cold and wind, though she rubbed salve into them every night.

The smith's daughter was a pretty dimpled girl and her husband a great strapping farm lad. She was obviously with child—their first, she said blushingly—and their happiness made Jane's heart ache for the loss of her baby.

The morning was clear and cold. The road passed through groves of chestnuts and beeches, their glowing golden-brown leaves a welcome change from the barren heath. On the second night they stopped at a village called Hales, which consisted of a few houses gathered near the road, and was just large enough to boast a small alehouse with one room to rent.

The afternoon of the third day took them to where the Yarmouth Road veered south to cross the London Road, and a blacksmith's shop, a few houses, and an inn lay at the crossroads. They had not covered many miles, but the brooding clouds promised rain.

"It's just as well we stop here," John said. "We're not like to find any place near so comfortable if we go farther tonight. And if we get a good start tomorrow we should be able to reach Yarmouth before dark."

The little taproom was crowded with people making their way to and from Yarmouth, Norwich, and London, as well as the locals, and the travelers exchanged news from their respective parts of the country.

Jane felt more hopeful than she had in weeks when they set off in the morning. From the crossroads, the road ran northeast toward Yarmouth. By nightfall they should be at the coast, and soon, perhaps even the next day, they would be away from England and danger.

The way now threaded through black, sticky, bullrush-fringed marshland, and here and there they had to pick their way across small streams or pay a wherry to take them across the larger expanses of water. Windmills dotted the fen. By afternoon the road ran through drier ground, like the heath between King's Lyn and Norwich, and as the breeze carried the scent of the sea air toward them, the way became marshy.

"So close now," John said as the road came alongside a river. "This is the River Yare. The sea lies just there."

Jane looked where he pointed, off to the right. She could not quite see the water, but the horizon dropped off to deep blue, as if at the end of the world. A little later, the sea appeared, a shimmering silver ribbon, its murmur carried on the wind.

And finally, an hour later, after more than six weeks of traveling, they were there. Yarmouth stood on a thin spit of land between the river and the sea, swept by cold winds. Jane had never seen the sea before, and stood and stared. The choppy blue water seemed to stretch out forever. Great roaring waves broke upon the strand. The air smelled of salt and fish, and gulls swooped and cried overhead.

Hundreds of ships and small boats rode side by side at anchor in the harbor. The quays were aswarm with activity, as men aboard the herring boats loaded their catch into great baskets, others rolled barrels to waiting carts, and sailors hurried to and from vessels. The air was suffused with the smell of fish. A town hall, customs house, and warehouses stood beside the water, and the nearby streets were lined with shops of chandlers and other merchants catering to the seagoing trade, and a few grand houses. Excitement surged through Jane. The last part of the journey lay before them, and at the end of it would be Charles.

Inside the town walls, they ventured into the rows of narrow side streets that ran between the marketplace and the river to find an inn, and Jane was a little taken aback at the number of sailors, ruffianly landsmen, and gaudily dressed women roaming from alehouse to alehouse. The sounds of music came from some of the doors, along with shrieks of laughter and voices raised in song or argument. John took Jane's arm protectively, and she ducked her head as they passed a trio of chattering and laughing wenches.

They found lodgings at an inn that seemed more sober than most and had supper sent up to their room. Jane could hardly believe that they did not have to set off walking in the morning, and after they ate, she washed her second shirt and a pair of stockings, hanging them to dry before the little fire.

"What sort of boat will we go on, do you think?" she asked, wrapping herself in her blanket and curling onto the bed.

"I don't know." John shook his head. "Perhaps a fishing boat, or there may be larger merchant vessels bound for France. I'll go in the morning to see what I can find. I'll warrant we're not the only English folk eager to seek passage."

Jane would have liked to see more of Yarmouth, but took the opportunity to stay abed in the morning while John went to the docks. He returned about midday, with the good news that he had been able to find the captain of a herring boat who was willing to take them to France, leaving on the evening tide the next day. The captain had carefully not asked questions, but there were soldiers about the town, John said, and he and Jane decided it would be safer for her to lie low until they were ready to depart.

"We'll land at Dieppe," John said. "It's much further by sea than Dunkerque or Calais, but it will save us a hundred miles or more of walking."

"Good," Jane said. "Whatever it cost, I'm sure it was worth it."

"It cost a pretty penny," John said.

"How much money is left?"

"Enough to get us to Paris, I think. After that—well, we'll see what we shall see."

LATE THE NEXT AFTERNOON THEY BOARDED THE HERRING DRIFTER, a single-masted vessel about sixty feet long, with a crew of a dozen men and boys. There was a tiny cabin, but Jane determined to stay on deck while there was light, wanting to see as much as she could, for who knew when she might have the opportunity to be at sea again? As they left the harbor for open water, the sea was rough, and the boat bounded up the steep green slopes and plunged into the troughs between the waves. Jane found it a little terrifying, but also exhilarating.

"Farewell, England," John said beside her as they watched Yarmouth disappear into the mist.

On the afternoon of the second day at sea, a brown shadow appeared on the horizon.

"That's France, Mistress," the captain said.

Jane gazed at the land ahead and said a silent prayer of thanks, for now she was nearly to safety and to being reunited with Charles.

DIEPPE WAS FRANCE'S MAIN PORT, JOHN TOLD JANE. FISHING VESSELS bobbed near the quays, but there were many more merchant and navy ships than at Yarmouth. Jane listened with fascination to the babel of languages. She understood French, and John identified Spanish, Dutch, and Flemish.

There was still a hundred miles to travel to Paris, but now that they were not in England and did not have to use such caution to avoid discovery, they could hire a horse, which could be changed at stages along the way.

"We should be able to reach Paris in about four days," John said as they made for a stable a little way from the waterfront.

Jane was eager to reach Paris as soon as they could, and chafed at the thought of how slow the trip would be if she rode pillion, but her body still felt broken and vulnerable and she didn't think she could ride astride, even if John did not object, which she knew he would.

The French countryside was beautiful, but it was December now, and each day the sun rose a few minutes later and dusk fell a few minutes earlier, enveloping the land in wintry dark. Jane was grateful that the road was well traveled, and they never had too far to ride to find food or an inn. The people they met accepted their presence with a lack of surprise that made it apparent that they were not the only English folk who had made their way to Paris recently.

"With luck we should be in Paris by sundown," John said on the fourth day of their ride

In the midafternoon two men on horseback galloped past them, and hearing a snatch of their conversation in English, John hailed them. As the men turned, Jane was astonished to see that one of them was their cousin Henry Lascelles, and the other Colonel William Carlis, a neighbor from Market Drayton in Staffordshire. It took the men a moment to recognize John and Jane.

"God's my life," Henry said, staring. "Jane. John."

He leaped from his horse and pulled Jane into his arms, holding her tight to him as if he thought she might disappear, and Jane clung to him, only now that she knew he was safe allowing herself to realize how worried she had been about him.

John had dismounted and he and Carlis were embracing, shaking their heads in wonder at being reunited so far from home and after so many dangers.

"John," Henry said over Jane's head, reaching out an arm to him. "I can scarce believe it's really you. Have you been traveling all this time since we parted?"

"Yes," Jane said. "It's been . . ."

Overwhelmed at seeing Henry again, she could think of no words to describe the ordeals they had suffered in the past weeks, and she found tears coming to her eyes.

"The king will be relieved to see you both safe," Carlis said. "He's told the story many times over of your travels together and of your bravery, Jane."

Will Carlis was a handsome chestnut-haired man of about thirty, and as he greeted her, Jane was acutely conscious of her appearance. She knew she must look fully the part of a poor countrywoman now, her clothes dirty and worn, her hands and face weathered and rough from sun and cold winds.

They rode along together, Henry and Will flanking Jane and John's horse. After the battle at Worcester, Will said, he had made his way back to Staffordshire, thence to London, and finally to Holland and the court of Charles's sister Mary, the recent widow of William of Orange.

"She didn't know until I arrived whether His Majesty was alive or dead. She had heard that he had been killed or captured, and you may imagine her relief to learn that he had escaped and that we had spent a day hiding in an oak tree together in the woods at Boscobel."

"I went to London, too," Henry said, "but came straight on to France. I brought the news that the king had reached Trent in safety, but no one knew where he was or in what condition until he landed at Fécamp and sent word ahead to his mother."

"I came hence to join His Majesty as soon as I knew that he was here," Will said.

"He was very distressed to learn that your part in his escape had been discovered," Henry said, "and will be overjoyed to see you."

"As will the queen and all our English friends," Will said. "Lascelles, let us haste back to Paris and bring him the happy news."

The sun broke through the clouds as Henry and Will spurred their horses southward, and Jane felt that its golden rays had chased away the fears that had lurked in her heart since she had been parted from Charles. He was alive and singing her praises, and she might be with him by nightfall.

. . .

JOHN AND JANE WERE AT THE OUTSKIRTS OF PARIS WHEN A CARRIAGE appeared on the road before them, a cloud of dust raised by its wheels.

"What a hurry they are in," John grumbled. "They're likely to run right over us if we're not careful. And Jesu, another carriage close behind."

But Jane's eyes were fixed on the face of the dark-haired man who was leaning out one of the windows of the carriage. Could it be? Now she could see that the man was peering toward her. She would know the tilt of his head anywhere.

"Charles!"

She called his name so familiarly before she could stop herself and ran toward the carriages. The doors of the front carriage flew open and Charles leaped out, followed by another young man, and he raced to meet her.

"Jane, my life, my life!" he cried, sweeping her into his arms. "Oh, Jane. I could scarce believe it when your cousin told me you were here."

Jane clung to him, overcome at the feel of his arms so solidly around her. She looked up into his eyes, touching his face as if to reassure herself that he truly stood before her.

"You are safe. You are safe. Thank God. There were such rumors . . ."

"I know; they reached me even here. Yes, I am safe, though if you will believe me, I was yet in England another month and more after we parted. Oh, Jane."

"No! Oh, I would never have left you if I had known," Jane cried.

"But you couldn't have known, no one could." He kissed Jane's hands. "But you—oh, my God, what grief I felt when I learned that no sooner had you returned home than you were discovered. Lascelles reached here before I did, and when there was no news of you, I feared the worst. Oh, my Jane."

He kissed her full on the mouth, the kiss of a lover. Having held back her terror and longing for Charles for so long, Jane now succumbed. Sobs racked her as Charles held her to his chest, and for a moment there was no one in the world but the two of them

"But I'm ignoring your brave brother," Charles said at length. "Colonel Lane, I bid you welcome. I am indebted to you more than I can ever hope to repay you, first for your help in conveying me from Staffordshire, and second for bringing Jane here to safety."

Henry Lascelles and Will Carlis had emerged from the coach, and were standing awkwardly by with the younger man.

"Forgive me," Charles said, releasing Jane from his arms but holding tight to her hand. "My brother, James, the Duke of York. This is Mistress Jane Lane and her brother Colonel John Lane, to whom I owe my life."

The young duke inclined his head in greeting as Jane and John made their bows.

"But come," Charles said. "My mother the queen is waiting in the carriage, and will rap my knuckles, no doubt, if I tarry any longer without presenting you."

"The queen?" Jane said, appalled. "But look at me!"

"I see you, my heart." Charles laughed. "But I assure you that she was most determined to come to greet you, and well knows the perils through which you have gone. She escaped from England disguised as a countrywoman herself, you know, during the wars."

Jane thought that even so, the queen would not be able to guess at the half of what she had experienced. She went with Charles to the carriage, where a handsome dark-haired lady of about forty in a black gown smiled out at her.

"Madam, allow me to present the famous Jane Lane and her gallant brother John."

"Your Majesty," Jane said, curtsying to the ground as John bowed beside her.

"I am so pleased to make your acquaintance, both of you," said Queen Mary. "And happy that we can spare you walking the last weary miles. Come, sit with me. Come, Charles."

So Jane and John rode with Charles and his mother, while Henry and Will followed with the Duke of York in the second carriage, and a footman mounted John and Jane's hired horse for the ride to Paris.

As the carriage rumbled along, Jane gazed at Charles, hardly believing that he was before her. It had been not even three months since they had parted, but so much had passed in that time that it seemed already that it had been in another life, another world, that they had known each other. She had missed him so desperately, prayed so fervently for his safety, and to be reunited with him was overwhelming. She wanted to enfold herself in the safe comfort of his arms, breathe in his scent, feel his heartbeat against her chest, to let loose the flood of tears that she had dammed up for so long, willing herself to be strong and to keep putting one foot before the other in the hundreds of miles between Bentley and Paris. Instead, she sat beside the queen, responding politely to her exclamations of what joyful surprise she and Charles had felt at hearing of Jane and John's approach.

Charles, seated opposite her, smiled at her and joined in the small talk, but his eyes were sad and tired. There seemed to be a veil between them and she longed to draw it aside, revealing the lover who had been so intensely with her on their journey through England.

There will be time, she reminded herself. *There will be time, now that we are together again. When we are alone, it will all be different.*

The countryside gave way to city streets lined with tall houses. Paris. They were here at last. The road ran close to the river now, and the towering spires of a church rose ahead, greater by far than any Jane had seen before.

"What beautiful church is that?" she wondered

"The cathedral of Notre Dame," Charles said, with a glance outside.

"Which means," said the queen, "that we are very nearly home."

The carriage was passing between grand buildings on both sides. It turned into a vast courtyard and clattered to a halt, and the footman threw open the door and helped the queen to step down. Charles waved him aside and climbed out himself before handing Jane down. With a clear view now of her surroundings, she looked around in awe. The courtyard belonged to a magnificent palace, and just adjacent stood an even more enormous and imposing structure.

"The Palais Royal," Charles said. "And the Louvre, over there, with the Palace of the Tuileries just beyond."

The queen took Jane's arm as they entered the palace, the men following behind.

"I'm afraid, Mistress Lane, that we have not very luxurious accommodation to offer you, guests as we are here. But we will do our best to make you comfortable. You will want to rest and bathe, no doubt, and this evening we shall celebrate your arrival."

All seemed a blur to Jane as they walked through endless passageways. Henry and Will took John off with them, and Charles halted at the door of his mother's apartments. Jane longed to be alone with him, but he took her hand and kissed it in farewell.

"My dear Jane," he said. "Rest. And we will see each other a little later."

"Martine will see that you have all that you need." The queen smiled at Jane as a middle-aged lady in dove gray appeared and curtsied to her.

Martine led Jane to her own bedroom, and as the door closed behind her, the realization swept over Jane that the long and anxious journey was finally over, and she sank onto the bed, overcome with exhaustion, barely getting her shoes off before she fell asleep.

When Jane awoke, a tub and bathwater were brought to Martine's room, and Jane submerged herself, letting the blissfully steaming water soak away the dirt, sweat, and blood of the past weeks. Her poor feet were callused and chafed, the skin around her fingernails cracked and raw, and the stubby remains of her fingernails were rough and grimy.

Martine cleaned and filed Jane's nails, produced a gown of lilac silk, a pair of stays, a chemise and petticoat, white silk stockings, and a pair of black kid shoes for Jane to wear, and helped her to dress and fix her hair in preparation for supper. Jane admired herself in a hand mirror, turning her head to see the effect of her back hair gathered in a bun at the nape of her neck and the rest falling in curls to her shoulders.

"Much better, no?" Martine asked, smiling.

"Better! A miracle is what it is!" Jane laughed. "Who will be at supper, mademoiselle?"

"Besides the queen and the young king," Martine said, "there will be the Duke of York, whom you met this afternoon, and dear Minette—Princess Henriette Anne, that is—the king's little sister. Elizabeth, the Princess Palatine, who is cousin to the king; and Lord Wilmot and Viscount Taaffe, His Majesty's great friends. And of course your brother, your cousin Mr. Lascelles, and Colonel Carlis."

Jane was awed at the prospect of an intimate dinner with the royal family. She wished she had some further decoration for herself, some jewelry perhaps.

"You are just the thing," Martine said, as if reading her thoughts. "No one has the money to dress in grand fashion. Poor little Minette has not even a second chemise."

AS THE PARTY SAT DOWN TO SUPPER IN THE QUEEN'S APARTMENTS, Jane saw that what Martine had said was very true. The queen wore a different gown than she had earlier, but it was plain and the silk showed signs of wear, and little Minette, a bright-eyed gamine of seven years old, wore a dress whose hem and sleeves were beginning to fray. Charles and the other men were simply dressed, in coats and breeches far less splendid than Jane's own father and brothers wore at home for special occasions. She and John smiled as they took in each other's changed appearance. He, too, had been outfitted in borrowed clothes, and he had shaved and cut his hair.

The queen was gracious in her welcome and presided over the table with regal aplomb, but Jane was astonished at the sparsely furnished room, the simplicity of the meal, and the attendance of only two servants, and she began to realize in what poor circumstances Charles must be living.

"Will you favor us with the story of your adventures?" Lord Taaffe asked, looking from John to Jane, as the soup was served.

Taaffe had led the king's forces in Ireland during the wars, Jane recalled. He was close to fifty, she guessed, wondering if his florid face was due to nature, drink, campaigning out of doors, or a combination of all three.

Jane and John told the story of their journey to exclamations of dismay at their encounter with the cavalry patrol and the distance they had walked through such wild land, sleeping rough with winter coming on. As if by silent agreement, they didn't mention the deserter or their stay with Marjorie.

All of the men present except Lord Taaffe and the Duke of York had been at Worcester, and inevitably, the talk turned to that terrible day.

"Carlis was among the last to get out," Charles said, turning to the colonel.

"Indeed, I think I saw the last man killed," Will said. "The sun had set on a day of such carnage and despair as I had never seen. The rebels were within the city walls and converging on our headquarters. We knew that His Majesty was in danger of capture and every moment we could give him was vital, and though there were only a hundred of us or so, we rallied and made a desperate charge on the enemy near Sidbury Gate."

"Only a hundred!" exclaimed Princess Elizabeth. She was about six or eight years older than Jane, pretty, though inclining to plumpness, with the same dark coloring as Charles, and like her aunt, her gown was sober black. "Out of how many to begin with?"

"We began the day with perhaps fifteen thousand," Carlis said. "The rest were dead or fled."

"My God," Jane murmured. She had known the defeat was terrible, but it was hard to imagine such losses.

"Many of those left were the poor Scots infantry," Carlis said, "reduced to fighting with their musket butts or fire pikes. The fighting was face-to-face, with any weapon that came to hand, and the streets ran with blood. I cut my way through the last of Oliver's men who stood before me and ran for St. Martin's Gate. It was full night, and I made my way northward to Tong, and there hid upon the heath for two days, a friendly countryman bringing me food once or twice."

"It rained so on those days," Jane said, recalling the late-night arrival of old Father William Walker.

"Yes," Will said. "And patrols were everywhere, and I knew I must find someplace better to hide myself. Charles Giffard of Boscobel had been under my command, and I knew if I could reach there, he would shelter me. So on the second night after the battle I set forth, and reached the house near dawn, to discover that His Majesty had miraculously been preserved and was also there."

"Dick Penderel took me there," Charles said, "after we found that there was no hope of crossing the Severn." He shook his head in disbelief. "What a night that was. The shoes I was wearing were too tight and my feet were bleeding and blistered, and my stockings were soaking wet and full of gravel, and it was such agony to walk that I really thought it might be preferable to give myself up."

All those present who had escaped from Worcester had suffered from blistered feet in the course of their travels, and they discussed the efficacy of washing the feet in vinegar, putting bits of rolled paper between the toes to prevent chafing, and a fervent mutual wish never to be forced to walk so many miles again.

"Cromwell's men were searching the houses roundabout," Will said, taking up their story, "so we hid ourselves high in an old oak tree. Will Penderel handed us up two pillows on a nut hook, and I desired His Majesty to lay his head upon my lap so that he might sleep."

"I had been three nights without sleep," Charles put in, "and laid my head down most gratefully."

The mention of sleep made Jane both conscious of how weary she was and how she longed to lie with Charles, to feel the heat of his body against hers and the murmur of his voice in her ear as they made love.

"As His Majesty slept," Will continued, "I could see soldiers going up and down, searching the woods. As they drew near, I feared His Majesty might wake and make some noise, and the only way I could think to alert him without speaking was to pinch him. Which I did."

The company dissolved in laughter at this, Charles laughing more heartily than anyone.

"We sat there, quiet and still, until the soldiers at last were gone," Will said. "Toward evening, we climbed down. It was grown late and we were hungry, and His Majesty expressed the desire for a loin of mutton."

"I was clumsy enough not to realize that these fellows had not the luxury of eating meat but once in a while," Charles said. "But William Penderel said he would make bold with one of his master's sheep. He brought it into the cellar and went to fetch a knife, but good Carlis here was too impatient to wait, and stabbed the sheep with his dagger."

"Dear me, how very bloodthirsty," Princess Elizabeth exclaimed, and Will shrugged.

"Ah, do you see?" Charles said, with a sly grin at Jane. "He looks sheepish, does he not?"

"We hung the sheep on the door and flayed it," Will said, "and then cut off a hindquarter, and His Majesty cut it into Scotch collops, which I put into the pan while His Majesty held it."

"Which brings us to the pretty quandary," Charles said, "of who was the cook and who the scullion? What say you all?"

There was a buzz of discussion, and then Princess Elizabeth held up a hand to still the talk.

"In my opinion, cousin, you were *hic* and *nunc,* both of them."

"Ah, well judged," Charles laughed. "Well, after our excellent supper, when it was grown dark, Dick Penderel took me to Mr. Whitgreaves at Mosely, where I met again with my lord Wilmot."

"And then he came that night to Bentley and told John that you were there!" Jane cried.

"Just so," Charles said. "And the rest of my story you know."

"The king tells me you are a very learned lady," Princess Elizabeth said, turning to Jane. "That you know Greek and Latin."

"I do love to read, Your Highness," Jane said. "It was one of the things I missed while we were traveling, not being able to distract myself with plays and poetry."

"Then you must certainly come and visit with me." The princess smiled. "And let me lend you some books while you are here."

"You do me much honor, Your Highness."

The princess waved away her thanks.

"We are all happy to do anything within our power to help you, mademoiselle, and you sirs"—she turned to John and Henry—"for the service you have done our royal cousin."

The little party lingered late into the evening, and despite her exhaustion, Jane was reluctant to miss a minute of it. To be reunited with Charles was heaven, and the undisguised enchantment of the royal family at meeting her was intoxicating. But at length the party broke up. Charles kissed Jane's cheek as they parted.

"I shall come and see you tomorrow," he said. "Alas, I am so poor that that is the best entertainment I can offer you."

"I want nothing more than to be by your side, wherever that might be," she whispered.

A few minutes later, wearing a borrowed nightgown, she climbed into bed next to Martine and dropped instantly to sleep.

CHAPTER FOURTEEN

JANE WOKE FROM A DARK DREAM TO SUN STREAMING IN THE window, unable for a moment to recall where she was. Martine appeared, and finding Jane awake, returned with a pot of hot chocolate and a plate with some little pastries of a kind Jane had never seen.

"So good," Jane said, wiping a crumb from her dressing gown. "What are they?"

"Croissants," Martine said. "Little crescent moons, you see?"

"Where might I find the king?" Jane asked as Martine helped her dress. "I should like to—thank him for his kind reception yesterday."

"He is paying a call at the Tuileries, I believe, mademoiselle, but will no doubt be back before long."

"And my brother?"

"He is with some of the other English gentlemen. Come, I will show you where."

"I thank you, mademoiselle, but if there is a way to get letters to England, I wonder if I might trouble you first for some ink and paper?"

Jane wrote to her family to tell them that she and John had reached

Paris, and also to Ellen Norton, telling her the truth of why she had left Abbots Leigh, and assuring her that nothing less than the future of the monarchy would have made her leave Ellen's side.

It was afternoon before she saw Charles. He appeared in the queen's sitting room wearing a new-looking coat of dark green, a very clean shirt, and white silk stockings. He was freshly shaved and wore a wig, its dark curls brushing his shoulders.

"Until my own hair grows back," he explained. "I was tired of looking like a Roundhead."

"It suits you," Jane smiled, studying him. "And it's certainly a change from Will Jackson."

"I thought you might like to see the cathedral," Charles said. "If you will not find walking outside too cold. I've brought a cloak for you, the gift of a friend, Mademoiselle d'Épernon, who says she can scarce wait to meet you."

Once outside, they crossed to the vast palace of the Louvre, and Charles led Jane through the maze of corridors and rooms until they emerged near the Seine. It was cold, with a brisk wind blowing off the river, but Jane hardly noticed. She felt safe for the first time in months, and supremely happy to be once more beside Charles. He took her arm, but seemed to feel no urge to make conversation, and as much as there was to say, Jane hardly knew where to begin.

The river sparkled in the sun, and Jane and Charles, as with one accord, stopped to lean against a stone railing along the bank and take in the view of the great cathedral rising ahead on an island in the middle of the river.

"There was a child," Jane said.

She had thought about what to tell Charles and how, but now that seemed all there was to say.

"Was?" Charles turned to her, his eyes dark with concern as they flitted from her face to her belly and back again. "Then . . ."

"I lost it. Near a month ago."

"Oh, Jane."

He took her into his arms and drew her against his chest, and she let the tears she had held back for so long flow, comforted by the murmur of his voice in her ear.

"I'm so sorry," he said after a time. "Your brother was with you?"

"Yes. He knows of the child; there was no way he could not."

"But did you have no doctor?"

"There was an old woman. A wise woman, a healer. She gave us shelter and cared for me."

"A month ago," Charles reflected. "I had not been here long then."

"I felt so alone," Jane murmured. "All I wanted was you with me. I didn't even know if you were alive. I had been happy to know I bore your child, come what might, and when—when it happened—it seemed I had lost you for good and all."

"Oh, Jane, what a shambles have I made of your life."

"If only I had not left you when I did," she said. "We could have been together through it all, and it would not have been so hard."

"Yes, but we could not have known what lay ahead for either of us."

Jane snuffled, and with the back of her hand wiped away the tears that threatened to freeze on her cheeks. Charles dug a handkerchief from his sleeve and handed it to her, and she blew her nose, and they both laughed as she hesitated over whether to return it to him.

"Keep it." He smiled. "God knows I have little enough to give you, but a handkerchief I can spare."

They walked on toward the cathedral, and Jane saw that the arched stone bridge that crossed to the island was lined with vendors' stalls and crowded with people. Music and voices rose on the breeze.

"Is that some fair?" Jane asked.

"No, the Pont Neuf is always like that, the gathering place for every mountebank, pickpocket, and whore in Paris. Perhaps we'll brave it another day."

They continued their stroll along the river, passing a high gate that opened onto another bridge. At the center of the island a third bridge, lined with tall houses on both sides, led toward Notre Dame, its high front jutting into the winter sky. Arm in arm they walked around the exterior of the cathedral, and Jane stared at the turreted apse, its graceful arching supports reminding her of the veins in a leaf.

"Extraordinary. When was it built?"

"It was finished about three hundred years ago. During the reign of my cousin Philip the Sixth."

Jane recalled with a start that Charles's mother was the daughter of the French king Henri IV.

"Yes," he said, as if reading her thoughts, "it is odd that I should be King of England when I am as much or more French, Scottish, Italian, Danish, and German as I am English, but there it is. My mother grew up at the Palais Royal, you know, and of course the present King Louis is her nephew, so she's back at home here."

"And you?"

"Me? I have no home. Nor no crown or throne but in name, no army to take them back, and not a shirt to my back but I must borrow the money to have it washed."

Inside the cathedral great vaulted ceilings soared overhead and sunlight filtered in through the clerestory windows high above. Candles burned on a tiered rack, and Charles dropped a coin into a box that stood nearby, and taking up a slender taper, lit a new candle, his eyes intent on the flame.

"In remembrance of my father," he murmured.

They sat on a bench in the sanctuary, comfortable with each other in the silence. The scent of frankincense hung heavy in the air, reminding Jane of the smell of peat burning on Marjorie's fire.

"I killed a man," she said quietly. "A deserter from Cromwell's army. He surprised us, and had taken John's pistol and purse. He had just realized I was not a boy, and would have taken me by force, I think, did I not shoot him."

"And likely killed you both, too," Charles said. "You had no choice."

"No. But I think about him—recall his face, and that instant of surprise."

Charles nodded.

"Aye, I've seen that surprise. Perhaps we none of us truly believe we shall die until the time is upon us."

The bells rang the hour.

"I would I had been there to protect you," Charles said, taking her hand. "What a farcical bad king I am, that I can neither protect nor provide for those who have served me so bravely and so well."

"The time will come," Jane said. "Marjorie saw it."

"Ah. Well, if Marjorie saw it, then I shall believe it true."

THAT EVENING JANE AND JOHN ONCE MORE SUPPED WITH CHARLES and his little court of exiles. He seemed in good spirits, she thought, watching his face in the golden candlelight. It seemed a year since she had parted from him at Trent, the birds outside heralding the break of day, and she longed to be alone with him and in his arms.

"I pray you, Your Majesty," she said during a lull in the conversation, "will you not tell us what befell you after Henry and I left you?"

"Why, my friends have heard the story so often already that I am afraid I shall weary them," Charles said, glancing around the table. The company murmured denials, and little Minette clapped her hands.

"I want to hear it again!" she cried. "Tell about the man locked in his room!"

"You see"—Charles smiled wanly—"she knows the story better than I."

He poured himself more wine and took a drink.

"Well, as you know, Frank Wyndham had good hopes that his friend could help me to a boat. But it proved that for sundry reasons, he could not, though he sent me a hundred pounds in gold. So it fell to Frank to try what he could, and he went to Lyme and spoke with a merchant there to hire a ship, being forced to acquaint him that it was I who was to be carried out. The merchant appointed a day to embark, and directed us to go to Charmouth, a little village hard by Lyme, where the boat should come for us. And that is when I truly wished I had you with me again, Jane."

Jane smiled not only to know that had he missed her, but to hear him declare it so.

"But as the tide would not serve until eleven o'clock at night, we had need to sit up all night at the inn and to have command of the house to go in and out at pleasure while we waited for the boat. To remove suspicion at such conduct, I hit upon the idea of a runaway bridal party. So the Wyndhams' servant wooed the landlady of the inn with a story of his gallant master's love for a lady whose family did not approve of the match. He told his tale so well that she swore she would do anything she could to help the couple."

He twinkled at Jane and she smiled in amusement.

"Riding before a lady had answered so well as a disguise that it seemed best for me to continue in the person of Will Jackson. But without you, I was forced to make what shift I could. So Juliana Coningsby consented to stand—or perhaps I should say to sit—in your place."

Jane's happiness dimmed. She did not at all like the thought of pretty Juliana on the pillion behind the king.

"Mistress Coningsby was to play the part of the bride," Charles said, taking up a knife and an apple and beginning to peel it, "and my lord Wilmot was the groom. We made ourselves comfortable in our room at the little inn, and full of good hope and humor, for the wind was then very good at north, and sat expecting the ship to come in, but she failed us, and there we still sat at dawn."

He triumphantly held up the deep red peel of the apple, which he had removed in one spiraling strip. Jane smiled, and he coiled the prize down into her palm, his eyes warm on hers.

"And why did the man not come, sir?" little Minette cried, a smile of impish glee on her face.

"That was exactly what I wondered, too!"

Charles pulled his little sister onto his lap and tugged one of her curls fondly, and she gazed up at him in pleased awe. He cut the apple into quarters and removed the core as he resumed his story.

"I sent Frank's man Peters and Lord Wilmot to know the reason of it, and we resolved to go to a place on the road toward London called Bridport, and there stay till my lord Wilmot should bring us news whether the vessel could be had the next night or no. So Frank Wyndham and Mistress Coningsby and I went in the morning to Bridport, and just as we came into the town, I could see the streets full of redcoats."

"Oh, no," Jane cried. "Just like at Stratford."

"Exactly. But even worse. It was a regiment of fifteen hundred men going to embark to take Jersey. So we at once rode out of town as if toward London, much fearing we might have been discovered. When we were gone about a mile off, my lord Wilmot overtook us, he having seen us in the town, and told us there had been some mistake between him and the master of the ship."

Minette emitted a little shriek of anticipation at what would come next, eliciting chuckles from the grown-ups.

"The 'mistake,'" Charles continued, "was that the captain's good wife had been at Lyme fair that day, and had heard the proclamation of the reward for our capture, and suspecting what her husband was about, and fearing what harm might come to him if he should carry us to France and be discovered, she locked him in his room."

Minette giggled with delight. "She locked him in his room!"

Frowning, the queen put a finger to her lips and shushed her youngest child.

"Lord Wilmot said he believed the ship might be ready next night," Charles said, "so we determined to make for Broadwindsor, a village about four miles in the country above Lyme."

"And then what happened, sir?" cried Minette as he handed her a slice of apple.

"Many more mishaps and misadventures!" Charles replied. "But methinks the telling of this tale has been long enough for tonight. Mistress Jane and Colonel Lane are still tired after their long journey, and surely it's time for young maids to be in bed. We'll finish the story another time."

The guests stood and took their leaves, and Charles led Jane to a quiet corner. Her heart beat fast as she looked up into his eyes, longing to feel his arms about her.

"My chaplain gives Sunday service at the home of Sir Richard Browne, the English ambassador," he said. "I will take you tomorrow, if you like."

"I would like that," she said.

"Good." He kissed her cheek and nodded his farewell, and as she watched him stride off into the shadows, she was conscious of John's eyes on her.

About twenty of the king's followers gathered in the home of Sir Richard Browne on that icy Sunday morning. It was the first time Jane had met most of them, but everyone quite clearly knew who she was. She noted one dark-haired young lady regarding her curiously. She bowed and the lady returned her bow, looking a little flustered, before turning back to the man beside her.

"Who is that?" Jane whispered to Charles.

"Hmm? Oh, Betty Boyle. She attends the queen my mother. Her father was Robert Killigrew, my mother's vice chamberlain."

He did not meet Jane's eye and she sensed there were things he was not saying about the lady, but the black-gowned cleric took his place at the head of the small congregation and there was no time for further talk.

After the sermon, Charles introduced Jane to the chaplain, Dr. Cosin, a stern-faced man of close to sixty years.

"An honor, Mistress Lane," he said. "We all have much to thank you for."

"I wonder, Father," Jane said, "if I could impose on you for a little private time with you when it is convenient."

"Why, I'm most happy to speak now, if it suits," Dr. Cosin smiled.

"Shall I wait?" Charles asked, but Jane thought she sensed a hint of impatience, and shook her head.

"No, I thank Your Majesty. John can see me back."

"I have the feeling I should leave my stole on," the minister said, leading her to a small parlor with a fire dancing on the hearth. "You have more on your mind than chat."

"Yes," Jane said. The warmth of the fire felt good, and calmed her. She was silent for a few moments, gathering her thoughts, and was grateful that Dr. Cosin sat beside her in silence, not pressing her to speak until she was ready.

"My brother and I faced many hardships during our journey," she said finally.

"Walking all that way, with winter coming on, I should think so."

"One day we met a soldier—a rebel deserter. He surprised us when John had just fired his pistol—hunting, you see—and he had us very much at a disadvantage. John had already thrown down his empty pistol and his purse and even the hare he had shot, when this soldier turned his attention to me. I was dressed as a boy so that I would be less likely to be recognized, but this man was very close to me and he saw that I was a woman. He touched me—he would have done more, I am sure, and John would have been helpless to prevent him. I had a pistol hidden beneath my coat and I shot him. Killed him."

Dr. Cosin made a noise of sympathetic alarm in his throat.

"You acted in your own defense, when there was no one else who could defend you."

"I did. But was it not still murder?"

Jane searched the chaplain's dark eyes, hoping for forgiveness and afraid of condemnation.

"You were defending yourself from assault, perhaps death. God knows the truth of that. Also, consider this. When a soldier goes into battle, he is doing his duty. You put off the tenderness of your sex and were acting as a soldier, defending king and crown. You were presented with the soldier's choice. Kill or be killed. It was no sin, I think."

"Thank you," Jane breathed.

It was a relief to have spoken of her fears. But a much greater weight yet enveloped her heart. Could she speak of it now? She watched the snow falling outside the windows and steeled herself.

She had better, she decided. For her silence was eating into her soul, and there might not be anyone else she could tell.

"There is another thing. When I was traveling with the king, he lay with me. I wanted him to, I didn't care about the consequences."

"I see."

Dr. Cosin's mouth tightened, and Jane was afraid of his disapproval, but she had to go on.

"I carried his child. And when I was walking with my brother—the day after I shot the man—I miscarried of it."

The pain of the memory was too much, and she began to cry softly.

"I fear God punished me for my sin by taking the babe. And perhaps for the killing of the soldier as well."

"The fornication was sin, most grievous sin, and no question. But perhaps God sought to protect you, rather than punish you."

"Protect me? How?"

"If the child had not died, perhaps your reception here would have been different." Just as John had feared, Jane thought. "But more than that, the king is destitute, you know, as are all his family and supporters here. The poor queen relied on the mercy of the Frondeurs who were rioting in the streets to give her food and wood for her fire. His Majesty has no means of supporting a child, and the burden you have taken up on his behalf, already so heavy, would have been heavier yet. And the child would have suffered."

"That's true." Jane sniffled and Dr. Cosin put a comforting hand on her shoulder.

"You have endured much for your sins already. Humbly ask God to pardon your offenses, sin with the king no more, and go in peace."

When Jane returned to the Palais Royal, Charles was nowhere to be seen. She was reluctant to keep asking after him, so she kept to Martine's room and rested until the noon meal. Charles was present, and after dinner, sat and visited with Jane, John, Henry, and Lord Wilmot in the queen's apartments. They had not gathered alone since they had all set out from Bentley, and it seemed unreal that now they should be sitting together in Paris.

"How very improbable that our wild scheme should have worked," Wilmot mused, looking around the little circle. "When I consider of the number of instances in which Your Majesty was in the midst of the enemy and they saw you not, and the dangers through which you passed, it seems that surely the hand of Providence must have been at work."

"So it does," Charles nodded.

"What happened after the boat failed to come to Charmouth?" Jane asked.

"After His Majesty left with Wyndham and Mistress Coningsby," Wilmot said, "I found that my horse had cast a shoe. The ostler was standing by as the smith began his work, chatting, as such fellows will, and said he was a soldier, and that he was only working at the inn for extra money. So you may imagine what a start it gave me when at that moment the smith looks most sharply at the horse's shoes, remarking that they had been set in three different counties, one of them Worcestershire."

"Oh, no!" Jane gasped.

"It did nothing to ease my mind when the fellow then asked about the lady and gentlemen who had sat up all the night, as if in readiness to depart. I passed it off with a laugh, repeating the story of the runaway bride and groom, but I could tell his curiosity was roused, and as soon as the horse was shod, I rode for Bridport as fast as I could."

"And now," Charles exclaimed, "we come to one more time when all should have been lost. For of course, when my lord Wilmot met us, he told us of the ostler, and we were looking over our shoulders, expecting to see soldiers at any minute. We had not rid a quarter of a mile when we came upon a little path that ran off to the left. None of us knew the country, but we agreed upon the instant to take that road, and make our way northward rather than south."

"And had we remained upon the main road for another five minutes," Wilmot said, "we would surely have been taken."

Jane felt her stomach heave at the thought of Charles imprisoned and executed.

"Meanwhile," Charles said, "we arrived at Broadwindsor, but the master of the ship, doubting that it was some dangerous employment he was hired upon, would not undertake to carry us over. Whereupon we were forced to go back again to Frank Wyndham's to Trent, where we might be in some safety till we had hired another ship."

Jane thought of her heartache at leaving Charles at Trent, and swore inwardly. If only she had not let Charles talk her and Henry into leaving so soon, it might have been she, not Juliana, who rode with him to Charmouth and back again. Maybe she would not have had to be parted from him at all.

At length the little gathering broke up, and Jane returned to Martine's room to make herself ready for supper. She was washing her face when she heard a noise behind her and turned to see a boy regarding her with intense curiosity. He was about thirteen and finely dressed, though his coat and the knees of his breeches were dirty.

"Are you Mademoiselle Jane Lane?" he asked.

Jane felt rather like an insect specimen pinned in a glass case, but bit back the impulse to ask what business it was of his.

"I am."

"I thought so." The boy nodded, evidently satisfied.

He started as a female voice at some distance called out, "Louis! Where are you?"

"Don't tell them I'm here, will you?" he begged.

Jane had only time to shake her head before he dove under the bed. An imperious-looking middle-aged lady in gold silk strode through the door and halted abruptly at the sight of Jane.

"Oh. I beg your pardon. I was looking for my son." She swept the chamber with an eaglelike eye.

"I'm all alone here," Jane said, gesturing as if to show the emptiness of the room. She didn't know why the boy wished to remain hidden, but he had looked at her so beseechingly that she couldn't help but sympathize with him.

The woman shook her head with exasperation and turned on her heel. After her tapping footsteps died away, the boy squirmed out from his hiding place, his clothes none the cleaner for having been under the bed.

"Thank you!" he grinned as he darted out the door.

It took Jane a moment to remember the name the woman had called, and to realize that she had just been responsible for the preservation of the King of France.

CHAPTER FIFTEEN

A week after Jane and John arrived in Paris it snowed. Jane looked out from her window at the rooftops of the city, their chimney pots jutting out of the white drifts on the slanting slates. She drew her robe about her and shivered, thankful that she and John were not walking through England or riding through the French countryside in such weather.

Simply not to be traveling at a harsh pace, worrying every time she heard the beat of hooves, was a relief. Now that she could let her guard down, and did not have to daily flog herself forward over the endless miles, her body was taken over with complete exhaustion and her mind felt numb and confused, and she found it difficult to focus beyond the moment at hand. She was grateful to have been welcomed so warmly at the court, small and impoverished though it was.

She spent the snowy afternoon visiting with the queen and Charles's cousin Elizabeth, the Princess Palatine. They were both engaged in needlework—the queen embroidering in silk and the princess making lace. Nearby, Martine sat with a basket of mending by her side, overseeing Minette's efforts on a sampler of tiny stitches worked on linen.

"I feel useless just sitting," Jane declared. "I pray you, Martine, give me something to occupy my hands as we talk."

"Very well, mademoiselle, if you insist," Martine said. "Here is a shirt belonging to His Majesty. The sleeve is pulling out from its seam, you see."

"Ah, much better," Jane said, putting a thimble onto her finger and threading a needle.

"Charles says that you quoted Virgil and Shakespeare to him as you traveled," Princess Elizabeth said.

"Yes," Jane said, "we have a shared love of poetry and plays, it seems. Though I have only had the pleasure of seeing one play performed."

"What a pity," tutted the queen. "We used to have many performances at court in the old days. My husband the king and I both had our companies of players, you know. And of course we frequently had masques—little performances, you know, with music and dancing, on allegorical or classical themes."

"Little?" Princess Elizabeth laughed. "Like *The Masque of Peace*? One hundred courtiers and musicians in costumes constructed for the purpose, the scenery designed and painted by the great Inigo Jones, weeks of preparation, and all this costing as much as would build a battleship. Was that little, madame?"

"Bah!" The queen brushed aside the gibe. "It was little enough for the entertainment it provided. I loved even better to take part."

"You performed, Your Majesty?" Jane couldn't hide the surprise in her voice.

"Oh, yes," the queen laughed. "There were no women among the players on the public stage, but the court masques were quite different. I danced as Divine Beauty in *Tempe Restored,* along with fourteen of my ladies."

"And don't forget *The Shepherd's Paradise,* Your Majesty," Martine said.

"Ah, yes," the queen sighed. "I am afraid the poor little Cockpit theater at Whitehall must be quite fallen into disrepair now."

"There is quite a beautiful theater here in the Palais Royal, you know," Princess Elizabeth told Jane. "Alas, with things in such an uproar as they have been, there has been no time for plays. But perhaps one day before too long . . ."

"What authors do you enjoy best, Your Highness?" Jane asked Princess Elizabeth, turning the shirt in her hand as she finished the first part of the seam.

"You may think it strange—or perhaps not, perhaps you will understand quite well—but I became quite fascinated with the writings of Monsieur Descartes. A philosopher, you know."

"Yes," Jane said. "I know his name, but have not read his work."

"He became a dear friend. He died last year, more is the pity."

Her eyes were sad, and she looked down at the needlework in her lap, absently smoothing away a knot in the thread.

"I miss him so. And of course the exchange of ideas," she added, glancing at Jane. "An interesting man, and one who welcomed debate. But he never did satisfactorily answer my one great question."

"And what was that?" Jane asked.

"He argued that our minds and our bodies are separate beings. If that was so, I queried, how comes it that they interact with each other as they do? For if they were truly separate, would not our minds wander off, free from our corporal bodies?"

"For myself," Jane said, "I can tell you that my mind wanders quite a bit, if I'm not careful."

The women laughed, and even little Minette joined in.

"Very good, mademoiselle," the queen said. "No wonder Charles enjoys your company so."

THE NEXT AFTERNOON CHARLES CAME TO SEE JANE AT HIS MOTHER'S apartments.

"It's a pity it's so cold," he said, looking out at the frost-tipped branches of the trees. "But my room is scarcely warmer, and I am so poor that walking is the only entertainment I can offer you. But come, I want to show you the Grand Gallery."

Snow sparkled on the ground before the palace.

"So beautiful," Jane said as Charles led her across to the Palace of the Louvre, holding her arm to keep her from slipping. "Like a field of diamonds."

Many English country houses had long galleries, useful for taking exercise in inclement weather, but Jane was not prepared for the sight of the Grand Gallery, which ran between the Louvre and the Palace of the Tuileries. It must have been close to a hundred feet wide and stretched before her, straight as a Roman road, for at least a quarter of a mile. High vaulted ceilings arched overhead from treelike columns along either side of the gallery, and windows high above admitted the pearly gray of the winter sky. Most enchanting, artists and artisans of various kinds were at work along the length of the gallery ahead.

"It's been a tradition for some two hundred years," Charles explained, "ever since my grandfather built the gallery, that it provide lodging and workspace for artists, for craftsmen, of whom the royal family of France makes so much use."

"A splendid idea," Jane said, pausing to watch an old man using a tiny brush to apply gilt to a stunning vase with a ground of brilliant blue.

"Yes," Charles agreed. "If I ever have a palace to my name, I'd like to do the same." They walked on, nodding and smiling to the artists who pulled off their caps and bowed to Charles.

"Tell me the rest of what happened, when you had to go back to Trent," Jane said as they walked on.

"Well, I left the story when we had escaped our pursuers so narrowly, did we but know it, and got to Broadwindsor. We went to the inn there, the George, taking the topmost room, thinking it the most private. But no sooner were we in, but comes in a great troop of soldiers."

"Like at the Crown in Cirencester!" Jane said. "Tell me you didn't blunder among them in the stable yard again?"

"No." Charles laughed. "The stakes were too high to play at that game again."

"What did you do?" Jane asked, pausing as her eye was caught by a weaver working on a great tapestry. The man bowed gravely first to Charles and then to her before resuming his work, threading the shuttle of his loom between the brightly colored threads.

"There was nothing we could do," Charles continued, "but stay within our room and pray that nothing should occasion them to come to search. And as it happened, there was a disturbance which proved a great help to us. For a wench that was with the soldiers was great with child, and began her travail."

The cave and Marjorie rose to Jane's mind, and the specter of the child that would never be. The weaver was at work on a depiction of the Madonna and Child, she noted with irony, the Virgin in vivid blue, the chubby face of the baby Jesus rose-petal pink and white.

"The poor girl was in the kitchen, delivering of her child," Charles said. "Somehow, the worthies of the village came to know of it, and fearful that the child and mother should become a burden to the parish, came to the inn, and a very hot conflict arose with the soldiers concerning provision to be made for the mother and the infant. As you may imagine, not a wink of sleep did we get, and yet the trouble likely saved us from worse."

"The poor girl," Jane said, imagining only too well the young woman's distress.

Charles nodded at the weaver and he and Jane resumed their strolling.

"We waited to take our leave until the company of soldiers was gone, and then we got us back to Trent as soon as ever we could. Wilmot endeavored to find me a boat, and all I could do was wait, locked in the bedchamber there."

"I wish I had been with you," Jane said.

"I wished so, too, every day." Charles smiled. "The time would have passed much more quickly."

They paused to watch a painter at work on a canvas, a still life of fruits and flowers, its vibrant colors jewel-like and almost glowing. Jane glanced sideways at Charles, longing to feel his mouth fierce on hers. She took his arm as they turned from the painter, and decided she must voice the question that had been rising in her heart since her arrival in Paris.

"Charles," she murmured, "why do you not take me to your bed? I long for you so."

Fire flared in his eyes, and he pulled her to face him, looking down into her face.

"I would not hurt you, my dear. It has not been long since you miscarried of the child . . ."

"I am well enough," she assured him, placing a hand on his cheek. She was conscious that they were watched, but she didn't care. She pushed from her mind the thought of the minister and his adjuration to sin no more. In Charles's presence, nothing mattered but her love for him.

He kissed her cheek. "I have little privacy here, as you know. But let us see if we can find a way."

He led her onward, her arm still in his. Two ladies in rustling silk were approaching from the opposite direction. At the sight of Jane and Charles, one whispered to the other. They bowed and smiled as they passed, and turning her head, Jane saw that the ladies had also turned back to look at her. Apparently what Charles did and with whom were matters of intense interest to the French court.

"Did you stay with the Wyndhams until Lord Wilmot found you a boat, then?" Jane wondered, wishing again that she had remained with Charles instead of leaving him at Trent.

"No. It seemed safest to leave. We made our way to another house, near Salisbury."

"You must have ridden the way that Henry and I did, then," Jane said. "Did you see the great stones?"

"Yes, I stayed looking upon them for some time, filled with a sense of something greater and infinitely more long-lasting than myself. I was glad of the accident in circumstances that took me there."

"Henry and I stopped there for the night," Jane said. "I felt in the presence of great magic and power, lying there among the stones with the stars wheeling overhead."

They had reached the end of the gallery, but rather than continue into the Palais des Tuileries, Charles led Jane back the way they had come.

"And then where did you go?" she asked.

He squeezed her arm, linked in his, and the familiar gesture warmed her.

"It's not worth the telling. Here and there for another fortnight before Wilmot was finally able to arrange for a boat at Brightelmstone."

THE ENGLISH COURT SQUATTED LIKE REFUGEES IN A TINY CORNER OF the vast complex of the French palaces, and for the first week or two she was in Paris, Jane had had almost no contact with any French people. She was touched and gratified, therefore, to receive a note from Charles's friend Mademoiselle d'Épernon, inviting her to visit. Mademoiselle was dressed for the afternoon in a gown of carnation trimmed with ribbon rosettes in gold and flame red, and Jane was acutely conscious of her own plain garments and weather-roughened face and hands as her new friend ushered her into her own apartments.

"I cannot tell you how grateful I am for the kind gift of your beautiful cloak, mademoiselle," she said, looking with admiration at the silk tapestries draping the walls and the intricate marquetry of the furniture.

"Mais non," Mademoiselle d'Épernon insisted. "It is the least I could do for someone who has risked so much and so bravely."

Jane wondered if Charles had told his friend exactly how much she had risked and what she had lost. The lady was very pretty, too, but her easy and open friendliness reassured Jane that she was not likely to be more than a friend to Charles.

Mademoiselle poured steaming hot chocolate from a gilded pot into delicate porcelain cups, and passed Jane plates of tiny iced pastries. What a change from heavy wheat bread and cheese rummaged from the bottom of a leather bag, Jane reflected, sipping the rich chocolate and biting into an almond-flavored pastry with rosebuds piped on the top.

"I shall be only too happy to provide you with any items you may need," Mademoiselle d'Épernon said. "I have too many things, quite too many things. The gloves, for instance—I think they breed when I am not looking."

Jane was grateful for Mademoiselle's easy smile, which somehow made it seem as if Jane would be doing her a favor by taking some exquisite garments off her hands.

"Tell me, please," Jane said, after they had exchanged small talk. "What is this Fronde that I hear about?"

"Why, it's a kind of revolution. Some of the nobles have taken a grudge against the young king, and there has been such violence—they burned the Hôtel de Ville!—that he and his poor mother fled, you know, and are only just come back."

"How dreadful," Jane said.

"Yes. And so we sympathize so much with your king, and he is rather a hero for his successful escape. And you a heroine, mademoiselle, for your part in it. And I must tell you, your coming has sparked much curiosity and speculation among the ladies here."

She tilted her head, an inquisitive but friendly smile curving her dimpled cheeks. Jane felt herself blushing and wondering how to respond as a flurry of questions flooded her mind. She had borne the flaming passion of her love for Charles as a secret for so long, and ached to confide in someone who would understand.

"Oh. Well. What do they wonder about?"

Mademoiselle blew out her cheeks in what Jane had already observed to be a quintessentially Gallic way.

"*Eh, bien,* it is said that you are the king's mistress. And there are those here who worry that perhaps you might push them from his thoughts and attentions."

Jane's heart clutched in panic. "Who?"

Mademoiselle saw the fear on her face, and took her hand gently.

"Mademoiselle Lane, he speaks very highly of you, your Charles, and clearly holds you in high regard. But you must know that of course he is an object of interest. Handsome, romantically tragic. It would be strange if he did not, young man that he is, respond to this interest."

"Of course." Jane said the words but her heart was twisting in pain.

"He spends time with the Duchess de Châtillon, a young widow," Mademoiselle said softly. "And also with Anne Marie Louise, Duchess de Montpensier, called the Grande Mademoiselle. But that is in the nature of a formal matter—for as a wife, she would bring him the money and power he so very badly needs."

Jane felt the tears start to her eyes, and Mademoiselle pulled a silk handkerchief from her sleeve and handed it to Jane before continuing.

"*Ma chère,* you will only make things harder for yourself if you expect him to be true to you. He is a man; he is a king; he is alone and in despair."

Jane sniffled into the bit of blue silk, feeling silly. How foolish she had been to think that he waited for her, denying himself the company of others. Out of his sight, she had been out of his mind.

"Forgive me for asking, mademoiselle, but you do not have much experience with men, I think?"

"No," Jane murmured, but thinking what a world of experience she had accumulated in the past four months.

"And you gave him your heart. Natural, under the circumstances. But you must also protect yourself. Do not give him all, as he cannot give the same to you."

At supper that evening Jane wore a gown of plum-colored silk, the gift of Mademoiselle d'Épernon, and blushed happily at the compliments she received. It had been so long since she had felt pretty and it was gratifying to see appreciation and desire in Charles's eyes. After supper she visited with Princess Elizabeth, who brought forth a dozen or so books, begging her to borrow whatever she wanted. Jane glanced with interest at the opening pages of Descartes' last work, *Passions of the Soul,* with its dedication to the princess.

"'Passions,'" she translated out loud, "'are perceptions or sensations or excitations of the soul which are caused, maintained, and strengthened by some movement of the animal spirits, which move the body in all the different ways in which it can be moved.'"

"I hope you will read Monsieur Descartes and tell me what you think." Princess Elizabeth smiled. "I do so miss my discussions with him. I think my royal cousin Charles is taken by the merit in his philosophies as well, though he baits me by pretending to incline more to Thomas Hobbes and this *Leviathan* he has just published. Hobbes was his tutor, you know."

Jane felt entirely at home with Princess Elizabeth, who was clearly accustomed to speaking her mind and being taken seriously, even in the company of learned men.

"I don't think I've ever met another lady who so shared my passion for knowledge," Jane said. "I had the benefit of my brother's tutor, as we were so close in age, but that is unusual, at least in England, I think."

"I have been extremely fortunate in that regard. When I was a little child, shortly after my father was deposed as King of Bohemia, I was sent to my grandmother in Berlin. She thought it very proper that young ladies should give serious thought to serious subjects. And later, in Leiden, I received a very complete education. My sisters called me 'La Grecque' because of my fondness for the classical languages, and though my mother, too, values learning, I am sure she has frequently despaired that I exhibited more interest in books than in young men. But books, in my experience, rarely disappoint, and young men are so very apt to do so."

Jane laughed. "I had never thought of it in those terms, but you are right."

She was feeling quite at home with Princess Elizabeth, and asked a question that had been burning in her mind since she had glimpsed

Charles speaking to a dark-haired young woman with a little boy a few days earlier

"I have heard whispers ever since I arrived about this Lucy Walter. She is the mistress of Lord Taaffe, I gather. But—forgive me if I seem to pry—it seems there is some connection to His Majesty as well."

Princess Elizabeth sighed. "Yes, you are correct, and I will tell you plainly. Lucy and my cousin were lovers for three years before he went to Scotland, and that pretty boy of hers is his son."

Of course, Jane thought. The child, with his dark eyes and curls, must be the very picture of what Charles had looked like as a little boy. Princess Elizabeth saw the questions in her eyes.

"They were much in love. She was a likable girl—even his sister Mary and his mother the queen received her—but of course he could not marry her. There were rumors that he did so, but that is nonsense. Charles knows very well that when he weds he must ally himself with a monarch whose money and power may help him to his throne. He courted my sister Sophie for a time, but it came to naught."

Jane had seen Lucy with a baby girl, surely too young to have been conceived before Charles left Europe a year and a half earlier.

"And her little daughter?"

The princess pursed her lips. "The child of Lord Taaffe, in whose care Charles left Lucy when he departed for Scotland."

"Then he is not—they are not . . ."

"Charles does not speak to me of Lucy, but when her name arises I see in his eyes sadness, guilt, and despair."

In the days following her conversations with Mademoiselle d'Épernon and Princess Elizabeth, Jane resolved to take the Frenchwoman's advice, to guard her heart, and observe what she could. She heard whispered references to the Duchess de Châtillon, to Anne Marie Louise, to Betty Boyle, and to Lucy Walter, and thinking about her love for Charles, she felt herself stranded on a small and rocky island in a rough and surging sea. She saw him most days, but always in company, and they had not had an opportunity for private conversation since their last walk.

One afternoon when the temperature had warmed a little, Charles suggested they enjoy the entertainments to be found on the Pont Neuf. Jane happily agreed, but made up her mind to be cautious in his company.

"I have talked so much of myself," Charles said as they strolled near the river. "Tell me of yourself, Jane. How do you?"

The question took Jane by surprise, but she decided there was nothing to be gained by pretense.

"I don't quite know, truthfully," she said. "I was vastly relieved to find you safe, and to reach France myself, of course. And yet now I am here I don't quite know where I fit in or what I am to do."

They walked a little way without speaking. Barges, boats, and all kinds of small vessels crowded the waterway, and ahead, the Pont Neuf was bustling. Jane wanted to wrap herself in Charles's arms, to lose herself in his presence, but she thought of what Mademoiselle d'Épernon had said about holding something of herself back. He was not hers alone. She wanted to ask him about the Duchess de Châtillon and the Grande Mademoiselle, and what they meant to him, but was afraid of the answer, and also felt that to do so would break the spell of their happiness together. Lucy, though—she felt a kinship with Lucy, who had borne the king a child. Was Lucy's story her own?

"Will you tell me about Lucy?" Jane asked.

"Ah, Lucy." Charles sighed. "I will tell you as best and as shortly as I can. I met her at The Hague. It was summer—July. She was beautiful and sweet and provided a most welcome haven when I was lonely and in despair."

As I did, Jane thought.

"But," Charles continued, "duty called me away within less than a fortnight of our meeting. My father was yet living, though imprisoned. I had gone to Holland because the English navy had mutinied and come to our cause, and I hoped to make use of that situation.

Alas, the naval expeditions came to nothing, and in August, with the defeat at Preston, our cause seemed once more lost."

They had come to the great arched bridge that led across to the Île de la Cité and then to the other side of the Seine. Stalls selling food and various goods stood on either side, and in the middle courtiers mingled with gowned students, prostitutes, and middle-class families out for a day of leisure.

"Shall we?" Charles asked. "Here, keep close. There are pickpockets about."

He took Jane's arm and they plunged into the eddy of bodies.

"I returned to Holland," Charles continued, "living upon the goodwill of my sister Mary and her husband, William of Orange. Lucy was there. She was with child—she must have conceived almost the first time we lay together."

As did I, too, Jane thought.

They came to a bottleneck, where their forward progress was blocked. A fire-eater vied for attention with a fiddler, but neither had drawn a crowd bigger than that gathered to watch a barber-surgeon pulling a tooth from a burly laborer, who was sweating and groaning with the effort not to cry out.

Charles led Jane around the edges of the crowd, and they passed a stall selling wooden legs and another where a man was clipping a large white poodle, which reminded Jane of sheep being sheared.

"My father was murdered in January, not long after I returned to Holland," Charles said. "And so I was proclaimed king in Jersey and in Scotland, though it meant nothing to my circumstances; I was as penniless as ever. Lucy bore the child—his name is James—in April, and left him in the care of her uncle and aunt to join me in France, then in Jersey, and thence back to the Low Countries once more. But all this time I knew well that it was my duty to my father and to the country to recover my throne. So when Scotland offered help, I was obliged to go. I entrusted Lucy and the child to the care of Lord Taaffe, and when I came to France after I left you, I found that she had borne him a child."

"Did you not feel betrayed?"

Charles shrugged. "Perhaps it was for the best. I had not—have not even now—the means to properly care for Lucy and our boy. Taaffe does, and for that I am grateful."

They had come to the place where the bridge crossed the foot of the Îsle de la Cité, and a bronze statue of a man mounted on horseback soared above them.

"My grandfather, Henri the Fourth," Charles said. "It was prophesied that he would be murdered if he had my grandmother crowned. Of course he paid no attention, and did have her crowned. And was murdered the next day."

"How terrible!" Jane said.

"Yes," Charles said. "But not unusual among kings. Sometimes when I stop to think about how many of my ancestors have been murdered, it seems quite extraordinary that I've lived as long as I have."

"Your father, of course . . ." Jane said, searching his face.

"My great-grandmother Mary Queen of Scots was executed by her cousin Queen Elizabeth, and her husband Lord Darnley was murdered. Of course it was my great-grandfather James the First who was the intended target of the Gunpowder Plot. And then of course there is that great teeming nest of the Medici on my mother's side. Intrigue for breakfast, mayhem for dinner, and murder for supper."

They leaned against the bridge's railing and looked back toward the palaces and the Grand Gallery. Paris in all its splendor lay before them, and Jane found it hard to remember that only a fortnight before she and John had been huddled in Marjorie's cave.

"You have other children," she said. She knew, but needed to hear it from his mouth.

"Yes. When first I fled England to Jersey, I was much in the company of Margaret de Carteret, daughter of the governor there. She had a boy, also named James. He's almost six now."

"They are still on Jersey?" Jane asked, thinking of the campaign being waged even now by Cromwell's army.

"Yes," Charles said heavily. "And there is one more I will tell you about, lest you hear it elsewhere and believe that I have withheld the truth. During a brief sojourn to France before I left for Scotland there was a lady—I will not name her, for she has a husband—and she has let me know that the daughter born to her last year is mine."

Dear God, Jane thought. *He only has to look at a woman to get her with child.* Suddenly the inquisitive eyes of the dark-haired lady at the home of Sir Richard Browne flashed into her mind.

"It was Betty Boyle."

Charles stared at her in astonishment.

"It was, wasn't it?"

"Yes," he said, and sighed. "You may well hate me now. I hate myself sometimes, to think of the children I have gotten who are so unprovided for."

And mine would have been another, Jane thought.

"I don't hate you," she said softly. "I'm glad you told me all."

"I thank you for understanding me," Charles said. "You have done that from the first, I think. We seem to have almost an understanding that needs no words."

"I think so, too," Jane agreed. But what did it matter, if he was not hers and never would be?

CHRISTMAS WAS DAYS AWAY, AND THE ENGLISH COURT GATHERED TO celebrate the day as best they could, despite the news from across the sea. Scotland had been under occupation since the battle at Worcester, and Jersey, succumbing to the invasion that had been in train when Charles was at Charmouth, had finally surrendered to the Commonwealth, so that now no inch of Britain was not under Cromwell's rule.

More of the royal family was gathered than had been together in several years, but on Charles's face and the face of his mother, Jane could see the shadows of grief for those who were not present. The first King Charles, of course, but also Charles's sister Elizabeth, who had died the previous autumn at the age of fourteen, after long captivity at Carisbrooke Castle. Charles had told Jane that Elizabeth's birthday was the twenty-eighth of December, and she thought the little girl's memory must weigh heavily on the queen at Christmastime. The youngest boy, Henry, the eleven-year-old Duke of Gloucester, was still imprisoned at Carisbrooke. The only other living sibling, Mary of Orange, had not thought it fit to travel. Her husband, William of Orange, had died the previous November from smallpox, only eight days before the birth of their son, also named William. And of course Jane knew that Charles must be worried about Margaret de Carteret and their child.

"You see how it is," Charles said to Jane as they watched servants hanging holly and ivy over a great stone fireplace in the queen's apartments. "We are as much as we may merry and more than we would sad."

As the company settled down to Christmas dinner, Jane looked at the faces around the table in the queen's apartment. Besides the intimate circle she had come to know well, there were also John Evelyn and his wife, old friends and supporters of the royal family, and Charles's lord chancellor, Sir Edward Hyde, had made the journey from Antwerp and was sharing cheap lodgings nearby with another of Charles's chief advisers, James Butler, the Marquess of Ormonde. Hyde was clearly in pain from the gout that plagued him, but making a mighty effort to be convivial. Princess Elizabeth's birthday was the day after Christmas, and the party drank her health, wishing her long life and happiness.

John reminded Charles that he and Jane had not yet heard the conclusion of the story of his escape, and Hyde had heard none of it, so Charles took up the tale over Christmas pudding and port wine.

"When at length we had reached Shoreham, and found that indeed the boat was there, Wilmot and I came into the boat in the wee hours and lay there waiting until the tide should turn. About seven o'clock of the morning, it being high water, we went out of the port."

"What was the date?" Jane asked, wondering what she had been doing on that day.

"The fifteenth of October. The same day, though I didn't know it at the time, that the Earl of Derby was executed. Six weeks after the Battle of Worcester."

"Six weeks." Edward Hyde shook his shaggy gray head.

"Only a few days before Jane and I set out from Bentley," John said.

"Even once we were on board, our adventures were not quite at an end," Charles said. "The master of the boat was bound for Poole laden with sea coal, and because he would not have it seen from Shoreham that he did not go his intended voyage, we stood all the day toward the Isle of Wight."

"No closer to France than when you set out," Queen Mary murmured, pouring more wine.

"The master came to me," Charles said, "and asked me to persuade his men to get him to set us on shore in France. Which I did, telling them that we were merchants that had some misfortunes and were a little in debt, that we had some money owing us at Rouen in France, and were afraid of being arrested in England."

"How very true, did they but know it," Wilmot interjected, smiling.

"I told them that if they would persuade the master to give us a trip over to Dieppe, they would oblige us very much, and gave them twenty shillings to drink."

"Always a sound investment, a shilling for drink," Taaffe laughed.

"The master pretended difficulty, but at last yielded," Charles said. "So about five o'clock in the afternoon we stood directly over for the coast of France, and the next morning, a little before day, we saw the coast."

He mopped his brow in exaggerated relief, and the company laughed.

"But"—he held up a cautionary finger—"there we espied a vessel, which by her nimble working I suspected to be an Ostend privateer."

"Dear God, and pirates, too!" Hyde marveled. "Better than a play!"

"I told my lord Wilmot my opinion of that ship and proposed our going ashore in the little cock boat, for fear they might plunder us and possibly carry us away and set us on shore in England."

"I think I would have jumped overboard and drowned," Wilmot said, "rather than face that!"

"So the master set us on shore, and as it turned out, the vessel which had so affrighted us proved afterward only a French sloop. We went up into the little town of Fécamp, and stayed there all that day to provide horses. The next day we got to Rouen to an inn, one of the best of the town, in the fish market, where they made some difficulty to receive us, taking us by our clothes to be thieves."

Jane laughed at the picture conjured in her mind of the suspicious innkeeper, searching the room lest the King of England should have made off with a chamber pot.

"We stayed at Rouen one day," Charles said, "to provide ourselves better clothes and give notice to the queen my mother of my being safely landed. After which, setting out in a hired coach, I was met by my mother short of Paris, and by her conducted hither. And now imagine how frighted I would have been had I but known this: Colonel Gunther, who got us the boat, had not gone out of Shoreham but two hours—and we had scarce set sail—but soldiers came thither to search for a tall black-haired man, six feet two inches high."

"To have it come to so close a pass after all you had been through since Worcester," said Hyde. "Surely the Lord has preserved Your Highness with a great purpose in mind, and will bring about your restoration."

After dinner there were Christmas games and songs, music, and a little dancing. But there was a sense of forced jollity that made Jane desperately sad. She was glad of John's presence, but she was homesick for the rest of her family. She had resolved to guard her heart, and Dr. Cosin's exhortation to sin no more hovered at the back of her mind. But tonight she was lonely and despairing and yearned for the comfort of Charles's arms. He sat next to her, smilingly watching Minette beam as she opened a little box of nuts and sweetmeats.

"Charles," Jane murmured to him. "I long to be alone with you."

She had not spoken to him with such yearning in her heart and voice since they had parted at Trent, and the eyes he turned on her were bright with returned desire.

"And I with you," he murmured. He glanced around at the laughing faces, absorbed in their gaming, and lowered his voice conspiratorially. "Come. Follow me in half a minute."

He slipped from the room and Jane followed shortly, finding him waiting in the shadows of the corridor. He pulled her to him and kissed her, and fire roared to life within her.

"Oh, Charles," she whispered. "I have ached for you so."

Inside his bedchamber, Charles turned the key in the lock, swept Jane into his arms, and carried her to the bed. He pulled the bed curtains closed, and they were in their own warm and cozy little world, the dim glow of the single candle in its wall bracket the only light.

"My darling," Charles murmured, his hands caressing her, and he kissed her deeply. He threw off his clothes as Jane kicked her shoes to the floor and fumbled at the fastenings of her gown.

Have a care, a voice whispered at the back of Jane's mind. *What if you get with child again?* But it was too late. She felt she would die if she had to wait another minute for the feel of his hands on her skin, and she trembled as he took her naked into his arms, his fingers whispering across her belly and descending to the soft nest between her thighs. He groaned as he entered her, and Jane cried out, in ecstasy both at the feel of him inside her and at her joy at being reunited with him at last.

After they had made love, Jane nestled against Charles's chest. She felt she had never been happier to be anywhere in the world than she was at that moment.

"What are we to do?" she whispered. "I cannot stay forever in your mother's apartments, hoping to be able to escape to you without their notice."

"No," Charles said, but a shiver of fear went up Jane's spine as he offered no further thoughts. He turned away and sighed. A curtain seemed to have dropped between them.

"Charles?" she whispered.

"Jane, Jane. Nothing would make me happier than to keep you with me. But I cannot. I live under my mother's roof here. After the first day she told me that if I wanted to take my meals with her, I must pay for them. Not out of unkindness, but because she is scarcely able to feed herself and my sister. And France is dangerous. This Fronde, this rebellion, is like to break out again at any time, and I will have no means to protect you."

"Then what am I to do?" Jane cried.

Charles pulled her into his arms and held her close, rocking her, and sighed so profoundly that Jane thought he was about to weep.

"Dear God, what have I done?" he breathed. "I have ruined your life as I have ruined so many others."

"No," Jane said. "I gladly did what I could, and would do it again. But I am not safe in England, and yet you tell me I cannot stay here."

"My sister Mary," Charles said. "I am sure that she would be overjoyed to have you as a lady-in-waiting. Her court is a sad place since the death of her husband, and she will be happy to have another face from home."

"But I speak no Dutch!" Jane cried.

"Nor does she," Charles snorted. "Believe me, you shall do very well with English and with some French. The Hague is full of Englishmen. Your brother will be welcome, too, and you will live safely and comfortably, which is far more than I could promise you here."

Dark fear and loneliness welled within Jane's soul.

"But will I see you?"

"Yes, yes," Charles said. "It is not so far, and I will come to see you as soon as ever I can."

TWELFTH NIGHT HAD PASSED, CHRISTMAS WAS OVER, AND THE DAY had come when Jane and John would travel to The Hague. Jane had cried herself to sleep the previous night, desolate at the thought of being parted from Charles, not knowing when they would meet again. But they still had an hour or two, and they were walking in the garden of the Tuileries, though the snow lay a foot deep on the ground and the bare branches of the trees sparkled with frost.

Their breath made little clouds in the frigid air, and Jane clung to

Charles's arm, not wanting to let go of him a moment before she had to. She was trying not to cry, not wanting to ruin their last precious time with each other, but at the thought of all the hindrances that might prevent their being together anytime soon, the tears began to flow. Charles glanced down at her and dug a handkerchief from his sleeve.

"Here." He gave her the handkerchief, and she scrubbed at her eyes and blew her nose, knowing that the weeping must make her look a fright.

"My Jane." Charles tilted her face up to his and bent to kiss her. "Why do you cry so?"

"Because I'm afraid you'll forget me."

"How could I forget you?" he asked gently, stroking a curl from her forehead. "You gave me my life. You are my life; I've told you that."

"Yet you send me away."

"Not forever. My friends here and in England are hard at work to bring me back to the throne, and when I can protect you and provide for you, as I cannot here, we can be together again. Remember how you wept when we parted at Trent, fearing we would never meet again? Yet here we are."

The feel of his body against hers comforted her, and she tried to imprint the feel in her memory, that she could recall him to her when they were parted. He kissed her, deeply and passionately, and all her worries were swept away. He did love her.

"My Jane," he murmured into her hair. "I swear on my life, it shall not be long before we are together again."

CHAPTER SIXTEEN

Jane and John arrived at the court of Charles's sister Mary of Orange at The Hague on a bitterly cold January day when sleet made it difficult to see the road ahead. They staggered into the Stadtholder's Palace numb with the cold, and Lady Stanhope, Mary's chief lady-in-waiting, greeted them and led Jane to the apartments of Mary's attendants. Mary's court was a far cry from the impoverished camp of exiles huddling around Charles in Paris. The ladies were gathered in a room bright with colorful painted wall paneling and ceiling and warmed by a fire roaring beneath a heavy marble mantelpiece.

"Come, warm yourself, you must be freezing," Lady Stanhope said. She was about forty years old, Jane guessed, much older than the other ladies, and though she exuded a sense of authority and a certain primness, her smile was welcoming.

A fair-haired young woman in sea-foam green helped Jane to take off her wool cloak and scarf, which were dusted with snowflakes.

"I'm Dorothy," she said, with a shy smile.

"And I'm Kate Killigrew," said a pretty girl with bouncing russet curls and a faint sprinkle of freckles across her cheeks.

As Jane joined Mary's ladies for hot chocolate and food before the fire, she was relieved to discover that they were all English. They had heard of her part in Charles's escape and begged her to tell them the story, and she favored them with a short version of her odyssey.

"We shall make arrangements tomorrow to have some clothes made for you," Lady Stanhope said, rising to leave. "The Princess Royal—that is how our mistress prefers to be styled, not by her Dutch title—wishes you to know that she values extremely the assistance you provided for her brother, and that you shall want for nothing."

After weeks of living in worn clothes filthy from her own sweat and the dirt of the road, and the few things she had been lent or given in Paris, the thought of new clothes sounded like heaven to Jane.

"Have you something to wear at supper?" Lady Stanhope asked. "Ah, yes, very nice," she said as Jane pulled forth the plum-colored silk she had received from Madame d'Épernon. "Of course someone can lend you anything else you need until your wardrobe is complete."

When Jane had rested, bathed, and changed her clothes, Lady Stanhope took her and John to the apartments of the Princess Royal to be introduced. Mary of Orange was tall and slender, and dark-haired like Charles, with hazel eyes and a nose that was perhaps just a bit too long for her face. She raised Jane from her curtsy and kissed her cheeks, and smiled radiantly at John as he bowed over her hand.

"Welcome!" she cried. "It gives me much pleasure to be able to repay in some small measure the dangers you underwent on behalf of my dear brother. Everyone here has been anticipating your arrival, and will be most eager to hear your adventures."

. . .

The small company gathered in Mary's lavish apartments that evening did indeed appear to be delighted to meet John and Jane, and crowded around them.

"Her Majesty Elizabeth, the Queen of Bohemia, my aunt," Mary said, presenting an imposing-looking lady of about sixty in whom Jane saw a strong family likeness to Charles. "And her daughter, the Princess Louise Hollandine of the Palatine."

Louise was fair, and somewhat resembled the Duke of York. Noting that both she and her mother were in black mourning dress, Jane recalled that Charles had told her that Queen Elizabeth's daughter Henrietta Maria had died in September and her son Philip the year before. The Princess Mary, too, was in black, for the death of her husband in November.

The rest of the guests presented the appearance of England in little. John and Jane greeted their cousin Edward Broughton, a sturdy man of about John's age who had been captain of the King's Lifeguard and had escaped from his imprisonment after the Battle of Worcester.

"Jane!" he cried, kissing her cheek, and then embracing John. "When did we last meet?"

"I think at Christmas two or three years ago," Jane said. "Who could have guessed that when we next saw each other it might be here?"

Jane curtsied as Mary introduced the other members of the party.

"Colonel Daniel O'Neill and Sir Edward Nicholas, both trusted friends and servants to my royal brother."

O'Neill, a tall man with dark hair and piercing blue eyes and a lilting Irish accent, looked to be about forty years of age, while Nicholas, like many of Charles's advisers in Paris, appeared to be of the generation of King Charles I.

"And finally," Mary said, "His Grace George Villiers, the Duke of Buckingham. Who is practically like our brother, you know," she added with a smile, "as his poor father was murdered when he was young, and he was entrusted to the king my father. None of us were yet born, so even Charles began life with an older brother waiting for him."

"His Majesty has told me so much of you, Mistress Lane," Buckingham said, bowing to her and John. He was a handsome and fair-haired man of about thirty, with a mischievous glint of humor in his eyes, and Jane suspected that Charles must in fact have told his near brother all there was to tell about what had passed between them during their travels. One of his arms was in a sling.

"How did Your Grace come to be injured?" Jane asked.

"Broke my arm in a fall when I was fleeing Worcester," Buckingham said. He glanced around the table. "What an improbable collection of tales we have among us of our escapes from England. I, at least, was not forced to dress as a wench, as the Duke of York did."

The young duke, who had accompanied Jane and John to visit his sister, flushed.

"Really, George," he said. "It was bad enough suffering the indignity, without you making it known to all and sundry."

Buckingham laughed. "I'm sorry, Your Grace. But it does tickle me, the picture of you in a gown and shawl."

"He was not the only one put to such a measure!" O'Neill exclaimed. "I made my escape from the Tower with the aid and the garments of a laundress, if you will recall. Come, Your Grace, if you impugn the honor or manhood of all the English gentlemen who donned skirts in the cause of their liberty, you would have more challenges to answer than would suit even a firebrand like you."

Buckingham grinned and bowed. "You are right, sir. And perhaps the rumors that the king himself was dressed as a wench helped him to avoid detection."

The supper was a merry one, the bright glow from the fire on the hearth and the flickering candlelight chasing away the wintry darkness, and wine and laughter warming Jane's spirits. She reached across the table to take John's hand and he returned her smile.

Over the next days, Jane met more of the numerous exiled English Royalists who were making their home at The Hague. Besides the many officers who had fought in the wars and had escaped after Worcester, there were courtiers, merchants, clerics, and countless others who had fled England with their families after the execution of Charles I, and from the conversations she heard or overheard, it seemed to Jane that the air was alive with one thought—how to return Charles to the throne.

Some weeks after Jane and John's arrival at The Hague, a letter from their father reached them.

"'Your mother and I thank Heaven daily for the news of your safe deliverance,'" John read aloud. "'Miraculously, Richard has also returned to us unharmed. Some thousands of the Scots captured at Worcester have been transported to the West Indies and the American colonies, and many of the English were conscripted into the army and sent to Ireland. But still the government has been quite overwhelmed by the number of prisoners and the lack of place to put them and means to feed them, and some, your brother among them, have been released, upon signing an engagement never to take up arms against the Commonwealth.'"

"Thank God," Jane sighed.

"'We were visited by soldiers after you left,'" the letter continued, "'but after some questioning they became convinced that we could tell them nothing of your whereabouts and so they departed. It is the same everywhere here. They seek and search, but miraculously none else have been taken up but poor Frank Yates.'"

Jane took the letter from John and read it over to herself.

"'After some questioning,'" she said. "He makes it sound like nothing, but, oh, John, I fear for them."

"Yes," John agreed. "It weighs heavily on me that I am not there to do what I can to protect them. And of course Athalia and the children."

They sat in silence for some minutes, watching the play of the flames in the blue-tiled fireplace.

"I must go back, Jane," John said at length. "You'll be safe and well cared for here, but I'm needed at home and must take the risk of returning. Father doesn't say so, but if I'm not there come spring for the planting, things will go hard at Bentley."

It was true, Jane knew. Her heart lurched at the mention of home. In spring the new-thawed earth would be growing a haze of green and the trees in the orchard sending forth the first tentative shoots of buds. Lambs, calves, and colts would be gamboling in the pastures. And she would not be there.

"Yes," she said. "You must return, if you think it safe."

The thought of parting from John after all that they had been through together overwhelmed her. She struggled to hold back tears, and John took her in his arms.

"Oh, Jane, what troubles have you endured, and so bravely. The king never had a better soldier."

JANE TRIED NOT TO WEEP AS JOHN RODE AWAY A FEW DAYS LATER, but with his departure she realized how truly alone she was now and how far from home.

"There, sweetheart," Kate Killigrew murmured, gathering Jane into her arms. "You'll see him and all your folk again before long, surely."

"And in the meantime," Lady Stanhope said, gently brushing a strand of hair from Jane's tear-streaked face, "we'll be your family as best we can."

SPRING HAD COME, AND THE SCENT OF BLOSSOMS WAFTED ON THE warm breeze. Jane inhaled and closed her eyes, and Princess Louise looked up from behind her easel and smiled. Like her sister Princess Elizabeth, Louise was a lively companion, learned and a keen reader, and Jane had become very fond of her and grateful for her company.

"Shall I paint you like that, then, with your head thrown back and your nostrils open wide?" Louise asked. "*English Lady Scenting the Air,* I shall call it."

"I'm sorry," Jane laughed. "I'll try to sit still."

"You're restless today," Louise said, squinting at her canvas and making a few deft brushstrokes.

"I had a letter from His Majesty," Jane said, feeling her cheeks flushing.

"Ah! And what does our royal cousin have to say for himself?"

"He is quite annoyed that the States General did not take up his offer to command some ships in their war with Cromwell. And he says he longs to visit, but has not even the money to hire a horse to get here."

Jane ached to be with Charles again, and wore his letter inside her bosom and against her heart, with the little silk bundle holding his father's watch.

"Surely the Princess Royal would be happy to have him here?" she asked. "Can't she help him with money for the journey?"

"Perhaps," Louise said. "But she's already laid out vast amounts on his behalf, you know. Munitions, gold—she and poor William, God rest his soul, have done more than any of his other cousin kings to bring him back to his throne. And she is so much troubled just now with the Electors. Besides, with things as they are in France just now, his mother probably wants him at her side."

After a lull of some months, the burning embers of the Fronde had flared into flames once more. Young King Louis and his mother had fled Paris to St. Germain, and now most of northern France was at war, her helpless towns flanked by the armies of the Royalist and anti-Royalist factions.

"Don't worry." Louise smiled. "Mary hates it here. As soon as the weather is warmer and the roads are safe, no doubt she'll pay Charles a visit, and I'm sure she'll take you along."

Jane was surprised to find that she had met a kindred spirit in Charles's aunt Queen Elizabeth of Bohemia, whose tart wit and forthright speech left many a court popinjay goggling in astonishment.

"I can well understand the terrors you must have faced when you were riding with Charles," Queen Elizabeth told Jane, her slight Scottish accent reminding Jane that the lady had been born Elizabeth Stuart, daughter of King James VI of Scotland. "For I had to run for my life as well, you know. When my husband was deposed shortly after he accepted the crown of Bohemia, I had four little children and was eight months gone with child, and we fled from Prague in the dead of winter, given a scant few hours' grace to escape with our lives. Poor little Rupert was left behind in the scramble, and his nurse ran after us and threw him into one of the carriages. Ten days' ride it was to Breslau, sometimes at the gallop. That was thirty years ago, and I have been an exile and a pauper ever since."

She sat silent for a few moments, stroking the little monkey who fidgeted in her lap before she spoke again, and behind the dark eyes Jane could see the shadows of memories.

"No one would have thought that my life would be thus, from where I began. Elizabeth of Scotland. That was what I was called when I was born, you know." She smiled at Jane. "My father had not yet become King of England, but the winds were blowing that way. For Queen Elizabeth had no children, and my father, the son of Mary Queen of Scots, was the closest heir she had."

She picked up a small piece of cake and held it out to the monkey. He popped it into his mouth, licked his lips, and looked at her expectantly.

"She was my godmother, you know. Gloriana, the Virgin Queen. And of course I was named for her."

"Do you remember her, Your Majesty?" Jane asked, fascinated.

"Oh, yes. I was six when she died. I was rather frightened of her. She wore an enormous farthingale and a great standing ruff, and her face stood out so white beneath that bright red wig." She laughed. "Of course now I see that she was just a lonely and vain old lady, like me, trying to hold off the ravages of time."

"Your Majesty is not old," Jane said. "And you certainly have no need of paint and wigs."

The queen patted her hand. "Thank you, dear girl, for your kind little lies."

"No lie, Your Majesty." Jane smiled. "I pray I may hold what beauty I have as well as you."

The monkey scrambled down from the queen's lap and went to sit on a little hassock near the fireplace.

"Such times I have seen," Queen Elizabeth mused. "Did you know that Guy Fawkes and his accomplices intended to put me on the throne, had they succeeded in murdering my father as they intended, in the Gunpowder Plot?"

"No, I didn't know," Jane said. "Thank God His Majesty your father was saved."

"Yes. Better that I kept my father than be Queen of England. I was Queen of Bohemia for only a year. We were so happy to begin with. But perhaps . . ."

Her eyes were far away again, and then she came back to the present and looked intently at Jane.

"I think sometimes, about the choices we make, not knowing how far-reaching the consequences may prove to be. Do not you?"

"Yes," Jane said, reflecting on how easily she had set off from Bentley with Charles. "Yes, I do."

As in Paris, Jane found herself the object of curiosity and admiration because of her adventure with Charles, and speculation as to what their exact relationship might be. She wondered the same thing herself. His letters always protested that he missed her and looked forward to the time when he would see her again, but he offered no definite plans. He was busy, she reminded herself, and his mind and time were much taken up with the business of trying to find a way to get England back—nay, with the daily worry of cobbling together enough money to eat and trying to help his straggling little court.

On this hot afternoon, Mary had retired to her bed with a headache, and her ladies, with neither duties to attend to nor leisure to do as they wished, fidgeted in the summer heat. Jane was restless and uncomfortably warm. She would go to her room, she decided, and bathe her face and chest in cool water. Halfway down the passage, she heard voices from outside. Glancing out the window, she saw Dorothy and Kate Killigrew sitting on a bench in the shade. Through some quirk of the air, their voices carried clearly.

"His Majesty and Lady Byron?" Dorothy breathed. Her eyes were wide with naughty delight. "But didn't her husband just die?"

"Yes!" Kate laughed. "The poor man is barely cold and his widow is stripping off her mourning clothes to play the strumpet to King Charles!"

Jane froze where she stood, her heart thudding in her chest.

"But what about the Duchess de Châtillon? The Duke of Buckingham told me that His Majesty was sore in love with her."

"And so he was. The whisper is that he asked her to marry him, and though she likes him well enough, he has not money enough even to buy new shoes, so she turned him down, and now he's drowning his broken heart in the lewd flesh of Lady Byron."

"Marry her?" Dorothy blew out a skeptical little puff of air. "He can't marry her. He needs a princess, with wealth and an army. I thought he was to marry that French wench"—she wrinkled her nose in disdain—"the Grande Mademoiselle?"

"He fair scuttled that ship." Kate shook her head. "He told some of his cronies that once he had married her, he would cut down her household and sell her properties, and that remark made its way back to her."

"Oooh!"

"Yes, quite. So that was the end of that. No, there's no princess in the offing and now he's tearing his way through the Paris beauties from what I hear."

"That'll be a blow to you know who," Dorothy mused. "She may fling her cap after him now."

Jane didn't want to hear any more. She fled to the room she shared with Kate and locked the door. So that was why she hadn't heard from Charles. What the eye ne'er sees the heart ne'er rues, as Nurse would say.

She heard voices in the corridor and hastily blotted her eyes. She would put Charles out of her mind, and make the best out of her life here until she could go home. And she would surely not make herself look foolish and fodder for gossip by letting on that there had ever been anything between her and the king, or that she had allowed herself to hope there might be more than what had happened.

Nurse's voice once more spoke in her head.

Hope is a good breakfast, but an ill supper.

JANE'S SPIRITS ROSE WHEN SHE RECEIVED A LETTER FROM SIR CLEMENT Fisher later in the summer.

"My dearest Jane: I scarcely know what to write, it seems so much has passed in the months since we walked together on that lovely summer evening at Bentley. When I heard that you had gone, I steeled myself to accept that you must have decided against accepting me. Very soon, however, I learned that you had been forced to flee. You may imagine what torment it was to me to think of you, to wonder what dangers you might be facing, and know that I was not there to protect you. John has been to see me, and now I know the full story. My great relief at knowing that you are safe is shadowed by the knowledge of what a great distance lies between us, and the uncertainty of when I shall see you again."

Jane lifted the letter to her nose. She fancied she could catch a faint whiff of tobacco smoke and the scent of Clement himself, and it brought him to her mind vivid and real as he had not been for her in the months since their parting. No, he was not Charles, not a warrior king.

He was a man. Take him for all in all, I shall not look upon his like again.

The line from *Hamlet* rose to her mind, and she smiled, and then tears came to her eyes. Yes, Clement was a good man. But far off, so very far off. And God knew when they would meet again. She took up her pen and at first she could get no further than "Dear Clement." But soon she felt she could imagine him sitting at her side, and then she could write quite easily of her life as it was now and her hope that it would not be long before she saw him once more.

In late November, Colonel O'Neill returned from a trip to Paris.

"A letter for you, Mistress Jane."

He smiled down at her, and Jane's heart skipped to see Charles's handwriting. Striving for the appearance of calm, she escaped to her room. Her fingers shook as she broke the seal and read.

"My dear Jane: I have hitherto deferred writing to you in hope to be able to send you somewhat else besides a letter; and I believe it troubles me more that I cannot yet do it than it does you. The truth is, my necessities are greater than can be imagined. But I am promised they shall be shortly supplied. If they are, you shall be sure to receive a share, for it is impossible I can ever forget the great debt I owe you, which I hope I shall live to pay in a degree that is worthy of me. In the meantime, I am sure all who love me will be very kind to you, else I shall never think them so to your most affectionate friend, Charles R."

There were no protestations of desperately missing her, no promises that he should see her soon. But he was thinking of her. And that made all the difference.

The new year of 1653 brought excitement and happiness, for Henry, the twelve-year-old Duke of Gloucester, was at last released from Carisbrooke Castle and sent to join his sister Mary at The Hague. The young duke and his sister Elizabeth had been held by Cromwell since 1646, and poor Elizabeth had died two years earlier, at the age of fifteen, longing for her far-flung family. Jane recalled that young Harry had not seen his sister Mary since he was two years old, when his family scattered in the face of the coming war, and she saw in his eyes the struggle to make sense of the bewildering transition from prisoner to petted prince.

The joy of Harry's arrival was quickly overshadowed by the news that the fleet commanded by Charles's cousin Prince Rupert of the Rhine, the dashing soldier son of Queen Elizabeth of Bohemia, had been scattered by a hurricane in the Caribbean Sea. In March, Rupert limped into port in France with five ships, but the *Defiance,* with his brother Maurice on board, was missing. After a terrible period of uncertainty, word came that the *Defiance* had sunk with the loss of all on board.

"This family is cursed," a distraught Queen Elizabeth declared, clinging to her daughter Louise, and a shiver went up Jane's spine. Could it be true? So much loss, so much grief.

"And the loss of Prince Maurice is not even the worst of it," Colonel O'Neill declared later, his eyes dark with grief. "Three years at sea Prince Rupert has been, privateering to raise gold for His Majesty's cause. And now much of that gold is at the bottom of the sea, and surely what he has brought safe will not be near what the king needs to make an assault on England. So much travail, and so little gained by it."

Prince Rupert arrived at The Hague in April. Jane had heard much of him when he was commanding the king's forces in Staffordshire during the war, and was curious to see how the man would measure up to the legend. Rupert had forced the surrender of Birmingham, Lichfield, and Leicester, and there had been shocked rumors of mayhem and plunder in the wake of his victories. Parliamentary broadsheets had even accused him of sorcery, claiming that his famous poodle, Boy, was his familiar, a demon hound that could catch bullets in his teeth.

Jane thought that Rupert seemed to fill the room when he swept into Mary's apartments.

He was about thirty, even taller than Charles, and like most of the Stuarts, his eyes and cascading curls were dark. He was also very well set up, strikingly handsome, and with more than a trace of the rogue about him. Jane felt a tingle of arousal as he kissed her hand, and not only because he reminded her of Charles.

Jane recalled Charles telling her about how he had worshipped his dashing cousin, ten years his senior, and she could well understand why. Rupert, then twenty-two and already a seasoned soldier and commander of the Royalist cavalry, had led the charge at Edgehill, the first real battle of the war, and had been with Charles during his wartime stay in Bristol.

"Ah, the beautiful lady who helped my royal cousin." Rupert grinned down at her. "I am longing to hear the tale."

"At Your Highness's pleasure," Jane murmured, blushing at the glint in his eyes.

"I know your brother John very well, you know," Rupert said. "He was one of the best men we had in Staffordshire."

"I thank you, Your Highness," Jane said. "He always spoke most highly of you."

This was not strictly true. John had fought with Prince Rupert and regarded him as a brutally effective commander, but also mercurial and impetuous.

The young Duke of Gloucester sidled up to his imposing cousin and offered a diffident bow. Rupert threw an arm around the boy's shoulder and shook him affectionately.

"I'm glad to see you, lad! I hear you're to be invested as Knight of the Garter soon?"

"Yes, sir, I am." Harry flushed with pleasure at the notice from his cousin. "I was hoping that you might be here when I am so honored. Especially as you have gone through it before."

He glanced down and Jane saw that Rupert wore a blue velvet garter that sparkled with diamonds just below his right knee.

"I'd not miss it for the world, boy," Rupert assured his young cousin, who seemed suddenly to stand several inches taller.

CHAPTER SEVENTEEN

PERHAPS IT WAS TRUE, AS LOUISE SAID, THAT MARY HATED THE Low Countries. Whatever the reason, she was restless, and moved her court from The Hague to Breda to Teyling to Antwerp and back, depending on her mood, the season, and what pleasures might be found at each of the palaces. In the autumn of 1653, her household embarked on the two-day journey to Breda, a pretty town built at the confluence of two rivers. Jane smiled as she recalled Charles describing it as "smelling with delight, gallantry, and wealth."

ONE AFTERNOON MARY TOOK JANE WITH HER TO PAY A CALL ON THE Hyde family, and as the carriage deposited them at their destination Jane admired the neat brick house near the old center of the city.

"You met Sir Edward Hyde in Paris, I'm sure," Mary said over her shoulder as they waited for the door to be opened to them. "He was chancellor of the exchequer to my father, you know, and during the war was guardian to my brother the king, and remains Charles's closest adviser now. The family fled England shortly after my father's murder and they have bounced from Antwerp to Brussels, never knowing how they are to live."

The door of the house opened, revealing the beaming face of a lady in her middle thirties who dropped into a deep curtsy.

"Your Royal Highness!" she cried as Mary raised her and kissed her. "Welcome!"

Lady Hyde's brood of children gathered to be introduced and to look on wide-eyed as their mother visited with the Princess Royal and Jane. Lawrence and Henry were about twelve and fifteen years of age, and little Frances was surely not yet ten, Jane thought. The eldest daughter, Anne, was a pretty dark-haired girl of about sixteen, old enough to sit with the ladies over chocolate and cakes.

"We cannot thank you enough, Your Highness, for your kindness and generosity in providing this house," Lady Hyde said, looking almost on the verge of tears.

"Why, it's the very least I could do, after the many years of loyal and wise service you have given us," Mary smiled. "It must be very hard on you to have your husband so far away for so long. At least there will be a home for him to come to when my brother can do without him for a few weeks."

"Have you word of His Majesty?" Anne Hyde asked. "My father wrote this summer that the king had been ill and had been bled several times."

"He is better now, thanks be to God," Mary said. "I'm sure the worry over money and what he is to do next affect his health."

"My husband's letters are full of the dire poverty of the poor young king and his followers," said Lady Hyde. "King Louis has granted His Majesty a pension, Edward writes, but is slow to pay it."

"Yes, poor Charles relies on money from Royalists at home for his very meals. And of course, if the French enter into an alliance with Cromwell, not only will the pension fail to come but Charles will have to leave Paris." Mary shook her head. "He thinks of going back to Scotland, but . . ."

She trailed off and Jane recalled the frustration and despair in Charles's voice when he had told her of his stay in Scotland before marching to his defeat at Worcester.

"Of course the right marriage would go a long way to helping him," Lady Hyde said. "A princess who would give him the armies and the money he needs to take back his throne."

"Yes," Mary sighed,"but it's easier said than done, I'm afraid. Charles may be king, but when monarchs go to market looking for bridegrooms for their daughters, there are many candidates whose prospects are much more certain."

MARY'S COURT MOVED TO TEYLING FOR CHRISTMAS, AND JANE WAS happy to receive a long letter from Charles, delivered once more by Colonel O'Neill along with a small package, which proved to be a volume of Shakespeare's sonnets.

"My dear Jane," Charles wrote. "I recalled you telling me how much you enjoyed the book of sonnets you received not long before we met, and how it grieved you to leave it behind. I hope you will take pleasure in this little gift, and think of me when you read it.

"There is no news here but the thought that never leaves my mind—how and when I may return to England. As you will no doubt have heard, that rogue Cromwell has recently taken upon himself the title of Lord Protector. What a travesty is there—it makes the bile rise in my throat!

"Hyde believes that I will be restored from within my country rather than by the efforts of those elsewhere, and that for a rising to be successful it must be planned carefully, to have the means and men to make it happen, and given the time to ripen, or all is lost. I am sure he is right, but I chafe with inaction, and murmur, 'If it were done, when 'tis done, then 'twere well it were done quickly.'

"Even as I write those lines I hear your voice in my head. You would remind me, I am sure, that the king who spoke those thoughts did not prosper, and counsel me to have patience, and so I will endeavor to heed your unspoken wisdom."

Jane smiled with pleased amusement that Charles knew exactly what she would be likely to have told him, and could very clearly picture him shaking his head in resignation.

"My brother James is lately returned from service in the army of my cousin Louis, full of reputation and honor," Charles's letter continued. "I am pleased for his success and the happiness it brings him—and for the sighing glances of the French ladies, I might add—and yet it makes me only too aware that I kick my heels with nothing to do.

"I will leave off here, for I can hear you cry, 'Pray you no more of this, 'tis like the howling of Irish wolves against the moon!' Please believe that you are ever in my heart, your affectionate friend, Charles R."

THE BITTER WINTER WINDS SHRIEKED THROUGH THE LOW COUNTRIES, and the brief respites of cold sunshine in the long black nights were never enough to warm Jane's bones or raise her spirits. But at last, spring breathed warmth into the frozen ground, the ice on the canals cracked and then melted, and the soft shoots of new plants created a green haze over the land.

"That son of mine is finally going to bring me to Heidelberg Castle!" Queen Elizabeth told Jane excitedly one day, waving a letter.

The queen had been waging an ongoing battle with her son, Charles Louis, Elector of Palatine, to get him to provide her with either a home or money on which to live, for she, like Charles, was entirely dependent on the charity of her friends and relations for her most basic needs.

"How wonderful!" Jane cried, taking the old lady's hands. "You will at last be reunited with your daughters!"

She knew what sorrow it had caused Queen Elizabeth that she could not afford to keep the Princesses Elizabeth and Sophie with her at The Hague, and that they had gone to their brother's court.

"Yes. But I wonder . . ." Jane found that Queen Elizabeth was regarding her with curiosity. "I wonder if you might like to come with me, dear Jane? I should miss your company very much, were I to leave here."

The idea was startling, but immediately appealing. Jane had little in common with most of Mary's other ladies, who were interested in little more than gowns and gossip. She would be happy to be able to resume the friendship with the Princess Elizabeth, which had budded only for them to be parted, and the court at Heidelberg was bound to be exciting and interesting. Moreover, the recent treaty between the United Provinces and the Commonwealth of England forbade The Hague from welcoming Charles. If she was in Heidelberg, she might stand a better chance of seeing him, she reasoned.

Over the next weeks, Queen Elizabeth's war of letters with her son continued, but by early summer, the plans for the move to Heidelberg had fallen through. Jane had barely had time to be disappointed, though, when she received a letter from Charles that made her heart sing.

"My royal cousin Louis has decided that the inconvenience of having me in Paris now outweighs the expense of making it possible for me to leave. He has promised that I shall have full payment of the pension he has long promised me if I am gone from France in ten days. I have written to my sister to join me at Spa for some little time of liberty, and I hope that I shall have the pleasure of your company there as well."

NESTLED IN A GREEN VALLEY IN THE ARDENNES MOUNTAINS OF Brabant, Spa in the summertime would have seemed like heaven to Jane even without Charles's presence, but she was elated to find him in good spirits, and his welcome of her was all that she had dared to hope for.

"My Jane!" he cried, sweeping her off her feet and into his arms. "Heaven and earth, but you are beautiful—positively blooming."

Jane laughed as he kissed her, giddy with joy.

Mary had taken the two best hotels in the town for the royal party. Besides Lady Stanhope, she had brought only Jane and Kate Killigrew as her attendants, but Charles had arrived with a boisterous party that included Lord Wilmot, recently created Earl of Rochester, whom Jane had not seen since Trent; Colonel O'Neill; the Marquess of Ormonde; his loyal friend and spymaster Nick Armourer; and, to Jane's joy, Henry Lascelles.

"His Majesty is right," Henry grinned, pulling her into his arms and kissing her cheek. "You are looking most fetching—the air at The Hague must agree with you." He tugged on one of her curls, as he had done when she was a young girl. "When His Majesty said you'd be here, I knew I must come."

That evening seemed tinged with magic. After a supper of rabbit stew and plenty of honeylike wine, the tables were cleared away for dancing, and the room glowed golden from the dozens of candles in their wall brackets and chandeliers. Charles danced with Jane again and again, and now, as the little band of musicians struck up the tune for a country dance, he drew her close to him. Her head was pleasantly fuddled from wine and she felt a surge of desire at the feel of his hand on her back. He leaned closer, whispering in her ear.

"Oh, Jane, I want you." The warmth of his breath sent shivers through her.

"Yes," she whispered back, feeling herself near to swooning with longing to have him take her.

"My room is just above. Meet me on the stairs in a minute."

His eyes were hot on her and she felt she could barely breathe as he squeezed her hand. The dance came to an end and he bowed and left the room, and Jane edged into the shadows, forcing herself to count to a hundred before she followed him.

He was waiting and pulled her to him fiercely, his mouth devouring hers, and she gasped with desire as he pulled away and led her up the stairs. He barely paused to bar the door behind them, hoisting Jane into his arms and carrying her to the bed. She moaned as his hand reached beneath her skirts, the roughness of his fingers sliding up her thighs, finding the molten core of desire at the center of her being.

She cried out as he entered her, so hard, filling her, conquering her, erasing awareness of anything but the feel of him within her and the weight of him above her. Low animal sounds came from her throat, mingling with his guttural breaths, and they clutched each other fiercely, as if they would meld themselves into one. A wave was roaring to a crest inside Jane and she cried out as it crashed within her, gasping for breath as the sensation ebbed, leaving a shimmering, bubbling joy on the sand of her being.

"How I have missed you," Charles murmured afterward, nuzzling Jane's ear as he held her close.

Of course Jane and Kate had to help Mary undress and prepare herself for bed, but after that Jane slipped away to join Charles once more, leaving his arms only when the first blush of dawn lit the sky. Kate sat up in bed when she crept into the room they shared, and raised an eyebrow.

"Sleep well, did you?"

"What sleep there was, was lovely," Jane grinned.

The day was glorious and sunny, and Jane sat happily next to Charles as the merry party rode out to the gurgling hot springs where they waded bare-legged, not minding their soaked skirts and breeches. As Mary and Lady Stanhope were not suitable partners for raillery, Jane and Kate alone basked in the full force of pent-up male energy now released in the holiday mood. Yet Jane sensed that though the young men teased and laughed with her, they kept a certain distance, and it was Charles who was closest to her side.

That night Jane once more spent with Charles, but when she stole into her own room in the morning, she was distressed to see Kate curled in bed, pale and drenched with sweat.

"What's amiss with thee?" Jane asked, putting a hand on Kate's forehead. "Faith, you're fair burning."

"Yet I cannot stop shaking," Kate whimpered, shivering miserably. "And my head's pounding."

Jane soaked a cloth in water and wrung it out, bathed Kate's face and chest, helped her into a clean nightgown, and gave her water to drink, and Kate dropped off to sleep, but Jane was alarmed at her ragged breathing, and stayed behind to sit with her while Mary went adventuring with Charles and his coterie.

By afternoon, Kate was writhing from pain in her belly, her discomfort only made worse by vomiting. Jane's blood ran cold when she noted the swellings in Kate's neck, armpits, and groin, and sent for a doctor.

The ruddy white-haired man examined Kate only briefly before motioning Jane to follow him from the room.

"*La peste,*" he said. "It is the plague."

Jane's heart stood still. The plague, and she had been touching Kate for hours, wiping the sweat from her face, bathing her pain-racked body, holding a basin and pulling back her hair while she vomited.

"It is better maybe you do not go back in," the doctor said, eyeing her steadily. Jane was afraid, but the thought of leaving Kate alone was unbearable.

"It's too late. If I'm to become ill, there's naught I can do about it now."

She started for the door and then was brought to a standstill and staggered with a wave of nausea as a further realization struck her—Charles. Of course no one knew just how the contagion passed from person to person, but she had been so close to Kate for days, and then so close—so very close—to Charles. Was it not likely that she had borne the seeds of the plague on her and that he might even now be falling ill?

Oh God, she prayed, *let not the wages of my foolish sin be paid to the king, on whom so much depends.*

The doctor gave Kate a brew to ease her pain, and Jane sat with her as the light faded and the little room was engulfed in shadow, and then by the light of a candle as the world darkened to black outside the window. Kate became delirious, thrashing and moaning and calling for her mother, and Jane wept for Kate's loneliness and pain and for her own, wishing herself home with her own mother and father, with John and her other siblings. And with Clement Fisher? He, too, hovered in the picture of home.

Kate died before dawn, her fever-bright eyes wreathed in shadow and the buboes in her groin and armpits swollen to purple-black eggs.

Jane had hot water for a bath brought to another room and soaked herself, scrubbing away the lingering scent of Kate's sweat from her skin and hair even as the tears ran down her face. Before she dressed, she peered anxiously at her reflection in the mirror for any signs of the plague. She felt gingerly in her armpits and groin, dreading the tenderness that might be the precursor to the deadly swelling, but found nothing amiss. She put on fresh clothes and sent those she had been wearing away to be burned, but still she felt alive to every sensation of her body, terrified that fever would seize her.

The terrible news of Kate's death spread rapidly through the followers of Charles and Mary, and those who were lodging in the hotel in which Kate had fallen ill hastily decamped to crowd into the other establishment. Jane, terrified at the thought that she might prove the means of the king's death after she and Charles and so many others had undergone such dangers to keep him safe, sequestered herself in a little room at the top of the inn. She huddled by the fireplace, wrapped in a blanket, shivering with fear and sorrow. A knock at the door that evening signaled that her supper had been left on a tray outside the chamber, and she clutched the stoneware mug of soup to her, warming her hands as she sipped the golden broth.

Jane stood at the window and watched the sun drop below the horizon and the shadows lengthen across the fields. Just over the road, she knew, were Charles and Mary and all the rest of their company, but she thought she had never felt so alone in her life.

A rapping at the door startled her.

"Who's there?" she called.

"It's me. Henry." Jane raced to the door and opened it. Her dear cousin stood there, and she longed to throw her arms around him, but instead took a step back.

"Henry, why have you come? You must not place yourself in such danger!"

A gust of wind from the corridor rattled the shutters outside the windows, and Henry stepped into the room, closing the door behind him.

"I had to come," he said, and Jane saw in his eyes what she had never properly noticed before. He loved her, not as her cousin, but as a man loves a woman.

"The king and the Princess Royal are gravely concerned about the plague, as well they might be," he said. "They are going to Aix-la-Chapelle in the morning."

"Oh."

Jane felt her stomach drop. She would be alone once more, truly alone, with the fear of the plague.

"But I am not," Henry said. "I shall stay here with you."

He sat on a chair before the fire and threw his hat onto the floor, and gave her a lopsided smile.

This was bravery, Jane thought. Not all the fighting in all the battles of the war equaled Henry's courage tonight.

"I have a note for you from the king," Henry said, holding out a folded and sealed paper. He walked toward the window and gazed out as Jane opened the letter with trembling fingers.

"My dear Jane," it read. "I hope you will understand that for the sake of many more people than you or me, I must put aside my strong wish to be at your side and instead remove myself. Aix-la-Chapelle is but a day's ride, and I swear I will not smile again until you are once more within my sight, healthy and whole."

That night as she lay curled in bed, listening to Henry's gentle snoring from the pallet before the fireplace, Jane could not erase from her mind the feel of Kate's hand in hers, warm with fever and clutching for some unseen thing or person, then going limp, the fingertips turning cool and waxy pale with astonishing swiftness.

Jane woke in the morning feeling exhausted and racked with emotion, but she had no fever, chills, or headache, and found no swelling when she examined herself with her hands. When she continued to feel well the next day, her hopes rose. And when a week had passed and she showed no sign of the plague, she threw herself into Henry's arms and wept for relief.

"Thank you," she murmured against his chest as he held her and stroked her hair. "Oh, Henry, I can never thank you enough."

As she smiled up at him, he bent his head to kiss her, and his mouth was on hers before she could stop him.

"I can't," she cried, pulling away from him, hands on his chest to keep him from grasping her to him, and her heart hurt to see the sadness in his eyes.

"Can you not love me?" he asked.

"I do, of course I do. But not—not like that."

It sounded so cruel, she thought, but it was the truth.

"Because of him? Because of the king?"

"Yes. No. I don't know. I know he cannot marry me, of course I know that. And yet—he holds my heart."

Henry nodded silently, his eyes downcast, then met her eyes with a sad smile.

"Then there's nothing for it but to get on as best I may."

JANE AND HENRY SET OUT FOR AIX-LA-CHAPELLE IN THE MORNING on a hired horse, Jane riding pillion, and it brought vividly to her mind the many miles they had ridden together three years earlier, all the long way from Trent to Bentley. The countryside was glorious in the summer sun, the fields on either side of the road golden with tasseled grain and the air heavy with the scent of grapes as they rode through vineyards, the gnarled vines curling on their stakes. They sang and exchanged stories of what their lives had been like since they had last met, and the sorrow of the previous night seemed to have evaporated.

A long day's ride brought them to Aix-la-Chapelle, where Holland met the lands of the Rhine. The royal party rejoiced when Jane and Henry made their appearance at the inn that had become their headquarters in the town, and Charles pulled Jane to him, heedless of the eyes upon them.

"Oh, Jane," he murmured into her ear. "Thank God you are well and with me once more. Can you forgive me for abandoning you?"

"Quite easily," Jane murmured, amazed that it was true. "What fools we all would have looked to have taken such pains to bring you safe out of England only to have you die of the plague."

"I MUST HAVE ANOTHER LADY TO REPLACE POOR KATE," MARY FRETted that evening. "But who am I to get?"

Jane suddenly thought of the Hyde family in Breda, and the look of admiration and longing on young Anne's face as she listened to Mary talk about the doings at her court.

"What about Nan Hyde?" Jane asked, and was relieved to see Mary's face brighten.

"An excellent idea! She is a good girl, most pleasant company, and surely would welcome a change from being cooped at home with her mother and the young ones. I'll write to Lady Hyde now."

BY THE TIME NAN HYDE AND HER MOTHER ARRIVED AT AIX-LA-Chapelle in the first week of September, Charles's merry band had swollen to near eighty. It seemed to Jane that every young Englishman within two days' fast riding had come to join the king and his sister in their holiday making. There were excited rumors that Queen Christina of Sweden, who had abdicated her throne three months earlier, had fled her country on horseback wearing man's apparel and might appear to join the royal siblings.

As they sat on a blanket spread on a green hillside sprinkled with little white flowers, Nan looked with keen interest at the tall young man laughing with Charles and Mary, his head thrown back and his long curls blowing in the breeze.

"Who is that?" she whispered. "I haven't seen him before."

"Prince Rupert," Jane said. "His Majesty's cousin. A fine-looking man, is he not?"

"Most handsomely made, indeed," Nan smiled. "And not so fierce as I would have thought, for such a celebrated warrior."

"He is not all fire and ice," Jane laughed. "Indeed, there are rumors that our mistress might marry him."

She looked again at Mary, who seemed happier and lighter of spirit than Jane had ever seen her, looking up at Rupert.

The days passed in a golden haze of pleasure. Charles and Mary, happy in each other's company, threw off their cares, and their attendants caught their happy mood. Mary spent blithely on merrymaking and entertainments for everyone, and there was nothing for Jane to do but enjoy herself. During the days they wandered the pretty streets of the city, visited the shrine to Charlemagne in the cathedral, bathed in the healing waters, and took long jaunts into the sun-drenched countryside. The evenings were filled with suppers, dancing, and card games.

Mary had either not detected the fact that Jane did not always sleep in the room she shared with Nan Hyde, or she was turning a blind eye, and Jane passed blissful nights in Charles's arms. He spent so much time with her that she knew there were no other women competing for his company. He was hers alone, and he had assured her that if she should get with child, he would find a way to care for them. This was the joyful time to which she had looked forward since their parting.

One afternoon they stole away from the others and walked arm in arm through the marketplace, admiring the medieval stone halls nearby. Charles was relaxed, hopeful about the possibility of his restoration, and in buoyant spirits. He bought a wreath of flowers and placed it on Jane's head after unpinning her hair so that it cascaded over her shoulders.

"There." He smiled down at her. "Now you look like a proper Queen of the May."

She laughed. "But it's September!"

He kissed her, his hand warm on her cheek, his fingers tangling in her hair. "My September Queen."

He bought bread, cheese, grapes, and a stone bottle of wine, and they sat on the edge of a fountain to eat and watch the passersby. Charles fed Jane the deep red grapes, bursting with juice, kissing her between bites.

"What do you think, my love?" he asked. "Is Aix-la-Chapelle to your liking?"

"Anywhere that you are is heaven to me," she murmured, resting her head against his shoulder.

Now that Charles had money from King Louis, Jane thought, perhaps he would keep her with him when Mary returned to The Hague. Her heart sang at the prospect.

After three weeks in Aix-la-Chapelle, the royal party traveled the forty miles to Cologne, where Mary took a sunny house with gardens for her and Charles and their closest attendants. Lord Taaffe arrived with a dancing master from Paris to teach the latest dances, and at Charles's entreaty, Mary hired a company of musicians to play every night. The royal party was honored at receptions at the Jesuit College, and the city magistrates welcomed Charles and showered him with gifts. The king's retinue continued to swell. Among the more lively new additions was a handsome young man named Henry Manning, only recently come from England, who was soon seldom apart from Charles, Wilmot, and Taaffe.

"He was educated in the household of the Marquess of Worcester," Wilmot told Jane one evening, "and not only did he lose both his father and brother in the wars, he was himself seriously wounded at Alresford."

"He's most likable," Henry Lascelles put in, refilling his wineglass, "and that, coupled with the fact that unlike most of us he seems to have plenty of ready money and he delights in treating his companions, makes him a most welcome addition to our little band."

Jane smiled at her cousin. He was still affectionate, but seemed to have thrown off his air of hurt at Jane's involvement with Charles, and all was well between them once more.

"Moreover," Wilmot said, lowering his voice and glancing around to be sure he was not overheard, "Manning brings news of men, horses, arms, and gold, ready to be put to use in the king's service in England when the moment should be right. A most valuable friend he may prove to the king."

Philip William, who had recently succeeded his father as Count of Neuberg, invited Charles and Mary to his court at Düsseldorf, and the English party floated down the Rhine through golden fields. Jane was astonished at the banquet that night, when roasted swans dressed in their own feathers were succeeded by suckling pigs and then by so many dishes that she lost count. There was music and dancing, and as she watched Charles, fine in new clothes purchased in Cologne, she wished she could always see him so free of cares.

In October, Jane reflected that she had never been so happy. She had been in Charles's company almost every day and most nights for three months. On this night, he lay next to her in the dark, his eyes closed. His breathing was slow and she had thought him asleep, but he rolled toward her and pulled her against him, nuzzling the back of her neck, and she felt the hardness of him rise against her. One of his hands closed on her breast, the other slid between her legs, his fingers slipping in her slick warmth, teasing and caressing.

"We 'fleet the time carelessly, as they did in the Golden World,'" he quoted, his lips nibbling at her earlobe, and she laughed, and then gasped as his fingers caressed more insistently. She wanted to stay in his company forever, never to be parted again.

"I've been thinking," he murmured. Jane's heart leaped.

"Yes, my darling?" She moved herself against him, tremors of pleasure shivering through her.

"I think I will settle in Cologne." He traced a finger around her nipple, and she felt his prick give a little jump against her buttocks. "The burghers here offer a most welcome sanctuary, and to tell you truly, I need a refuge now more than ever, after Aix-la-Chapelle. A most expenseful place."

Jane waited. Surely he was about to tell her that she would stay with him, that her company was all he needed to complete his happiness. But he said nothing.

"And I?" she whispered.

"Hmm?"

His hands were busy on her breasts, and he rolled her onto her back and slid down to fasten his mouth on one of her nipples, his tongue moving teasingly over her flesh.

"Will I stay with you?" she asked, pulling his head up so that she could look into his eyes.

"In Cologne? Oh, Jane, the money from Louis is not all that much, really only enough to keep myself. And my time will be much taken up with the business of raising money and men. When things are more settled perhaps."

"But . . ."

No words came that could adequately express Jane's dismay and disappointment at the prospect of being parted from him again.

Charles rolled himself on top of her, nudging her thighs apart with his knee, but Jane put a hand to his chest, stopping him.

"But when will I see you again?"

"Why, I don't know, Jane, but surely before long. I shall come to visit you."

He was kissing her throat now, his mouth leaving tongues of flame on her skin. He thrust his fingers inside her, opening her to him, and she felt her resolve slip away at his touch.

"Will you?" she asked, her breath coming in short gasps. "Will you come to see me?"

"Of course," he said, easing himself inside her. "You're my Jane."

CHAPTER EIGHTEEN

MARY AND HER TRAIN LEFT CHARLES IN DÜSSELDORF TO return to The Hague while he made his way back to Cologne. Mary wept and clung to her brother, declaring she would not live until she was in his company again. Jane commanded herself not to weep at their parting, and succeeded in holding back her tears until he was out of sight only by the thought that she would see him again in several months, as he and Mary had already made plans to spend the next summer together.

Shortly after her return to The Hague, Jane was happy to receive a letter from Charles, delivered by Colonel O'Neill.

"My dear Jane: As the cold settles across the land here, so, too, it seems to settle into my bones and heart. You and my dear sister did more than you can imagine to lighten my spirits over these past months, and now that you are gone and I am left to my own company, the shadows seem to creep toward me.

"To pass the time I read—I am become most industrious in my studies of French and Italian—and hunt when I am invited. When I can read no more and must be active, I walk, as I have the means to do no more. My lord Wilmot chides me like a mother hen not to go bareheaded as I do lest I take cold, but upon my soul sometimes I think it cannot make much difference whether I live or die.

"My friends remind me that a wealthy bride is like to help me to my throne, and propose first one and then the other, but the prospect raises nothing in my heart but despair. I hate these princesses of cold northern climates.

"Were this not bad enough, scarcely had you left but I received a flock of letters from Paris with the alarming news that the queen my mother is most earnest in her efforts to change my brother Harry to a Papist, directly contrary to the last words of my dead father, and what is more, like to have grave effect upon my efforts to return into England. I have writ to her, to my brothers both, to Jermyn, to all who have a hand in it, that she must desist, and that if I have not my desire granted, it will be such a breach between the queen and me as can never be made up again."

Queen Elizabeth of Bohemia was pleased to have her niece back home, and welcomed Nan Hyde and her mother to Mary's household as she had welcomed Jane. Jane was coming to like Nan very much. The girl was smart and forthright, vivacious and good-humored, and regarded Jane, twelve years older than she, with a gratifying awe.

The Christmas season seemed brighter to Jane than any she had celebrated in years. At the palace at Teyling, the court presented a masque, with Mary dressed as a Gypsy, and Jane and Nan as shepherdesses. Jane delighted in the dancing and music, and observed with amusement how Sir Spencer Compton, the youngest son of the Earl of Northampton, followed Nan with calflike eyes wherever she went.

"He would be quite a catch," Jane whispered as Sir Spencer glanced at Nan anxiously from across the room.

"Oh, I suppose," Nan shrugged. "But somehow he doesn't appeal to me. I've never been in love. Have you?"

Jane was taken aback at the sudden blunt question and found herself stammering.

"I—yes."

"Really? With whom? Is he here? Or where is he?" Nan's brown eyes danced with excitement.

Of course Jane couldn't admit her feelings for the king. The image of Geoff Stone rose to her mind.

"He's in England. We knew each other before the war, but then his family fought against the king."

"Oh." The merriment faded from Nan's eyes. "So many possibilities ruined by the arch rogue, as Her Majesty calls Cromwell."

THE PRINCESS ROYAL ANNOUNCED THAT SHE WOULD VISIT HER mother in Paris, and as Jane packed for the journey, she recalled Princess Louise's comment that Mary hated the Netherlands. Perhaps it was true, for Mary certainly spent much time away from there, though it meant leaving her little son William, now four and a half years old, in the company of his nurses. Child though he was, he was a prince of Orange, and must remain in his lands.

Jane had thought that perhaps Charles would join them in France, but as she was packing for the journey, she received a letter from him that disappointed her hopes of seeing him, but raised bright prospects for his future.

"March 15, 1655. My dear Jane: I write to you in haste from Middleburg, whither I have come to be ready to embark for England, for though I scarce dare write it, there are risings afoot at home that promise much. I have thought much of you these last days, as I rode hither from Cologne with only my lord Ormonde and a groom, using once more the name of Jackson. I would you had been with me; it would have lightened my heart and my spirits much. I will write to you when I can. Your most affectionate friend, Charles R."

The hopeful news from Charles added to the holiday spirit as Mary's entourage set out on their journey. Jane, Nan, and Lady Stanhope rode with Mary in her carriage, followed by a string of carriages and wagons bearing servants and the clothes and household items without which the Princess Royal could not travel, and guards to watch over them. The party made its way from The Hague to Antwerp and then to Brussels. At Mons they were greeted by the celebratory firing of cannon and the city magistrates accorded to Mary the customary honor of setting the watchword for the night. On the train went through Flanders, finally crossing into France. Smiling country folk waved from the side of the road, awed by the royal cavalcade, and when they reached Peronne, Mary cried out in delight to learn that her brothers, the Duke of York and the Duke of Gloucester, had come to meet her and accompany her the rest of the way to Paris.

The young dukes galloped toward Mary's carriage on two fine dark geldings, and Mary leaped out to embrace them.

"Harry!" she cried, holding the Duke of Gloucester at arm's length. "Look at you—standing head and shoulders above me now!"

It was true; the boy Jane had met more than two years ago was now fifteen and had turned into a young man, who greeted Jane with grown-up gravity.

The Duke of York had arranged a lavish supper for his sister and her attendants, and the castle in which they were to lodge was far more grand than any place they had stopped since leaving The Hague. As Jane followed Mary into the great hall, she surveyed the room happily. She was much more comfortable than she had been in days, having had a bath and put on clean clothes, and she was looking forward to the meal that promised to be delicious, judging by the smells wafting on the air.

"Mistress Lane!"

Jane turned at the sound of the familiar voice to see the Duke of York approaching her, followed closely by two elegantly dressed gentlemen.

"Mistress Lane, I didn't greet you properly before. What a great pleasure to see you again," the duke said, raising Jane from her curtsy.

"I thank you, Your Highness," she smiled. "What a lovely welcome."

The duke's looks had much improved in the three years since she had seen him, Jane thought. At nineteen he had been almost as tall as Charles, but slender and gawky, looking hardly more than a boy. Now he had fleshed out. His shoulders were broader, and Jane thought it was more than just the elegant blue officer's coat he wore that gave him an air of self-assurance and command. He wore his own hair, which lightened from a golden brown at the top of his head to a rich honey in the curls that fell over his shoulders.

"Lord Gerard and Sir Charles Berkeley," the duke said, indicating the men who stood at either side of him.

"Of course." Jane smiled at the duke's companions, handsome men both. Perhaps the remainder of the journey to Paris would be quite pleasant, if they were along. Jane felt rather than saw a presence just behind her right elbow, and turned to see that Nan Hyde was standing there, her eyes shining with excitement as she gazed at the three young men before her.

"Your Highness," Jane said. "May I present Mistress Anne Hyde, the eldest daughter of Sir Edward, who has lately joined me in service of Her Royal Highness."

Nan sank in a graceful bow, the cloud-blue silk of her gown pooling on the floor around her, and as she raised her eyes to meet the duke's, Jane noted the look of thunderstruck enchantment that passed over his face, and the blush that spread over Nan's roselike cheeks as he kissed her hand.

"Mistress Anne," the duke murmured. "The next time I see your father I shall have to chide him for denying us your acquaintance until now."

Nan giggled, almost wriggling like a puppy, Jane thought, and Gerard and Berkeley exchanged a knowing look behind the duke's back.

The evening's supper and dancing were merry, and Jane's enjoyment was heightened by the knowledge that they were now within a few days' journey of Paris. She was struck by the image of golden rays, like those of the sun, reaching from Paris to warm the reaches of the French countryside.

LATER THAT NIGHT, AS JANE UNDRESSED FOR BED, SHE NOTED NAN staring dreamily at her own reflection in the mirror as she brushed her hair.

"You look as though you've got a bit of moonbeam caught in your eye," she murmured. Nan did not respond at first, and when she realized Jane had spoken to her, laughed self-consciously.

"Oh! I was only thinking that I hope the Duke of York shall remain in Paris once we get there."

"I expect he shall," Jane said, looking closely at Nan's face. "You like him, do you?"

Nan flushed to the roots of her hair but nodded emphatically. "I think he's the most beautiful man I've ever seen."

Jane smiled. So there was a man who could pique Nan's interest. Too bad that aside from Charles himself, the Duke of York was about the only man in the world that Anne Hyde could not hope to marry.

THE COUNTRYSIDE THROUGH WHICH THE CONVOY PASSED NOW WAS close to the way that Jane and John had traveled from Dieppe to Paris after their long walk to Yarmouth, and Jane reflected what a difference, from that last exhausted leg of their terrifying journey, to this luxurious jaunt.

Queen Mary and Minette, now eleven years old, met Mary's retinue at Bourget.

"Oh, what a beautiful thing you are," Mary cried, taking Minette into her arms. "What a treasure!"

The queen embraced Jane like a long-lost daughter.

"Mistress Jane, how happy I am that you are here with us. You must come and visit with me when you are settled and tell me all your news."

The royal family, all together except for Charles, were feted by the French court. Suppers, dancing, music, theater, every day some new excitement. Nan Hyde and the Duke of York were frequently near each other, and one night at supper Jane noted the sour look on Queen Mary's face as she watched the duke lean close to Nan to whisper something to her, and Nan blush and giggle in delight.

"He told me he loves me!" Nan told Jane that night as they undressed for bed. "Oh, Jane, I have never been so happy in my life."

"I'm glad for you, sweetheart," Jane said, taking in the glow that suffused Nan's face. "But have a care."

"What do you mean?" Nan demanded, her forehead puckered with sudden worry.

Tread carefully, Jane told herself. She recalled her pain when Mademoiselle d'Épernon had warned her against giving her whole heart to Charles.

"I mean that though no doubt he loves you, if he says so, it does not mean that he can marry you. Should something happen to the king, the duke would succeed him. The choice of his bride will not be his alone."

"Oh, pooh," Nan scoffed. "I'll not worry about that now. It scarce seems likely that His Majesty will ever sit on the throne, let alone that his brother will, does it?"

Jane thought of her last letter from Charles, and his hopes for the risings at home.

"Perhaps it doesn't seem likely now. But we cannot tell what may come."

Her heart ached to see Nan looking sad now, and she went to the girl and stroked her cheek and smiled. "Take pleasure in his company, by all means. But keep your mind open to other possibilities if you can."

The following week, Nan fell ill, and the doctors gave the dreaded news that it was smallpox. Jane sat with Nan in the evening, reading to her and coaxing her to drink some broth to keep up her strength. When Nan had at length fallen asleep, Jane left the room to find the Duke of York lurking outside the door.

"How is she?" he asked anxiously. "Can I see her?"

"She's sleeping now, Your Highness," Jane said, looking up into his gray eyes, clouded with worry. "I'll tell her in the morning that you were here. But surely it would be more wise not to endanger yourself by visiting her until she's better?"

She was surprised to see tears in his eyes.

"I don't care what happens to me," he whispered. "If she should—if she should not recover, I don't know what I'll do."

"I'll come to you in the morning," Jane promised, "and tell you how she does. But I pray you have a care for yourself, Your Highness. Sleep, and hope for the best."

Against all odds, Nan's condition improved over the next few days, and soon the doctors pronounced her out of danger.

"Thank God," Nan said, examining her reflection anxiously in a hand mirror as she lay in bed. "My face is not scarred. I don't think I could have borne that. How could I have faced His Highness with a pockmarked face?"

"You are most fortunate indeed," Jane agreed. "But if he loves you, surely it would not have made any difference in his feelings."

The spirits of the English in Paris were downcast by the news that the uprisings at home had been found out and put down, and that Charles had returned to Cologne, seemingly further than ever from being restored to his throne. Jane received a letter from him, and hurried to read it in private.

"My dearest Jane: As you will hear by others, my great hopes were disappointed. Of course many lay the failure at my door, and I am sure the talk is even more blameful where you are, but I pray do not give credit to those people who take upon them to censure whatever I do, and have no way to appear wise but to find fault with whatever is done. They who will not believe anything to be reasonably designed except it be successfully executed had need of a less difficult game to play than mine is. I hope we shall shortly see a turn, and (though it be deferred longer than I expected), I shall live to bid you welcome to Whitehall. Your most affectionate friend, Charles R."

Hard on the heels of the discouraging news from England, a mud-spattered messenger arrived from The Hague with word that Mary's little son William was ill with the measles, and within hours, Mary's carriage was clattering away from Paris and toward home as Jane and Lady Stanhope tried to comfort the weeping Princess Royal. Nan was tearful, too, and Jane knew it was because she had been parted from the Duke of York.

Little William was out of danger by the time his mother reached him, but the hurried trip had been wearing, and Jane sank exhausted into bed, glad to be done with traveling.

MARY WAS STILL PLANNING TO SPEND THE SUMMER WITH CHARLES in Cologne, and Jane was eagerly counting the days until she would see him again. In June, less than a week before they were to leave, she received a letter from her mother. She opened it eagerly, always glad of news from home. But her face fell as she read, and Nan looked up in alarm at Jane's little cry of dismay.

"What is it?"

"My brother and my father have been arrested," Jane said, the blood draining from her face. "And my uncle. They were not told the cause, my mother writes, but she is in great fear that it is to do with our helping the king."

Her mind raced with helpless anxiety. Her poor father was sixty-five years old, and his health would surely suffer if he were imprisoned for long. And if it were proved that John had helped the king to escape, and had then helped her, it would mean his death, and his large family would be left to struggle without him. The thought that her father, brother, and uncle could already be dead overwhelmed her.

She could not go to see Charles now, she realized with a pang. She must stay and wait for further news, for she would not be able to live with herself if she had gone gadding to Cologne, losing herself in carnal ecstasy in Charles's arms, while her brave old father and uncle and John met their deaths.

Jane retreated to her room and wept. Waves of homesickness washed over her. Particulars of Bentley and the family sprang to her mind in vivid detail. Nurse's faint fragrance of the lavender in which she kept her clothes, the clouds of blossoms when the orchard was in bloom, the old mark in the dark paneling of the great hall to mark the height of Walter Parsons, the Staffordshire giant. The raven with the crooked beak that lurked near the banqueting house. And her cat, Jack. She could see his tranquil pale green eyes and stumping gate, and wished desperately she could clasp him to her and feel the rumble of his purr against her. The thought of him was more than she could bear, and she clung to her pillow and sobbed.

The terrifying news from home reawakened Jane's anxiety about her place in Charles's heart. She wrote to tell him that she would not be able to accompany Mary on the summer's visit, and added, striving to keep her tone light, that he must surely forget her after such a long absence. Charles's letter was reassuring in its promptness and bluntness.

"My dear Jane: I did not think I should ever have begun a letter to you with chiding, but you give so just cause by telling me you fear you are wearing out of my memory, that I cannot choose but tell you I take it very unkindly, after the obligations I have to you, that 'tis possible for you to suspect that I can ever be so wanting to myself as not to remember them on all occasions to your advantage. Which I assure you I shall, and hope before it be long I shall have it in power to give you those testimonies of my kindness to you which I desire.

"I am very sorry to hear that your father and brother are in prison, but I hope it is upon no other score than the general clapping up of all persons who wish me well. And I am the more sorry for it since it hath hindered you from coming along with my sister, that I might have assured you myself how truly I am your most affectionate friend, Charles R."

Jane read the letter over again, smiling at the thought of how he would have assured her how truly he was her most affectionate friend if they were together. So he did miss her.

Mary departed for Cologne in July, and Jane consoled herself with the company of Queen Elizabeth and Princess Louise, and awaited further news from home.

Clement Fisher wrote, assuring Jane that he had been to Bentley to offer any assistance that her mother and family might need while John and Thomas Lane were in prison.

"It is a troubling time," he wrote. "There are rumors that Cromwell might be crowned king, a sad and ironic thing, if it should come to pass. There are even wild whispers that the king might marry one of Cromwell's daughters, and so find his way back to some kind of rule, though it seems to me that such a beast, half monarchy and half republic, would not live long, and from what I have heard of the king it scarcely seems a thing to be believed."

No, Jane thought. She couldn't imagine Charles meekly accepting joint rule with Cromwell, and sitting down at a council table with the men who had been responsible for his father's murder.

She received a letter from Charles a few weeks later. "My sister and I have made a jolly journey to Frankfurt. We have come incognito, but 'tis so great a secret that not above half the town knows it. There is a company of English players here, and I thought of you, Jane, and how you would have enjoyed their show, perhaps especially because there were women among the players—actresses! What a novel idea it is—it improves the playing, I think, to have real women. And not only for the reason you may suppose I think of!

"One night at the theater there was a scene that did not take place upon the stage. We entered only to see that my cousin Charles Louis, the Elector Palatine, was there. He and his brother Rupert spent much time at my father's court when I was a boy, and he was with us early in the difficulties with Parliament, but he soon turned his back on our cause. Worse yet, he made peace with the rebels, and took up residence at Whitehall, hoping that Cromwell would make him king in place of my father. Most shameful, especially as he had often importuned my father to help him regain the Palatinate.

"As you can imagine, I cannot stomach him now, and we turned on our heels and strode from the theater, leaving him stammering and red-faced in our wake.

"Cologne is not a little altered, for from having very little company, and some of those worse than none, we have now as good as can be, and pass our time as well as people can do that have no more money, for we dance and play as if we had taken the Plate Fleet, though I am confident our losses are not so great as Cromwell's are, who for certain has received a very considerable one at Hispaniola, and we are in great hopes of the breach between Spain and England.

"We have here a very great intrigue between Sir A.H. and Mrs. P., which I believe will end in matrimony, and I conclude it the rather, because I have observed a cloud in his face at any time these two months, which Giov. Battista della Porta in his *Physonomia* says foretells misfortune. Ever your loving friend, Charles R."

Mary was back at The Hague in October, bearing gifts for Jane from herself and Charles.

"I fear my poor brother is losing hope of being restored," she told Jane. "And his penury gnaws at him, at his pride and his sense of himself. He told me he was so poor he had not eaten meat for ten days together in July, and of course his followers are in the same state."

Jane heard little from Charles over the next months, and her heart bled to think of him dispirited and sad.

Soon after the New Year, Jane was cheered by a visit from Henry Lascelles, but dismayed at his news.

"Do you recall Henry Manning?" Henry asked, grim-faced.

"That convivial young man who joined us in Cologne? Yes, why?" Jane wondered.

"That convivial young man proved to be a spy," Henry growled. "He followed His Majesty to Middleburg last spring and reported on his movements to the rebels, as well as betraying the much he knew of loyalists at home. The failure of the risings owed somewhat to his intelligence, and there were many died in England because of him."

"What happened to him?" Jane asked, afraid to hear the answer.

"We took him in the act of writing to Cromwell's man Thurloe. He attempted to tear up the papers but we prevented him, and he had about him plenty more that damned him. The king and others questioned him. He denied and equivocated, the cowardly dog, but at last he admitted all, and we shot him in the woods outside Cologne."

Jane could imagine only too well how such betrayal must eat at Charles's heart, make him wary of trusting anyone, and how he must despair at ever returning to his kingdom.

"I hope you will remember," she wrote to him, "the constancy and love shown to you by so many of your subjects during those weeks we were together and afterward. Poor people, to whom the reward of a thousand pounds for betraying you would mean the ability to keep them and their families in comfort for the rest of their lives, yet they kept their silence and did for you whatever they could, though to do so put them in great peril. Pray do not let the treachery of one man blind you to the loyalty of many more."

She read the letter over, feeling once more the excitement of the days and nights they had shared.

"My darling, it breaks my heart to think that one you thought your friend should prove so false. I wish I could hold you to me, give you the comfort of my arms as I did in those nights we were together. I would smooth your brow with my hand and kiss away the sting of treachery. If I could march on England alone and vanquish the rebels, you know I would do it, and gladly, too. Take heart, my love, for I am sure in my soul that the day will come that the king will enjoy his own again. With love always, your Jane."

Some weeks later Mr. Boswell, a hanger-on at Mary's court, came to The Hague from Cologne. Jane hated his leering insinuations, his constant preening and boasting, and her heart sank as he approached her, a smirk on his fat red face.

"Mistress Lane! The sage who counsels the king!"

"What do you mean, sir?" He had the look of a cat stalking a mouse, and she struggled to keep her voice calm.

"Why," Boswell cried, pouncing once she had taken the hook, "I was in His Majesty's bedchamber t'other day"—he drawled with elaborate carelessness—"and His Majesty read out your letter to him."

Jane felt her face burn. Surely Charles had not read out her letter, such private thoughts and memories meant only for him, to a crowd of strangers? All that day the thought lay heavy in her mind. She pictured Charles in the midst of his friends, laughing at her care and advice. Throughout the week she teetered between thinking it would not be like him to do so, and fearing that perhaps she had so fallen in his esteem that he would mock her. That notion infuriated her, and she sat down to write another letter.

"Mr. Boswell says that you read my letter to your friends. It was meant for your eyes alone, and I would not have written in such unguarded terms had I known that it should be made public. I regret it much if my writing is unwelcome or my love to you is troublesome. I would not for the world thrust myself where I am not wanted."

She folded the letter, stamped the seal into the hot wax, and handed it off to the messenger who would leave shortly for Cologne before she could change her mind.

Once more, Charles's response was swift, accompanying Henry Lascelles to The Hague.

"My dearest Jane, I hope you do not believe that hearing from a person I am so much beholding to can be in the least degree troublesome to me, that am so sensible of the obligations I have to you, but on the contrary, 'tis a very great satisfaction to me to hear from you; and for that which Mr. Boswell is pleased to tell you concerning your giving me good counsel in a letter, and my making it public in my bedchamber, is not the first lie that he has made, nor will it be the last, for I am certain there was never anything spoken in the bedchamber in my hearing to any such purpose, nor, I am confident, when I am not there, for I believe Mr. Boswell's end is to show his frequent being in my bedchamber, which is as true as the other. Your cousin will let you know that I have given orders for my picture for you, and if in this or in anything else I can show the sense I have of that which I owe you, pray let me know it, and it shall be done by your most assured and constant friend, Charles R."

CHAPTER NINETEEN

Soon after the New Year of 1656 had begun, Jane heard that Charles's once-love Lucy Walter had arrived at The Hague.

"She's living with Thomas Howard!" Nan Hyde whispered. "With the king's bastard and that of Lord Taaffe!" Howard, the brother of the Duke of Suffolk, was one of Mary's household, with apartments in the Stadtholder's Palace. "Mary's in a mighty rage about it, but what's the poor girl to do? Taaffe has done with her, and the king has no money to keep her."

A few days later, Jane came upon Lucy and her two children in one of the long galleries of the palace. Lucy smiled at her tentatively.

"Mistress Lane! What a pleasure to see you here."

"And you." Jane's eyes went to the young boy seated on the floor before the fireplace, engrossed in laying out toy soldiers in ranks. He was about seven, cherub-cheeked and rosy-lipped, but the eyes he turned on her were somber and purposeful.

"I am going to invade England," he explained solemnly, pointing at his wooden soldiers. "And then the king my father will have his crown again."

"His Majesty is lucky to have such a general as you," Jane said, kneeling next to the boy. He nodded and straightened a soldier's position. He was as like Charles as if he had been spit out of his mouth, she thought. Lucy was sitting in a chair nearby, her little daughter on her lap asleep, her thumb tucked into her mouth. The girl was about five, and angelic looking in her sleep, but Jane could tell at a glance that she lacked the Stuart blood.

"May I ask your counsel, Mistress Lane?" Lucy asked. The question took Jane off guard, but she nodded and drew up a stool next to Lucy's chair.

"I think of going home to England," Lucy said. "It is hard here, with the children. Charles has promised me a pension of five thousand pounds, but it never comes."

Five thousand pounds, Jane thought. In a recent letter Charles had told her he ate but one meal a day, so dire was his poverty, and that the well-meant gift of a pack of hounds had mortified him extremely, as he could not possibly afford to feed them. Without a miracle he wouldn't be able to send Lucy five shillings.

"He sends me cheerful notes and little gifts." Lucy shrugged her shoulders hopelessly. "I fear he thinks to fob me off with empty words because I am a trouble to him. My lord Taaffe and Colonel O'Neill both tell me that the king desires me to be gone from here. Indeed, I think he wishes I would simply disappear. I know you know him well. Perhaps you know his heart better than I these days."

Lucy's stark pain and honesty were unsettling, and Jane's heart went out to the girl, who looked at her so wretchedly and with such trust.

"I know he cares for you," she said. "And of course for your boy."

Lucy nodded uncertainly, as if weighing the truth of the statement.

"I would go home at once if I could," Jane said. "You have family there who would help you?"

"I have family. What they could or would do for me I know not, but at least I would be in England. It's warmer there." She shivered, and Jane glanced at the snow falling outside the window.

"I will write to His Majesty," Jane said. "And urge him to find a way to do more for you."

"Thank you," Lucy murmured. "Perhaps he'll listen to you."

THAT NIGHT JANE REREAD CHARLES'S MOST RECENT LETTER.

"February 5, 1656. My dearest Jane: In my affairs I am able to send you some better hopes than I could ever yet do. In Spain the war is declared against Cromwell, and I look every day it should be so in Flanders, and I believe I shall find my account very well in this change. If the things I look for fall out, our ill fortune will forsake us, and then we shall be happy together. Your most affectionate and constant friend, Charles R. P.S. I have given O'Neill a note for you to keep the mill going; it should have been more if I had had it."

"My dear Charles," Jane wrote to him. "I share your joy and hopes for happier times than you have seen of late. I hope that perhaps your better prospects will mean that you might find a way to provide more for the care of Lucy and your son. She is most sad and fearful, looking like a dog that expects to be whipped. Money would help her greatly, but I think it would lighten her soul just to know that you are thinking of her."

Charles wrote back, sending money for Lucy, and exultant at the promises he had recently received from the Spanish officials in Brussels.

"At first I found them dry, yet at last they began to be very free with me and have promised a monthly allowance of three thousand crowns for me and fifteen hundred for my brother James. The Spanish ports will welcome my cousin Rupert and other English privateers, and best of all, Spain will provide arms and men in the cause of restoring me to my throne."

Mary was displeased, though, by Charles's alliance with Spain, the hereditary enemy of the United Provinces.

"He has promised not only that all Royalists in foreign armies shall now join the Spanish army, but that he will withdraw his Irish soldiers from their service in France and give them to Spain, who shall use them to fight against France," she stormed. "The Duke of York is furious."

Well he might be, Jane thought, as he had prospered and flourished by serving in Louis's army, and he now must resign from that service or find himself allied against his brother. Moreover, Charles's mother and sister Minette still made their home at the Palais Royal. What a tangle of royal cousins ruled Europe, and what complications arose from their disputes and alliances.

The Duke of York arrived at The Hague a few weeks later in a cold fury.

"The Duke of Gloucester has gone to join the Spanish army already!" Nan whispered to Jane, happy to have her lover nearby and enjoying the drama unfolding around her. "But James says he won't go to the king, no matter what!"

Jane noted Nan's casual use of the duke's name. Things must be moving along apace in their secret romance. Close though she was to Charles, she would never refer to him to another person as anything other than "His Majesty" or "the king."

By May Mary's temper had cooled, she had repaired the breach between her brothers, and the Duke of York accepted a command with the Spanish forces. But, almost as if to assert that she would not be limited by Charles's alliances, Mary journeyed to Paris to visit her mother. Of course Jane and Nan were with her, and so was the Duke of York.

In private with Jane, Nan spoke of practically nothing but the duke, her descriptions of their secret meetings growing more rapturous by the day.

"I think he will marry me," she confided to Jane one night, looking out over the moonlit Seine and breathing in the sweet scent of blossoms on the summer air.

"Nan, he can't!" Jane cried. "The king will make him marry some princess. I beg you keep hold of yourself. You wade so blithely into very deep waters, and I fear the waves will close above your head."

But Nan only shrugged, and Jane knew that further words would be wasted.

Jane visited her old friend Mademoiselle d'Épernon, and their stroll in the gardens of the Tuileries brought back memories of her walks with Charles when she and John had first arrived in Paris, now almost five years earlier.

"One hears that your handsome king is courting his cousin Princess Henrietta, the Princess of Orange," Mademoiselle said, with a sidelong glance at Jane from under her parasol.

"Yes," Jane said, keeping her voice level. "One does hear that."

"It is not to the liking of the queen his mother," Mademoiselle giggled. "Of course she wishes for him to have a Catholic bride."

"Nor of the Princess Royal," Jane said. Mary had made quite clear what she thought of the possibility of Charles marrying the hated sister of her dead husband.

"I think His Majesty will follow his own counsel," Jane smiled, "though certainly Her Majesty may wish otherwise."

A breeze fluttered the leaves in the trees around them, and threatened to blow away Mademoiselle's wide-brimmed hat of pale straw trimmed with blossoms and ribbons.

"And what of this Mistress Hyde?" she asked, clamping a hand to the top of her head. "She has many suitors, yes? Sir Spencer Compton, and the Viscount of Newburgh. But one also hears that perhaps she looks higher. As high as a duke, perhaps?"

This was not good, Jane thought, that stories about Nan and the Duke of York were circulating freely at the French court. During Mary's previous visit, Charles's mother had not taken much trouble to disguise her displeasure at her son's being so much at Nan's side. His sister Mary would certainly not like a serious intrigue between her lady-in-waiting and her brother. And as Jane had tried to tell Nan, Charles would not be pleased if James entangled himself deeply with her, when he was a valuable pawn in the marriage market with European royalty.

"Oh, Nan is young and delights in the attention," Jane said breezily. "It means nothing. If I were to lay money on who Mistress Hyde might wed, I should wager on Sir Spencer Compton. Do you not see the way he looks at her?"

"Most true!" Mademoiselle cried delightedly, and to Jane's relief, she began to gossip about intrigues among the French courtiers. Perhaps that red herring drawn across the trail had worked, Jane thought.

While in Paris, Jane was shocked to learn that Lucy Walter had indeed gone back to England with her children, and that she had been arrested and imprisoned in the Tower.

"Her captors questioned her, but did not keep her long," Boswell pronounced, "apparently coming to the opinion that she knew nothing that would be of use to them. Now she has crept back to Brussels, but Thomas Howard has forsaken her, and now she's little better than a common whore."

"And what is she to do, pray?" Jane cried. "She must keep herself and her children fed and housed, and without help from the king, she has no choice but to seek male protection and support, wherever she may find it."

She wrote again to Charles, who had moved his court to Bruges, begging that he might find some way of providing for Lucy and her children. He responded that he would do so, and urging her to do what she could to get his sister Mary and brother James to leave Paris, their presence there growing more awkward by the day as France was on the verge of entering into an alliance with Cromwell.

Sir Spencer Compton had gone to join Charles, and Jane had guiltily included in her letter a gossipy reference to his infatuation with Nan Hyde, seeking to keep Charles off the scent of Nan's romance with the Duke of York, and Charles wrote back jovially; "I will try whether Sir S. Compton be so much in love as you say, for I will name Mistress Hyde before him so by chance, that except he be very much smitten it shall not move him."

Jane read with relief that he found life in Bruges much more bearable than anyplace he had settled in his exile. Thanks to generous patrons, he was living in a pleasant house with a garden in back sloping down to the canal. The burghers treated him with great courtesy, and he had been made patron of the guilds of Saints George and Sebastian, for archers and crossbowmen, respectively. He had formed his own regiment of guards, had put another under the command of Lord Wilmot, as well as a regiment of Irish under Ormonde and one of Scots under Middleton, and the latter, he wrote, in their "right Highland apparel," caused amazement in the town.

But as the months wore on, and Spain failed to come through with its promised support, the tone of Charles's letters changed to one of despair. He had not the money to pay his soldiers, and they grew disorderly, and begged and starved. His supporters lacked their most basic necessities, and he was powerless to help them.

"Nothing would lighten my spirits more," he wrote, "than being able to relieve the wretchedness that envelops those that attend me so loyally. We are all cold, hungry, and shabby. Lord Norwich chanced to singe his coat by the flame of a candle, and as it is his only coat, he had no remedy but to cut off the blackened part and wear it still. Another of my followers was distraught with efforts to get money for the care of his sick wife and child, and my helplessness to do anything for the poor fellow cast me low indeed.

"The truth is, this scurvy usage by the Spanish puts me beyond patience, and if I were with Don Juan, I would follow your counsel and swear two or three round oaths. I am so vexed with the delay I see is like to be in obtaining of money, and consequently my not being able to get from hence until that be, that I have lost all patience, and give all men that have or shall have to do with money to the devil.

"I am no better now with the money promised but not paid by Spain than I was with that promised but not paid by France. I cannot choose but think of the Irish footman that would needs leave his master to seek a better. His master asked him, 'But what if you cannot find a better?' to which he answered very discreetly, 'Why, faith, then I will come to thee again!' "

Whatever money Charles found to spend on the desperately important matter of intelligence, he was always outspent by Cromwell. The possibility of assassination was a constant threat. And Charles felt deeply betrayed when the Duke of Buckingham, who had been raised like a brother to him, returned to England and married the daughter of the Parliamentary general Fairfax.

Spain was at war with France, but would not allow Charles to go to the front, and kept him sitting in Bruges, while the dukes of York and Gloucester gathered glory about them in service of the Spanish.

In June of 1657, when it was reported that the dukes had been slain or taken prisoner, Nan Hyde was in a state of collapse until they arrived safe in Bruges. Then she went into further panic at the rumors that the Duke of York might marry Fatima Lambert, the daughter of another Parliamentary general, or even one of Cromwell's daughters, regaining her composure only when the duke arrived at The Hague and assured her he had refused both matches.

Jane marveled first that the duke was apparently truly in love with Nan and second that the depth of their relationship had somehow not become widely known. She was extremely uncomfortable knowing their secret and keeping it from Mary of Orange, from Elizabeth of Bohemia, and from Charles.

And a further resentment crept into her mind, push it down though she would. Over the years since she had come to Mary's court, she had forced herself to put out of her thoughts any idea that Charles might marry her, or even that he could marry her. It was true that the Duke of York was not the king, but until the day might come that Charles had a legitimate son, the Duke of York was heir apparent, and could someday be king. If Nan could hope to wed him, why could not Jane keep her hope alive?

And that discontent brought to mind the vexed problem of Lucy Walter, who wrote distraught letters to Jane, claiming that Daniel O'Neill and Lord Taaffe were trying to take away her son, accusing her of ridding herself of two more bastard children, of the murder of a serving maid, of being mad. And that Taaffe, who held her allowance, would not give it to her.

Jane confronted O'Neill.

"She must have means to live. How can you—can the king—be so callous to the girl?"

"No one wishes her harm, Mistress Lane. But every idle action of hers brings His Majesty upon the stage in a most discreditable light. Perhaps you can advise her to give up the boy and take herself someplace quiet. Then shall she have all she needs."

Toward the end of the year Lucy returned to The Hague, and looking like a gray-faced wraith, crept out of a shadowed corner as Jane approached.

"I beg you to speak to the king for me," she wept, clutching at Jane's hand. "All I want is to keep my boy, and I will never make trouble for him."

Jane didn't see how Lucy's wanting to keep her own son with her was causing trouble.

"Why do they want to take him?" she asked. "What trouble could you do?"

Lucy fixed her with haunted eyes, and glancing down the empty corridors, drew Jane close to her, huddled against a cold stone wall.

"I could tell the truth," she whispered.

"The truth?"

"That I am his wife."

The shock hit Jane's stomach like a blow.

"Wife?" Her voice was barely above a silent breath. "Of . . ."

"Of Charles. Of the king."

JANE LAY STARING INTO THE DARK THAT NIGHT, UNABLE TO SLEEP. Was Lucy to be believed? She did truly seem to be on the edge of madness. Perhaps her fevered brain had seized on the idea that Charles had married her and she had convinced herself it was true. Or perhaps she knew it was not true, but wished it so, or said it in the vain hope that it would give her some purchase on the tilting, slippery deck her world had become.

But what if it were true?

Charles had met Lucy on Jersey, when his father, though imprisoned, yet lived, when the chance of his becoming king, or even of returning to England, probably seemed far off. He had loved Lucy, had been happy with her. He had told Jane so himself. And Jane suddenly recalled Elizabeth, the Princess Palatine, telling her that Charles's sister and mother had liked and accepted Lucy. Accepted her. As his wife?

And if she was his wife, of course Charles's men would try to control her, to quiet her. For now that he was king, and desperately needed a way to take back his throne, Lucy Walter could only stand in the way of his acquiring a bride who would bring him the gold and armies he needed. And of course they would want to take Lucy's son from her, lest he catch her contagion and come to believe himself to be the king's rightfully gotten son and heir.

The thoughts made Jane's head spin, and the emotions raised by the thoughts were overwhelming, for if Lucy's tale was true, then Charles was a far blacker character than Jane could bear to think him.

"Dear Jane," wrote Clement Fisher in the autumn of 1657. "Each time I write to you, I wish so much that I had good tidings to send you, and each time I am saddened that my words must bring nothing but disappointment. Your father and brother and uncle are still imprisoned, with no word of when they may gain their release.

"As you no doubt know there have been more risings, but each has been put down, and I do not think it is putting it too strong to say that the king's supporters here are heartbroken, for our hopes of seeing him on the throne seem to grow ever more dim, though we pray for some extraordinary act of Providence.

"The only bright spot in the gloom is that Cromwell has decided not to have himself crowned, though that is little enough."

Clement. Jane wished she could look into those bright blue eyes and feel their warmth. She was feeling more lonely than ever lately, far from home and with little hope that she could return anytime soon. And her loneliness was not comforted by thoughts of Charles. She had not seen him since they parted in Düsseldorf more than three years earlier, and she had heard from many sources that Catherine Pegge, an English lady in Bruges, was with child by him.

She would have been angry, except that when Charles wrote to her, his letters were so bleak that they broke her heart.

"I am not only without money but have been compelled to borrow all that I have spent these three months. Meat, candles, coal, the very washing of my ragged shirts, all is upon credit, and I content myself with but one dish at my meals.

"I need not put you in mind of the season of the year and how soon winter will be upon us, and you will easily believe I am in some pain for the preparations which ought to be ready against that time. Every week brings me letters from my friends in England, to know against what time I will expect them to be ready and what they may depend on from me; and if this winter pass without any attempt on my part, I shall take very little pleasure in living till the next."

Princess Louise disappeared from the palace on a snowy morning in December. The first alarm and fear for her safety was quelled only slightly by the discovery of a letter she had left. Queen Elizabeth of Bohemia stood staring at the letter in disbelief, and looked up to Jane with desolation in her eyes.

"She has gone. She has deserted me." She seemed to totter on her feet, and Jane rushed to guide her to a chair.

"Surely not, Your Majesty?"

"Yes. She writes, 'It has pleased God to discover to me the surest way of salvation, and to give me to know that the Catholic religion is that only way. I have been obliged to withdraw from Your Majesty from fear of being desired to receive the sacrament against my conscience.'"

Jane thought of Charles's aunt as a warship under full sail, gun ports lifted and cannon at the ready, and she had never seen her appear less than in command of herself, but now the queen let the letter drop to the floor and clung to Jane, weeping.

"Thirteen babies I bore," she sobbed. "Seven dead. And now they have all gone, and none remain to me."

Jane patted the frail back and stroked the soft white hair.

"I will stay with you, Your Majesty," she said. "I will be a daughter to you."

At the end of February 1658 Henry Lascelles arrived at The Hague with grim news. Lord Wilmot was dead, having succumbed to camp fever in the overcrowded regimental headquarters of Charles's forces, still languishing at Bruges.

Jane recalled when she had first seen Lord Wilmot, that rainy night in the kitchen at Bentley, when he had come to plan Charles's escape and to convey in advance the king's thanks for the risks she was undertaking on his behalf.

Little did I know, she thought. That night had changed her life. Would she go back and do it differently if she could? Surely if she had known what lay ahead of her, she would never have had the courage to set forth. But what if she had not? Almost certainly Charles would have been taken, imprisoned, beheaded.

"Do you think we shall ever be able to go home again, Henry?" she asked, striving to make her tone far lighter than she felt.

"I don't know."

He shook his head, and Jane noticed for the first time that there were gray hairs among the chestnut, and that lines channeled his forehead and cut from his nose to his mouth.

"There were stirrings in England, and we got messages imploring the king to come once more, that this time a rising might be successful. Ormonde went to England—in disguise." He laughed grimly. "For all the traveling in disguise there has been, king and court might well set themselves up as a company of players."

Jane had a sudden and vivid image of Lord Wilmot, his great bulk balanced with careful dignity on his horse, a hawk on his wrist the only concession he would make toward a disguise, when she had caught sight of him with John away across the fields as she and Charles had set out on their journey so long ago.

"The king pawned his George to pay for Ormonde's journey." Henry shook his head in sorrowful disbelief. "Ormonde had some difficulty, but returned with encouragement, saying that he thought His Majesty might safely land at Yarmouth."

Yarmouth. Jane could smell the salt in the air as she had first smelled it when she and John had neared the coast after that long and desperate journey.

"But—" Henry began.

"There is always a 'but,' it seems."

"And this 'but' is the same there has been for so long—not enough men, not enough money, not near the certainty of success if we should chance an invasion."

"And no one wants another Worcester."

"No."

The year did not seem likely to improve. Lucy Walter wrote begging Jane's help. Her boy had been wrested from her in Brussels by some piece of trickery, she said. Jane stared at the tearstained letter in disbelief. What Lucy claimed—that the boy had been snatched while her attention was distracted—seemed unbelievable. But when Jane questioned Colonel O'Neill, he only seemed to confirm Lucy's story.

"It had to be done," he said. "The wench has been growing a greater thorn in His Majesty's side every year, and the boy couldn't be permitted to stay with her, running barefoot and wild in the streets."

"But he's her son!" Jane cried.

"And the son of the king. He'll be better off in Paris with his grandmother the queen."

The deed was done, and though it broke Jane's heart, she didn't see how she could help Lucy to get her son back. She wrote to Queen

Mary, urging that Lucy be allowed to visit her boy, but received no reply.

Her anger at Charles's treatment of Lucy hardened into cold bitterness at the news that Charles's mistress Catherine Pegge was with child again.

Early in 1658 the Duke of York came to visit his sister Mary at Breda, bringing with him Harry Jermyn, the nephew of Henry Jermyn. The older Jermyn had long served Queen Mary in England as vice chamberlain and master of the horse and had remained with her as her secretary since she had been in France, and there were rumors that she had secretly married him.

Nan Hyde and the duke were so much in each other's company that surely Mary would have known that something was afoot between them, Jane thought—had not Mary been as much with Harry Jermyn. The Princess Royal had been widowed as long as she had been a mother, Jane reflected, watching Mary laugh with Jermyn over supper—more than seven years. Perhaps love was in the air as spring began to creep over the frozen ground and canals.

The duke and Jermyn had not been at Breda three weeks, however, when Mary received a letter from Charles that had her more furious than Jane had ever seen her.

"He declares that there are reports in Paris that I have married Harry Jermyn, and tells me he is calling Harry back to him, to still the rumors!" Mary raged. "'What I advise you in this matter proceeds purely out of that kindness which I will ever have for you,' he writes, the hypocritical devil!"

But Jermyn could not defy the king's command, and departed for Brussels, leaving Mary just as bereft and tearful as was Nan Hyde at being parted from the Duke of York, who went to Antwerp to join Charles, ready for another possible invasion of England.

Once more it seemed that success was at last within Charles's grasp. Spanish forces battled on his behalf against the united might of France and Commonwealth England. The dukes of York and Gloucester were in at the thick of the fighting, and even Charles led a charge at Mardyke. But with the loss at the Battle of the Dunes in June, once more hope slipped away.

"The king is in even a worse case than he was before," Henry Lascelles told Jane when he came to visit her for her birthday. "Cromwell's navy is blockading the Spanish ports so they are bottled up and cannot help. The King of Spain has told His Majesty he would not be welcome in Spain, and of course any hope of help from France is now lost."

"But what of action on his behalf in England?" Jane asked. "Surely his friends at home have not given up?"

"Perhaps not given up," Henry said, shaking his head. "But the risings in England this year were put down as soon as they were begun. One great difficulty is that Cromwell's spies are many, and have insinuated themselves everywhere, even into the Sealed Knot, to which His Majesty gave credentials, so that scarce can those loyal to the king make a move but it is already known in London."

I shall never be able to go home, Jane thought, and suddenly she was weeping.

"Oh, Henry," she cried against his shoulder as he held her hard, "had I known that I was banishing myself from England forever, I never should have had the courage to do as I did. I want to go back to Bentley. I don't care what happens."

"Jane, Jane," he murmured. "I would go with you myself to make sure you got safely back, did I think you would not still be in danger. Your poor father and uncle and John are prisoners still. If you went back you would certainly be arrested."

Jane could not stop the tears. The long years of loneliness and disappointment stretched behind her. First she had lived on the memory of the passion that she had shared with Charles, sure that someday she would be at his side once more. As the years had gone by, the long separations broken only by letters, all that had kept her going was the hope that someday—surely not too far off—she could go home and take up her life. And now it began to seem that perhaps even that would never be.

Henry held her, letting her cry out her despair until there were no more tears to come.

And then came a thunderbolt. On the third of September, the seventh anniversary of the Battle of Worcester, Oliver Cromwell died.

"The king was playing tennis at Hoogstraten when he heard of it," Henry told Jane, having ridden hard to bring the news to Mary's court. "He went white, and then flushed red, and then sank to his knees in prayers of thanks. And then ordered wine and supper, and was in better spirits than any had seen him in years."

"I should think so!" Jane cried, laughing and weeping at once. "Oh, Henry, it's a miracle!

Henry glanced at Jane and then away, and coughed uncomfortably.

"He's asked to marry his cousin Henrietta Catherine. If he's to have his throne, he'll need a queen."

"Of course," Jane said, her voice sounding distant to her own ears. She knew Charles must wed some royal bride now. And yet it was hard, to have such joyful news followed so soon by the stark reminder of what she had known all along and had tried to put from her mind. Willing away the tears, she smiled at Henry.

"I knew it must come, Henry. The king values my—friendship. That is enough."

Only three weeks after Cromwell's death, Lucy Walter died destitute and distraught in Paris, where she had followed in hopes of being allowed to see her son. Jane had always felt that Lucy lived in some shadow world parallel to her own—what might have happened if she had borne that child she had lost on the heath—and Lucy's death shook her to the core. Poor Lucy. She had loved Charles with her whole heart, it seemed, and he had sailed off to Scotland in pursuit of his crown. She—helpless and alone with his child—had taken refuge where she could—first in the bed of Lord Taaffe and later that of Thomas Howard. And for that—that pitiful instinct for survival, that desperate gamble to buy herself time until Charles might take her back—for he had jollied her along with letters, little gifts, and the promise of a pension which had never been paid—she had been ridiculed and reviled, accused of living a life of open depravity. And the final cruel indignity—she had been kept from seeing her boy and had been treated like a mad dog.

And it was Charles who had made it so. Jane had tried not to see that, had told herself that it was Hyde, it was Taaffe, it was O'Neill, it was Princess Mary, Queen Mary, the Duke of York—anyone but Charles. But now she faced the truth. He was king, poor though he might be, and he had hidden in the shadows and watched as his first love, the mother of his child—his wife, if Lucy was to be believed—had been humiliated and broken.

Quite the Machiavelli, Your Majesty, Jane thought. *Perhaps only the fact that I lost that child prevented me from receiving such treatment at your hands.*

In the fall Jane received a letter from John. He and her father and uncle had finally been released from prison. Her heart broke at the news that her father was weak and ill after his long ordeal. She longed to sit with him, to hold his hand and read to him as he had read to her when she was a little girl, to love him and comfort him in whatever time he had left. But John warned very clearly that it would still be dangerous for her to return. *But soon,* she murmured to herself, *perhaps now it will not be long before I can go home.*

And yet the time was not yet, it seemed. Sir George Booth's rising in England was defeated. France and Spain ended their war, and the dukes of York and Gloucester, now without military careers to pursue, came to stay with their sister Mary. Mary's mother-in-law, the Princess Amelia, declined to marry her daughter Henrietta Catherine to Charles, still a king without a country, and he languished in Antwerp, his poverty as grinding as ever.

CHAPTER TWENTY

JANE FOUND THE WINTERS IN HOLLAND NEARLY UNBEARABLE. The cold seemed a living thing, gnawing its way into her bones and making her joints ache. No sooner had the sun risen, it seemed, than it began to set, the blue shadows creeping across the frozen canals as the sky darkened into interminable night.

So Jane was happy when on a cold evening in Breda in late November 1659 she heard Nan's laughter from a little parlor. She could use some cheerful company, she thought, and went to investigate. She found Nan with the Duke of York and his friend Sir Charles Berkeley, gathered before the hearth, where a fire crackled and glowed.

"Oh, Jane!" Nan cried, beaming. "I was about to go to find you! Come join us in a glass of wine."

The Duke of York handed Jane a glass, toasted her health, and said, with a conspiratorial glance at Nan, "Will you excuse me for but a moment, Mistress Lane?"

"Of course, Your Highness," Jane said, baffled.

Nan drew her down to sit on a low bench before the fire, and Sir Charles sank onto a stool, his long booted legs thrust out before him.

"Where is Her Highness?" Nan whispered to Jane, glancing at the door.

"Mary? Why, she's gone to bid little William good night, and is probably still in the nursery."

"Good," Nan giggled, leaping up as the Duke of York returned with a black-clad priest, closing the door behind them as they entered. "This won't take long. Come, Jane, stand up with me."

She pulled Jane to her feet, and before Jane had a chance to realize what was happening, the priest had produced a *Book of Common Prayer* and was reading the marriage service.

"But—" Jane began to object, but the duke raised a hand to stay her.

"It is quite all right, Mistress Lane. I am of age and free to wed where I love."

"Please, Jane?" Nan pleaded, tears coming to her eyes. "We haven't long! If Mary finds out she's sure to make trouble. Oh, Jane, I've waited so long!"

Jane stared at Nan, clutching the duke's hand. It was unbelievable. The Duke of York was going to wed Nan Hyde, surely without the knowledge or permission of the king, and come what might. And who was she to object? Jane thought. Let Nan have her happiness.

"Yes, of course I'll stay," Jane said.

"And you won't tell?" Nan begged.

"No," Jane said, a black weight settling on her heart. "I won't tell."

A YEAR AFTER LOUISE LEFT THE HAGUE, QUEEN ELIZABETH'S DAUGHTER Sophie, known since her marriage as Sophia of Hanover, came to visit Mary's court for Christmas. She was a beautiful girl, bloomingly with child, and she brought with her the seven-year-old Elizabeth Charlotte of the Palatinate, nicknamed Liselotte, the daughter of Sophie's brother the Elector of Palatine.

Queen Elizabeth glowed with happiness as she held her little granddaughter on her lap, and the rest of the court was just as charmed by the smiling fair-headed child.

"Soon you will have a little cousin to play with!" Queen Elizabeth smiled. "Will that please you?"

"Perhaps," Liselotte said, considering. "Can I dress it up like I do my dolls?"

"You funny girl!" Sophie laughed. "It will be a baby, not a doll. But that is better, you see, for it will be like a little brother or sister to you."

Jane regarded Sophie with interest, recalling Princess Elizabeth's comment that Charles had been captivated by his cousin, who was almost exactly his own age, and that he had at one time many years ago wanted to marry her. Sophie was stunning, with fair skin and luxuriant dark curls, her eyes sparkling with humor. Jane thought a little grudgingly that Sophie would likely have been a very suitable wife for Charles, and wondered why the match had not come off.

Jane noticed Nan Hyde watching Sophie intently, with an expression that was hard to read, her eyes darting to where Mary sat with her son William, now eight years old, who was boasting to little Liselotte of the horse he had received as a birthday present. *It must be very hard for Nan to keep her secret,* Jane thought. *She longs to be able to say that she is the wife of the Duke of York, instead of being thought his sister's lady-in-waiting.* How long could the secret keep? she wondered.

In December Jane received a letter from John, delivered by Lord Ormonde.

"My dear sister," John wrote, "I hardly know where to begin to tell you in what turmoil and confusion things are here in England. I am sure that word will have reached you of the increasing hostility between the Rump, as the recently recalled remnant of the old Parliament is known, and the army faction. Since Richard Cromwell resigned in the spring, these factions have moved and countermoved, attacked, parried, and riposted, and it seems to me—I scarce dare to hope it—that there are rumblings beneath the earth that presage great upheaval to come—earthquakes that may throw some from their places and restore others."

Jane read the letter again, hope rising in her breast. Was it possible that events in England were finally moving in the king's favor?

Mary removed her household to Teyling for Christmas, and the court was merrier than at any time since Jane's arrival, for now a rush of encouraging news flowed from England, and the English exiles were at last filled with the sense that after so many years of darkness and despair, the sun was about to break through the clouds.

Mary's court busied themselves with feasts and music and masques, and Jane sat happily with Queen Elizabeth late into the night, listening to her stories of her childhood in the exciting early days of her father's reign as King of England, and of the first untarnished joy she and her husband had felt when he was in Prague, newly crowned as King of Bohemia, and a glittering future seemed to lie before them.

Henry Lascelles came to see Jane in Breda in late January, in high spirits

"General Monck met with Fairfax at York," he said. "And there are murmurs that both are now for restoration of the monarchy."

"Truly?" Jane gasped. After so many disappointments she hardly dared to believe it might be so.

"Truly," Henry grinned. "Moreover, His Majesty has word that Londoners do now openly speak of the king, and say that General Monck will bring him back." He took Jane's hand and squeezed it. "Oh, cousin. I think that our labors of so long ago are about to bear fruit."

Jane was restless that night. She could not quiet her mind nor still the excitement that surged through her body. At last, at last, at last. The day for which she had hoped for so long might be at hand.

A week later Nan dashed into Jane's bedchamber and grasped her hands in elation.

"Have you heard? General Monck has reached London! The apprentices are rioting against the Rump, the old army is in disarray as Monck's men come in to replace them, and all is in Monck's hands!"

"It's like a house of cards," Henry said. "It wants but a breath to make it topple."

The breath came. In February, with the might of the army behind him, Monck demanded that the Rump Parliament be dissolved by the sixth of May and an election held to bring in a full and free Parliament.

And in early April, Charles himself arrived unannounced at Breda, spattered with the mud of the road, having ridden all night from Brussels. Jane had begun to think that she would never see him again, and to have him solidly and vibrantly present was overwhelming. Her disappointment and heartbreak of the past years melted away as he greeted her with a grin and swept her into his arms.

"My Jane, my savior! Your sacrifice was not in vain, you see."

Jane looked up into his eyes and for the first time in years felt that here was her Charles, the man she had known and fallen in love with on the road from Bentley to Abbots Leigh. She reached up to stroke his cheek, but stopped herself, conscious of the curious gazes of Mary's court. Charles was suddenly the most famous man in Europe, and his every move and word were noted and commented on.

The dukes of York and Gloucester arrived, and Jane smiled at the joy in Charles's face as he sat down to supper with his brothers and sister Mary.

"How long has it been since we've all been together?" he asked, looking to Mary.

"Eighteen years. When Mother took me to go to my husband."

A shadow of sadness came over Mary's face, and Charles took her hand.

"What grief that our sister Elizabeth did not live to join us here." He looked at his brothers. "But soon we will all meet in England. Minette, too. And then we need never be parted again."

. . .

One morning in mid-April, Jane entered her room to find Nan Hyde vomiting violently into a chamber pot, her face flushed and damp with sweat.

"Shall I ask for a doctor to be sent for?" she asked, hastening to Nan's side.

"No," Nan gasped. "I'm quite well."

"You're not," Jane said. "Do you have a fever?"

She put her hand to Nan's forehead, remembering with dread those first few hours when Kate Killigrew had been taken ill at Spa.

Don't let it be the plague, she prayed.

Nan's skin was cool to the touch; at least she didn't have a fever.

"I'm not ill," Nan said, thrusting the chamber pot under the bed and wiping her face with a cloth. "I'm with child."

She jutted her little chin defiantly at Jane, as if expecting Jane to argue or criticize her.

So now it had come, Jane thought. The secret marriage would not be secret for much longer.

"Does the duke know?" she asked.

"Not yet. I didn't want to tell him until I was sure."

On the fourteenth of May, Jane and the rest of Mary's household accompanied Charles from Breda to The Hague, where he would receive a delegation from Parliament. They traveled by boat, arriving at dawn, and by the rosy morning light Jane saw that the shore was thronged with thousands of people. Cannons boomed in celebration of Charles's arrival, and their way to the palace was lined with cheering crowds.

Jane waited anxiously with Mary and her son William, the dukes of York and Gloucester, and their aunt Queen Elizabeth for

Charles to return from his meeting with the Parliamentary commissioners. Everyone seemed too anxious for conversation. The Duke of York paced, Queen Elizabeth absentmindedly stroked the little monkey that chattered on her hap, and Mary kept standing and then sitting down again. Jane had a piece of needlework in her lap, but found herself too nervous to sew without pricking herself, so she simply sat. She suddenly had a vivid recollection of sitting just so in the kitchen at Bentley years ago, waiting for John to return with news of the king's whereabouts.

Jane's heart jumped at the sound of Charles's voice. He strode in, face alight, closely followed by Colonel O'Neill, struggling with the weight of a large portmanteau.

Queen Elizabeth stood and took a faltering step toward Charles, and when she spoke, her voice was strained with hope. "Good news?"

"The best news!" Charles crowed, going to her and kissing her. "Miraculous news! Parliament has invited me to return."

There was a moment of silence, as if the royal family was too stunned to react.

"And look at this!" Charles cried, pulling the portmanteau from O'Neill's hands. "Come and look!"

He dropped the bag onto the floor before him, and it landed with a heavy thud and the clink of metal within. He opened the clasp and Jane saw with astonishment that the portmanteau was full of gold coins.

"How much is there?" she breathed.

"Four thousand pounds," Charles said. "A payment in earnest on a grant of fifty thousand pounds that Parliament has voted to me. They told me that when they left London, bells and bonfires and the report of artillery had already begun to proclaim me king and publish the joy of the nation."

He looked around at them, his eyes brimming with tears, and when he spoke again his voice was hoarse.

"It is truly beyond belief. After all these years, to have it happen of such a sudden and without bloodshed."

"God be praised," Jane said.

And suddenly she knew she was going to faint, and reached for Charles as she fell. He caught her in his arms and lowered her to the ground, supporting her on his lap.

"Jane, my dear, are you ill?"

"No," she murmured, looking up at him. "I am well. It's only that I just realized—I can go home now."

THE ROYAL FAMILY, THE ENGLISH EXILES, ALL OF THE HAGUE, ALL OF Europe, it seemed, were seized with a wild joy. The years of despair and poverty seemed forgotten in the face of the fact that in a matter of days Charles would be on his way to England, to the throne and crown that had eluded him for so long.

Jane felt as if she had woken from a nightmare. Only now, when her sentence was near its end, did she let herself feel how much she had hated the Low Countries and life at Mary's court with its petty rivalries and disputes. Her heart had been in England all along, and soon she would be there again—and with a king on the throne that she had helped to put there!

Charles's mother, Queen Mary; his sister Minette; and his cousin Princess Louise arrived from France. Prince Rupert, Elizabeth the Princess Palatine, and Queen Elizabeth's son Edward flocked to The Hague and were packed into the palace to join in the celebrations. Of the siblings only Sophie was absent, as she had returned to Osnabrück in March and would shortly be brought to bed of her first child.

Jane and Mary's other ladies were in a flurry of preparing for the many balls and feasts that would pack the coming days. For now that Charles was truly king again, everyone wanted to shower him with honor and congratulations, even those who had failed to come to his aid when he was in most dire need of it.

To Jane's dismay, Charles was now always at the center of a crowd. She had barely seen him, had not even had an opportunity to speak privately with him since they had returned to The Hague, and now he was surrounded by all these people. Who were they? They had come from everywhere, out of nowhere, and all at once. The English who had grimly endured the past ten years or more, living from hand to mouth in Holland and France and elsewhere now came scurrying to jostle for the king's attention, fighting for a moment in his reflected glory. And what galled her almost more than anything was that they treated her as if she was one of them rather than an intimate of the king's.

Never mind, she told herself. *Tomorrow night at the ball he will dance with me and talk with me. All eyes will be on us, and then they'll know that I hold a special place in his heart.*

JANE STUDIED HER REFLECTION IN THE MIRROR AS THE DRESSMAKER pinned up the hem of the new gown she would wear at the ball the next evening. It was a spectacular creation, gold satin, glowing with a sheen like honey in the sun, the skirt falling in rich folds, the sleeves and overskirt trimmed with bows in shimmering deep brown. The deep neckline, cut so low and close to her shoulders that she could scarce raise her arms, thrust her bosom into prominence.

"You will be the most beautiful lady there, mademoiselle," the dressmaker enthused, adjusting a bow and stepping back to look at her work.

Jane smiled with satisfaction. She would dress her hair in ringlets, and wear the great tear-shaped pearl earrings that Mary had given her. Yes, she would turn heads in her new gown, and when Charles was at her side, she would feel like a queen. And in the days to come, there would be plenty of time to spend together, making up for the lost years.

THE GREAT HALL WHERE THE BALL WAS TO BE HELD WAS ALREADY packed when Jane entered behind Mary. It had been a brilliant and sunny day, and the rays of sunlight, lingering into the spring evening, competed with the hundreds of candles in their wall brackets. The room buzzed with chatter and laughter. The bright rustling silks of the ladies' dresses caught the flickering candlelight. The air was scented heavily with perfume and with the apple blossoms that weighed down the branches of the trees outside the tall open windows. The excitement and anticipation seemed tangible. Jane, Nan, Lady Stanhope, and Mary's other ladies followed Mary to where Queen Mary sat with Queen Elizabeth of Bohemia and the Princesses Elizabeth and Louise.

"Where's this king son of yours, then?" Queen Elizabeth asked in an undertone that carried easily around the room. "Wants to make an entrance, I expect."

The musicians at the other end of the chamber had been playing, their music underlying the hum of conversation, but now, as if on cue, they stopped. The room went silent. A horn blazed out a fanfare, and Charles entered.

He was resplendent in a suit of black velvet trimmed with bows and knots of red ribbons, matching the heels of his black shoes, his gloves, and the fluttering ostrich plumes in the crown of his hat. The lace-edged sleeves of his shirt and his lace collar were snowy white. He had shaved clean except for a small mustache, and his dark curls tumbled over his shoulders.

Jane caught her breath at the sight of him. She had always thought him handsome, even in the humble guise of Will Jackson, but tonight he shone like a star, the embodiment of grace and power and beauty.

Every inch a king. Jane chuckled to herself as she recalled Charles quoting the line from *King Lear* to her on one of the nights they had shared at Abbots Leigh. And he was now, every inch of his six feet two inches, dazzlingly royal.

The crowd applauded and cheered, and Charles gave a regal nod in reply before breaking into a grin. The formal moment past, there was a stir as if everyone at once would make their way toward the king. But he turned away, his attention caught by something to his side, and the crowd stopped where it stood. Jane craned to see. What had arrested the king's attention was a girl. A stunningly beautiful girl. The most beautiful woman Jane had ever seen, she thought. The stranger was dressed in a blue so pale as to be almost white, but with enough color that it reflected and intensified the violet of her eyes. Her hair, a deep auburn that shone in the candlelight, hung in ringlets around her face and cascaded over the creamy white of her bare shoulders and the surge of her full breasts.

A murmur went through the room. And then Charles reached out a hand and the girl went to him. He took her hand and looked down at her, and Jane's soul turned to ice.

"Who is that?" Dorothy whispered behind her.

"Barbara Palmer." It was Boswell's voice. "The king's mistress. She arrived with her husband in February. They say she was in the king's bed within a fortnight and has scarcely left it since, except when he was at Breda."

Jane's heart froze. February? She had been at Breda then. So for the last three months, while her heart had soared at the thought of seeing Charles again, he had been at The Hague, and bedding this girl.

She rushed from the room, fighting to hold back her tears. The musicians struck up a dance tune, and applause broke out. The king taking the floor, no doubt, with Barbara Palmer. She stumbled into her room, slamming the door behind her, and sank onto the floor, shaking with grief and rage.

This was the day she had longed for, prayed for, for which she had given up her life as it had been and spent the long years away from home. And now she was forgotten, lost in the crowds of fawning subjects and favor seekers. And Charles as she had known him, the memory that had sustained her through the long winter of their separation—the lazy grin, the eyes shining just for her, his voice joining hers in song—was gone, and in his place was a gilded stranger. They had been as intimate as two people could be, and now a vast gulf yawned between the king and his subject.

And with the unearthly picture of Barbara Palmer lingering mockingly in her mind, for the first time Jane felt old. On their journey, when Charles was twenty-one and she twenty-five, the difference in their ages had seemed insignificant. But now, when he was not yet thirty, with legions of beautiful young girls crowded around him, with their smooth and perfect skin, their lush bosoms, their unlined faces and clear eyes, and all of them willing to give themselves to him utterly, she suddenly saw herself as she feared others must see her—aging, sad, pathetic. No dish to tempt a young king who might have any woman in Europe.

On a table in her room stood a miniature that Princess Louise had painted of her soon after her arrival at Mary's court. She took it up and stared at it. She had not truly looked at it in—how long? Years? She had glanced at it with unseeing eyes, taking for granted that it represented her as she was.

Now she picked up a hand mirror and held it up, comparing her reflection to the portrait, and what she saw made her weep the more. The firm and determined chin of the Jane of then was now softened by a roll of flesh. The eyes that had stared so bright and clear were now red with tears, the lids swollen and puffy. Fine lines cobwebbed from the corners of her eyes, bracketed her mouth, cut channels in her forehead. Her décolletage was no longer the silken damask it had been, but roughened and mottled.

Jane threw the mirror onto the floor and watched it explode in a shower of silvered shards. She flung herself onto the bed and sobbed, great wrenching animal cries tearing her throat. She wanted to stop feeling, to end her existence. To hurt and kill. Charles. Mary. John. Lord Wilmot, in his grave. Barbara Palmer. All the pretty young creatures who sighed after the king and caught his eye. And most of all she just wanted to feel no more.

She gave herself up to the ocean of grief and rage, losing herself in it. The tears and the wrenching sobs lasted a long time, but finally she had cried all that she could cry and had no emotions left to vent.

CHAPTER TWENTY-ONE

ON THE MORNING OF THE TWENTY-THIRD OF MAY, JANE JOINED Charles; his mother, Queen Mary; his aunt Queen Elizabeth; his sisters, Mary and Minette; and his brothers, the Dukes of York and Gloucester, aboard the *Naseby,* touring the ship that would take Charles back to England. The royal family dined in state, and afterward, Charles rechristened the ship the *Royal Charles* and gave other ships in the fleet names more appropriate to a royal flotilla than those they had borne under Cromwell.

There were plans afoot for a reunion of the family at Christmas, but Charles's brothers were the only members of the royal family who would sail with him now. Nan Hyde had left Mary's service and was traveling to England, ostensibly because her father was accompanying the king, but Jane wondered, with a glance at Nan's belly, how much longer the secret marriage could be kept a secret.

Jane could scarcely believe that she would not be present when Charles set foot on English soil after all she had done to ensure that he might do so. But she knew that Barbara Palmer was with him, and she would have been hard-pressed not to feel miserable and bitterly resentful had she been in their company.

A FEW DAYS AFTER THE KING'S DEPARTURE, JANE'S MOOD WAS LIFTED by the news that on the twenty-eighth of May, Sophie had been safely delivered of a healthy baby boy named Georg Ludwig.

"'We call him Görgen,' Sophie writes," Mary sniffed. "Not a very English name."

"Well, after all," Queen Elizabeth said, beaming with joy at having a new grandchild, "the wee mite will not only be heir to his father, the Duke of Brunswick-Lüneberg, but his three uncles have no children either! He'll be a little German ruler. Who knows, perhaps one day he'll even be the Holy Roman Emperor!"

NOW THAT MESSENGERS COULD TRAVEL FREELY TO AND FROM ENGland, news of Charles's homecoming reached Mary's court rapidly. Jane listened as Queen Elizabeth read a letter from Charles's friend John Evelyn.

"'May the twenty-ninth. This day came in His Majesty Charles the Second to London after a sad and long exile. This was also his birthday . . .'"

Yes, Jane thought. Charles had turned thirty on the day that he had ridden into London to claim his throne. He had been but twenty-one when she rode with him, combining both the hope and impetuousness of youth with the toughness and melancholy born of the shocks and hardships he had already suffered.

"'He rode with a triumph of above twenty thousand horse and foot,'" Queen Elizabeth read, "'brandishing their swords and shouting with inexpressible joy. The ways strewed with flowers, the bells ringing, the streets hung with tapestry, fountains running with wine, the windows and balconies all set with ladies, trumpets, music, and myriads of people flocking the streets, so as they were seven hours in passing the City, even from two in the afternoon till nine at night. I stood in the Strand and beheld it and blessed God. And all this without one drop of blood, and by that very army which rebelled against him. But it was the Lord's doing, *et mirabile in oculis nostris,* for such a Restoration was never seen, nor so joyful a day and so bright ever seen in this nation.'"

Jane's eyes were full of tears as she listened. It was astonishing that everything had turned out better than anyone would have thought possible only a few months before. But she had made that glorious day possible, and she should have been at Charles's side, not stuck across the cold North Sea and far from home.

She would accompany Mary to England soon, but Mary would not stir from The Hague until she had used her brother's newfound power to force the Electors to confirm her ten-year-old son, William, in his position as Elector-General and to arrange for his schooling.

At the end of June a letter arrived in Jane's mother's handwriting. That was not unusual; during the time that John and her father were in prison, her mother's letters had been her main source of news from Bentley. But for some reason on this day the spidery ink on the white paper set off alarum bells in Jane's head. She broke the wax seal and read.

"My dear daughter, it grieves me to tell you that your beloved father died yesterday, on the thirteenth of June. He had been in poor health after his imprisonment, and was taken of a sudden with an ague . . ."

The letter fell from Jane's fingers and her hands flew to her throat. She suddenly felt as though she could not breathe.

"Jane, dear, what is it?" Queen Elizabeth cried in alarm.

"My father—dead."

Queen Elizabeth, Mary, and Lady Stanhope rushed to her and held her as she wept. But she felt as though there were a wall of ice between her and them, and her mind whirled, disbelief fighting with grief and rage.

Her father, gone. It could not be. She had longed for home for so long, and though she missed her mother and the rest of the family, now she realized that home had always meant her father, and without him Bentley would seem but a shadow of itself.

"It should not have been this way," she cried. "He risked so much and paid so dear. He should have lived to rejoice at the king's return, with no more thought than to read, and walk, and play with his grandchildren."

She thrust herself away from the women and snatched up the letter from the floor. Was there any word of comfort in it?

"I would have you know that almost his last words were of his dear Jane, and of your courage and the great deeds you have done for England. Others of the neighborhood have lately been honored for the part they played. Mr. Whitgreaves and Father Huddleston of Mosely and the Penderel brothers of Whiteladies were sent for to London last week that they should receive the thanks of the king at his own hands . . ."

IN SEPTEMBER, MARY HAD AT LAST SETTLED HER SON'S AFFAIRS SATisfactorily, and her household was in frenzied preparation for their departure to London. The Earl of Sandwich arrived in the *Resolution*, to conduct the Princess Royal and her entourage to England, and they would depart as soon as the weather permitted. Jane sang as she packed, and ran to ask Queen Elizabeth if she needed help in making ready. But Charles's old aunt shook her head.

"The king has not invited me to court."

Jane stared at her. "But surely—"

"No. He has not. And without his invitation I cannot go, for I have no place to live nor means to live on once I got there."

"I will write to him," Jane said, quaking with rage. "You, above all people, must be there!"

"No, no. Perhaps he has forgotten. I will wait a little longer. He has so much on his mind just now, and I would not be a trouble to him."

Jane stared in dismay at the old lady, who would be left quite alone. She took a deep breath. "Then I will stay here with you."

With tears in her eyes, Queen Elizabeth embraced Jane and patted her cheek.

"You are a good girl, Jane. But you must go home to your dear brother and the rest of your family. Loving you as I do, I know how much your mother must long to have you back with her."

The bad weather cleared, and the *Resolution* put to sea, but Jane thought that perhaps they would have been better to wait. Mary and half her ladies were violently ill. The seas were rough, the ship climbing walls of glassy green water and then plunging into foamy troughs, the crew struggling to keep the vessel afloat and on course, battling with the sodden sails, desperately cutting away rigging when a mast came crashing down to prevent the ship from being pulled onto her side. Everyone was wet and cold throughout the voyage, and there was no hope of hot food. Jane was terrified, sure with each violent pitch and roll that the ship would be laid on her beam ends and swamped. Even within sight of land, the *Resolution* nearly foundered. How unfair it would be, Jane thought, to have survived these last nine years only to perish before she reached England.

At last the ship lay at anchor at Margate. A boat put out from shore, and as it drew near, Jane saw that it carried Charles and the Duke of York. Their faces were somber as they climbed onto the quarterdeck, and Jane noticed with a start that beneath their dark cloaks they wore mourning clothes.

"Jane." Charles raised her from her curtsy and kissed her cheek. "Pray lead me to my sister. I'm afraid I bear bad news, and she should receive it in private."

Jane's mind seethed with alarm. The king would only put on full mourning for the death of someone very close to him. Who could it be? His mother? Or was it possible that dear old Queen Elizabeth had died at The Hague while Mary was en route to England, and the news had outstripped them? But she only nodded and conducted the royal brothers to Mary's cabin. Whoever had died, she would learn of it soon enough. Mary had washed and dressed and was managing to stay upright in a chair, but her face was still almost green from the effects of seasickness. She rose with a weak smile on her lips and then froze as she noted her brothers' somber attire.

"Who . . ."

She swayed on her feet, and Jane ran to give her a steadying arm. Charles and the Duke of York rushed to their sister's side and eased her back into her chair.

"Oh, Mary," Charles said, stooping before her. "It's Harry."

The Duke of Gloucester, Charles's youngest brother. Jane's heart went out to Mary, who had immediately come to love the little brother she had hardly known when he had arrived at The Hague.

"Smallpox," Charles went on. "He seemed to rally and be out of danger, and then suddenly he worsened."

"No!" Mary's wail was animal. She started to her feet, arms flailing, head thrown back in wild grief. "No! No!"

Lady Stanhope took Mary into her arms, Mary clinging to her like a small girl as she sobbed, and Jane was reminded that Lady Stanhope had been with Mary when she left England to join her husband when she was only ten years old, and had been Mary's governess and the closest thing to a mother she had known since then.

Perhaps the curse of the Stuarts had not been lifted after all, Jane thought.

CHARLES AND THE DUKE OF YORK STAYED ABOARD THE *RESOLUTION* that night, but the royal siblings sat in quiet grief together, and Jane had no chance to see Charles until the next day. He had brought a procession of barges to meet his sister and her entourage, and the convoy set forth up the river to London. Mary stayed below, and for a few hours Jane basked in the warmth of Charles's welcome.

"This is hardly the joyful homecoming you pictured, I'm sure," he said, coming to her side.

"I'm so sorry," she murmured, noting the lines of sadness around his eyes. "What desolation, to lose your dear brother, and just when the future holds so much promise."

"Yes. A lesson to seize the day, for we never know what tomorrow may bring."

The river swept in a great horseshoe-shaped bend, and Charles pointed out the old Palace of Greenwich and the dockyards of Deptford on the south bank. Suddenly London lay ahead. Jane was awed by the sight of the many church steeples rising from amidst the streets of tall houses packed cheek by jowl, stretching away from the riverbank for what looked like a mile or more to the fields and meadows beyond, and the gentle twin hills that Charles told her marked Highgate and Hampstead. The quays teemed with sailors and dockworkers, and vessels large and small plied their way through the sparkling water of the Thames.

"It's beautiful!" Jane cried to Charles. She laughed, for the first time in weeks.. "Remember when we were in Bristol, and I asked you if London was like that?"

"Aye, I do," he said, grinning.

"I never thought I'd get the chance to come here."

"And now that you are, how does it compare with Paris and Breda and The Hague?"

"A thousand times better." Jane smiled. "Because it lies in England."

The Palace of Whitehall seemed enormous, but oddly rambling and arbitrary, due no doubt to the fact that it had not been designed and built all at once but rather had grown over the centuries. As they had approached on the river it had more the appearance of a town than a palace. And so it was a town, in a way, Jane thought, with its gardens, kitchens, breweries, bakeries, and butcher shops, its theater and its tiltyard, its banqueting house and official chambers, and the series of landing stairs along the Thames. The palace's resemblance to a town was strengthened by the fact that the Holbein Gate stood open, and the street before the palace was choked with the passage of Londoners of every level of society—lords, clerks, army and navy officers, soldiers and sailors, street merchants, whores, and thieves.

A few days after her arrival, Jane stood in the Banqueting House, where Charles held court each day. It seemed to her that all of England and much of the rest of the world had flocked to London now that Charles was back on the throne. All around her was a press of people. Some she knew from Paris or The Hague, and a few were from near her own home. The previous day, in a solemn ceremony in Westminster Abbey, she had seen the Bishop of Lichfield invested as Archbishop of York.

"Here's a fellow countryman of yours, Jane," Charles called to her. "Mr. Izaak Walton, also of Staffordshire. Do you remember I told you that I had given my Garter and my George to Colonel Blague when I was at Whiteladies? Well, they were passed on for safekeeping, and I shall never be able to thank my good friend Izaak for restoring them to me."

He stuck out his leg to display the Order of the Garter around his silk-stockinged calf, and tilted the George so that its diamonds twinkled in the candlelight.

"A great pleasure, sir," Jane said, curtsying to Walton. "I most enjoyed reading your collection of Wooten's poems."

"The pleasure is mine, Mistress Lane," Walton returned, bowing. "An honor to meet the lady who preserved the life of the king through such perils as he has described."

"And that reminds me," Charles said to Jane. "I am endeavoring to procure you a pension. If it were up to only me, you should have a wheelbarrow of gold before you this minute, but alas, these things must work their way through Parliament. But surely it will not be long."

Jane was not the only one who was to be rewarded for her loyalty and help to the king during his long years of exile. Every day he created new earls, viscounts, and baronets, restored lands that had been sequestered, and promised gifts and pensions. And when she had written home to tell her family that she was at last in England, and would return to Bentley after the coronation in January, she had included Charles's invitation that her brother Richard should come to Whitehall to be a groom of the bedchamber.

Jane had not been in London a week before she noticed a familiar striking figure making his way toward her through the chattering courtiers in the Banqueting House. Prince Rupert stood head and shoulders above most of the crowd, and Jane thought he was even more handsome than when she had last seen him. She curtsied low, and felt herself flush at the intensity of his gaze.

"Mistress Lane. I am most gratified to see you. Not only on my own account, but because my mother the queen has entrusted to me a letter for you."

With a devilish twinkle in his eyes, he pulled a little square of folded paper from his pocket.

"Oh, how does Her Majesty?" she cried, breaking the wax of the letter. She had worried about Queen Elizabeth of Bohemia every day since leaving The Hague, and the sight of the familiar handwriting filled her with joy.

"She was very well when I left her a few days since," Prince Rupert said, smiling down at her.

"I am so relieved to hear it. And so grateful to Your Highness for taking the trouble to carry the letter to me."

That evening Jane sat down to write to Queen Elizabeth, letting her know that she and Mary had arrived safely, and to give all the news that she had.

"I have had the honor to receive Your Majesty's letter by Prince Rupert. Methinks His Highness looks very well. Everybody here seems to look very graciously on him. We are like to have the queen very suddenly here, which many are discontented at."

Charles's aunt had insisted that she wanted to be informed how Charles was rewarding Jane, so with a wry smile, Jane wrote on.

"The king has done nothing for me but puts me off with good words, but that will not go to market. The princess is very well. She has never been abroad but once, at Hampton Court, and has eat but once in public with the king since she came. I appear not above once a day at court and then I choose my time when there is least company. I pray God bless Your Majesty with all happiness"

As Jane had written, she did not choose to spend much time at Whitehall, with its press of timeservers and glavering fools. But she did make a daily appearance, and about three weeks after her arrival heard Boswell in whispered conversation with Dorothy.

"I've heard that the duke says the child is not his at all!" Boswell sneered.

"She's a fool," Dorothy whispered. "He'll never marry her, sure. He must marry some princess to strengthen the family ties to the other royal houses and get a good dowry, not saddle himself with a merry-begotten child."

Boswell snorted. "He that doth get a wench with child and marries her afterward, it is as if a man should shit in his hat and then clap it upon his head."

It was surely Nan Hyde they were talking about. So her belly could not be kept a secret any longer, and now the troubles had begun.

Jane had no sooner got back to Somerset House than she had a visit from Nan's maid, Nell Stroud, her eyes anxious.

"My mistress begs that you will come to see her, Mistress Lane, as soon as you possibly may."

Jane's mind began to tally the possible problems Nan was facing.

"I will come with you now," she said, "but what is the matter?"

"Oh, Mistress, I'll leave it to her to tell you in full, but she's in the briars right enough."

Jane put on her cloak and hat and hurried with Nell the short way along the river to Worcester House, where Nan was living with her parents.

"Oh, Jane, thank God you've come!" Nan exclaimed, breaking into tears as she rushed to Jane and threw her arms around her. She was heavily pregnant now, but her face was streaked with tears and her eyes sunk in shadows. She led Jane to a little table before the fireplace and Nell disappeared to fetch some refreshment.

"Nan, what's amiss?" Jane cried, alarmed at her friend's state.

"Everything," Nan said, shaking her head as though lost. "We were married again here in secret a few weeks ago, lest there be any question about our marriage in Breda. James told the king that we were wed, and that if His Majesty did not accept it we would leave England forever. The king was not happy but said as it was done there was naught he could do. He sent my lord of Ormonde and the Earl of Southampton to tell my father."

She broke off and started sobbing, mopping her face with a handkerchief that was already sodden and wrinkled.

"My father declared that he would rather I was the duke's whore than his wife."

"But why?" Jane asked, appalled.

"Because he fears it will be thought that he seeks to rise above his station, that he has pushed me to James for what he may gain by it. He said—he said he would beg His Majesty to put me in the Tower and cut off my head."

"Surely he didn't mean it?" Jane gasped.

"He did!" Nan wailed. "They thought he was mad, James said, he was roaring so. He said I was no daughter of his anymore, that he disowned me."

Jane thought of Lord Capulet railing at poor Juliet.

Hang, beg, starve, die in the streets
For by my soul I'll ne'er acknowledge thee,
Nor what is mine shall never do thee good.

"He ordered my mother to lock me up, and she has done so!"

"But what of the duke? Surely he can make your father see sense?"

"He—he—he—"

Nan was sobbing so hard now that she couldn't get the words out.

Jane gathered the girl into her arms and held her, stroking her damp hair from her face, until the sobs subsided into hiccups and at last Nan could speak again.

"That is the worst of it, and why I am so afraid! He was coming by night to visit me, secretly. Oh, my mother knew, but my father did not. But now he has not come for more than three weeks! And Nell tells me that Sir Charles Berkeley, that very devil, has poisoned his mind, telling James that the marriage is not lawful because the king did not give his consent beforehand, and moreover that he—Sir Charles, I mean—has lain with me, and sundry other men besides!"

It grew more and more like a plot from Shakespeare, Jane thought, with Sir Charles acting a very Iago to the Duke of York.

"But sure the duke does not believe that?" Jane said. "He couldn't!"

"But he does!" Nan's eyes were hopeless. "Or at least he must have come to think it may be so, for I'm told he thinks of throwing me over, of denying that we were ever wed!"

"But you are, and I was there," Jane said.

"Yes, and that is why I need your help. Oh, Jane, I beg you, go to him. Remind him that I am indeed his true and loving wife, and tell him that on my soul I could never play him false and never have. I would rather die, tell him."

"I will," Jane said, anger boiling within her. "He'll answer to me, I assure you. And that rogue Sir Charles as well."

GUILT AND ALARM SUFFUSED THE DUKE OF YORK'S FACE WHEN JANE stomped up to him in his chambers at St. James's Palace.

"Your Highness," she began. "I must needs speak with you of your wife."

"Here, in here, I p-p-pray you," he gulped, his stammer rising to trouble him as it always did when he was upset. He ushered her into his privy chamber and shut the door behind them, regarding Jane as he might a mad dog.

"For shame, Your Highness. For shame, sir."

The duke dropped his eyes and drew breath to speak, but Jane carried on.

"Surely you know better than to believe the damned lies of that cur Berkeley? Nan is true to you, and has been ever since the day you met, I swear upon my life. And if it is true that you are trying to wriggle away from the poor girl, and claim you were never wed, by God I will go to the king and tell him of that marriage in Breda, and of all that went before it."

She was breathing hard, and found that she had been shaking her fist at the duke.

"Don't do that, I implore you, Mistress Lane." He looked truly alarmed, Jane was glad to see. "I didn't mean to say she lied. I didn't really think—only Sir Charles said—"

"Sir Charles is a lying vermin, and you know it. And I will not set foot from here until I see you on your way to your wife—your poor wife, great with your child—to tell her you will not play her false nor never will—and until you swear that you will go next to that snake Berkeley and demand that he recant his filthy lies or that you will have satisfaction with sword or pistol!"

"I can't challenge him! The king—"

"Yes, the king has forbidden dueling, so Berkeley had better eat his words, hadn't he?"

The duke's mouth worked, like that of a fish out of water, but Jane could tell he knew he was beaten.

"Yes. You're right. Oh, my poor Nan."

Jane was alarmed to see that his eyes were filling with tears, and threw up her arms in frustration.

"'Fore God, sir, don't weep. Just go and put things right."

IN THE MORNING NELL STROUD WAS BACK AT SOMERSET HOUSE ONCE more.

"My mistress is in labor, Mistress Lane! And the king has ordered her father to admit to her chamber a delegation to get to the truth of the matter."

"To her chamber? Now, while she is abed?"

"Yes, Mistress, and she needs you!"

At Worcester House Lady Hyde greeted Jane with a haunted expression on her face.

"Oh, Mistress Lane, I can scarce believe what's occurring, but my poor girl is as good as on trial, it seems."

Gathered outside Nan's bedchamber were Ormonde and his wife, Sir Edward Nicholas, the Earl of Manchester, the Countess of Sunderland and Cork, and the Bishop of Winchester. The bishop nodded a silent greeting.

"Good. Now Mistress Lane is here, we can begin."

The crowd filed into Nan's room and took their places around the bed. Poor Nan was doing her best to look dignified, which was not easy, Jane thought, as her great belly rose in a hill before her, its quakes and rollings visible even under the bedcovers. A midwife stood by, glowering at the intruders.

"Mistress Anne," the bishop intoned gravely. "We are come at His Majesty's behest to settle the truth of this matter. You have nothing to fear, just tell the truth before these witnesses."

Nan swallowed and clutched her mother's hand, but nodded.

"Who is the father of your child?" the bishop demanded.

"His Highness James, the Duke of York," Nan said, her voice steady, sticking out her chin in that way Jane knew so well.

"And have you ever known any other man but the duke?"

"No!" Nan cried, her face flushing. "Before my mother and my God and all that is holy, I have not!"

She was seized by a pain, and cried out. Her eyes went to Jane, imploring, and Jane hastened to the opposite side of the bed from where Lady Hyde stood, displacing the bishop with her glare, and took Nan's other hand in hers. Nan writhed with the pain, crushing Jane's hand in hers. The inquisitors shuffled and muttered in embarrassed uncertainty.

Jesu, Jane thought. *That it should come to this. Can they not leave the poor girl in peace?*

Nan panted as the wave of pain crested and passed. The bishop cleared his throat, and with a wary glance at Jane, once more took up his position close to the side of the bed.

"And are you and the duke married?" he asked, peering solemnly at Nan's face.

"Indeed we are. Twice over we are," Nan said, her eyes blazing. "We were wed first at Breda last autumn, and then once more at about midnight on the evening of the third of September of this year."

The third of September, Jane thought. The anniversary of the Battle of Worcester and of the death of Oliver Cromwell. Surely Charles would hold his breath when that date rolled around for the rest of his life, wondering what new cataclysmic event was about to unfold.

Nan was seized once more in the grip of her pain, and the midwife pushed her way through the observers and put her hand beneath the bedclothes.

"The babe is coming!" she snapped at the bishop, and then turned her eyes on the committee. "For pity's sake, get out!"

The bishop scurried a few feet away, to the side of Lord Ormonde. The other observers seemed frozen where they stood. Nan made no attempt to suppress her cries this time, and gave a great roaring groan that echoed off the walls before subsiding into heavy panting breaths. The midwife's hands were busy between Nan's thighs and she glared across Nan's belly at the bishop. He struggled to retain his composure and once more took up his examination.

"Mistress Lane. Mistress Hyde has averred that you were a witness to the marriage in Breda. Will you confirm that this is true?"

Nan's whimpers were rising again, and the members of the royal delegation looked as if they would like to sink into the earth.

"I will, sir," Jane said. "And so was Sir Charles Berkeley, as I will take any oath you like."

There was a murmur from the witnesses around Nan's bed, and she squeezed Jane's hand and gave her a damp little smile.

"Thank you," the bishop said, backing away from the bed. "I will report what you say to His Majesty, and pray that this matter is now at rest."

Nan broke into tears of relief as the committee fled from her room, and then gave a groan as a pain took her once more.

"Thank you, Jane," she gasped out. "Thank you. Pray for me, will you, that my child and I may come through this night in safety?"

"I will," Jane said, bending to kiss Nan's forehead. "But I'm sure you'll be fine."

NAN'S SON WAS BORN ON THE TWENTY-SECOND OF OCTOBER. THE DUKE of York had publicly declared that Nan was indeed his wife. Sir Charles Berkeley had recanted his lies. Sir Edward Hyde had accepted that he had no power to change what was already done. But no one but Nan, and possibly the Duke of York, was happy about the situation.

Mary of Orange was furious.

"I'll not have the baggage taking precedence over me," she vowed, her lips compressed in fury, as Jane helped her to dress for bed that night. "The queen my mother is on her way from Paris, and when she gets here she'll soon put a stop to any talk of Nan Hyde being made the Duchess of York."

It would be a bitter pill indeed, Jane thought, to one as prideful as Mary, to have her lady-in-waiting suddenly her superior. Nan had stepped into a hornet's nest indeed when she had given her heart to the duke.

THE RUMORS ABOUT NAN'S PREGNANCY AND HER MARRIAGE TO THE duke had reached The Hague, and Queen Elizabeth of Bohemia wrote to Jane, anxious to know the truth of what was happening. She liked Nan well enough, she said, but surely the wench was not really married to the Duke of York? Jane sighed in shame at the lies she had told, by omission or commission, to keep the marriage secret. She could not bring herself to admit that she had witnessed the marriage, and struggled to write a reply that would not deny the queen's sense of outrage, but would tell her truly that there was no point in wishing that the rumors were false.

"I have little encouragement to write of to Your Majesty," she wrote. "For the present news is that Mistress Hyde is brought to bed of a boy, which she vows to be the duke's and he married to her. She is owned in her father's family to be Duchess of York, but not at Whitehall as yet, but 'tis very sure that the duke has made her his wife. The Princess Mary is much discontented at it, as she has great reason. When Queen Mary comes we shall see what will be done about it. The duke and princess are gone to Dover to meet her. The king and Prince Rupert are to follow on Saturday. Your Majesty desired to know when the court goes out of mourning. As yet, everybody is in mourning clothes, and 'tis thought will continue so till after Christmas. I pray God bless Your Majesty. That prayer I must ever end with."

The arrival of Queen Mary did nothing to still the storm at Whitehall over Nan Hyde and the Duke of York. The queen refused to see her daughter-in-law, to acknowledge the child, or meet with Nan's father, recently created Baron Hyde. Jane heard that a weary and angry Charles had brokered a meeting between the reluctant grandparents, enforcing his mother's bending to his wishes only by the threat of withholding the pensions she needed so badly.

CHAPTER TWENTY-TWO

SINCE HIS RETURN TO LONDON, CHARLES HAD TOLD OVER AND over again the story of his escape from Worcester and his subsequent travels, and it was both astonishing and pleasant to Jane to discover that she was famous. She had been shown at least eight broadsheets and ballads, with crude woodcut depictions of her riding behind the king. "The Memorable Tragedy of Mrs. Jane Lane," "His Majesty's Miraculous Preservation by the Oak, the Maid and Ship," "The Five Faithful Brothers, a True Discourse Between Charles II and the Five Brothers at His Escape from Worcester, with Mrs. Lane's Conveying His Majesty Through All His Difficulties," "The Royal Oak, or the Wonderful Travels, Miraculous Escapes, Strange Accidents of King Charles the Second," "The Wonderful and Miraculous Escape of our Gracious King from that Dismal, Black, and Gloomie Defeat at Worcester."

Already a book had been published entitled *Boscobel, or the History of His Majesty's Preservation After the Battle of Worcester,* and another called *Monarchy Revived* was in the works, and would have a dedication to Jane.

At the end of October Jane learned that the Right Worshipful Company of Merchant-Tailors were to preside over celebrations, which, according to the handbills papering London, would feature a pageant, *The Royal Oak, with Other Various and Delightful Scenes Presented on the Water and the Land.*

Jane and several of Mary's ladies took a coach to Cheapside, and watched the festivities from the upper windows of the Key Tavern. A huge wagon served as a movable stage, with an elaborately painted backdrop depicting the woods of Shropshire and Staffordshire, and one noble tree in particular helpfully labeled "The Royal Oak."

First came three or four tumblers, who delighted the crowd with their rolls, handstands, flips, and other feats of agility. There followed members of the Merchant-Tailors company presenting the king's miraculous escape. Jane watched with a sense of disbelief to see herself personified by a boy of about fourteen, an apprentice with the company, mounted on a hobbyhorse behind the player-Charles.

"It's you!" Dorothy squealed. As word spread to the folk gathered nearby that Jane herself, the heroine of the play and the king's savior, was among them, there were cheers and toasts in her honor, and after the pageant was done, she found herself at the center of an admiring knot of people wanting to hear firsthand about her travels with the king.

Life at Charles's court was vastly different from the impoverished existence his followers had endured in France and Holland, and far grander, too, than Mary's court. Charles was tearing through the fifty-thousand-pound grant from Parliament, rewarding his faithful friends, adorning himself and Barbara Palmer with clothes and jewels, hiring musicians and acrobats, pastry cooks and confectioners, goldsmiths and upholsterers, and setting to rights the Palace of Whitehall, much of which had fallen into sad disrepair during England's years without a king. One of the first areas to get attention was the small private theater known as the Cockpit. Carpenters, plasterers, and painters labored by day and by night, and Jane was thrilled when she heard that on the nineteenth of November, the newly re-formed King's Company, under the management of Thomas Killigrew, would present Ben Jonson's play *The Silent Woman.*

That night Charles and his court shoehorned themselves into the little theater, still smelling of paint and sawdust, the light of the hundreds of candles in wall brackets and on great cartwheel chandeliers above dancing and glinting off the jeweled crowd. Jane, seated with the royal family and their attendants on the dais facing the stage, had a perfect view of the actors as well as the rest of the audience. Her heart leaped as the curtain rose, and the actors swept onto the stage. She laughed in delight to hear spoken aloud the scenes she knew from her father's book of Ben Jonson's plays. Jests that had seemed dull and inexplicable on the page brought the house to tears of laughter.

After that, she saw plays as often as she was able. The King's Company returned to the palace on several nights, but Jane also accompanied Charles and others when they went to the Vere Street Theatre, the converted tennis court that had just opened as the new home of Killigrew's company.

Her pleasure in the theater made Jane think of Queen Elizabeth's stories of the grand masques at the court of her father, King James I, and of the elderly queen's enjoyment of the Christmas masques at Mary's court. Jane missed Queen Elizabeth, fretted at her being left alone at The Hague, and wrote to encourage her to come to London with or without Charles's invitation. There was plenty of room at Whitehall, and after all, the king could hardly send his aunt away once she was there. In early December she was touched to receive a letter from Queen Elizabeth informing her that the queen had written to Charles to tell him in no uncertain terms that he must reward Jane richly for her help to him.

"I am so infinitely obliged to Your Majesty for your gracious favor toward me," she wrote, "that I am not able to express the great sense I have of it. All that I can say is that whilst I have breath I shall pray for Your Majesty's prosperity. I wish I could send Your Majesty the good news that the king had settled something upon me, but as yet it is not done. But Queen Mary promises me she will see it done before she returns. Her journey is deferred for some time longer."

Queen Elizabeth had demanded to know the latest turns of events in the saga of Nan Hyde and her baby, wondering once more if it could really be true that the duke had married her.

"The child is not yet christened," Jane wrote, "but it is confidently reported that it shall be within a few days, and owned. The Princess Mary is very much troubled about it. Queen Mary is politic and says little of it. There is no question to be made but that they are married. I do not think that Princess Mary will stay long here after the queen is gone."

Jane could picture Queen Elizabeth, hungry to know every detail of how things stood at Whitehall.

"Queen Mary is very obliging to all people," she wrote, "and she is much more liked than the Princess Royal. The young Princess Minette is indeed very handsome. They have not yet left off mourning, and be in black still. I most humbly thank Your Majesty for my wine."

In early November, Jane received a message from Worcester House that Nan Hyde wanted to see her. Nan received her in her bedchamber, fully recovered now from the birth of her child, who snored peacefully in his cradle.

"He's to be christened Charles," she said proudly. "Oh, Jane, it's all come about perfectly. I never thought it would."

Nan called for coffee and cakes, and it seemed to Jane that Nan had a new imperiousness about her, and that not only the servants, but Lady Hyde, who came in to greet Jane, treated Nan with far greater deference than they had before.

Nan seemed to be bursting with excitement, and once they had settled before the fire, she could not contain herself any longer.

"I'm to be made Duchess of York."

It took Jane's breath away. It had all happened, she thought. Everything that had seemed so impossible when she first saw Nan sighing over the Duke of York so long ago in Peronne. Now Nan Hyde was married to the duke. She was to be Duchess of York. And the fair-haired sleeping child was second in line to the throne. And Jane? Who loved the king, had risked her life to save him, who had been loved in return, who had borne the king's child in her belly? She had swallowed her disappointment and hurt, as she had thought she must. *What if I had made a fuss?* she wondered. *And what if the child had lived? Was there at any time the chance that he would have married me?*

She realized that Nan was waiting for her reply to the momentous news.

"I give you my congratulations, Nan," she said. "Your Grace."

Nan giggled.

"Not quite yet. But soon. Oh, Jane, I cannot thank you enough. Where I should be without your help, I dare not think."

"Nonsense," Jane said. "I only reminded the duke of what he knew to be true and of his duty to you."

"Only that!" Nan said. "When I was so nearly lost."

She leaned toward Jane conspiratorially.

"I must have a household, Jane. Will you come to me, and be one of my ladies?"

No, Jane thought. *No, I will not come to be maid to you, who are no better than me, and have not deserved to be where you have got. And yet,* she thought, *What harm? I will go home in January, just as soon as the coronation is done. Mary is in a black rage already, and this is like to make her even more fretful.*

"Yes," she said, forcing herself to smile. "Thank you. It will be my honor to serve you."

And so Jane's belongings were moved from Mary's household at Somerset House to Worcester House, where the Duke and Duchess of York were making their home, and on the ninth of December she stood by while the infant Charles was christened, with the king, Prince Rupert, and the wife of General Monck, now the Duchess of Albemarle, serving as godparents.

. . .

Charles had commissioned from Isaac Fuller a series of five paintings of his miraculous escape, and one of them was to portray him on horseback, with Jane riding pillion behind. When she was informed that she was needed for a sitting, she looked forward to some time in Charles's company. But when she arrived at the room where Fuller was at work, Charles was nowhere to be seen, and she was helped onto a seat placed sideways on a tall sawhorse.

"His Majesty will sit separately," Fuller explained. "I make sketches from life, and then put the elements together when I come to work on the canvas itself."

Other pictures would show the king changing into his disguise as Will Jackson at Whiteladies, sheltering in the woods near Boscobel, hiding in the oak tree with Colonel Carlis, and riding on the Penderels' mill horse. The five Penderel brothers, along with Thomas Whitgreaves and Father Huddleston, had sat for Fuller when they visited Whitehall in June, and he showed Jane the painting of them escorting Charles through the dark woods.

The paintings brought back vividly to Jane's mind her travels with Charles, the days when they had been as close as two people might be. She longed for that closeness again, and on a whim, decided to go and see him.

She made for the king's privy chamber. Perhaps she would be fortunate enough to find him alone. She was pleased to see that no one waited in the outer chamber, but just as she was about to give her name to the guard, the door to Charles's room opened, and a richly dressed young woman and a little girl stepped out. Charles kissed the woman on the cheek before he saw Jane, and she noted his look of guilty surprise as his eyes met hers. The woman turned to see who was coming, and Jane recognized her as the former Betty Killigrew Boyle, who had been made Viscountess Shannon in September. She had been one of the ladies-in-waiting to Charles's mother in Paris, and another of his lovers. And the little girl by her side, with her near-black ringlets and shining dark eyes, was unquestionably Charles's daughter. The two women stared at each other for a moment before bowing coldly, and then the viscountess swept past Jane and away, her heels clicking on the marble floor.

"Jane," Charles said. "Is there something I can do for you?"

He seemed a little awkward. Quite polite, as he might be to a stranger. Not the Charles she had hoped to find. Not her Charles.

"No, Your Majesty," she said. "I just—I have just been admiring Mr. Fuller's paintings and wanted to compliment you."

"Oh, yes," he said, pulling out his pocket watch and tilting it to catch the light. Jane thought of the watch he had given her on that morning when they parted at Trent.

"Good, aren't they?" Charles smiled vaguely in her direction. "I'm sorry, Jane, but I'm late for Edward Hyde. Perhaps we can talk later?"

"Of course, Your Majesty," she said, curtsying, and managed a smile as she left him.

That night, Jane could not sleep, and stood staring out a window of the darkened palace. She could just discern the ripples in the river below, shining in the moonlight. She thought she had never been so lonely in her life. Seeing Charles's little girl that afternoon had made her think once more of what would have happened had she borne that lost baby. Would she have received a title, as Elizabeth Killigrew had? Would Charles pay any more attention to her? Or would she feel as cast aside as she now did, only more so, with a child to care for and no prospect of a husband, either in the person of the king or someone else?

The face of Clement Fisher rose to her mind, and she suddenly longed to see him. He was still unmarried, she knew. But perhaps there was someone, someone he had contracted with but not yet wed. After all, it had been nine years since they had seen each other last. Well, that was just one more thing she would learn when she went home. In January, after the coronation. Not very much longer now.

. . .

THE COURT, STILL MOURNING THE DEATH OF THE DUKE OF GLOUCESTER, was preparing for a subdued Christmas. Jane's brother Richard had come, and she scarcely recognized him from the fire-breathing young man she had last seen a few days before the Battle of Worcester. It warmed her heart to have him with her at Whitehall, among the ever-growing sea of strangers.

She had not yet received further news of the promised pension, but she was overjoyed to learn that Parliament had voted her a gift of a thousand pounds to buy herself a jewel. She would be glad of the money, but had no intention of spending so much on a jewel when it might let her live in independence and comfort for many years.

She was just sitting down to write to inform Queen Elizabeth of Bohemia of her good news when Dorothy darted into her room, looking terrified.

"Have you heard? The Princess Royal is taken ill."

Mary had never been quite well since they had arrived, but Jane had put it down to grief over her brother's death, distress at having been forced to leave her son William behind at The Hague, the dreadful voyage to England, and then the protracted stress over the Duke of York's marriage.

"You mean more ill than she has been?" she asked.

"Oh, yes." Dorothy blinked, on the edge of tears. "A raging fever, and red spots all over."

Jane's heart stopped. Red spots sounded very like smallpox. Jane hurried to Somerset House, where a group of black-gowned doctors gathered, looking like a flock of ravens. By that night, Mary was worse, out of her head with delirium. The next afternoon Mary seemed somewhat improved, but Jane thought she had better write to Queen Elizabeth.

"I believe Your Majesty will hear the hot alarum of the Princess Royal's being in great danger of death, which indeed this morning was sadly apprehended by many. But because Your Majesty should not be frighted at what news perchance you may hear, I have just now been with her and God be praised she is much better. The doctors do not yet know whether it is the pox or the measles, but I fear it will prove the smallpox.

"Let it be what it will, I am confident the trouble about her brother's business has thrown her into it. The duke is much at Worcester House with his wife and is as all people say very fond of her. She takes an abundance of servants, and 'tis said great lords' daughters are offered her to be maids of honor to her. I confess I am now glad Your Majesty is not here, for all things go very cross. The queen has deferred her journey a week longer because of the princess being not well.

"The Parliament has given me a thousand pounds this week. I will not fail to write Your Majesty word how the princess does by the next post. I pray God bless Your Majesty."

Mary's doctors decided that it was not measles she had, but smallpox, which had so recently carried off the Duke of Gloucester, and all of London seemed to hold its breath, hoping for news of Mary's recovery but fearing the worst. Charles sent his mother and sister Minette to St. James's Palace to be out of danger of contagion, but visited Mary daily himself, sitting by her bedside as she grew weaker.

Jane returned to Somerset House to see Mary again the day after she had written to Queen Elizabeth. Mary's room was stifling, a fire burning on the hearth and heavy coverings over the windows, and a whimper of misery came from the figure beneath the bedclothes.

"Your Highness," Jane said softly as she approached the bed.

Mary's eyes flickered open. They were bright with fever, and her face seemed to have aged ten years. Flat red spots flared on her face, her forearms, and the palms of her hands.

"Jane," Mary murmured. "Don't touch me. I would not have you ill."

She closed her eyes, as if the effort of keeping them open was too exhausting. Jane sat beside the bed, horrified at Mary's condition.

"Is there anything I can do, Your Highness, to make you more comfortable?"

The faintest of smiles crossed Mary's face.

"My little William. Make sure that the king cares for him as he ought, champions my son as I have done in dealing with the stadtholders. Ask my aunt Elizabeth of Bohemia to never let him forget me."

"Oh, Your Highness, surely you will recover to see your son again," Jane murmured, her heart breaking at the thought of William, just turned ten, being orphaned.

Mary shook her head, her eyes closed once more, as if gathering her strength to go on.

"Tell Nan Hyde I'm sorry I have not been more kind to her these last weeks. I know she loves James, and he must love her to have withstood what he has on her behalf."

Her eyes opened again, burning into Jane's.

"And thank you, Jane. For what you did for His Majesty. I know that you have suffered these years, and I can never thank you enough, for without you surely he would not have come safe away from England, nor would he now be back in London, and truly king."

"I would do it again a hundred times," Jane said, wondering if it were true.

"What courage," Mary said. "Never forget, Jane, what you have done for England."

THE NEXT DAY MARY SEEMED TO RALLY, BUT ON CHRISTMAS EVE SHE died, and the stunned court greeted the first Christmas after Charles's restoration with renewed sorrow.

On the twenty-ninth of December, Jane walked behind Mary's coffin to Westminster Abbey, flanked by Lord Ormonde and Edward Hyde. As was the custom, the king was not present, and the Duke of York served as chief mourner.

The funeral was conducted by the Reverend Gilbert Sheldon, as had been the christening of Nan Hyde's son. He was a man of the generation of Jane's parents, who was also from an old Staffordshire family, and listening to his accent made Jane acutely homesick. Very soon now, she would go home. There was no reason for her to be in London once the coronation was done.

Except . . . The word whispered at the back of her mind. Except what? Except to feel once more Charles's love, to know that she was special to him and that their days together had not been forgotten.

On the first of January, Jane went with Nan Hyde to Whitehall, where the Duke of York presented her formally as his wife to his mother, Queen Mary, who, with as much grace as she could muster, embraced the new duchess and kissed her cheeks.

A little later, Nan's baby Charles was created Duke of Cambridge, though what should have been a joyful celebration seemed almost an afterthought in the gloom following Mary's death.

The next day, Queen Mary and Minette set out for Paris, and Charles and his brother James were left to themselves, all that remained of the royal family that had returned so hopefully to England.

Twelfth Night brought to a close the Christmas season that had started with such joy and ended in such grief. In the Banqueting House, Jane chatted with Dr. Sheldon, exchanging memories of Christmases long past, of Morris dancers with antlers stepping the horn dance of Abbots Bromley. He knew her parents and John, and Jane was sure she must have met him when she was small.

"Will you go home now, Mistress Lane?" Dr. Sheldon asked.

"Very soon," she answered. "I tarried here so that I might attend the coronation, but now . . ."

"Yes, now with the loss of the Princess Royal that must be put off for some time."

"Until after Easter, I am given to understand," Jane said.

And now there really is no reason for me to tarry here, Jane thought. *Except* . . .

She pushed the thought from her mind.

. . .

Jane had received a Christmas gift of a dozen bottles of wormwood wine from Queen Elizabeth. They had been dispatched before the queen learned of Mary's death, and arrived with a letter full of good wishes for the new year. Jane had just sat down to write back to Charles's aunt, when Dorothy rushed in to inform her that word had come that Minette had been taken ill on the voyage back to France. Jane's first thought was what terror that news would strike into the heart of the poor old queen, already distraught over the loss of her favorite niece, and she bent her head and prayed before she took up her pen to write her letter. *I must give her the news but not alarm her,* she thought. *Not until there is need for her to be alarmed.*

And please, God, let there not be the need. Let there not be another blow to one who has withstood so many.

"I have yesterday received Your Majesty's gracious present of wormwood wine, which is extremely good," she wrote. "Which in all humbleness I do present my duty and humble thanks for."

And now for the difficult part, she thought.

"Here is no news that I know can be pleasing to Your Majesty," she wrote on, "but yet after so many and great afflictions that Your Majesty has had, I hope nothing will have cause to afflict you more. This morning news is come that your niece has the measles a-shipboard and that the queen is returned to Portsmouth. I would give anything that I were with Your Majesty."

I can't leave it like that, she thought. *Give her something to distract her.* She smiled, thinking of the old queen's most recent letter, full of indignation that Nan Hyde should have been made Duchess of York.

"I have this morning been to wait on the duchess," she wrote. "She lies here, and the king is very kind to her. She takes upon her as if she had been duchess this seven year. I wish Your Majesty did but see how perfectly I am mortified, but no one lives that is more Your Majesty's most humblest most obedient servant than I am and will ever be."

Jane reread the letter and sighed. She wanted to beg the queen to embark for England now so that at least she would be among family and friends, but she could see the proud old head shaking her refusal. When the king invited her, then she would come. *Can I tell her that I love her?* Jane wondered. She dipped her pen in the ink bottle and held it over the paper, hesitating, but could not quite summon the courage to write those words.

"Madam," she wrote, "for God's sake, have a great care of yourself, for if Your Majesty should come to harm that loss were never to be repaired. God in His infinite mercy protect you."

JANUARY HAD COME AND GONE, AND THE CORONATION WOULD NOT take place until April, and yet Jane had not gone home to Bentley. What held her there? she asked herself. Nothing.

Except . . .

On the twenty-fifth of February, almost nine months to the day since Charles had returned to London, Barbara Palmer gave birth to a daughter. The baby was called Anne Palmer, but no one thought that Barbara's husband was the father.

Jane tried to tell herself that the news didn't hurt, but it did, to her very soul. Whitehall echoed with the whispers, and Charles strutted amidst the crowds of courtiers. Like a rooster among the hens, Jane thought. And as at The Hague, when she had first seen Barbara Palmer, she was consumed with a helpless despair. She had given nine years of her life to the preservation of the king, nine years that had taken her from youth, with possibilities still before her, to this hell in which it seemed that her choices had slipped away while she was not looking.

It is past time I go home, she told herself. *How much evidence do I need that Charles has forgotten me, if indeed he ever cared for me at all?*

She had thought that she could not feel more miserable, but the next day she found that she could.

"James tells me that my father has been most industrious to find a wife for the king," Nan Hyde said, smiling, as Jane brushed her hair, "and that the choice has been made."

Jane stopped, brush in hand, blinking her astonishment. Of course she knew that Charles must have a queen, but she had not known that the search for a bride had begun in earnest, much less that the matter had been settled. Most of all it hurt that she had heard of it from someone other than Charles.

"There were three quite good possibilities," Nan went on, happy to have the rapt attention of everyone within hearing. "The Princess of Denmark, the Infanta of Portugal, and the sister of the Prince of Parma. But—though it's still secret, so do not breathe a word—it's to be the Portuguese princess."

Jane felt the blood rushing to her face. There was a roaring in her ears and she could no longer hear Nan's voice. She longed to grapple Nan around her throat and choke the simper off her face. She clapped a hand to her mouth, whether to keep herself from vomiting or screaming, she did not know.

She turned and fled from Nan's presence, ignoring the questioning cries behind her. She was almost to the king's privy chamber before she knew where she was going. She stalked past the guards at the door before they had time to stop her. Charles was alone with Edward Hyde.

"I must needs speak to Your Majesty. Now."

Hyde gaped at her.

"Well, Charles?"

The king paused only a moment before dismissing Hyde with a wave of his hand. Jane waited, but barely, before the door closed behind him.

"How dare you!" she shouted. It wasn't a very dignified beginning, she knew, but she was past caring.

"What have I done?" Charles asked, blinking.

"You are to be married! And you have not even the consideration to tell me yourself!"

The thought flitted across her mind that at last she was alone with

Charles, as she had not been in seven years, and that this scene was nothing like what she had hoped for.

"You know I must marry. I need an heir."

"But you—you—how can you do this to me?" Jane knew the words were absurd, made no sense, but there was no stopping them. "After what I have given you?"

"I can never repay you, Jane, for what you did for me. For England."

For you, she thought. *It was all for you, once I knew you. I love you, not England. The you with the laughing eyes, and the strong arms that held me, and the mouth that crushed mine in the heat of your passion. My lover, the father of that babe lost so long ago. Not the king, not this stranger who sits here before me.*

"Go home, Jane." His words were soft, but they hit Jane like a blow. "You see how it is here. I am always at the center of—of something. Some dispute, some urgent business, some suit for money or honors. During our time together, I could be myself, but I fear me I will never have such leisure again."

"You have time enough for Barbara."

Charles spoke so quietly that Jane could scarce hear him.

"You're better than that, Jane. You deserve better. You would not be happy with balls and card games and supper parties and the constant backbiting that has only just begun but now will never leave off. You long for discourse that will stretch your mind, for experience that will test your strength and courage, and for attention from a man that is constant and whose fire never dies. I cannot give you that. I wish I could, but I know myself too well."

Jane felt her heart tearing in two. She was drowning in a lake of her own blood deep within her breast. She should leave, before she made a worse fool of herself, but she could not.

"But before?"

"Before was a time out of time, a place that had no place, when you and I were all there was except the burning need to find my way to safety. That time is gone, and what we had will never come again."

Jane stared at him. It would never come again. He had said it, so bluntly. In one moment shattering the hopes she had nursed for so many years, though she thought she had let go of them long since. He was smiling, and the smile enraged her.

"I could have—" she began. She thought of Henry Lascelles, the love shining in his eyes. Of the men she had dismissed from consideration without a thought over the years. Because always it had been Charles who held her heart. "I could have loved someone else. Been happy."

"You shall have a pension of a thousand pounds a year. Enough that you need never do anything that you do not want to do, or bind yourself to any man except in love."

What a fool she had been. It was all over now, it didn't matter what she said.

"Why didn't you tell me before that you didn't want to be with me?"

"I did—"

"You didn't. All you had to say was, 'Jane I cannot love you,' and I would have heard you."

"But I did love you," he protested.

Jane winced at the past tense, and saw in the same moment that Charles realized what he had said. He opened his mouth to speak, but she waved him silent and turned her back to him, choking on her tears. She felt his eyes on her and she wanted to be gone from him, away from this torture of humiliation. But she could not leave yet. All the rage and hurt and bafflement of the long years bubbled to the surface, hot as molten metal, and would not be stilled.

"All you had to say was that I should not hope."

Her voice sounded unnaturally calm to her own ears. Torrents of pain raged within her.

"It would have hurt, but I would have survived. God knows I survived worse for you."

The long weeks of the walk to Yarmouth, the cold, the exhaustion, the killing of the rebel deserter, the days lying in Marjorie's cave after the loss of the child.

"I would have turned my thoughts from you, carved you out of my heart if need be. Why didn't you tell me? You had so many chances."

He threw up his hands helplessly.

"You knew I could not marry where I loved; I had to put the good of the country first."

Jane thought of poor Lucy Walter. Had she been the king's bride, denied and cast aside when it did not suit him to have a wife?

"Your purse first, you mean."

"Jane," he cried. "What would you have me do? I needed money, an army to take back my country—and all I had to offer was myself as husband to some princess with a father or brother with the means to help me. I tried to find a wife, God knows, not for my contentment but out of duty, but none would have me. My person alone was not enough, without I had a throne and a crown. And now I am back, now I am king in fact, the choice rests not with me alone."

"'His greatness weighed, his will is not his own,'" she quoted.

"Exactly," he said.

"You think you're Hamlet?" There was venom in her voice.

"He wrote it because it was true!" He ran his hands through his hair despairingly. "Jane, I never led you to believe that I could marry you."

"Marry me, no, but you said you loved me. Did that not mean anything?"

"Of course it did," he said, moving swiftly to her side.

"What? What did it mean? That you wanted to bed me at that moment but had no thought for me as soon as I was out of your sight?"

"Of course I wanted to see you."

"Then why did you not send for me? Why have I spent these many years—nine years, Charles!—waiting for you to want to be with me as you said you did? I loved you. I love you still."

She was sobbing and turned away from him in shame. When she had mastered herself, she went on.

"There has been no one else for me but you. But for you, there has always been someone else. I tried to tell myself that they didn't matter to you, that you needed the comfort, that you were sad and lonely and that I was the one you truly loved, and that the time would come that we would be together. But always it was someone else. Poor Lucy—"

"She was long gone to Taaffe by the time you came to Paris."

"The Duchess de Châtillon," Jane pressed on relentlessly. "Lady Byron, Catherine Pegge, Betty Killigrew—it was always someone else who had your company while I waited, longing for you. And now, now that you can do as you will—"

"I cannot!" he exploded.

"You can spend your days and nights with whom you please, whoever you must wed. And now it is still not me—it is Barbara Palmer." She didn't try to stop the tears now. "Barbara Palmer! So beautiful, so young. How can I compete? I can't. I've given you my youth and hopes, when you never loved me, never wanted me."

"Jane—" He tried to take her into his arms but she shoved him away, eyes blazing.

"I wish I had never seen you. I wish they had taken you at Worcester and hanged you at Tyburn. I wish England had gone up in flames and the monarchy ended and you suffered in hell for what I have been through for you."

She was suddenly aware of the little silk bundle pinned inside her bodice—the watch he had given her when they parted at Trent, wrapped in his handkerchief. She yanked it out and held it up for him to see.

"Take it back again. 'Rich gifts wax poor when givers prove unkind.'"

She hurled the watch at Charles, but it sailed over his head and crashed against the wall. Her last sight of him was the anguish in his eyes as she turned and fled, slamming the door shut behind her.

CHAPTER TWENTY-THREE

THE COACH RATTLED DOWN THE WOLVERHAMPTON ROAD, AND Jane's heart beat fast as the familiar turnoff to Bentley Hall came into view. The house was unchanged from when she had seen it last, but as she approached it seemed still and empty. Perhaps it was the dogs. There used to be a pack of dogs that set up such a clamor at the approach of any vehicle, animal, or person, but now only two rose from the shadows to give halfhearted barks.

The door opened, and with a shock Jane realized that the old lady who peered out at the approaching coach was her mother. Her hair had gone completely white, and she seemed stooped, and far thinner than Jane remembered her. And there was John behind her, and Athalia, both gray-haired and sad behind their smiles. She looked beyond them, and realized with an enormous tug at her heart that it was the sight of her father she sought. But he was gone, and she would never again see the love for her in his eyes or smell the comforting scent of his pipe as they sat together in his little library. Tears came to her eyes.

John helped her to alight, and awkwardly they all began to talk at once, and then all stopped at once to let one another speak, and again began to speak at once. Jane hugged her mother to her, careful at her fragility. Had she always been so small?

"You'll be tired," her mother said. "Your room is waiting for you, just as it was."

The memory of her room as it had been on that morning so long ago came sharp into Jane's mind, and suddenly she wondered why she had not come home so soon as she had landed in England, or indeed as soon as she had known that Charles would take his throne and she no longer had to fear for her life. What magic had she thought that Charles or London held, that they had kept her from the home and the people she loved so dearly?

"The others?" Jane asked.

"We'll have everyone to supper tomorrow," John said. "When you've had a chance to rest. Everyone is fair aching to see you again, Jane."

The servants had taken Jane's baggage upstairs, and she opened the door of her room to the scent of the fir boughs burning in the fireplace. And to the sound of a creaking call she knew so well and had not heard for so long.

"Jack!"

The cat leaped off the window seat and came stumping across the floor toward her, his tail held high. She could hear his purring from halfway across the room. She knelt and he came to her, and she kissed his head, stroked the soft white fur of his throat, inhaled the dusty and alive scent as he butted against her cheek.

"Oh, Jack. I'm sorry I've been gone so long."

JANE FELT LIKE A STRANGER AT THE FAMILY SUPPER THE FOLLOWING evening. John's children were all grown. Mary, Anne, and Elizabeth had married and were no longer at home. Thomas, whom she had last seen as a slight boy of eleven, was a tall and strapping young man who had just reached his majority. Grace, Lettice, and her namesake Jane were past twenty-one, though as yet unmarried. Even the youngest girls, Dorothy and Frances, were young ladies. The gathering was so small that there was no need to use the banqueting house; the entire family fit comfortably in the dining room.

Nurse, the steward, and a few other old retainers were still at Bentley, but so many of the others that Jane had known were gone, and the household now had only nine servants in all.

"We've done far less mining and farming than in the old days," young Thomas said. "There was no point in the labor as the more we earned, the more we were levied."

"But that will all change now," William said. "Now that the king is back, and we have nothing more to fear."

Jane noted with shock that even he, only a couple of years older than she, had a dusting of gray hair at his temples.

"Many things will change, and for the better, too," John said. "So many years of hardships are behind us now."

JANE STOOPED TO LAY THE APPLE BLOSSOMS ON HER FATHER'S GRAVE. It still looked so new, with the shoots of grass covering the mound of earth a fresher and brighter green than that of the surrounding sod. She sat, not caring for the dirt on her skirts, and with a finger traced the letters of his name, the dates of his birth and death, the edges of the carving in the stone still sharp and clean.

"I'm sorry, Father," she whispered. "I wish I had been here for you."

The whole orchard at Bentley was a cloud of pink and white blossoms, their sweet scent permeating the air. *Nine springs I missed,* Jane thought. *Nine times the winter-dark branches shooting forth their tiny buds, nine times those buds exploded in riotous blossom, nine times those blossoms showered the earth as the green leaves uncurled, nine times the nubs grew steadily into the heavy fruit. Did you walk here among the trees and think of me and wish me with you? Did you know that every day I thought of you and prayed for you, dear Father?*

She cried, as she had not been able to release herself to cry for her father's death until now, laying her head upon the sod, her fingers clutching at the cold ground. And when she had finally done, wiping her grimy cheeks with dirt-streaked hands, the question sprang into her mind, as it had done so many times before. Was it worth it?

Not long after Jane's return, she received a letter from Sir Clement Fisher, welcoming her home and asking if he could visit. Jane thought back to the last time she had seen him, at that birthday supper so long ago, just before Charles had arrived to change her life forever. She was an entirely different person now than she had been then, she thought. Could she hope to explain to Sir Clement what her life had been? Would she need to? After some thought she wrote back that she would be pleased to see him, and a week later she watched from her bedroom window as he came riding up the drive. He was still very handsome, she thought, little changed outwardly from the man she had known almost ten years earlier. She glanced in the mirror. She knew how much she had changed. Would he still find her to his liking?

"Jane."

Clement's voice was warm and his eyes told her that he still saw beauty in her face and form. She was surprised at how the sight of him stirred her heart. He had aged well, and seemed somehow more solid than she remembered. As he took her hand and kissed her, she felt at home and very safe.

"Jane," he said. "And now you are not just my Jane but the heroine of the country, the friend of the king and the darling of the courts of London, Paris, and the United Provinces."

"Hardly that," Jane laughed. "Were I that darling, they would not have let me leave. There is refreshment in the small parlor. Shall we sit there?"

As they settled before the fire, Jane recalled the evening long ago when Clement had asked her to be his wife. She poured hot chocolate for him, and sipped her own, not sure what to say.

"Will you tell me of your time abroad?" he asked.

"There's not much to say. Or rather, there's so much that I scarce know where to begin. Ten years . . ."

"Yes. Oh, Jane, I thought of you so often in those years. I carried you ever in my heart and longed for your return."

Jane was surprised at his words, and moved that he should be so candid.

"I'm gratified at such esteem," she said. "But I am not who I was. I fear I must disappoint you, when you find that the woman you have held in your mind's eye is gone."

He looked sad, and Jane spoke again.

"I do not mean in any way to reject your friendship."

"Is it friendship only that you think I offer you?"

There was love in his eyes, and with a flood of longing Jane realized how she had yearned for love and how little she had received in recent years.

"What I mean," she said, "is that I welcome your company more than I knew. And yet I am afraid, I find."

"Afraid? Of me?"

"No, not afraid of you. But of being known by you, perhaps."

She thought about the lost child, and the pain, and what Marjorie had told her, that she might never hold a child in her womb again. Could she ever tell Clement that? What if he wanted a child, what if that was his chief reason for seeking a wife? They sat in silence for some moments before he spoke.

"I would not have you share with me more of yourself than is comfortable for you. Let us begin anew. We'll get to know each other as the people we are now, rather than who we were before. I'll take nothing for granted, and hope that with time you may come to trust that you are safe with me."

Jane smiled, grateful.

"Thank you. Once more you offer me more patience than any woman has a right to expect."

"But it is not any woman to whom I give it. It is you. Oh, Jane, you cannot know what it means to me to have you here beside me."

. . . .

Charles's coronation would take place on the twenty-third of April. St. George's Day, the feast day of the patron saint of England. Well chosen, Jane thought. There was no day in the calendar that could be more heavily freighted with Englishness, with tradition, with the monarchy stretching back so many centuries. She had a pang of longing that she would not be in London for the event. She could imagine the streets thronged with the rejoicing populace, the church bells pealing, the king's stately procession to Westminster Abbey, and the ranks of the nobility there to witness the restoration of the monarchy. She thought of Charles bowing his head to receive the crown and smiled to wonder who would place it on his head, and whether whoever it was would have to stand a-tiptoe to reach. A-tiptoe. The phrase jolted words long forgotten into her mind.

. . . will stand a tip-toe when this day is named,
And rouse him at the name of Crispian.

It was the speech of King Henry V to his outnumbered troops before the Battle of Agincourt.

We few, we happy few, we band of brothers;
For he to-day that sheds his blood with me
Shall be my brother; be he ne'er so vile,
This day shall gentle his condition,
And gentlemen in England now a-bed
Shall think themselves accursed they were not here . . .

The thought shot through Jane like a bolt of lightning. As those men with Henry upon the field in France, she had been there, side by side in battle with the king. Her king. Her Charles. As Charles had said atop that windswept hill in Dorset, if Shakespeare were yet living, he might have written of it, her place no less in glory than those soldiers of old.

The dogs set up a furious barking and Jane went to the window to see what had them so stirred up. A coach was coming up the drive toward the house. A coach was an unusual thing in the country, and certainly a coach such as this, with an ebony-black finish so glossy that the rays of the sun striking it shone as though on a mirror. The old groom Maycumber was hastening as fast as his stiff legs would allow him from the back of the house to meet the strange equipage, and as it turned Jane saw with a shock that the door was painted with the royal coat of arms. Her heart skipped. But as the coach clattered to a halt, a liveried footman emerged, alone. It was not, as she had so wildly hoped for a moment, Charles, come to see her.

THE ENTIRE LANE HOUSEHOLD STARED IN AMAZEMENT AT WHAT the coach had brought, now spread before them on the long dining table. A pocket watch, worked intricately in gold. A great clock. A gold snuffbox with a tiny portrait of the king decorating its lid. A gold poncet box engraved with the Canton of England and the Lane arms. And what Jane could scarcely look away from, a life-size portrait of Charles, in a heavily carved gilded frame, in full regalia as he must have been for his coronation—a robe of purple velvet trimmed in ermine, the heavy golden orb in one hand and splendid scepter in the other, and on his head, a heavy crown of gold, adorned with jewels of monstrous size. The crown that she had helped to put on his head.

Along with the gifts had come a letter from Charles. The king was pleased to provide for each of John's daughters a marriage portion of a thousand pounds, and John would receive a yearly pension of five hundred pounds. And a title.

John looked stunned when he read out the letter, to the gasps and squeals of excitement of his wife, daughters, and mother. But he glanced at Jane, and then carefully folded the letter and put it away in the inside pocket of his coat, his expression unreadable. And to the cries asking when he should assume his title, and if they could all go to London when he should do so, he shook his head, and said only, "We'll see."

There was more—a long parchment, heavily weighted with seals and ribbons. John opened it, and then passed it to Jane.

"You read it. It's really for you."

She glanced down at the ornate letters on the creamy vellum, and read aloud.

"'To all and singular to whom these presents shall come, we the king's heralds and pursuivants of arms send greeting. We calling to mind the great and signal service performed to us by John Lane of Bentley in County Stafford concerning the preservation of our royal person after the Battle of Worcester, at which time condemning and threatenings published by the murderers of our royal father against any whosoever should conceal or assist us, and disdaining the rewards proposed to such as should be instrumental in the discovery and destruction of our person, and he not valuing any hazard his family might run, he with duty of an unspotted allegiance did by his great prudence and fidelity so conduct us as that we were able at length to retire to places of safety beyond the seas, have therefore of our own proper motion and free will given and granted to John Lane and his lawful descendants this honorable remuneration, as a notable mark or badge of his constant fidelity, that henceforth they shall bear an augmentation to their paternal arms, three lions passant guardant or, in canton gules.'"

There was a moment of silence.

"Dear God," Jane said. "It's the royal lions of England. The king has added the royal lions to your coat of arms."

THE ROYAL FOOTMAN HAD ALSO BROUGHT A SMALL PACKAGE WHICH he put into Jane's own hands, telling her that the king had charged him to do so. She saved this to open privately, and went up to her room and closed the door as soon as she could leave the rest of the family without causing comment.

Inside the package was the watch wrapped in the silk handkerchief, which Jane had last seen when she threw it at Charles. There was a letter, too.

"My dear Jane: Of all it is now within my power to give you and your family in thanks for your help to me, this, my father's watch, is the most precious in my eyes. I beg that you will accept it once more with my most humble apologies, in remembrance of our time together. As you will see if you examine it, the handkerchief preserved the crystal of the watch in its whole and perfect state, and I take leave to hope that what is between us, which has been similarly buffeted and tossed, will likewise survive. Your most affectionate friend, Charles R."

Jane laughed despite herself as she examined the watch, and shook her head. *God damn you, Charles,* she thought. *You will never let me hate you, however I might try.*

IN MID-MAY JANE RECEIVED A LETTER FROM QUEEN ELIZABETH. THE familiar handwriting brought tears to her eyes.

"Now I hear that the coronation is so happily passed, I have no more patience to stay here, but am resolved to go myself to congratulate that happy action. I would not do it before, not to give the king too much trouble at once, except he had commanded me to go, and now I assure you I shall give very little trouble, for I bring with me not above twenty-six or twenty-seven persons." Jane laughed out loud at the thought of dear Queen Elizabeth and her retinue descending on Whitehall. "I go with a resolution to put myself wholly in his hands, and obey him in all things, and trouble him for nobody. Your most affectionate friend, Elizabeth."

"I rejoice at Your Majesty's news," Jane wrote back. "I am sorry I shall not be in London to welcome you, and I hope that it may be possible that I shall have the pleasure of seeing Your Majesty soon. But be assured, wherever I am in the world, my prayers shall be for Your Majesty and will serve you with my life."

. . .

Jane had left London with the thousand pounds Parliament had bestowed on her. She had insisted on paying for the many things which the household at Bentley badly needed—another cow, work on the stables and the orchard—and of course she had brought gifts for her family. But still she had more than enough money to do whatever she wished. So she had given in to her mother's urging to have a portrait painted, something grand that would hang above the mantel in the great hall. The painter, Mr. Rowntree, had come from Stafford and was staying at Bentley Hall while he worked.

They had finished the afternoon's sitting, and she had come to stand beside the artist to survey the canvas. She was pleased. It showed her in one of the new gowns she had had made in London, rich pearls around her neck. In her hand she held a crown, draped with a veil of filmy black. Rowntree had suggested the idea and she had gone along with it, though the symbolism was perhaps too unsubtle, she thought.

Yes, she had hidden the crown, in the person of the king, thus preserving him and the monarchy. And he had gone on to his kingdom, leaving her behind. Like Dido and Aeneas. A smile suddenly quirked Jane's lips as an inspiration struck her. She considered. Was it silly? Silly be damned. It was her portrait, she would have it painted to please herself.

"I have an idea," she said, turning to Rowntree with a catlike smile.

Clement Fisher was true to his word. He visited Bentley regularly, but never pressed Jane for more closeness than she could easily give, and let her set the pace. She felt herself relaxing in the warmth of his love as summer came on, and could almost imagine being his wife. Almost. For at the back of her mind lay yet the shadow of Charles. She still dreamed of him, still thought of him almost daily, as she had done for so long. She knew it was foolish. She would not likely see him again, and could not let the ghost of a man who would never be hers rob her of a life with a man of flesh and blood who waited so patiently for her to come to him. She must find a way to let go of Charles, to lay him to rest, but yet she knew not how to do it.

Her birthday came. She was thirty-five. What an age, she thought, laughing that she had considered herself an old maid at twenty-five. And now she really must make up her mind to wed Clement, or release him from all hope, for to continue any longer if she did not mean to marry him would be unfair. *I will give myself until Michaelmas,* she thought. *He gave me so long those ten years ago, and so I will give myself the same length of time, and give him the answer he waited for then and waits for still.*

And then, as though he had heard her longing for him, Jane received a letter from Charles.

"As you well know, this third of September shall be the tenth anniversary of the Battle of Worcester and my deliverance. I mean to take the opportunity to visit now in happiness those places where I hid in despair, and thank in person those I could not thank before, and of course you are chief among them whose company I hope to have. My aunt the Queen of Bohemia will accompany me. She declared she would venture to the ends of the earth to see you once more, and until then bids me send you her fond love."

Jane smiled. Leaving London before Queen Elizabeth's arrival had been only slightly less painful than her heartbreak over Charles, and she was glad she would see her old friend again.

The king's advent in Staffordshire was a more momentous event than anything that had happened in the county in living memory or beyond. Every person within a day's ride, it seemed, had come to see the king and to marvel. His retinue flocked behind him as he made his royal progress through the countryside, visiting in turn each of the houses that had sheltered him. At each of the stops—Whiteladies, Boscobel, Mosely—the crowds watched rapt as the king greeted the legions of people who had taken a part in keeping him safe. The Penderel brothers, who had sequestered him—and his horse—in the house at Whiteladies as dawn rose on the morning after the Battle of Worcester. Dame Joan Penderel, who had brought him food as he sheltered in the woods nearby. Father John Huddleston, who had taken him to Mosely and given him his shirt.

At Boscobel, Charles and Colonel Will Carlis stood smiling beneath the oak tree—now known by all as "the Royal Oak"—where they had spent a day hiding from Cromwell's troops. Charles gathered up a couple of dozen acorns, putting them in the pockets of his pea-green coat.

"I shall plant these at Hyde Park and in St. James's Park," he declared, "that in the future I may always have a place of safety in time of need!"

The crowd laughed in delight, and there were calls of "No need for that, Your Majesty!" and "You're always welcome in Staffordshire, Your Majesty!"

He has a knack for it, Jane thought, standing companionably beside Queen Elizabeth. She watched the king nod and smile and chat with each of the country folk who had risked their lives for him, watched them beaming in his presence. *He makes each of them feel that they are special to him, that he truly cares and will never forget them. As he made me feel. But when he is back in London in a week's time? Or even tonight, when he lays his head comfortably to rest after a feast and carousing into the evening, will he give them a second thought? No. And now I am one of them. Just one more of the many, useful to him once upon a time, but now forgotten when the need is past.*

Having retraced in sunlight the route along which he had fled ten years earlier in darkness, Charles arrived at Bentley Hall. The household had trooped along with him, basking in his reflected glory, and now they welcomed him to the house that had been his last hiding place before he set out on his historic odyssey.

"I'd know that kitchen door anywhere!" Charles declared, to a delighted laugh from the little crowd that stood in the stable yard. "I recall as if it were yesterday stumbling through that door bone-tired and frightened, and looking like a scarecrow that had fallen into a pig's trough."

"And yet your majesty shone through," John said, to a pleased murmur.

Jane thought of that night, and her first sight of Charles. She felt again the thrill that had gone through her the next morning when she reached her arms around his waist to steady herself behind him on the horse, the sound of his voice as he spoke low to her over his shoulder, and how her spirits had soared as his voice had joined hers in song while they rode. She thought about that first kiss, so unexpected and overwhelming, in the stable at Long Marston. And the feel of his mouth and hands on her burning skin, the delicious shock as he had entered her, the fierce joy she had felt as she lay in his arms on those nights so long ago. They had been the most exciting days of her life. Her heart wrenched to think how she would have felt had she known that she would be so utterly forgotten after all they had gone through and what they had been to each other.

And then she saw that Charles was looking to her, waiting. She felt the many eyes upon her and flushed. He had spoken, and she had not even heard what he said. He spoke again.

"Will you walk with me, Mistress Lane? I should like to see this famous orchard of which you have told me."

Jane blinked and found her voice. "Gladly, Your Majesty."

Charles held out his hand to her, and as she moved to take it, the little crowd surged forward to join them. But Charles held up a hand to stay them.

"I pray you wait for me here. For I would have Mistress Jane alone as my guide."

He smiled down at Jane as he took her arm in his and led her toward the orchard. Jane could feel the stares and hear the whispers behind them, and remembered how she had thought to hear such whispers at the ball at The Hague the previous spring, and her shock at seeing Barbara Palmer take her place beside Charles.

Now they were among the apple trees, and out of sight and earshot of the crowd. Charles sighed, looking around him at the branches heavy with their fruit.

"I see why you love this place so," he said. "I understand what you meant when you said that you liked to come here and feel yourself lost in another world, and that you wondered if the fairies were watching you."

"You remember that?" Jane asked in astonishment.

"Of course," Charles said. "Why should I not?"

"Because . . ." Jane stopped. She could not put into words the yearning she had felt for so long.

"I remember it all, Jane. The sight of you trying not to look shocked when I blew in that kitchen door. The feel of you against me in the saddle. The conversations through those dark nights, that lifted my spirits so. The songs.

"Cast care away, let sorrow cease,
A fig for melancholy . . ."

He pulled Jane toward him and bent to kiss her gently. As she looked into his eyes, the years dropped away. He was hers again. Not the august person of the king, but the Charles with whom she had fallen in love, smiling down at her.

"I thought you had forgotten."

"I could never forget you. And though no doubt I have done an ill job of showing it, I love you, Jane. In another world . . ."

He looked away as his words trailed off, and Jane was amazed to see deep sadness in his eyes. He turned to her again.

"As perilous as they were, those days felt to me like the most real and joyful of my life, and it was you with whom I shared them. I had nothing to give you, did nothing but put your life in danger, yet you cared for me. I felt—free. Perhaps that seems odd. But with no end in mind but the saving of my skin, and the threat of death so close, I was truly myself. And you were truly yourself with me. We were as one, and happy. And if I had been any young country lad, free to choose for himself and where his heart lighted, I would have looked no further."

"Charles."

Jane put up her hand to stroke his cheek, realizing as she did so that it had been years since she had touched him, and how familiar was the feel of his skin beneath her fingers and the scent of him.

"If we were a simple lad and lass, courting in the orchard," Charles said, "I would ask you for a lock of your hair to carry with me near my heart."

He let go of Jane's hands to reach into his pocket, and pulled out a tiny penknife. He held it up, smiling.

"Wilt thou give me a lock of thy hair, sweeting?"

Jane smiled at his use of that most intimate "thou," now grown old-fashioned, but still the language of lovers.

"I will."

He carefully snipped a tendril of her hair, wrapped it in a silk handkerchief, and put it into his pocket.

"And wilt thou give me the same?" Jane asked.

"I will."

He handed her the knife, and lowered his head so that she could shear a dark curl. She, too, folded it into a handkerchief, and thrust it down the front of her bodice, where it would be safe and next to her heart. He put the knife away and took her hands in his.

"Then there it is. We have exchanged favors, and now we belong to each other."

"We will be far apart," Jane said.

"No matter the distance or the time, Jane. You shall always hold your place in my heart."

MICHAELMAS WAS COMING. SIR CLEMENT FISHER INVITED JANE TO visit him at Packington Hall, and she knew that he wanted to show her the house and lands that he hoped she would share with him. John accompanied Jane on the trip, and she rode pillion, calling vividly to her mind her travels with Charles. The air was crisp and cool, billowing clouds drifting across the clear blue of the sky.

"Why, it's the ninth of September!" Jane exclaimed to John. "Ten years to the day that the king came to Bentley and it all began."

So much had changed in those years, but the fields rolling away on each side of the road, the tawny stubble of the harvest shining gold against the red earth, the birds singing in the trees, the baaing of sheep and the lowing of cattle, the scent of autumn in the air, all that was the same, and what Jane had missed so much when she was abroad.

Clement showed them around his estate, the land stretching away in all directions as far as Jane could see, with deer grazing beneath the sturdy oaks. There was no sound but the gentle murmur of the wind in the leaves, and Jane thought she had never been anywhere that was more beautiful or where she felt more safe. It felt like home.

They stopped at the chapel of St. James, the parish church of Great Packington and Clement's tenants, the ancient headstones in the churchyard stretching back through the centuries. Clement had saved the house for last, but Jane knew she would love it even before they entered. Three stories of warm red brick with high dormers on the roof, Packington Hall was in ways very much like Bentley Hall. But Athalia was mistress of Bentley, and there Jane would always be the guest of her brother and sister. Packington and all its comfort and beauty could be hers, along with Clement's love.

John absented himself, leaving Jane and Clement gazing out the window of the cozy parlor over the rolling acres. Clement took Jane's hand, and she could sense the unspoken question.

"It lacks yet a fortnight until Michaelmas," she said. "But . . ."

He smiled down at her.

"But?"

"But if I may give you my answer now, I will."

He drew her toward him and brushed a strand of hair from her forehead.

"Yes," Jane said. "That is my answer. I will be happy to be your wife."

He kissed her, first tenderly and then passionately, and Jane relaxed into his arms, knowing that he was hers alone and always would be.

. . .

JANE MARRIED SIR CLEMENT FISHER JUST BEFORE CHRISTMAS, THE ceremony performed by the Most Reverend Gilbert Sheldon, newly consecrated as Archbishop of Canterbury, as befitted a man of Sir Clement's stature and the lady who had saved the life of the king. The tenants of Packington gathered to greet the newly married couple outside the chapel of St. James and to cheer the wedding party as they made their way to Packington Hall. Jane smiled and waved, happy to be at the center of her and Clement's little village, blushing and laughing as he swept her into his arms and carried her across the threshold of their home.

ON THE LAST NIGHT OF THE YEAR, JANE AND CLEMENT SAT CLOSE together in the parlor, a fire dancing bright on the hearth.

"I have kept meaning to ask you," Clement said, kissing her hand and looking up at Jane's portrait above the mantelpiece. "Surely the quotation in the corner of the painting is Virgil? '*Sic, sic, iuviat ire sub umbra.*'"

"Yes," Jane said, "From *The Aeneid*. 'Thus, thus, it pleases me to go into the shadows.'"

"I thought so. Very fitting." Clement nodded. "For indeed you did serve your king, and then go into the shadows."

Jane smiled at him and squeezed his hand, but could barely keep from chuckling as she recalled to herself the rest of Dido's curse, spoken just before she plunged the sword into her breast.

Let the cruel Trojan's eyes, from far out at sea,
Gaze long on the flames from the pyre
And bear with him the evil omen of my death.

YES, SHE HAD DESPAIRED, AND SHE HAD WANTED CHARLES TO SUFFER. But the rage and pain had lifted. She was free.

Ninth of September, 1689—Packington Hall, Warwickshire

WHEN JANE GOT UP THAT MORNING THE CRISP BITE OF THE autumn air and the golden and brown leaves swirling over the red earth of the stubbled fields brought back to her mind that day so long ago—could it really be thirty-eight years now?—the ninth of September, 1651—when she had met Charles, dirty and disguised, in the kitchen at Bentley.

Every year it was the same. The ninth of September brought back a rush of memories and thoughts and feelings. It seemed almost like a dream now, that she had ever ridden half across the country behind the king, with Henry too, fearing for their lives every moment. Of course it had all come out well eventually.

Or had it? Yes, Charles had escaped and lived to return and claim his crown. But he had had no legitimate child, and when he died four years earlier his brother James, the Duke of York, had succeeded him on the throne, and last year the Catholic James had been forced to abdicate in favor of his daughter Mary, child of Nan Hyde, and her husband and cousin, the reassuringly Protestant William of Orange, who Jane had first met as a fat little baby at the court of his mother Mary. So much unpleasantness could have been avoided if only Charles had married his cousin Sophie of Hanover, Jane thought. But at least there had been no war or bloodshed when James was removed from the throne. England had had enough of that. Even James wanted to live more than he wanted to rule, and he had gone quietly, with his head intact, and was now far away, in peaceful exile in France.

But Jane's life had been disrupted, never to be the same, on that distant September morning. To be sure, she had welcomed the chance for adventure, and had gone where her heart took her, though it was into the arms of a man who could never marry her.

Had it been worth it? What would her life have been like if Charles had turned up in some other kitchen and ridden some other horse? Would she have married Clement just the same, but a decade earlier? How had she been changed? She and Clement had been very happy, but would they have had children if she had not lost that babe so long ago? She would never know.

She felt a sharp twinge in her chest, and winced. Probably heartburn. She was getting too old to eat anything spiced, she thought, and sighed.

She picked up the square of silk on which she had been working embroidery for the past few months. She had completed the heads of Charles, his father Charles I, his brother James II, and her own father. She had meant it as a tribute to them, and to all that they had seen. But it had all been so long ago. Who now even remembered what had happened? For many years, people had worn oak leaves on Oak Apple Day, as Charles's birthday on the twenty-ninth of May had come to be called, commemorating his salvation. But now the wearing of oak leaves was forbidden, and this year villagers in nearby Meriden had been arrested and threatened for doing so. The young William and Mary must be mighty nervous about their place on the throne to be so adamantly against something so innocent, Jane thought. But that was the way it was, and nothing to be done about it.

Jane realized that she was the only one left alive to remember that

September dawn when they had set off for Abbots Leigh. Charles, Henry Lascelles, Lord Wilmot, John and Athalia, Withy and her husband John Petre, her mother and father, were all long gone.

Of course many others had written down their parts in the story when it was safe to do so, once Charles was back on the throne. Whitgreaves, the Penderels, Father John Huddleston, Anne Wyndham, and those whose parts had come after Jane had left the stage, Colonel Gunther and Mr. Ellesden. Yes, the Royal Miracle, as it had come to be called, had been thoroughly chronicled. But no one knew the real story. Her story. The story of how she had been swept off her feet by a warrior king, like a princess in some fairy tale, and had accompanied him on a journey worthy of the stage or an epic poem.

She could not have told her story then, for her love and her pain had burned too sharply to put to paper. Maybe she should write it now. Jane smiled at the thought. What would the world think of old Lady Fisher dredging up tales of dalliance from long ago? They would probably think she was cracked. If they even took any notice. No, the story was better kept in her heart and memory. She put her hand to her bosom, and felt the knot of Charles's handkerchief and watch pinned inside her gown. It had been a matter of habit for her to wear it for so long that now it had almost become a part of her. She hadn't opened the little bundle in years, but in her mind's eye she saw each detail of the silver watch nestled within.

With fingers shaking a bit—damn this old age, it was so tedious—she unpinned the handkerchief and drew it forth. She put it to her nose. Was it possible that she could still detect a faint ghost of Charles's scent? It scarcely seemed likely, and yet she could swear it was so. His face came bright and clear into her mind, those dark eyes shining down at her, and she heard his laughter and the husky whisper of his voice as he held her close and spoke words of love. It was almost as if he stood in the room with her. Why now, after so long, should he make himself so vividly present?

The knot was hard to open, reluctant to release its prize after so long, but at length she managed to untie it. She held the watch up to the sunlight. The crystal still sparkled and the tiny etched designs in the tarnished silver still seemed to hold some arcane secrets in their rune-like shapes.

And then, though Jane could hardly believe it was happening, the hands of the watch moved. How was it possible? It had been decades since it had been wound. But that barely audible tick was exactly as she recalled from that morning in Trent when Charles had given her the watch.

She held it up and peered at it, turned it about. Nothing. It was still again now. Silent as the grave. She looked at the face of the watch. The little hands stood at twelve. Noon. No. Midnight! Of course, midnight. And then Jane understood, and smiled. For it had been midnight on the ninth of September when Charles had come into that dark kitchen and stolen her heart.

She felt the merest whisper of a breeze. The windows were closed, but yes, a breath of air had caressed her cheek.

"Are you impatient to lie with me again, Charles?" she asked softly. "So importunate that you must need move the hands of the clock forward to gull me into coming to bed to you? You need not resort to such trickery, my love. I am weary, and I ache for the touch of your lips and your hands."

She went to the bed. She could almost see him there, his head propped on one elbow as he gazed at her, patting the coverlet beside him. She lay down, her hand where she knew his must be, and closed her eyes. She was very tired and would welcome a long sleep.

ACKNOWLEDGMENTS

I'm happy and astonished to have a fleet of editors and agents to thank: Kate Seaver at Berkley Publishing Group in the U.S., Helen Bolton and Kate Bradley at Avon U.K., Kevan Lyon of Marsal Lyon Literary Agency, foreign rights agent Taryn Fagerness, Arabella Stein of Abner Stein Agency in London, and Diane McGee of McGee Creative, who represents me for film rights.

I'm very pleased to have Caitlin Mulrooney-Lyski at Penguin handling the publicity for this book as she did for *The Darling Strumpet.*

I owe great thanks to Derek Wilson, because it was from his book *All The King's Women*, which I read in the course of my research for *The Darling Strumpet*, that I learned about Jane Lane's amazing story.

This book required an enormous amount of research, and there are many people to thank in connection with that endeavor!

My dear friend Alice Northgreaves accompanied me on a blitzkrieg research trip in England, playing Watson to my Holmes and doing most of the driving as we followed the route that Charles took after the battle and on his travels with Jane. We visited Worcester, Boscobel House and Whiteladies, Mosely Old Hall, tried to find the site of Bentley Hall and got pretty close, zoomed up to Stafford, were enchanted by Packington, drove on through Bromsgrove, Long Marston, Mickleton, Chipping Camden, and Cirencester to Bristol and Abbots Leigh, spent a lovely couple of nights in Shepton Mallet, went south to Castle Cary and Ansford, on to adventures in Trent, and stopped to see Castle Nunney, home of my ancestors the Prathers, before heading back to London. Alice gamely braved the nearly impossible schedule I had set, being used to driving on U.S. highways instead of small back-country roads and lanes in England, came up with good suggestions about sources of information, intrepidly plunged into pubs with me to ask for help finding long-gone sites, and helped me track down information about riding pillion. I also used her wonderful description of Norfolk as "black, sticky, bullrush-fringed marshland." You can read about our travels and see the photos on my blog www.theroyalmiracle.blogspot.com. Thanks, Alice; I couldn't have done it without you, and even if I could it wouldn't have been so much fun!

We very much enjoyed our stays at the Admiral Rodney in Martley, Burgage House in Worcester, Leys House in Gnossal, and Maplestone in Shepton Mallet.

Heather and Stuart at the Rose and Crown in Trent (the one that is mentioned in the book, which stood and still stands across the road from Trent Manor) went way out of their way to be helpful, putting me in contact with Margaret Hohler, giving me much useful information and a copy of *A King in the Oak Tree*, and serving up one of the best meals I've had anywhere.

I cannot begin to be grateful enough to Margaret Hohler, the present owner of Trent Manor, who graciously invited Alice and me not only into her home but into her own bedroom, which was the very chamber where Charles stayed, with the priest hole in a little closet. As at Mosely and Boscobel, it gave me shivers to be in the places he hid.

I'm very grateful to the Earl and Countess of Aylesford for allowing us to wander around Packington's beautiful and extensive park, which is probably not much changed from what it was like when Jane lived there and was very evocative, and to visit St. James's Church, where Jane and Clement Fisher were buried. Thanks also to Kay Gleeson for arranging the visit.

David Lee, the property manager for the National Trust at Mosely Old Hall was very helpful and welcomed Alice and me, suggested research sources, gave us directions to find the site of Bentley Hall, and arranged for volunteer Tony Wilcox to take photos of the lovely portrait of Jane as a young woman that hangs at Mosely. Tony was kind enough to send me a selection of photos, one of which appears on my website, courtesy of the National Trust. Carol Gosling conducted a very informative tour of the house and also let me record her further thoughts about Mosely Old Hall—all in her wonderful accent, which must be something like what Jane sounded like!

Steven Gregory, Ella Harrison, and the staff at the lovely Boscobel House were welcoming and helpful, and Sean Farnworth gave us a most enjoyable and informative tour.

When Alice and I swooped into Stafford late one afternoon, Andrew Pearsall and Nick Thomas at the Stafford Borough Council at the Ancient High House went out of their way to provide as much information as they could about the 1642 visit to Stafford by Charles I, Prince Rupert, and possibly Charles II, as well as whether the King's Company might have played in Stafford or nearby, and suggested other possible resources for research. A young man at the Staffordshire and Stoke on Trent Archive Service whose name I unfortunately didn't get was also very helpful, and staff at the William Salt Library told me about Henry Murray Lane's 1898 publication *The Lanes of Bentley Hall,* which proved to be extremely useful.

For much of the time I was working on this book I was fortunate to have the feedback of the members of my writing group, Willow Healy, Gil Roscoe, and Elizabeth Thurber. Elizabeth also gave me useful information about horses and riding in general.

Kirsten Shepard, one of my oldest and dearest friends, was in Paris with her mother, Margaret Shepard, while I was writing the part of the book that takes place in Paris, and they helped me immensely by providing information about and pictures of the Palais Royal, Louvre, Tuileries, Grand Gallery, and many others. Kirsten also translated a letter written in French by Anne Hyde describing Mary of Orange, which was wonderful to have.

My father, Dick Bagwell, provided information about popular songs of the day that would be appropriate for Charles and Jane to sing as they traveled, giving me the music and words to "The World Turned Upside Down/When The King Enjoys His Own Again," "The Hunt is Up," "Come O'er the Bourne Bessy," "Jog on the Footpath Way," and others.

Alan Stone, a local historian at Shepton Mallet, spent an hour or more with Alice and me, giving us very useful and entertaining information about Somerset, the Civil War, Roman roads, and more.

The staff of the Humanities and Manuscript reading rooms at the British Library were very good about helping me find much very useful material.

Pauline Gibson of Bentley, who writes the *Bentley Banter*, has been very helpful in providing information about the site of Bentley Hall and the surrounding area.

Anne Mello and the staff at the Pasadena Public Library filled my numerous requests for interlibrary loans.

Samuel Pepys invested a great deal of time and care to ensure that the story of Charles's escape after the Battle of Worcester was preserved for posterity. Charles told Pepys the story in May 1660 aboard the *Royal Charles* as he was returning to England to take his throne. In the autumn of 1680, Pepys spent two three-hour sessions with Charles at Newmarket, using his famous shorthand to take down Charles's account of his odyssey, which Pepys later edited with his characteristic skill and flair. He also collected all the other contemporary accounts and bound them together, giving us a very complete picture of an amazing piece of history from the point of view of the people who participated in it.

My quest for information about riding pillion lit up email lists and organizations all over England and the U.S. Alice Northgreaves did the initial digging. Many people in the equestrian and historical reenactment communities, including the Society for Creative Anachronism, the Sidesaddle Association, and the American Sidesaddle Association, gallantly came to my aid. Natalie Wooldridge, known in the SCA as Lady Ariadne De Glevo, gave me lots of information about horse breeds, their gaits and speeds, how much ground a horse could travel in a day, etc., as well as riding pillion, and sent me a wonderful photo of Steve and Jean Emmit in beautiful period garb on a caparisoned horse, he astride and she riding pillion. Mike Glasson of the Walsall Leather Museum sent me some photos of pillions. Margie Beeson sent me information about and photos of pillions provided by Rhonda of the ASA. Others who helped along the way were archivist Sue Hurley of the Worshipful Company of Saddlers, Jeremy Smith at the Guildhall Library, Karol Kafka of California Aside, Stephanie Hutcherson at Georgia Ladies Aside, Melodee Spevak, VP Marti Friddle of the ASA, Jim Myers, Lynda Fjellman, Jane Pryor and Shirley Oultram of the SA, Jo Strange of Hazlemere in Surrey, Frances Dorrian, and King's Saddlery in Walsall.

I was overjoyed to find Michael Shaw and Danny McAree's article "The Rediscovery of Bentley Hall, Walsall," originally published in *West Midlands Archaeology* Vol. 50 (2007), pages 2–5. I discovered it by using my iPhone to Google "Bentley Hall Staffordshire" when I was standing near that site but couldn't find it, and was relieved to learn that I was more or less in the right place. You can find the article at http://www.localhistory.scit.wlv.ac.uk/articles/Hall/BentleyHall.htm. I was charmed by the article's description of the Banqueting House at Bentley as being "built in the eccentric Flemish style with high chimneys and dormer windows—a fanciful edifice designed to surprise and delight," and took the liberty of using that phrase in this book.

Thanks to the people who have posted videos on You Tube showing how to load and fire a flintlock pistol. And how not to do it!

Thanks to the staff and patrons of the Red Lion in Bromsgrove, the Crown in Cirencester, and the George in Castle Cary for their helpful information about Jane and Charles's progress through those towns and how to find sites that Alice and I were looking for.

AUTHOR'S NOTE

Jane Lane's heroic part in helping Charles escape, putting herself in enormous danger to do so, made her famous after the Restoration. I was enthralled when I read Derek Wilson's account of it, and was convinced by the evidence he presented for his belief that Jane and Charles became lovers during their travels. I was surprised and delighted to learn that no one had previously told the story in fiction.

After the Restoration, many people who had helped Charles wrote their stories, so that there is an almost hour-by-hour record of what he did, said, wore, and ate during parts of his odyssey. But Jane never told her story publicly, so I had very scant information to use in writing the parts of the book that took place after she left Charles in Trent. There are references to her learning that she had been discovered, walking with her brother to Yarmouth in disguise, being welcomed by Charles and his family and followers in Paris, joining the court of Mary of Orange, becoming a lady-in-waiting to the Duchess of York after the Restoration, receiving gifts and a pension from Parliament, and marrying Sir Clement Fisher. Some letters from Charles to Jane and from Jane to Elizabeth of Bohemia survive. I filled in the enormous blanks with as much fact as I could glean from research and then by surmise and invention. I don't know if Jane was intimately involved in the events surrounding Anne Hyde and Lucy Walter, but she certainly knew them and could have been.

Three of the letters from Charles to Jane in this book are real letters from Charles to Jane. Some of the others contain excerpts of real letters from Charles to other people. Some of the letters are my own invention. I wasn't able to find any letters from Jane to Charles, so I wrote all of her letters myself. Jane's letters to Queen Elizabeth of Bohemia are her real letters, with a little cutting, clarification of who she's talking about, and I think the addition of one sentence in her last letter. I found it very touching to learn of their friendship and overwhelming to hold Jane's actual letters in my hands at the British Library and see her bold, very modern-looking handwriting.

Charles did visit Staffordshire and Shopshire for the tenth anniversary of the Battle of Worcester and his escape, and it seemed like a good opportunity for me to have him and Jane meet and come to a resolution.

I undertook my research trip somewhat on the fly immediately after my agent made the deal to sell the book, as Boscobel House and Mosely Old Hall would soon be closing for the winter, and traveling around England wasn't going to get any easier as it got colder and wetter. It was not until I returned home that I learned that the Yarmouth Jane walked to was probably the one on the east coast rather than the smaller one on the Isle of Wight, as I had been led to believe from one book. There was no possibility of returning to England to retrace that part of Jane's journey (much less going to Paris, The Hague, Breda, Spa, Aix-la-Chapelle, Dusseldorf, and other places.). Fortunately I found a 1939 facsimile of John Ogilby's 1685 *Britannia*, an atlas of the roads between principal cities and towns in England, and using that and Google Maps and Google Earth (ain't technology amazing?) I was able to determine Jane and John's likely route and learn what the road and terrain were like, mile by mile, from Staffordshire to Yarmouth.

I used Charles's own words, as recorded by Pepys, in the sections of the book in which he recounts his adventures, but had to cut much of the story, which is worth reading in full. His blundering through the inn yard full of soldiers actually happened at Bridport, after Jane had left him, and I moved it to Cirencester, so Jane could be there.

If you want to read more about the Royal Miracle, as Charles's escape came to be called, I can recommend *Charles II's Escape from Worcester*, edited by William Matthews, which presents Pepys's transcription of Charles's account and his edited version side by side, as well as other contemporary accounts; *The Escape of Charles II After the Battle of Worcester* by Richard Ollard; A. M. Broadley's 1912 *The Royal Miracle: A Collection of Rare Tracts, Broadsides, Letters, Prints, & Ballads Concerning the Wanderings of Charles II After the Battle of Worcester,* which also chronicles the delightfully daffy 1911 reenactment of the events; both the 1897 and 1908 editions of *The Flight of the King* by Allan Fea, as well as his *After Worcester Fight; The Boscobel Tracts*, a collection of contemporary accounts edited by J. Hughes and published in 1857; *The Wanderings of Charles II in Staffordshire and Shropshire* by H. P. Kingston; and Jean Gordon Hughes's *A King in the Oak Tree*. I'll try to post a more complete bibliography on my website by the time this book is published!

I was intrigued by Derek Wilson's discussion of the quote from *The Aeneid*, "*sic, sic iuvat ire sub umbra*," which is on Jane's portrait at the National Portrait Gallery in London. He translates the phrase as "Thus, thus it pleases me to go into the shadows" without saying whose translation it is, and argues that it is inconceivable that Jane didn't know that Dido says that line just before she curses Aeneas for his faithlessness and kills herself. I looked up several translations of the relevant passage, and I don't recall any more that I used or if I melded them, so yes, it's possible I used a translation that didn't exist in 1651!

Pretty much the same is true of the brief quote from Descartes.

Francis Yates was the only person executed for his role in helping Charles escape. He was hanged at Oxford, but I moved the event to Wolverhampton because I needed Jane to have a vivid experience of what could happen if she were discovered.

The next time you see a pub or anything else called the Royal Oak or Boscobel Oak, now you know where the name came from. I've been amused to discover a street in L.A. and a company in Canada called Royal Oak, as well as the numerous more likely namesakes.

Jane's exact birthdate, year of birth, and where she stood in the order of her siblings isn't known, but it seemed likely she was among the youngest, so that's where I put her, and I liked the idea of her sharing a birthday with Juliet.

Jane married Clement Fisher in December 1663, though in the interest of the story I've made it seem as if they were married in 1661. I don't know if they were engaged or involved before Charles interrupted her life, but it seems likely. They did not have any children. Clement died in 1683. Jane died on September 9, 1689, thirty-eight years to the day after Charles blew into Bentley.